周銀卿——著
黃薇之——譯

用6句英文,和外國人輕鬆話家常

和外國人

職場、旅遊、交友都萬用,最快上手的英語會話學習術!

육하원칙 영어회화 : 6개 의문사로 네이티브와 막힘없이 대화하기

透過「六何法英語會話訓練法」，再也不怕與母語人士對話了！

使用英語對話時，只能回答簡短的句子嗎？

　　身處全球化時代的我們，無論是公司業務、海外旅行或職場生活，總免不了碰上要用到英語會話的情況，不論是有所需求，或是為了自我成長，英語會話已成為現代社會中不可或缺的要素，學好英語也幾乎是所有人夢寐以求的心願。儘管已是老生常談，但為了增強會話實力，**要盡可能地多練習英語口說才行，無論對方是外國人或本國人都無妨，不停地用英語對話才是最好的方法。**不過有些讀者的問題在於，假使面前馬上出現英語對話的機會，也無法將對話變長、延續下去，只能用簡短句子來回答對方的提問，或是在對方的話語中，插入幾個感歎詞就結束。

讓英語對話變長的祕密武器——六何法疑問詞！

　　想讓英語對話延伸得長一點的話，該怎麼做呢？思考一下用自己的母語對話時的情形，當對話中斷或是處在尷尬的情況時，自己還能向對方提出問題，並且延續話題嗎？其實，用英語對話也是一樣，當然要以提問來展開防守！不過提問和說話一樣並不容易，提問一兩次之後，就再也沒有可問的話題了。

　　本書要告訴你此時能派上用場的祕密武器——「六何法疑問詞」，用「誰？何時？在哪裡？做什麼？如何做？為什麼？」的「六何法疑問詞」來展

開得力防守。不只能讓對話變長,還能使對話更為深入。像這樣熟練提問之後,接著再練習回答的技巧,也就是稍微仿造對方的提問來回答。這就是「六何法英語會話訓練法」,不但可以不用再害怕與英語母語人士對話,還能讓英語程度初級者感受到引導對話的神奇經驗!

英語只是第二種語言而已!別氣餒!

　　雖然英語在韓國真的很重要,但諷刺的是這裡並非能輕鬆學習英語的國家,因為我們沒有形成「就算說錯了也能繼續使用」的風氣,讓人無法自由地練習會話。我的願望非常簡單,就是「不要忘記英語只是第二種語言,用錯是理所當然的!就算錯了也要理直氣壯地用英語說出來!英語不好不用氣餒!」在英語會話中,最重要的是積極的態度,完美學成了「六何法英語會話訓練法」之後,請積極地活用在實際生活中。即使和英語母語人士對話也不會畏縮,還能引導對話。

蘿拉老師 周銀卿

本書的構成

PREVIEW 暖身

進入正式學習之前，先用短短的文章來暖身吧。不只能認識與主題相關的文化小常識，還能附加學習各種英語表達。

STEP **1** 我先提出問題

試著活用六何法疑問詞，向對方提出問題。接著再嘗試用 be 動詞、助動詞等等，來延伸練習提問。

STEP **2** 反向利用提問來回答

別再簡短回答！其實只要好好利用對方的提問，你也可以回答得很充實。試著利用提問中出現的句型，來練習回答的方法。

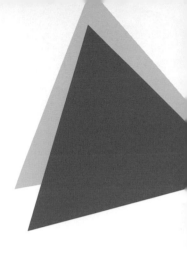

利用前面練習的六何法疑問詞提問與回答，
挑戰看看與英語母語人士對話吧。仔細觀察
如何在實際對話中活用六何法疑問詞。

從每次的對話範例中，挑出三個母語人士常
用的片語，並附加說明與例句。

mp3 活用法

掃描各章第一頁右上角的 QRCode，即可收
聽本書所有例句的 MP3，聆聽母語人士的發
音後，跟著複誦一次，能讓學習效果加倍！

目 錄
Contents

Part 3 Leisure activities spice up your life
讓生活更豐富的休閒活動

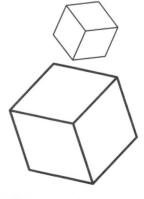

目 錄
Contents

Part 4

The real and virtual worlds
現實生活及網路世界

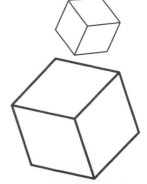

Part 1

人生的八成，
民以食為天

各位在何時感到最快樂呢？我是在吃東西時最開心！最近隨著大眾對於食物的關心增長，出現了許多美食餐廳和料理節目，無論何時，食物都是很好的對話素材。接下來，就用六何法疑問詞來聊聊關於食物的話題吧！

Eating and drinking well

Let's eat out today!

→ → → 今天外食吧！

　　在美國或英國等國家外食（eating out）時，通常會給 10 至 20%的小費（tip）。結算之後，小費會加在帳單（bill）上，沒有零錢（change）時，會將小費金額寫在帳單上，再一起用信用卡付款。雖然韓國人還不習慣給小費，但這在美國是很基本的禮儀。由於服務生要仰賴小費維生，顧客在這方面最好不要太過小氣。如果非常滿意服務的話，給得比基本的還要多也無妨。

　　小吃店、飯館、餐廳、自助吧，這些詞用英語怎麼説呢？一般的餐館叫做 **diner**，是從「用餐」（dine）衍生出來的單字，很容易和 dinner（晚餐）搞混吧？**diner** 發音為 [ˈdaɪ.nɚ][1]，和 dinner 是不一樣的。如果是稍微昂貴一點的餐館，則是 **fine diner**，販賣辣炒年糕或飯卷等食物的小吃店，則是 **snack bar**，在美國主要是販售漢堡或三明治等。販售簡單料理的小餐館為 **bistro**，可以挑選、盛裝各種料理來享用的是 **buffet**，販賣咖啡和三明治的是 **café** 或 **coffee house**，而販售漢堡的則是 **fast food restaurant**。看著看著，肚子突然就餓了起來，Let's grab a bite to eat.（吃點簡單的東西吧。）

1　此處原文直接用韓文拼音，本書改以國際音標（IPA）標示發音。

STEP 1 我先提出問題　01-1.mp3

試著用「誰、何時、在哪裡、做什麼、如何做、為什麼」的六何法疑問詞來問問題。直到沒有可以再進一步詢問的疑問詞時，就能更自然地引導對話。

✪ 用六何法疑問詞來提問

1. Who is your favorite cook?　最喜歡的廚師是誰？

2. When do you normally eat out?　通常會在什麼時候外食？

3. Where do you like to eat out?　喜歡去哪裡外食？

4. What is your favorite restaurant/cuisine?　最喜歡的餐廳／料理是什麼？

✪ 不用六何法疑問詞來提問

5. Do you like to eat out?　喜歡外食嗎？

6. Can you recommend a good Korean restaurant?　可以推薦一家不錯的韓國餐廳嗎？

STEP 2 反向利用提問來回答　01-2.mp3

如果以前只能簡短回答問題的話，現在試著說出完整的句子吧。將疑問句變成陳述句，就能簡單變成一個句子了。開始練習用句子回答吧！

1. Who is your favorite cook?　最喜歡的廚師是誰？

   My favorite cook is _____.　最喜歡的廚師是 _____。

   my mother 我媽媽 | my school chef 我學校的廚師 | Jamie Oliver 傑米奧利佛（英國知名廚師）| Sam Kim 金山姆（韓國知名廚師）

2. When do you normally eat out?　通常會在什麼時候外食？

   I normally eat out _____.　通常 _____ 會外食。

   every day 每天 | on Fridays 在星期五 | on weekends 在週末

3. Where do you like to eat out?　喜歡去哪裡外食？

   I like to eat out at _____.　喜歡去 _____ 外食。

a diner near my office 辦公室附近的餐廳 ▎ a buffet downtown 市區的自助吧 ▎ a fast food restaurant in front of my house 我家前面的速食店

4. What is your favorite restaurant?　最喜歡的餐廳（名字）是什麼？

My favorite restaurant is _____.　我最喜歡的餐廳是 _____ 。

Olive Garden 橄欖園（美國知名餐廳）▎ McDonald's 麥當勞 ▎ a bistro called 'Alice's' 一家叫做 Alice's 的小餐館

5. Do you like to eat out?　喜歡外食嗎？

→ Yes, I like to eat out. Because _____.

是，我很喜歡，因為 _____ 。

❶ I am not a good cook. 我不太會做菜。

❷ I don't have time to cook. 我沒有時間做料理。

→ No, I don't like to eat out. Because _____.

不，我不喜歡，因為 _____ 。

❶ when I cook, I can use fresh ingredients so it is healthier. 自己做菜的話，就能使用新鮮的食材，對健康也更好。

❷ I am a good cook so my food is delicious and it is cheaper than eating out. 我擅長料理，因此會比外食要來得美味又省錢。

6. Can you recommend a good (Korean) restaurant?　可以推薦一家不錯的（韓式）餐廳嗎？

→ Sure, I would like to recommend （餐廳）（位置）.

我推薦在 _____ 的 _____ 。

❶ a Korean restaurant　韓式餐廳，in my neighborhood　我家附近

❷ a snack bar　小吃店，in front of my office　我辦公室前面

→ No, I'm sorry. I can't recommend any.　Because _____.

不，很抱歉，我不能推薦，因為 _____ 。

❶ I don't like eating out so I don't know any good restaurants.　我不喜歡外食，所以不知道有什麼好餐廳。

❷ I'm new in Seoul so I am not aware of good places to eat at.　我才剛來首爾沒多久，不知道哪裡比較好吃。

確認前面練習的提問如何活用在和母語人士的對話中，請不要忘記一邊聽一邊跟著說。

Min Hey James, what a nice surprise to **run into**① you! How are you doing?

James Good morning, Min! **I can't complain.**② How about you?

Min I'm good. Did you watch the cooking show last night?

James Yes, I did. I like watching cooking shows.

Min **Who is your favorite cook on that show?**

James Um, from last night's show? Well... I guess my favorite cook is Kim Ha-young. I want to go to his restaurant one day.

Min That would be nice. **When do you normally eat out?**

James I normally eat out on weekends. I eat at home on weekdays.

Min **Where do you like to eat out?**

James I like to go to famous restaurants. I search the web to pick the restaurant.

Min That sounds fun! **What is your favorite cuisine?**

James Well, I like to eat Japanese, Korean and Italian cuisine. I especially like Italian foods such as pizza and pasta.

Min Pizza and pasta sound yummy. Can you cook them? Do you like to cook?

James Well, I'm not a good cook so my food is not that delicious.

Min That's okay. I'm a poor cook too. Anyway, **can you recommend a good Japanese restaurant?**

James Sure, there is a sushi bar called 'Kiku' in front of my office. Here is the business card of that restaurant.

Min Thank you. I will **try** this place **out**③ this Saturday.

 解說請見 P276

① run into

run（跑）再加上 into（進去～）成為 run into 的話，就變成「偶然遇見」這樣完全不同的意思。

- **I ran into** Tom on my way to school. 我在上學途中偶然遇見了湯姆。
- **Running into** people unexpectedly is always a pleasant thing. 偶然遇見誰通常都是一件很開心的事。

② I can't complain

聽到「How are you?」通常都會想到用「I'm fine, thank you. And you?」來回答，但其實還有許多不同的回答方式。試著用「I can't complain.」來表達沒什麼不順利，並且過得很好的意思吧。

- **I can't complain** about my life these days. 我最近的生活沒什麼好抱怨的。
- **I can't complain** about the wage I get. 我對於收到的薪水沒什麼不滿。

③ try out

有「嘗試看看～（是否不錯）」的意思，單用 try 也可以。差別在於 try 有試圖要去做什麼的意思，而 try out 則有參加某團體的選拔、試驗之意，或是在要確認物品、服務品質時使用。

- Why don't you **try (out)** the new restaurant? 要不要試試那家新開的餐廳？
- I **tried out** for the school soccer team but didn't make it. 我參加了學校足球隊的選拔，但是不太順利。

Delivery food is convenient

→ → → 外送餐點很方便

　　這一章節要來認識有關外送餐點（delivery food）的說法。若要說明外帶，我們通常會用 take-out 吧？在韓國，我們稱打包餐點為 take-out，不過美國並不會這麼用，而是會說 to go。點餐時，服務生會問 For here or to go? 在這裡吃會說 **for here**，而打包帶走則是說 **to go**。

　　打電話點餐（order by telephone）時，該怎麼說呢？電話撥通後，對方會說 May I help you?，這時只要回答 **I'd like to place an order for delivery.** 即可，然後對方會繼續詢問要訂購的餐點以及地址，What would you like to have?（要點什麼呢？），What's the address?（地址是什麼？）。為了讓通話順利進行，最好先決定要訂購的餐點，並確認好地址再撥電話。

　　雖然近來可以透過網路（order online）或智慧型手機訂購餐點，但不妨把訂餐想成是口說練習，試著鼓起勇氣打電話訂餐吧！

STEP 1 我先提出問題

 02-1.mp3

試著用「誰、何時、在哪裡、做什麼、如何做、為什麼」的六何法疑問詞來問問題。直到沒有可以再進一步詢問的疑問詞時，就能更自然地引導對話。

✪ 用六何法疑問詞來提問

1. How often do you get delivery food?　你多常叫外送餐點來吃？

2. What is your favorite delivery food?　最喜歡的外送餐點是什麼？

3. What is an advantage of delivery food?　外送餐點有什麼優點？

4. When do you usually get delivery food?　通常會在何時訂購外送餐點？

✪ 不用疑問詞來提問

5. Do you like to get delivery food?　你喜歡叫外送餐點來吃嗎？

6. Is it unhealthy to eat delivery food often?　常叫外送餐點來吃的話，對健康不好嗎？

STEP 2 反向利用提問來回答

 02-2.mp3

如果以前只能簡短回答問題的話，現在試著說出完整的句子吧。將疑問句變成陳述句，就能簡單變成一個句子了。開始練習用句子回答吧！

1. **How often** do you get delivery food? 你有多常叫外送餐點來吃？

   I get delivery food _____.　_____會叫外送餐點來吃。

   every Friday 每個星期五 │ twice a week 一星期兩次 │ once a month 一個月一次

2. **What** is your favorite delivery food?　最喜歡的外送餐點是什麼？

   My favorite delivery food is _____.

   我最喜歡的外送餐點是 _____。

   Chinese food 中華料理 │ pizza 披薩 │ fried chicken 炸雞

3. What is an advantage of delivery food?　外送餐點有什麼優點？

An advantage of delivery food is that _____.　外送餐點的優點是 _____。

❶ I can taste exotic food that I can't cook.　可以吃到自己做不出來的異國料理。

❷ I don't have to cook or clean up afterward.　不用做菜，之後也不需要收拾。

4. When do you usually get delivery food?　通常會在何時訂購外送餐點？

I usually get delivery food _____.　通常會在 _____ 訂購外送餐點。

on weekends 週末 ｜ when I have guests 有訪客時 ｜ when I'm too tired to cook 當我太累無法做菜時

5. Do you like to get delivery food? 你喜歡點外送餐點來吃嗎？

→ Yes, I like to get delivery food. Because _____. 是，我喜歡，因為 _____。

❶ I can save a lot of time and still have a decent meal.　可以節省時間，又能吃到像樣的一餐。

❷ I can have delicious foods that I can't cook myself.　可以品嘗到自己做不出來的美味料理。

→ No, I don't like to get delivery food. Because _____.　不，我不喜歡，因為 _____。

❶ I think delivery food is unhealthy and unhygienic.　我覺得外送餐點對健康不好，而且不衛生。

❷ they are much more expensive than cooking meals yourself.　比自己做菜花得更多錢。

6. Is it unhealthy to eat delivery food often?　常叫外送餐點來吃的話，對健康不好嗎？

→ Yes, it is unhealthy to eat delivery food often. Because _____. 對，對健康不好，因為 _____。

① restaurants normally use a lot of artificial seasoning. 餐廳通常都會使用很多人工調味料。

② most delivery foods are deep fried or too sweet. 大部分外送餐點都是油炸的，或是太甜。

→ No, it is not unhealthy to eat delivery food often. Because _____.
不，不會危害健康，因為_____。

① these days, many restaurants deliver healthy food. 最近很多餐廳都會外送健康餐點。

② I get delivery food often and I am neither fat nor unhealthy. 我很常吃外送餐點，但沒有變胖也沒有變得不健康。

STEP 3 和母語人士對話

 02-3.mp3

確認前面練習的提問如何活用在和母語人士的對話中，請不要忘記一邊聽一邊跟著說。

Min James, **do you like to get delivery food?**

James Sure! As a matter of fact, my ideal weekend is watching a good movie at home while eating delivery food.

Min That **sounds yummy**① and comfy. **How often do you get delivery food?**

James It's a bit embarrassing but I must say, almost once a week.

Min That's okay. **When do you usually get delivery food?**

James I usually get delivery food on weekends when I **can't be bothered to**②cook.

Min **What is your favorite delivery food?**

James I like to get Chinese and fried chicken. What about you?

Min I also like fried chicken. But I'm not **a big fan of** ③ delivery food.

James Why? **Do you think it is unhealthy to eat delivery food often?**

Min Yes, to be frank, I do. Delivery food is usually unhealthy, fattening and greasy.

James You might be partly right, but it is so delicious.

Min I can't disagree with that. Anyway, **what is an advantage of delivery food?**

James Well, first of all, you don't have to cook or clean up afterward. And you can have exotic food you can't cook.

解說請見 P276

① sound yummy

很常聽到 yummy 吧？意思是指「美味的」。sound 則是「聽起來像～一樣」的意思，sound yum 也可以説成 sound delicious。

⊃ A：I'm going to get a burger with fries. Do you want to come?　我要去吃漢堡和薯條，要一起去嗎？

⊃ B：Sure. That **sounds yummy**.　好啊，聽起來很好吃。

② can't be bothered to (do)

意思為「很懶得做～」，用來表示懶得做什麼，或是覺得做什麼很勉強。在英國較常使用，美國也會使用。

⊃ I **can't be bothered to** do my homework.　我很懶得做作業。

⊃ I didn't clean the room because I **couldn't be bothered to**.　因為懶得做，所以我沒有打掃房間。

③ a big fan of

big fan 有「熱血粉絲」之意，形容非常喜歡某件事物，沒有那麼喜歡時就會説 not a big fan of ～。

⊃ I'm **a big fan of** Korean soccer.　我很喜歡韓國足球。

⊃ I'm not **a big fan of** American movies.　我沒有那麼喜歡美國電影。

Coffee wakes me up!

→ → → 喝咖啡趕走睡意！

　　美國人是出了名的愛喝咖啡，有許多知名的咖啡連鎖店（coffee franchise），這一章節要告訴大家在星巴克（Starbucks）用英語點餐的方法。如果服務生問你 **What can I get for you?**，感覺沒辦法立刻回答吧？這種時候，可以用以下的祕密公式來回答：

1. 先挑選尺寸，星巴克的杯子由小至大分別為 **tall**、**grande**、**venti**，一般咖啡店則是從 **small**、**medium/regular**、**large** 中挑選你要的大小。
2. 接著決定要熱咖啡還是冰咖啡，不是 **hot** 的話就是 **iced**，iced 是過去分詞吧？也就是「做成冰的」的意思。
3. 如果想要去咖啡因的話，説 **decaf** 即可。
4. 接著説你要不要追加 **espresso shot**。
5. 再來挑選牛奶的種類，有 **whole milk** 和 **2% milk**，whole milk 是一般的牛奶，2% milk 或 **skimmed milk** 則是低脂牛奶。
6. 最後説你想要的咖啡種類即可。

那麼來實際演練一下吧？

店員：**What can I get for you?**

我：（想要喝涼爽的「冰拿鐵」，尺寸是 tall，因為很睏所以要多加一份 espresso，又怕發胖所以要低脂牛奶。）**I would like a tall, iced, extra-shot, skimmed-milk latte.**

STEP 1 我先提出問題

🎧 03-1.mp3

試著用「誰、何時、在哪裡、做什麼、如何做、為什麼」的六何法疑問詞來問問題。直到沒有可以再進一步詢問的疑問詞時，就能更自然地引導對話。

✪ 用六何法疑問詞來提問

1. What is your favorite coffee?　最喜歡什麼咖啡？

2. Why do you drink coffee?　為什麼要喝咖啡呢？

3. When do you drink coffee?　何時會喝咖啡？

4. How often do you drink coffee?　有多常喝咖啡？

✪ 不用六何法疑問詞來提問

5. Do you think you are addicted to coffee?　覺得自己是咖啡上癮嗎？

6. Can you make your own coffee?　你會自己沖咖啡嗎？

STEP 2 反向利用提問來回答

🎧 03-2.mp3

如果以前只能簡短回答問題的話，現在試著說出完整的句子吧。將疑問句變成陳述句，就能簡單變成一個句子了。開始練習用句子回答吧！

1. **What** is your favorite coffee? 最喜歡什麼咖啡？

   My favorite coffee is ＿＿＿＿＿.　我最喜歡的咖啡是 ＿＿＿＿＿ 。

   espresso 義式濃縮咖啡 ┃ americano 美式咖啡 ┃ cappuccino 卡布奇諾 ┃ caramel latte 焦糖拿鐵

2. **Why** do you drink coffee? 為什麼要喝咖啡呢？

   I drink coffee **because** ＿＿＿＿＿.　因為 ＿＿＿＿＿ 所以喝咖啡。

   ❶ it keeps me awake. 要讓我保持清醒

   ❷ it helps me focus. 有助於集中精神

3. **When** do you drink coffee?　何時會喝咖啡？

   I drink coffee ＿＿＿＿＿.　＿＿＿＿＿會喝咖啡。

   in the morning 在早上 ┃ in between meals 在兩餐之間 ┃ after a meal 用餐後 ┃ when I wake up 起床時 ┃ when I'm tired 疲倦時

4. How often do you drink coffee? 有多常喝咖啡？

I drink coffee _____. _____會喝咖啡。

every day 每天 | every 3 hours 每三個小時 | once a week 一星期一次

5. Do you think you are addicted to coffee? 覺得自己是咖啡上癮嗎？

→ Yes, I think I am addicted to coffee. Because _____. 是，我好像對咖啡上癮，因為_____。

  ❶ I can't concentrate if I don't drink coffee. 沒喝咖啡的話就無法集中精神。

  ❷ my hands shake when I don't drink my morning coffee. 早上如果沒喝咖啡手會發抖。

→ No, I don't think I am addicted to coffee. Because _____. 不，我應該沒有咖啡上癮，因為_____。

  ❶ I sometimes drink tea or juice instead of coffee. 偶爾會喝茶或果汁來代替咖啡。

  ❷ I don't get cravings for coffee. 沒有想要喝的念頭。

6. Can you make your own coffee? 你會自己沖咖啡嗎？

→ Yes, I can make my own coffee. Because _____. 會，我會自己沖咖啡，因為_____。

  ❶ I have a coffee machine in my house. 家裡有咖啡機。

  ❷ I took a coffee making course. 我上過沖煮咖啡的課程。

→ No, I can't make my own coffee. Because _____. 不會，我不會自己沖咖啡，因為_____。

  ❶ I have never tried making my own coffee. 我沒試過自己沖咖啡。

  ❷ I don't have a coffee machine in my house. 家裡沒有咖啡機。

STEP 3 和母語人士對話

🎧 03-3.mp3

確認前面練習的提問如何活用在和母語人士的對話中，請不要忘記一邊聽一邊跟著說。

James Good morning, Min. Do you want to get some coffee?

Min Hi James, I would love to.

James **What is your favorite coffee?**

Min I like to drink latte. What about you?

James My favorite is americano. I drink it quite often.

Min It sounds like you really like coffee. **Can you make your own coffee at home?**

James Yes, in fact I have a coffee machine in my house. I make coffee for my wife every morning.

Min You're very kind. **When do you drink coffee?**

James I drink coffee when I wake up and **in between meals**[1] . I guess I drink a lot of coffee.

Min It sounds like you do. **How often do you drink coffee?**

James I guess if I average it out, about 4 cups of coffee every day.

Min That's really a lot. Would you say, I mean **do you think you are addicted to coffee?**

James Yes. I definitely am. I **can't live without**[2] coffee. I can't concentrate without it.

Min If you don't mind me asking, **why do you drink coffee?**

James Coffee helps me stay focused, and when I'm tired, coffee keeps me awake.

Min I **get the picture**[3].

 解說請見 P277

① in between meals

meal 是「餐」，吃東西時雖然也可以用 food，但如果要明確表示「餐」的意思，就要用 meal。in between 意思是「在～中間」，in between meals 就有「在餐與餐之間」之意。

- ⊃ I get hungry **in between meals**.　我在兩餐之間都會肚子餓。
- ⊃ My mom drinks coffee **in between meals**.　我母親會在兩餐之間喝咖啡。

② can't live without

用來表現「沒有～就活不下去」，適合表示對某個事物上癮，或是對愛人告白時使用。

- ⊃ To be honest, I **can't live without** my smartphone.　老實說，沒有智慧型手機我活不下去。
- ⊃ My darling, I **can't live without** you.　親愛的，沒有你我活不下去。

③ get the picture

「可以描繪出是什麼情況」的意思，和 understand 同義。

- ⊃ After your explanation, I finally get the picture.　在你說明之後，我終於可以理解了。
- ⊃ Do you get the picture now that I have explained everything?　全部都解說完了，現在你能夠理解了嗎？

It is a plate of heaven

→ → → **甜點是來自天堂的料理**

dessert 這個單字是從法語 desservir（收拾餐桌）演變而來，因為甜點是在收拾好餐桌之後才會出現的。中世紀以前，容易取得的蜂巢或堅果類（nuts）都可當作甜點；到了中世紀，隨著砂糖的生產，也出現了加入砂糖熬煮的香甜甜點。如同韓國有傳統韓菓（traditional Korean sweets）或糕點（rice cake），美國也有傳統的甜點，就是 **apple pie**，蘋果派不但是一整年都很受歡迎的甜點，也是喚醒美國人鄉愁的食物。因此有 **motherhood and apple pie**（象徵大部分美國人認為重要的價值或物品），**as American as apple pie**（像蘋果派一樣很美國）這樣的說法，兩者皆代表了美國人覺得的典型美國社會與文化價值。

有不少人會搞混 dessert（甜點）和 desert（沙漠）的拼法，這裡告訴大家簡單分辨的方法。一旦感受到壓力時，就會想要吃甜點吧？壓力的英語是 stress，「感受到壓力」就是 stressed，把它倒過來寫寫看，變成 desserts 了吧？也就是「甜點」。只要記得「感到壓力的話，就會吃很多甜點」，就能輕鬆分辨 dessert 和 desert 了。

試著用「誰、何時、在哪裡、做什麼、如何做、為什麼」的六何法疑問詞來問問題。直到沒有可以再進一步詢問的疑問詞時,就能更自然地引導對話。

✪ 用六何法疑問詞來提問

1. Who made this cake/cookie/pie?　這個蛋糕／餅乾／派是誰做的?

2. How often do you have dessert?　有多常吃甜點呢?

3. Where do you like to buy your sweets/doughnuts/desserts?　通常喜歡在哪裡買糖果／甜甜圈／甜點呢?

4. What is your favorite dessert?　最喜歡的甜點是什麼?

✪ 不用六何法疑問詞來提問

5. Do you like to have dessert?　喜歡吃甜點嗎?

6. Can you take me to a good dessert café?　可以帶我去不錯的甜點咖啡館嗎?

STEP
2 反向利用提問來回答

 04-2.mp3

如果以前只能簡短回答問題的話,現在試著說出完整的句子吧。將疑問句變成陳述句,就能簡單變成一個句子了。開始練習用句子回答吧!

1. Who made this cake?　這個蛋糕是誰做的?

_____ made this cake.　是 _____ 做的。

My mother 我媽媽 ┃ My friend Jane 我朋友珍 ┃ A famous patissier 有名的甜點師

2. How often do you have dessert?　有多常吃甜點呢?

I have dessert _____.　我 _____ 會吃甜點。

every night 每天晚上 ┃ on a special day 在特別的日子 ┃ when I eat out with my friends 和朋友外出吃飯時

3. Where do you like to buy your doughnuts?　你通常喜歡在哪裡買甜甜圈呢?

I like to buy my doughnuts at _____. 我喜歡在 _____ 買甜甜圈。

a doughnut shop in front of my house 我家前面的甜甜圈店 | a famous bakery in my apartment complex 我家公寓社區裡的知名麵包店

4. What is your favorite dessert? 最喜歡的甜點是什麼？

My favorite dessert is _____. 我最喜歡的甜點是_____。

apple pie with ice cream 冰淇淋蘋果派 | Italian gelato 義式冰淇淋 | Christmas pudding 聖誕布丁

5. Do you like to have dessert? 喜歡吃甜點嗎？

➔ Yes, I like to have dessert. Because _____.

是，我喜歡，因為_____。

① I feel happy when I have something sweet. 吃甜食會讓心情變好。

② I have a sweet tooth. 我喜歡甜食。

➔ No, I don't like to have dessert. Because _____.

不，我不喜歡，因為_____。

① I am not a fan of something sweet. 我不太喜歡甜食

② I want to lose weight so I try to stay away from sweets. 我想減肥，所以會避吃甜食。

6. Can you take me to a good dessert café? 可以帶我去不錯的甜點咖啡館嗎？

➔ Yes, I can take you to a good dessert café. Because _____.

好，可以帶你去，因為 _____。

① I know a good dessert café near my house and I go there quite often. 我知道在我家附近有一間不錯的甜點咖啡館，我也很常去。

② I have a friend who owns a good dessert café and I can take you there today. 我有朋友開了一家不錯的甜點咖啡館，今天可以帶你去。

➔ No, I can't take you to a good dessert café. Because _____.

不，我不能帶你去，因為_____。

① I don't know any good dessert cafés. 我不知道有什麼不錯的甜點咖啡館。

② I don't like dessert and I am on a diet right now. 我不喜歡吃甜點，而且正在減肥。

確認前面練習的提問如何活用在和母語人士的對話中，請不要忘記一邊聽一邊跟著說。

Min Hey James! Come and **have a bite**[①] of this cake.

James Thank you. (Takes a bite) Yummy! It's delicious! **Who made this cake?**

Min Well, **I don't want to brag**[②], but I baked it myself.

James That is amazing! I didn't know you can bake!

Min Well, it's my hobby. **Do you like to have dessert?**

James Sure! Don't we all?

Min I guess so. **How often do you have dessert?**

James Once or twice a week?

Min That's not that often! I have dessert almost every day!

James Every day? That's too often! Do you bake all your desserts? Or do you buy them?

Min I bake some and I buy some.

James **Where do you like to buy your desserts?**

Min I like to go to a dessert café called A to Z in front of City Hall.

James I would love to go there once. **What is your favorite dessert from that place?**

Min I love their chocolate soufflé. It's really good.

James So **can you take me to a good dessert café**, maybe the one you mentioned?

Min Sure, let's go right now! **Tag along!**[③]

▶ ▶ ▶ 解說請見 P277

用 **6** 句英文，和外國人輕鬆話家常！

① have a bite

bite 當成動詞使用的話為「咬」，當成名詞使用的話則有「一口」之意，因此 have a bite 就成了「吃一口看看」的意思。建議對方品嘗自己正在吃的食物，或是品嘗一些簡單的點心時使用。

⊃ Pleasc have a bite of this pie.　吃一口這個派吧。

⊃ Can I have a bite of your sandwich?　我可以吃一口三明治嗎？

② I don't want to brag

brag 有「炫耀」的意思，要炫耀什麼之前，先謙虛地用 I don't want to brag 開頭會比較好。

⊃ I don't want to brag but my sister just passed the bar exam.　我沒有要炫耀的意思，不過我姊姊通過司法考試了。

⊃ I don't want to brag but this bag is worth my month's salary.　我沒有要炫耀的意思，不過這個包包等於我一個月的薪水。

③ Tag along!

Tag 當作名詞有「標籤、標牌」的意思，也就是跟隨著的標誌，另外也有「捉迷藏」的意思，因此如果朋友問你 Do you want to play tag?，就是指「要不要玩捉迷藏？」。將 tag 當成動詞和 along（一起～）併用，就成了「跟著～」。

⊃ Do you want to **tag along** to my friend's house warming party?　要跟我一起去我朋友的喬遷派對嗎？

⊃ Can I **tag along** to the shopping mall?　我可以跟著去購物中心嗎？

What do I love to eat?

➔ ➔ ➔ 我喜歡吃什麼？

在美國生活中常會用到片語動詞（phrasal verb）和慣用語（idiom），由此可以看出英語更善於使用巧妙的隱喻，而不是單純直接的説法。接下來介紹幾種和飲食相關的慣用語。

1. **big cheese**：意思是「重要的人」，而不是「大起司」。It seems that Mr. James is a big cheese in the car industry.（看來詹姆士先生是汽車產業的重要人物。）

2. **buy a lemon**：不是真正的檸檬，而是意指「上當購買了沒有用處、只能丟掉的物品」。把 lemon 理解成不良品即可。I was tricked and bought a lemon.（我被騙買了不良品。）

3. **in a nutshell**：就是「簡略説明的話」，適合在整理要點時使用的説法。In a nutshell, I failed the test.（簡單來説，就是考試搞砸了。）

4. **pie in the sky**：「天空裡的派」，就像在韓國會説「畫中的年糕」，都是指現實中不可能達成的期望。Talking about buying that house is just pie in the sky.（討論買房子的事，根本就是鏡花水月。）

STEP 1 我先提出問題

🎧 05-1.mp3

試著用「誰、何時、在哪裡、做什麼、如何做、為什麼」的六何法疑問詞來問問題。直到沒有可以再進一步詢問的疑問詞時，就能更自然地引導對話。

✪ 用六何法疑問詞來提問

1. What is your favorite food? 　最喜歡的食物是什麼？

2. Why is it your favorite food? 　為什麼最喜歡那種食物呢？

3. When did you first taste your favorite food? 　第一次吃到最喜歡的食物是在什麼時候？

4. Where did you try your favorite food for the first time? 　第一次吃到最喜歡的食物是在哪裡？

✪ 不用六何法疑問詞來提問

5. Is your favorite food healthy? 　你最喜歡的食物是有益健康的嗎？

6. Can you cook your favorite food? 　你會做自己最喜歡的食物嗎？

STEP 2 反向利用提問來回答

🎧 05-2.mp3

如果以前只能簡短回答問題的話，現在試著說出完整的句子吧。將疑問句變成陳述句，就能簡單變成一個句子了。開始練習用句子回答吧！

1. What is your favorite food? 　最喜歡的食物是什麼？

   My favorite food is _____. 　最喜歡的食物是_____。

   kimchi jjigae 泡菜鍋 ▏braised short ribs 燉排骨 ▏chicken soup 雞湯 ▏pepperoni pizza 義式臘腸披薩

2. Why is it your favorite food? 　為什麼最喜歡那種食物呢？

   It is my favorite food because _____. 　因為 _____ 所以最喜歡那種食物。

   ❶ it is healthy and delicious. 　有益健康又美味。

   ❷ my mom used to make it for me when I was sick. 　我生病時，媽媽會做給我吃。

3. When did you first taste your favorite food?　第一次吃到最喜歡的食物是在什麼時候？

I first tasted my favorite food _____.　我在 _____ 吃到我最喜歡的食物。

on my elementary school graduation day 小學畢業典禮時 ｜ when I traveled to the US 10 years ago 十年前去美國旅行時

4. Where did you try your favorite food for the first time?　第一次吃到最喜歡的食物是在哪裡？

I tried my favorite food for the first time _____.　我 _____ 吃到我最喜歡的食物。

in my uncle's house 在叔叔家 ｜ at a local Chinese restaurant 在當地的一家中國餐館

5. Is your favorite food healthy?　你最喜歡的食物是有益健康的嗎？

→ Yes, it is healthy. Because _____.

是，對健康有益，因為 _____。

❶ the main ingredients are vegetables.　主要材料是蔬菜。

❷ it is low in calories.　熱量低。

→ No, it is not healthy. Because _____.

不，對健康不好，因為 _____。

❶ it is greasy and fattening.　是油膩又會發胖的食物。

❷ it is salty and too sweet.　太鹹太甜了。

6. Can you cook your favorite food?　你會做自己最喜歡的食物嗎？

→ Yes, I can cook it. Because _____.

會，我會做，因為 _____。

❶ my mother taught me an easy recipe.　我媽媽教了我簡單的料理方法。

❷ it isn't difficult so I have made it several times.　不難所以試做過幾次。

→ No, I can't cook it. Because _____.

不會，我不會做，因為 _____。

❶ I couldn't find the recipe.　我找不到食譜。

❷ it is quite difficult to cook.　不太容易料理。

確認前面練習的提問如何活用在和母語人士的對話中，請不要忘記一邊聽一邊跟著説。

Min Have some of this rice cake.

James Thanks. Yummy! This is delicious. What is the name of this rice cake?

Min We call this chapsalttock or glutinous rice cake.

James I have never had this before. Is this your favorite rice cake?

Min Yes, it is. **What is your favorite Korean food?**

James My favorite Korean food is ramen.

Min **Why is it your favorite Korean food?**

James It's simply the best. The noodles and the spicy soup are always **mouthwatering**[①].

Min **When did you first taste Korean ramen?**

James Let me see. I think it was 3 years ago.

Min **Where did you try ramen for the first time**[②]?

James It was when I went camping with my friend. We had ramen for dinner and it was just perfect.

Min I know it's a silly question, but do you think ramen is healthy?

James I don't think so. Everybody says it's unhealthy and I understand why. It contains a lot of MSG, right?

Min Yep, you're right. So try not to have it too often.

James I will. You sound like my mother.

Min Oops, sorry. **Can you cook ramen?**

James Sure I can. It's **a piece of cake**[③]. I can cook it in 5 minutes.

▶ ▶ ▶ 解說請見 P278

① mouthwatering

「流口水」的意思，要表達「好吃」時，別再用常見的 delicious 或 yummy，試著改用特別一點的 It's mouthwatering. 吧。

- ⊃ Here are top **mouthwatering** recipes.　這裡有讓人流口水的厲害食譜。
- ⊃ That restaurant's pancakes are **mouthwatering**.　那家餐廳的鬆餅好吃到讓人流口水。

② for the first time

「第一次」的意思，任何事情第一次做時都可以使用。因為電影《冰雪奇緣》中出現的歌曲〈For the First Time in Forever〉，讓這個說法變得更知名。

- ⊃ I stayed up the whole night to study **for the first time**.　我第一次為了唸書而熬夜。
- ⊃ Tom submitted his essay on time **for the first time**.　湯姆第一次準時交論文。

③ a piece of cake

直譯就是「一塊蛋糕」，和韓文的「吃冷粥」或「躺著吃年糕」意思相同，用來表達非常簡單的事。

- ⊃ Cooking ramen is **a piece of cake**.　煮泡麵非常簡單。
- ⊃ Convincing somebody is **a piece of cake** for me.　對我來說，要說服別人是非常簡單的事。

HOME COOKED MEALS

A home cooked meal is the best!

→ → → 家常菜最棒了！

CNN 選出了美國人最喜愛的五十道家常菜，以下介紹其中幾道我們也很熟悉的料理。

第一名當然非 **Thanksgiving Day dinner** 莫屬了，有烤火雞（roasted turkey）、玉米麵包（cornbread）、馬鈴薯泥（mashed potatoes）、南瓜派（pumpkin pie）等等傳統感恩節的食物。

第二十五名為 **baked beans**，較多以罐頭的形態出現，按字面解釋就是「烤豆子」的意思。烤豆子加入了洋蔥、培根、醬汁一起烤，常會抹在吐司（toast）上吃，由於擁有豐富蛋白質，吃完會很有飽足感。

第三十一名是常出現在電影和美國電視劇中的 **macaroni and cheese**，韓國的美式家庭餐廳也有這道菜。在煮好的（boiled）通心粉上，加了滿滿的各種起司，再放入烤箱烤，是一道簡單的料理。

第三十八名是 **biscuits and gravy**，為南方料理，在類似肯德基也有販售的圓形大比司吉上，淋上肉汁（gravy）一起吃，醬汁是由烹煮肉類後剩下的肉汁和胡椒製成。之後不妨到美式家庭餐廳挑戰看看吧。

試著用「誰、何時、在哪裡、做什麼、如何做、為什麼」的六何法疑問詞來問問題。直到沒有可以再進一步詢問的疑問詞時，就能更自然地引導對話。

✪ 用六何法疑問詞來提問

1. Why do you like home cooked meals?　為何喜歡家常菜呢？

2. How often do you have a home cooked meal?　有多常吃家常菜呢？

3. What is an advantage of home cooked meals?　家常菜有什麼優點？

4. When do you normally have a home cooked meal?　通常什麼時候會吃家常菜？

✪ 不用六何法疑問詞來提問

5. Can you prepare a nice home cooked meal?　你會準備一桌美味的家常菜嗎？

6. Do you like home cooked meals?　喜歡家常菜嗎？

如果以前只能簡短回答問題的話，現在試著說出完整的句子吧。將疑問句變成陳述句，就能簡單變成一個句子了。開始練習用句子回答吧！

1. Why do you like home cooked meals?　為何喜歡家常菜呢？

   I like home cooked meals because _____.　因為 _____ 所以喜歡家常菜。

   ➊ the food is healthy.　食物有益健康。

   ➋ the food is hygienic.　食物是衛生的。

2. How often do you have a home cooked meal?　有多常吃家常菜呢？

   I usually have a home cooked meal _____.　通常 _____ 會吃家常菜。

   almost every day 幾乎每天 ┃ once or twice a month 一個月一、兩次

3. What is an advantage of home cooked meals?　家常菜有什麼優點？

An advantage of home cooked meals is they are _____.　家常菜
的優點是 _____ 。

made from fresh ingredients 用新鮮的材料製成 ｜ cheap and delicious 便宜又美味

4. When do you normally have a home cooked meal?　通常什麼時候會吃
家常菜？

I normally have a home cooked meal _____.　通常 _____ 會
吃家常菜。

on a special day 在特別的日子 ｜ when I get off work early 提早下班時 ｜ when I visit my
parents' house 去父母家時

5. Can you prepare a nice home cooked meal?　你會準備一桌美味的家
常菜嗎？

→ Yes, I can prepare a nice home cooked meal. Because _____.

是，我會，因為_____。

❶ I took a cooking class.　我去上了料理課。

❷ I like cooking and I know quite a few recipes.　我喜歡做菜，知道一些烹飪方法。

→ No, I can't prepare a nice home cooked meal. Because _____.

不，我不會，因為 _____ 。

❶ I am really bad at cooking.　我真的不太會做料理。

❷ it is too difficult for me to do.　對我來說太難了。

6. Do you like home cooked meals?　喜歡家常菜嗎？

→ Yes, I like home cooked meals. Because _____.

是，我喜歡家常菜，因為 _____ 。

❶ I think they are healthier and more delicious.　感覺更健康而且更美味。

❷ I am on a diet and eating out can be very fattening.　我在減肥，外食會變胖。

→ No, I don't like home cooked meals. Because _____.

不，我不喜歡家常菜，因為 _____ 。

❶ I hate cleaning up afterward.　我討厭之後還要收拾。

❷ my mother is not a good cook so homemade meals are not delicious.　我媽媽不太會做
菜，所以家常菜不好吃。

確認前面練習的提問如何活用在和母語人士的對話中，請不要忘記一邊聽一邊跟著説。

James What's the hurry?

Min I'm going to my mother's house today.

James She'll be happy to see you. **What's the occasion?**[①]

Min It's my brother's birthday so the whole family is gathering for dinner.

James **Lucky you!**[②]   That sounds fun.

Min It will be fun. I'm excited to have my mother's home cooking. **Do you like home cooked meals?**

James Of course I do. I think home cooked meals are the best.

Min I totally agree. **Why do you like home cooked meals?**

James Above all, they are healthy. I know my mother uses the best ingredients and the food is way more hygienic than restaurant food.

Min You are absolutely right. **Can you prepare a nice home cooked meal?**

James Well, I can't cook like my mother, but I do **look up**[③] some recipes and can make a few decent dishes.

Min So do you cook often? **How often do you have a home cooked meal?**

James I have a home cooked meal almost every day.

Min You have time? **When do you normally have a home cooked meal?**

James I cook breakfast at home every day.

Min You have a healthy habit. **What do you think is an advantage of home cooked meals?**

James I think the biggest advantage is that the ingredients are fresh. If you eat outside, you have no idea how old the ingredients are.

Min I can't disagree with that.

 解說請見 P278

① What's the occasion?

適用於談話的對象看起來和平常不太一樣時，有「今天是什麼日子啊」、「怎麼回事啊？」之意，occasion 有「特別場合」或「活動」的意思。

⊃ You are all dressed up today. **What's the occasion?**　今天盛裝打扮耶，是什麼日子啊？

⊃ You are looking good today. **What's the occasion?**　今天看起來很帥氣，是什麼日子啊？

② Lucky you!

有「你的運氣真好！」之意，當羨慕或妒忌對方時，是很適合的用法。

⊃ A：I'm going to get an award for being the employee of the month.　我將得到本月的員工獎。

⊃ B：**Lucky you!** When is the ceremony?　好羨慕啊！頒獎典禮是什麼時候？

③ look up

直譯的話是「向上看」，但在對話中則是用來表示「找找看」的意思，主要用於查找字典、參考資料、目錄等等資訊的時候。

⊃ Can you **look up** Tom's number for me?　你可以幫我找湯姆的電話號碼嗎？

⊃ I need to **look up** the definition of this word.　我得找一下這個單字的意思了。

Fast food is delicious!

→ → → 速食真好吃！

　　説到代表性的速食，應該有漢堡（hamburger）、三明治（sandwich）和熱狗（hot dog）吧，不過，你知道叉在竹籤上的炸熱狗，英語不叫 hot dog，而是 **corn dog** 嗎？在英語系國家，hot dog 指的是在長長的麵包中，夾入熱狗和蔬菜，再淋上醬料來吃的食物。

　　我小時候曾去過加拿大一家叫做溫蒂漢堡（Wendy's）的速食店，只是為了點漢堡，整個背後就冷汗直流，因為我不知道該怎麼用英語表達自己想要的、以及不想要的食材。**I would like to have lettuce and relish but I don't want onion.**（請幫我放生菜和醃漬物，然後不要洋蔥。）應該要這樣説才對。

　　來學一些可以夾在漢堡裡的材料吧，從蔬菜類開始，有 lettuce（生菜）、tomato（番茄）、red onion（紫洋蔥）、pickles（醃漬物）、cucumber（黃瓜）、spinach（菠菜），切碎的醃漬物又叫做 relish。其他還可以加入 cheddar cheese slice（切達起司片）或 smoked bacon（煙燻培根）等等，基本的醬料有 mustard（芥末醬）、ketchup（番茄醬）以及 mayonnaise（美乃滋）。

STEP 1 我先提出問題

🎧 07-1.mp3

試著用「誰、何時、在哪裡、做什麼、如何做、為什麼」的六何法疑問詞來問問題。直到沒有可以再進一步詢問的疑問詞時，就能更自然地引導對話。

✪ **用六何法疑問詞來提問**

1. What is your favorite fast food?　最喜歡的速食是什麼？

2. When do you normally have fast food?　通常會在什麼時候吃速食？

3. Where do you go to have fast food?　會去哪裡吃速食？

4. How often do you have fast food?　有多常吃速食呢？

✪ **不用六何法疑問詞來提問**

5. Do you like fast food?　喜歡速食嗎？

6. Is fast food bad for children?　速食對孩童不好嗎？

STEP 2 反向利用提問來回答

🎧 07-2.mp3

如果以前只能簡短回答問題的話，現在試著說出完整的句子吧。將疑問句變成陳述句，就能簡單變成一個句子了。開始練習用句子回答吧！

1. What is your favorite fast food?　最喜歡的速食是什麼？

   My favorite fast food is _____.　我最喜歡的速食是 _____。

   a cheeseburger 起司漢堡 ｜ pizza 披薩 ｜ a sandwich 三明治

2. When do you normally have fast food?　通常會在什麼時候吃速食？

   I normally have fast food _____.　通常 _____ 會吃速食。

   on weekends 在週末 ｜ when I'm very busy 我很忙的時候 ｜ when I'm with my friends 和朋友在一起時

3. Where do you go to have fast food?　會去哪裡吃速食？

   I go to _____ to have fast food.　會去 _____ 吃速食。

the 'McDonald's' in my neighborhood 我家附近的麥當勞 | the 'Burger King' in front of my office 辦公室前面的漢堡王 | the 'Sandwich Joe' near my apartment complex 我家公寓社區附近的 Sandwich Joe

4. How often do you have fast food? 有多常吃速食呢？

I have fast food _____. 我 _____ 會吃速食。

once a week 一星期一次 | more than three times a week 一星期三次以上 | once or twice a year 一年一兩次

5. Do you like fast food? 喜歡速食嗎？

→ Yes, I like fast food. Because _____.

是，我喜歡速食，因為_____。

❶ it is delicious and cheap. 好吃又便宜。

❷ I don't have to wait for the food to be cooked. 我不用等待食物煮好。

→ No, I don't like fast food. Because _____.

不，我不喜歡速食，因為 _____。

❶ it is unhealthy and fattening. 對健康有害，還會發胖。

❷ it doesn't have enough nutrients. 沒有足夠的營養。

6. Is fast food bad for children? 速食對孩童不好嗎？

→ Yes, it is. Because _____. 是，對孩童不好，因為 _____。

❶ the ingredients are usually frozen and not fresh. 材料通常都是冷凍的而且不新鮮。

❷ it causes children obesity. 會造成兒童肥胖。

→ No, it isn't. Because _____. 不，它不會，因為 _____。

❶ children don't have fast food that often. 孩童並沒有那麼常吃速食。

❷ we can add a salad and balance the meal. 再加上沙拉就能保持飲食均衡。

STEP 3 和母語人士對話

 07-3.mp3

確認前面練習的提問如何活用在和母語人士的對話中，請不要忘記一邊聽一邊跟著說。

Min It's finally lunch break! It seemed like the morning went on forever.

James **Tell me about it.**[①] I'm starving.

Min What do you feel like having for lunch?

James I feel like having a burger today. **Do you like fast food?**

Min Yes, I do. Let's go to the fast food restaurant downstairs.

James **I'd love to.**[②] **What is your favorite fast food?**

Min My number one favorite fast food is hamburgers. What about you?

James I also love burgers. My favorite is a crispy chicken burger.

Min That sounds yummy too. **Where do you go to have fast food?**

James There is a decent fast food restaurant in front of my house. I go there whenever I get a craving for fast food.

Min **When do you normally have fast food?**

James I guess I prefer to have fast food on weekends when I don't feel like cooking.

Min I love fast food, but I wouldn't want to feed it to my children too often. What do you think? **Is fast food bad for children?**

James I do agree with you. Fast food is fattening and lacks enough nutrients. I do think it is bad for children.

Min Yes. My nephew is quite big and I think it's because of all the fast food he has. Child obesity is a serious issue.

James Yes. Fast food is okay only when you have it **once in a while**[③].

解說請見 P279

① Tell me about it

直譯的話為「告訴我那件事」，但實際上有「就是說啊」的意思。在完全同意對方的意見時可以使用。

- ⊃ A：I can't believe John was elected as the class representative. 我不敢相信約翰竟然選上學年代表。
- ⊃ B：**Tell me about it.** Jack is so much better. 就是說啊，傑克還比較優秀。

② I'd love to (do)

有「想做～」的意思，可以簡單解釋成「好啊」，也可以把想做的行為接在 to 的後面。

- ⊃ A：Can we meet again later? 我們能再見面嗎？
- ⊃ B：**I'd love to** see you again. 我想再跟你見面。

③ once in a while

意思為「偶爾一次」，說明偶然發生一次，不是經常發生的事情。

- ⊃ My boyfriend and I have a fight **once in a while**. 我男友和我偶爾會吵架。
- ⊃ My computer is old so it stops working **once in a while**. 我的電腦太舊了，偶爾會停止運轉。

COOKING

Cooking can be fun!

→ → → **料理真有趣！**

雖然大家都說英國料理不好吃，但其實還是有美味的食物，只是不太為人所知。英國的代表性料理是烤牛肉（roast beef），搭配約克郡布丁（Yorkshire pudding），還有煮、蒸或烤（boiled, steamed or roasted）的蔬菜一起吃的週日烤肉（Sunday roast）。而美國和加拿大由於是各種民族移居的多民族國家，料理也和他們的民族一樣多元。若要從中挑選的話，美國以傳統的感恩節料理——烤火雞（roasted turkey）最具代表性，加拿大則以鮭魚或小龍蝦等等海鮮（seafood）料理較為知名。

接著來學習受邀作客時的禮節吧？首先，最基本的就是要吃得津津有味，沒有剩餘的話會更好。也不要忘了用 **It's delicious.**（好吃），**How did you make this?**（這是怎麼做的？），**It smells so good.**（聞起來真棒）等等句子來稱讚做料理的人。不要只是專心於吃，也要和其他人有眼神交流，分享愉快的話題也很不錯。但要避免政治和宗教等敏感主題，最好聊些和興趣嗜好相關的話題。

試著用「誰、何時、在哪裡、做什麼、如何做、為什麼」的六何法疑問詞來問問題。直到沒有可以再進一步詢問的疑問詞時，就能更自然地引導對話。

✪ 用六何法疑問詞來提問

1. Why do you cook?　為何要做料理？

2. When do you normally cook?　通常何時會做料理？

3. Who do you usually cook for?　主要是為了誰做料理？

4. What can you cook the best?　最擅長的料理是什麼？

✪ 不用六何法疑問詞來提問

5. Is cooking at home better than eating out?　在家做料理會比外食來得好嗎？

6. Do you prepare a packed lunch?　你會準備便當嗎？

如果以前只能簡短回答問題的話，現在試著說出完整的句子吧。將疑問句變成陳述句，就能簡單變成一個句子了。開始練習用句子回答吧！

1. Why do you cook?　為何要做料理？

I cook because _____.　因為 _____ 所以我做料理。

❶ I'm good at cooking　擅長做菜。

❷ it is healthier to have home cooked meals　吃自己在家做的菜更健康。

2. When do you normally cook?　通常何時會做料理？

I normally cook _____.　通常 _____ 會做料理。

on weekends 在週末 ┃ in the mornings 每天早上 ┃ on a special day 在特別的日子

3. Who do you usually cook for?　主要是為了誰做料理？

I usually cook for _____.　主要是為了 _____ 做料理。

myself 我自己 ┃ my family 家人 ┃ my girlfriend 我的女友

4. What can you cook the best? 最擅長的料理是什麼？

I can cook _____ the best. 最擅長的料理是 _____。

curry 咖哩 | vegetable soup 蔬菜濃湯 | tuna porridge 鮪魚粥 | roast turkey 烤火雞 |
mashed potatoes 薯泥

5. Is cooking at home better than eating out? 在家做料理會比外食來得好嗎？

→ Yes, I think cooking at home is better than eating out. Because

_____.

是，我覺得在家做料理比外食來得好，因為 _____。

❶ it is hygienic and cheaper. 比較衛生而且便宜。

❷ I can use fresh ingredient so it is healthier. 可以吃到新鮮食材，比較健康。

→ No, I think eating out is better than cooking at home. Because

_____.

不，我不覺得在家做料理比外食來得好，因為_____。

❶ it is more expensive to buy fresh ingredients. 買新鮮食材更花錢。

❷ eating out is quick and convenient. 外食快速且方便。

6. Do you prepare a packed lunch? 你會準備便當嗎？

→ Yes, I prepare a packed lunch. Because _____.

是，我會準備便當，因為 _____。

❶ it is much more economical than buying food. 比起買外食要來得經濟實惠。

❷ it is less fattening than buying food outside. 比起買外食比較不會發胖。

→ No, I don't prepare a packed lunch. Because _____.

不，我不會準備便當，因為 _____。

❶ I don't have time to prepare it. 沒有時間準備。

❷ I'm not good at cooking. 我不太會烹飪。

確認前面練習的提問如何活用在和母語人士的對話中，請不要忘記一邊聽一邊跟著說。

Min Is this your lunch box? **Do you prepare a packed lunch?**

James Yes, I do. I cook quite often so I bring food from home.

Min That's really nice. I didn't know you like to cook.

James Yep. **I'm fond of cooking**[1]. It's one of my hobbies.

Min If you don't mind me asking, **why do you cook?**

James Well, there are many advantages. It's healthier for sure and it is cheaper if you cook often.

Min I see. **Who do you usually cook for?** Do you live with your family?

James Nope, I live alone. So I just cook for myself.

Min It must be a lot of work to cook and to have a full-time job. **When do you normally cook?**

James Yep, you are right. I am busy on weekdays so I usually cook on weekends.

Min That sounds wise. **What can you cook the best?**

James I'm really good at cooking Korean style curry. It's easy, quick and delicious. You should try it.

Min I'm a lousy cook, but I will **give it a try**[2]. So you think that **cooking at home is better than eating out**, right?

James **You bet!**[3] Cooking can help you lose weight and save money at the same time.

▶ ▶ ▶ 解說請見 P279

用 6 句英文，和外國人輕鬆話家常！

① be fond of

意思為「喜歡」，和 like 同義，是比 like 更高級的說法，聊天時可多使用。

- ➲ My mother **is** quite **fond of** dogs.　我媽媽非常喜歡狗。
- ➲ I didn't know you **were fond of** Jack.　我不曉得你喜歡傑克。

② give it a try

try 有「嘗試、挑戰」的意思，give it a try 則是「挑戰某事物一次看看」之意，it 可以代換成挑戰的行為或事物。

- ➲ A：Kimchi is not that spicy. You should **give it a try**.　泡菜並沒有那麼辣，你嘗試一次看看。
- ➲ B：I just **gave it a try** and unexpectedly, I succeeded.　我只是嘗試看看，沒想到卻成功了。

③ You bet!

bet 為「打賭」之意，但 You bet! 則有「當然囉！」、「就是那個！」之意，用於強烈同意對方的話時。

- ➲ A：It was an amazing movie.　真是一部驚人的電影。
- ➲ B：**You bet!** I can't stop thinking about the perfect ending.　就是說啊！一直會想起完美的結尾。

Would you like to go out for a drink?

→ → → **要去喝一杯嗎？**

　　説點輕鬆的，韓國的飲酒文化很盛行吧？美國或是英國則是因為重視家族文化，家人之間也很常去酒吧（bar），聚餐時幾乎沒有勸酒的行為，酒吧早早就會關門，路上很難看到喝醉的人。不過，住在城市的年輕人則常常喝酒。來認識一下喝酒相關的説法吧！

　　Do you like to drink?，雖然在 drink 的後面省略了酒（alcoholic beverage），不過這句話有「你喜歡喝酒嗎？」的意思。酒喝多的話就會醉吧？「喝醉」是 **get drunk**、**be drunk**，「微醺」則是 **be tipsy**，如果説 I am tipsy.，就是「我有點醉了」的意思。

　　喝酒的隔天還留有醉意的時候，叫做 be hungover，這種時候就要喝解酒湯（hangover soup）來解酒。如同韓國有解酒湯一樣，其他國家也有 **hangover food**（解酒食物），美國會吃又鹹又油的食物，通常是培根、雞蛋、起司三明治和油炸料理。從科學的角度來看，喝酒之前最好吃一些油膩的食物，而喝酒後吃雞蛋的話，則是能分解酒精。在英國，會將生雞蛋拌進伍斯特醬（Worcestershire sauce）用來解酒，可樂和咖啡也常被當成解酒食物。

試著用「誰、何時、在哪裡、做什麼、如何做、為什麼」的六何法疑問詞來問問題。直到沒有可以再進一步詢問的疑問詞時，就能更自然地引導對話。

✪ 用六何法疑問詞來提問

1. What is your favorite alcoholic beverage? 最喜歡的酒是什麼？

2. When do you normally go to a bar? 通常何時會去酒吧？

3. Where do you usually go drinking? 通常會去哪裡喝酒？

4. Who do you like to drink beer with? 你喜歡跟誰一起喝啤酒？

✪ 不用六何法疑問詞來提問

5. Do you like to drink beer? 喜歡喝啤酒嗎？

6. Have you tried soju/sake? 喝過燒酒／清酒嗎？

STEP 2 反向利用提問來回答 ∩ 09-2.mp3

如果以前只能簡短回答問題的話，現在試著說出完整的句子吧。將疑問句變成陳述句，就能簡單變成一個句子了。開始練習用句子回答吧！

1. What is your favorite alcoholic beverage? 最喜歡的酒是什麼？

   My favorite alcoholic beverage is _____.

   最喜歡的酒是 _____。

   wine 紅酒 | beer 啤酒 | soju 燒酒 | sake 清酒

2. When do you normally go to a bar? 通常何時會去酒吧？

   I normally go to a bar _____. 通常 _____ 會去酒吧。

   on weekends 在週末 | on Fridays 每個星期五 | on a special day 在特別的日子

3. Where do you usually go drinking? 通常會去哪裡喝酒？

   I usually go drinking at _____. 通常會去 _____ 喝酒。

   a pub 酒館 | a nightclub 夜店 | a lounge 酒吧 | a hotel bar 飯店酒吧

4. Who do you like to drink beer with? 你喜歡跟誰一起喝啤酒？

I like to drink beer with _____. 我喜歡跟 _____ 喝啤酒。

my colleagues 我的同事 | close friends 好朋友 | my spouse 我的伴侶 | my boyfriend 我的男友

5. Do you like to drink beer? 喜歡喝啤酒嗎？

→ Yes, I like to drink beer. Because _____.

是，我喜歡喝啤酒，因為 _____。

❶ I like having fun at a bar with my friends. 我喜歡和朋友一起去酒館玩樂。

❷ when we get tipsy, we have a lot more fun. 稍微有些醉意會更開心。

→ No, I don't like to drink beer. Because _____.

不，我不喜歡喝啤酒，因為 _____。

❶ my body can't take alcohol well. My face turns red when I drink beer. 我的身體不太能適應酒精，喝了啤酒臉就會變紅。

❷ it's too filling. I like to drink wine. 肚子太脹了，我喜歡喝紅酒。

6. Have you tried sake? 喝過清酒嗎？

→ Yes, I have tried it. Because _____.

有，我喝過，因為_____。

❶ I traveled to Japan last year and I had a chance to try it. 去年我到日本旅行時，有機會喝到。

❷ my best friend loves drinking it so he recommended I try sake a while ago. 我最好的朋友很喜歡喝清酒，不久前推薦我喝過了。

→ No, I haven't tried it yet. Because _____.

沒有，沒喝過，因為 _____。

❶ I rarely go to Japanese restaurants. 我很少去日本料理店。

❷ I don't like to try new alcoholic drinks. 我不喜歡嘗試喝新的酒。

STEP 3　和母語人士對話

🎧 09-3.mp3

確認前面練習的提問如何活用在和母語人士的對話中，請不要忘記一邊聽一邊跟著說。

James　Hey Min, what did you do last weekend?

Min　Good morning James! I had a great time with my husband.

James　What did you do? **Fill me in.**[①]

Min　We **stopped by**[②] a new bar that opened in front of my house.

James　Nice. How was it?

Min　We had sake and it was really good. **Have you tried sake?**

James　Not yet. It's a Japanese drink right? I would love to try it later.

Min　You should. **Do you like to drink beer?**

James　Yes, I love to drink beer.

Min　**Who do you like to drink beer with?**

James　I like to drink beer with my friends, colleagues, family members and so on.

　　　　I guess I just like to drink.

Min　I understand. **What is your favorite alcoholic drink?**

James　Well, I guess my favorite is wine. These days I like drinking white wine.

Min　I am a wine lover as well. **When do you normally go to a bar?**

James　I normally go to a bar on special days like birthdays, anniversaries and

　　　　when I have something to celebrate.

Min　I see. So **where do you usually go drinking?**

James　I usually go drinking at a bar near my office. I don't like to go someplace

　　　　far away.

Min　Next weekend, we should get together for a drink. **What do you say?**[③]

James　I would love to. Give me a call.

▶ ▶ ▶ 解說請見 P280

① Fill me in

fill in 是「填滿」的意思，fill me in 則有「提供情報填滿我不知道的部分」之意，也就是「再多給一點情報，再多說一點」。

- How was your week? Please **fill me in**.　你這個星期過得如何？再說仔細一點吧。

- I missed the meeting so you need to **fill me in**.　我沒有去開會，請告訴我錯過的部分。

② stop by

「臨時路過」的意思，也可以用來表示「暫時訪問一下」，嚴格來說是去某處的路上順路經過，但用在會話中就沒有特別區分。

- Can you **stop by** my office tomorrow?　明天可以順路來我辦公室一下嗎？

- I will **stop by** your house to give you the book.　我明天會經過你家，把書拿給你。

③ What do you say?

和 How about you?、What do you think? 一樣，有「怎麼樣？」的意思，適合在詢問對方的意見時使用。

- A：Let's go shopping this Friday. **What do you say?**　這個星期五去逛街吧，你覺得呢？

- B：That's a great idea. I would love to.　這點子不錯，我想去。

Let's talk about street food!

→ → → 來聊聊路邊小吃吧！

　　冬天走在街上，總是不知不覺地被路邊販售的鯛魚燒或魚板吸引。像這種在路邊販賣的 **ready-to-eat**（即食的）、**portable**（可攜帶的）、**cheap**（便宜的）食物，叫做 **street food** 或 **street snack**。

　　在路邊販售食物的攤販則是 **food stall**、**food cart**、**street vendor** 或是 **cart bar**。那麼就來認識一下不同國家街頭賣的代表性小吃吧？美國知名的是在麵包中間夾入熱狗（hot dog）和醃漬物的小吃；土耳其有名的是土耳其烤肉（kebab）；而加拿大的路邊小吃──肉汁奶酪薯條（poutine），是一種將薯條（french fries）淋上醬汁和起司的食物；在韓國很受歡迎的珍珠奶茶（bubble tea），則是來自台灣的食物。義大利的黏稠冰淇淋（gelato），以及西班牙的吉拿棒（churros）都是受到喜愛的路邊小吃；泰國人喜歡吃街邊的麵食，而中國人則常在路邊買餃子（dumpling）來吃。

STEP 1 我先提出問題

 10-1.mp3

試著用「誰、何時、在哪裡、做什麼、如何做、為什麼」的六何法疑問詞來問問題。直到沒有可以再進一步詢問的疑問詞時，就能更自然地引導對話。

✪ 用六何法疑問詞來提問

1. What is your favorite street food?　最喜歡的路邊小吃是什麼？

2. When do you have street food?　何時會吃路邊小吃呢？

3. Where do you go to have street food?　會去哪裡吃路邊小吃呢？

4. How often do you eat street food?　有多常吃路邊小吃呢？

✪ 不用六何法疑問詞來提問

5. Do you like street food?　喜歡路邊小吃嗎？

6. Can you cook street food at home?　你會在家裡做路邊小吃嗎？

STEP 2 反向利用提問來回答

 10-2.mp3

如果以前只能簡短回答問題的話，現在試著說出完整的句子吧。將疑問句變成陳述句，就能簡單變成一個句子了。開始練習用句子回答吧！

1. What is your favorite street food?　最喜歡的路邊小吃是什麼？

   My favorite street food is _____.

   我最喜歡的路邊小吃是_____。

   gimbap 紫菜飯卷 ｜ tacos 墨西哥夾餅 ｜ crêpes 可麗餅

2. When do you have street food?　何時會吃路邊小吃呢？

   I have street food _____.　_____ 會吃路邊小吃。

   ❶ when I don't have enough time　時間不夠時

   ❷ when I go shopping with my friends　和朋友去逛街時

3. Where do you go to have street food?　會去哪裡吃路邊小吃呢？

   I like to go to _____ to have street food.　我喜歡去 _____ 吃路邊小吃。

a food stall in front of my office 公司前面的攤販 | a snack bar in Gangnam 江南的小吃店
| a food truck in my neighborhood 我家附近的餐車

4. How often do you eat street food? 有多常吃路邊小吃呢？

I eat street food _____. 我 _____ 會吃路邊小吃。

once a month 一個月一次 | on Sundays 每個星期天 | once or twice a year 一年一兩次 |
almost every day 幾乎每天

5. Do you like street food? 喜歡路邊小吃嗎？

→ Yes, I like street food. Because _____.

是，我喜歡，因為_____。

❶ it is cheap, delicious and convenient. 便宜、美味又方便。

❷ it is light and affordable. 簡單又便宜。

→ No, I don't like street food. Because _____.

不，我不喜歡，因為_____。

❶ I think it is unhygienic and unhealthy. 感覺不衛生而且對健康不好。

❷ it is not a proper meal. 不是正常的一餐。

6. Can you cook street food at home? 你會在家裡做路邊小吃嗎？

→ Sure, I can cook __（食物名稱）__. Because _____.

那當然，我會做 _____，因為 _____。

❶ fish cake, it is easy to cook. 魚板，做法簡單。

❷ tteokbokki, my mother taught me how to make this. 辣炒年糕，媽媽教了我做法。

→ No, I can't cook street food at home. Because _____.

不，我不會，因為 _____。

❶ I can't really cook at all. 我真的完全不會做料理。

❷ I don't know the recipes for these foods. 不曉得這些食物的食譜。

確認前面練習的提問如何活用在和母語人士的對話中，請不要忘記一邊聽一邊跟著說。

Min That was a long meeting. Did you have lunch?

James Yeh, I did. But I'm a bit hungry. Do you want to grab a snack?

Min Yes, I'm starving. I feel like having some street food. **Do you like street food?**

James Sure. **It's like you read my mind.**[①] **What is your favorite street food?**

Min I like tteokbokki and fish cake. They are the perfect combination.

James That sounds yummy. Let's get those.

Min **How often do you eat street food?**

James I really like tteokbokki so I eat street food quite often. Maybe once a week?

Min That's not too often. **When do you normally have street food?**

James When I **feel like having**[②] something spicy. I sometimes **have cravings for**[③] spicy tteokbokki.

Min I didn't know you like spicy food that much. **Where do you go to have good street food?**

James I like going to a snack bar called 'Jaw's.' It's a well-known place.

Min Since you like street food so much, **can you cook street food at home?**

James Yes, I can cook tteokbokki. I think I make it well.

Min I'm sure you do. I would love to try it one day.

 解說請見 P280

① It's like you read my mind

意思為「好像能讀懂我的心一樣」，用於表達強烈同意。

- ⊃ A：Do you want to go to a movie tonight?　今天晚上要去看電影嗎？
- ⊃ B：Yes, I'd love to. **It's like you read my mind**.　好啊！真是心有靈犀。

② feel like having

表達想要吃什麼。having 如果改用其他動詞的話，就是想做該動詞所表示的行動，例如 I feel like studying. 即「我想唸書」。

- ⊃ I **feel like having** some chocolates.　我想吃巧克力。
- ⊃ She said she **feels like having** some fruit.　她說想要吃水果。

③ have cravings for

crave 基本上有「想要～」的意思，是比 want 更強烈的表現，可解釋成「渴望」，for 後面如果按上食物名稱，簡單來說就是「對～嘴饞」。When I'm stressed, I have cravings for chocolates. 即「我感受到壓力時，就會想吃巧克力」，這樣就能理解了吧？

- ⊃ I **have cravings for** some meat.　我想吃肉。
- ⊃ I heard when you are pregnant, you **have cravings for** random foods.　我聽說懷孕的話就會想吃奇奇怪怪的食物。

Part 2

興趣與嗜好，
發現自我的時間

各位有什麼興趣嗎？興趣是因為喜歡，以一顆愉悅的心去做的事，能讓身心變得健康。因興趣而開始的學習，不但能成為有用的才能，亦可能會帶來財富，所以和興趣、嗜好相關的話題，也是不錯的對話素材。那麼，就試著用六何法疑問詞來聊聊興趣和嗜好吧！

請掃描 QRCode，
收聽例句的 mp3 音檔吧！
聆聽後跟著複誦一次，
能讓學習效果加倍！

Hobbies make who you are

Bon voyage!

→ → → 旅途愉快！

　　對要出發去旅行（travel）的人說 **Bon voyage!**，你一定曾在電影中看過這樣的場景吧？這句話是「祝旅途愉快」的意思，它其實是法語，但在英語系國家也很常使用。另一個常用的說法是 **Have a safe trip!**，則有「願旅途平安」之意。從現在開始，對要去旅行的朋友就說 **Bon voyage!** 或 **Have a safe trip!** 吧。

　　要去旅行時，最傷腦筋的就是找住宿的地方吧？除了飯店（hotel）和民宿（guesthouse），還有其他方法可以找到省錢的住處（accommodation），聽過 **couch surfing** 嗎？這是 couch（沙發）和 surfing（網路搜尋資料）的複合名詞。**couch surfing** 是一個旅行者的社群，能幫忙旅行者聯繫旅遊地的當地人（local），並住進他們家裡。想在其他國家或地區 **couch surfing** 的話，也要出借自己的家給其他旅客。雖然可以免費住宿，還是要帶上小禮物或請對方吃飯來表示謝意。

STEP
1 # 我先提出問題

🎧 11-1.mp3

試著用「誰、何時、在哪裡、做什麼、如何做、為什麼」的六何法疑問詞來問問題。直到沒有可以再進一步詢問的疑問詞時，就能更自然地引導對話。

✪ 用六何法疑問詞來提問

1. What is the best trip you have ever had?　什麼是你目前為止最喜歡的旅行？

2. Who do you like to travel with?　喜歡和誰一起旅行？

3. Where would you like to travel to next?　下次想去哪裡旅行？

4. How often do you travel abroad?　有多常出國旅行？

✪ 不用六何法疑問詞來提問

5. Do you like to travel?　喜歡旅行嗎？

6. Is Korea a good place to travel in?　韓國是旅行的好去處嗎？

STEP
2 # 反向利用提問來回答

🎧 11-2.mp3

如果以前只能簡短回答問題的話，現在試著說出完整的句子吧。將疑問句變成陳述句，就能簡單變成一個句子了。開始練習用句子回答吧！

1. What is the best trip you have ever had?　什麼是你目前為止最喜歡的旅行？

The best trip I have ever had was to ＿（地點）＿. I went there ＿（時間）＿.

目前為止我最喜歡去 ＿＿＿＿＿＿ 的旅行，是 ＿＿＿＿＿＿ 去那裡的。

Thailand 泰國，last summer 在去年夏天 ｜ America 美國，a few months ago 幾個月前 ｜ Australia 澳洲，in 2001 在 2001 年時

2. Who do you like to travel with?　喜歡和誰一起旅行？

I like to travel with ＿＿＿＿＿＿.　我喜歡和 ＿＿＿＿＿＿ 一起旅行。

my best friend 最好的朋友 ｜ my family 家人 ｜ my spouse 伴侶

3. Where would you like to travel to next?　下次想去哪裡旅行？

I would like to travel to ＿＿＿＿＿ next.　下次想去 ＿＿＿＿＿ 旅行。

Brazil 巴西 ┃ Greece 希臘 ┃ Turkey 土耳其

4. How often do you travel abroad?　有多常出國旅行？

I travel abroad ＿＿＿＿＿.　我 ＿＿＿＿＿ 會出國旅行。

every month 每個月 ┃ at least once a year 至少一年一次 ┃ once every three or four years
三到四年一次

5. Do you like to travel?　喜歡旅行嗎？

→ Yes, I like to travel. Because ＿＿＿＿＿.

是，我喜歡，因為＿＿＿＿＿。

① I like to explore different cultures and try new cuisines.　我喜歡探索不同的文化，並且
嘗試新的食物。

② I like adventure and I love to meet new people.　我喜歡冒險，又熱愛認識新朋友。

→ No, I don't like to travel. Because ＿＿＿＿＿.

不，我不喜歡，因為＿＿＿＿＿。

① I am not a fan of adventure and I am not an outdoor person.　我不喜歡冒險，又討厭戶
外活動。

② I prefer to stay home and rest during the holidays. 假日我偏好在家休息。

6. Is Korea a good place to travel in?　韓國是旅行的好去處嗎？

→ Yes, Korea is a good place to travel in. Because ＿＿＿＿＿.

是，韓國是旅行的好去處，因為 ＿＿＿＿＿。

① there are numerous historical monuments.　有許多歷史遺跡。

② the local people are kind and friendly.　當地人親切又善良。

→ No, Korea is not a good place to travel in. Because ＿＿＿＿＿.

不是，並非旅行的好去處，因為＿＿＿＿＿。

① most of the signs are in Korean. It is difficult to find the way.　幾乎所有的標示都是韓
文，要找路不容易。

② traveling expenses are higher than most other Asian countries.　旅行費用比大多數的
亞洲國家要來得高。

STEP 3 和母語人士對話

🎧 11-3.mp3

確認前面練習的提問如何活用在和母語人士的對話中，請不要忘記一邊聽一邊跟著説。

James Min, how was your holiday? What did you do?

Min It was amazing. I went to Thailand with my husband. We **had a blast**①.

James Wow. It sounds like you really enjoyed your break.

Min Yep. We love to travel. **Do you like to travel?**

James Sure. I also love to travel abroad.

Min Oh, really? **How often do you travel abroad?**

James Well, I guess I try to go abroad at least once a year.

Min **Good for you!**② You must have been to many places. **What is the best trip you have ever had?**

James The best trip I have ever had was to Spain. I went there a few years ago.

Min I really want to go to Spain. Who did you go with?

James I went with my best friend. **Who do you like to travel with?**

Min Me? Hmm, I like to travel with my family. So James, **where would you like to travel to next?**

James I'm planning to go to Greece next summer. **I have always wanted to**③ go there.

Min That sounds amazing. In your opinion, **is Korea a good place to travel in?**

James Well, yes and no. Korea does have many historical monuments that are very interesting to see, but it is difficult for foreigners to find their way because sometimes there aren't any English signs.

 解說請見 P281

① have a blast

blast 有爆炸的意思，用在口語中有「一大樂事，高興的狀態」之意，have a blast 能用來表示「度過愉快時光」。

- A：What are you doing tonight?　今天晚上要做什麼？
- B：I'm going to a club with my friends. We are going to **have a blast**.　要和朋友去夜店，我們一定會玩得很開心。

② Good for you!

直譯為「對你來說很不錯」的意思，但沒有諷刺的意味，單純是稱讚「做得好」的說法。

- A：I passed the mathematics exam.　我數學考試合格了。
- B：**Good for you!** I'm so proud of you.　做得好！我以你為榮。

③ I have always wanted to (do)

「想要～很久了」的意思，適合用來表達長久以來的心願。

- **I have always wanted to** go to Europe.　我一直很想去歐洲。
- **She has always wanted to** be a pianist.　她一直都想成為鋼琴家。

Be smarter with a smartphone
➜ ➜ ➜ 利用智慧型手機變得更聰明

　　根據二〇一四年的新聞報導，韓國民眾的手機持有率達 94％，為全世界最高，很驚人吧？也因此有許多韓國人對手機成癮。（Many Koreans are addicted to smartphones.）

　　人們為何會沉迷於手機呢？或許是因為裡面什麼都有吧。網路（the Internet）、遊戲（games）、音樂（music）、書（book）、記帳本（account book）、健康檢測（heath check）、社群軟體（SNS）、相機（camera）、修圖程式（photo editing application）等等。使用者（user）可以隨身攜帶，簡單就能下載（download）或移除（remove）應用程式（application），依自己的喜好來使用，的確可以說是沉迷於「自己的世界」。有一些單字特別能表現智慧型手機的特色，像是 **ubiquity**、**accessibility** 以及 **portability**，ubiquity 對韓國人來說是很熟悉的單字，確切的意思為「無所不在」，意指「非常常見」。access 是「接近某地、某人的機會或方法」，加上 ability 變成 accessibility，則是「可接近性」的意思。portable 意為「容易攜帶」，加上 ability 之後，就成了「可攜帶性」的意思。

STEP 1 我先提出問題　🎧 12-1.mp3

試著用「誰、何時、在哪裡、做什麼、如何做、為什麼」的六何法疑問詞來問問題。直到沒有可以再進一步詢問的疑問詞時，就能更自然地引導對話。

✪ **用六何法疑問詞來提問**

1. Why do you use a smartphone?　你為何使用智慧型手機呢？

2. What is your favorite application?　最喜歡的 APP 是什麼？

3. When did you buy your first smartphone?　第一次買智慧型手機是在什麼時候？

4. How often do you use your smartphone?　有多常使用智慧型手機？

✪ **不用六何法疑問詞來提問**

5. Are you addicted to your smartphone?　有手機成癮症嗎？

6. Do you think a smartphone is a necessity or a luxury item?　你覺得手機是必需品還是奢侈品？

STEP 2 反向利用提問來回答　🎧 12-2.mp3

如果以前只能簡短回答問題的話，現在試著說出完整的句子吧。將疑問句變成陳述句，就能簡單變成一個句子了。開始練習用句子回答吧！

1. Why do you use a smartphone?　你為何使用智慧型手機呢？

   I use a smartphone because _____.　我使用智慧型手機是因為 _____。

   ❶ it is useful and convenient 好用而且方便。

   ❷ I can access the Internet wherever I am 無論在哪裡都能上網。

2. What is your favorite application?　最喜歡的 APP 是什麼？

   My favorite application is _____.　最喜歡的 APP 是 _____。

   MotionX GPS Drive 美國導航程式 ┃ CNN Radio News CNN 廣播新聞 ┃ Facebook 臉書

3. When did you buy your first smartphone?　第一次買智慧型手機是在什麼時候？

I bought my first smartphone _____.　_____ 買了第一支智慧型手機。

last December 去年十二月 ┃ several years ago 幾年前 ┃ in 2007 在 2007 年

4. How often do you use your smartphone?　有多常使用智慧型手機？

I use my smartphone _____.　_____ 使用智慧型手機。

all the time 一直 ┃ every single day 每天 ┃ once in a blue moon 久久一次

5. Are you addicted to your smartphone?　有手機成癮症嗎？

→ Yes, I am addicted to my smartphone. Because _____.

是，我有手機成癮，因為_____。

① I check my smartphone continuously.　老是在確認手機。

② I use my smartphone to play and to work　玩樂或工作時都會使用手機。

→ No, I am not addicted to my smartphone. Because _____.

不，我沒有手機成癮，因為 _____。

① I don't check my smartphone too often.　我不會經常確認手機。

② I can leave the house without my smartphone.　沒有帶手機還是能出門。

6. Do you think a smartphone is a necessity or a luxury item?

你覺得手機是必需品還是奢侈品？

→ I think a smartphone is a necessity. Because _____.

我覺得手機是必需品，因為_____。

① a lot of people communicate using smartphone applications.　很多人利用手機 APP 來聯絡。

② many smartphone functions are very useful.　手機有許多功能都很實用。

→ I think a smartphone is a luxury item. Because _____.

我覺得手機是奢侈品，因為 _____。

① it is too expensive.　太昂貴了。

② many functions are not really helpful.　許多功能不太實用。

確認前面練習的提問如何活用在和母語人士的對話中，請不要忘記一邊聽一邊跟著說。

Min Why didn't you reply to my text message last night?

James My smartphone is broken. I have to get it fixed.

Min You use a smartphone? **Why do you use a smartphone?**

James It's convenient. I like to check my email frequently. Do you have a smartphone?

Min I use a regular cellular phone. **When did you buy your first smartphone?**

James **It's been a while.**[①] I bought my first smartphone about 5 years ago. Why don't you get a smartphone?

Min Because I see my friends wasting a lot of time playing games and so on.

James Well, you are right. I also **lose track of time**[②] when I use my smartphone.

Min **How often do you use your smartphone?**

James I check my smartphone every hour.

Min But you work with it, right? **What is your favorite application?**

James I use my company application the most. I can easily check emails, messages and notifications.

Min See, you work with it. So my next question is, **are you addicted to your smartphone?**

James Hmm, I definitely am. I **can't function without**[③] my smartphone.

Min **Do you think a smartphone is a necessity or a luxury item?**

James For me it's a necessity. I do a lot of work with it. Do you think it's a luxury item?

用 **6** 句英文，和外國人輕鬆話家常！

Min Yes, I don't think I need one. I can work fine with my regular cellular phone and my laptop.

▶ ▶ ▶ 解說請見 P281

① It's been a while.

有「滿久以前、很久」的意思，提到關於很久之前的事情時可以使用。

⊃ A：Have you ever studied about World War II?　你研讀過第二次世界大戰的相關資料嗎？

⊃ B：Yep, but **it's been a while.** I don't think I remember much.　嗯，不過是滿久以前了，好像不太記得了。

② lose track of time

意為「跟不上時間的流逝」，適合用來形容做某件事的過程，時間過得很快。將 lose 改成 keep 的話，則是「掌握時間的流逝」，即為相反的意思。

⊃ A：Aren't you late? It's already 3 pm.　你沒遲到嗎？已經三點了。

⊃ B：Already? I **lost track of time** reading this book!　這麼快？看這本書都忘記時間了。

③ can't function without

直譯的話為「沒有～就無法運轉」，意思為「沒有～就無法好好工作」。

⊃ A：What's wrong with you today?　你今天怎麼了？

⊃ B：I left my smartphone back at home. I **can't function without** my phone. 我把智慧型手機放在家裡了，我沒有手機就無法工作。

I want to be beautiful

➔ ➔ ➔ **我想變漂亮**

　　這一章節要介紹不同於韓國的歐美時尚（fashion），北美和歐洲喜歡穿簡單的牛仔褲（jeans）以及緊身的衣服，也喜歡將薄衣物疊加、穿搭在一起，並且常用飾品（accessories）、帽子（hats）和太陽眼鏡（sunglasses）來展現個性。通常不會依照季節，而是配合當天的天氣來穿搭，如果稍微有陽光的話，就會穿得比較薄。

　　韓國稱很會穿衣服的人為「時尚達人」，英語是 fashionista，或是用 **have a good sense of fashion** 來形容，很有造型叫做 **have a good sense of style**，**have an eye for fashion** 則是指「有時尚感」。如果你的朋友很有時尚感，試著用這句話來炫耀看看吧：My friend has an eye for fashion so I like going shopping with her.（我朋友很有時尚感，所以我喜歡跟她一起逛街。）

　　工作或上學的穿著跟參加派對的穿著一定不一樣吧，若是「很會依情況穿衣服」，叫做 **dress for the occasion**；穿了不符合潮流（trend）的衣服叫 **It is old-fashioned.** 或是 **It looks outdated.**。但是請別忘記，It seems that real fashionistas do not believe in trends.（真正的時尚達人並不相信流行。）

STEP 1 我先提出問題 🎧 13-1.mp3

試著用「誰、何時、在哪裡、做什麼、如何做、為什麼」的六何法疑問詞來問問題。直到沒有可以再進一步詢問的疑問詞時，就能更自然地引導對話。

⭐ **用六何法疑問詞來提問**

1. How much money do you spend on clothes a year?　一年花多少錢在衣服上？

2. Where do you usually buy clothes?　通常在哪裡買衣服？

3. What kind of clothes do you usually wear?　通常穿什麼類型的衣服？

4. Who do you like to go clothes shopping with?　喜歡和誰去買衣服？

⭐ **不用六何法疑問詞來提問**

5. Are you a shopaholic?　你是購物狂嗎？

6. Do you read fashion magazines?　你看時尚雜誌嗎？

STEP 2 反向利用提問來回答 🎧 13-2.mp3

如果以前只能簡短回答問題的話，現在試著說出完整的句子吧。將疑問句變成陳述句，就能簡單變成一個句子了。開始練習用句子回答吧！

1. How much money do you spend on clothes a year?　一年花多少錢在衣服上？

   I spend _____ on clothes a year.　一年花_____買衣服。

   around 1,000(thousand) dollars 約 1000 元美金 ┃ about 300,000(three hundred thousand) won 30 萬韓元左右 ┃ a minimum of 1,000,000(one million) won 至少 100 萬韓元

2. Where do you usually buy clothes?　通常在哪裡買衣服？

   I usually buy clothes _____.　通常 _____ 買衣服。

   at an outlet store 在暢貨中心 ┃ at a department store 在百貨公司 ┃ online 在網路上

3. What kind of clothes do you usually wear?　通常穿什麼類型的衣服？

   I usually wear _____.　通常穿 _____。

casual clothes 休閒 | formal clothes 正式服裝 | jeans and a t-shirt 牛仔褲和 T 恤 | a uniform 制服

4. Who do you like to go clothes shopping with? 喜歡和誰去買衣服？

I like to go clothes shopping with _____.

我喜歡和 _____ 去買衣服。

my best friend 最好的朋友 | my husband 丈夫 | my colleague 同事

5. Are you a shopaholic? 你是購物狂嗎？

→ Yes, I am a shopaholic. Because _____.

是，我是購物狂，因為_____。

❶ I go shopping every weekend. 每個週末都會去逛街。

❷ I sometimes buy things I can't afford. 偶爾會買負擔不起的東西。

→ No, I am not a shopaholic. Because _____.

不是，我不是購物狂，因為_____。

❶ I don't go shopping often. 我不常去逛街。

❷ I don't buy things I don't need. 我不買不需要的東西。

6. Do you read fashion magazines? 你看時尚雜誌嗎？

→ Yes, I read fashion magazines. Because _____.

是，我看時尚雜誌，因為_____。

❶ I can get useful fashion tips. 可以獲得有用的時尚技巧。

❷ I'm interested in fashion. 我對時尚很有興趣。

→ No, I don't read fashion magazines. Because _____.

不，我不看時尚雜誌，因為_____。

❶ I don't find them informative. 沒有實用的資訊。

❷ I'm not interested in fashion. 我對時尚不感興趣。

STEP 3 和母語人士對話

 13-3.mp3

確認前面練習的提問如何活用在和母語人士的對話中，請不要忘記一邊聽一邊跟著說。

James Nice dress! Are you going somewhere special today?

Min Thank you. I just felt like dressing up today. **No special plans.**①

James I have never seen you so dressed up.

Min I do dress up from time to time but just not to work.

James You do? How often do you get dressed up?

Min Once or twice a month, when I have a wedding or dinner party to go to.

James I see. **What kind of clothes do you usually wear?**

Min Whatever looks neat. I usually wear a simple skirt and blouse.

James Well, you do dress neatly. **Where do you usually buy clothes?**

Min I like to go shopping **at** an outlet store near my house.

James **Who do you like to go clothes shopping with?**

Min I usually go with my mother. She has a good sense of fashion.

James That sounds nice. So do you go shopping often?

Min I think I do. At least once a month.

James Would you **consider yourself to be**② a shopaholic?

Min Absolutely not! I never buy things I can't afford.

James That's wise. So **how much money do you spend on clothes a year?**

Min That is **a sensitive question**③. Let me think. I think I spend about one million won on clothes a year.

James That sounds reasonable. **Do you read fashion magazines?**

Min I do. I like to get fashion tips from magazines.

 解說請見 P282

① no special plans

意指「沒有特別的計畫」。被問到週末計畫時，如果沒有什麼該做的事，就可以這樣回答。

- I have **no special plans** today. Do you want to spend time with me?　我今天沒有特別的計畫，你要和我一起過嗎？
- I like to spend my weekends with **no special plans**.　我喜歡沒有什麼特別的計畫來度過週末。

② consider oneself to be

consider 是「認為、考慮」的意思，be 的後面可以加上任何形容詞，這個說法有「認為自己～」的意思。

- Do you **consider yourself to be** diligent?　你覺得自己認真嗎？
- **I consider myself to be** a good housewife.　我認為自己是一個好主婦。

③ a sensitive question

sensitive 是「敏感的、感性的、需要慎重的（情報、主題等等）」的意思，a sensitive question 的意思就是「（需要慎重回答的）敏感題目」。

- In Korea, asking someone's age is **a sensitive question**.　在韓國詢問別人的年齡是很敏感的問題。
- It's always hard to ask **a sensitive question**.　敏感的問題總是難問出口。

14
SOCCER

Let's cheer for my soccer team!

→ → → 為我們的足球隊加油吧！

　　喜歡足球嗎？英語裡有許多足球用語，現在就來確認看看你是否真正理解相關用法了吧？

　　足球在美國稱作 soccer，英國叫做 football。在美國如果說 football 的話，會認為是美式足球，因此使用時要特別注意。

　　比賽是 **match** 或 **game**；比賽場地美國叫做 **the soccer field**，而英國則是 **the pitch**；裁判是 **referee**，副裁判為 **assistant referee**；運動選手叫做 **athlete**，而足球選手一般稱作 **soccer player**；觀眾則是 **spectator**。

　　若以位置（position）來看，後衛是 **defender**；前鋒是 **attacker**，也可稱為 **striker**；候補球員稱為 **substitute**。

　　技術（skill）方面的話，運球是 **dribble**，同一隊之間的傳球是 **pass**，搶走敵隊的球是 **tackle**，犯規則是 **foul**。日常生活會用到的英語如果能像這樣確認過的話，英語實力就會變得更加扎實。

STEP 1 我先提出問題

 14-1.mp3

試著用「誰、何時、在哪裡、做什麼、如何做、為什麼」的六何法疑問詞來問問題。直到沒有可以再進一步詢問的疑問詞時，就能更自然地引導對話。

✪ 用六何法疑問詞來提問

1. What is your favorite soccer team?　你最喜歡的足球隊是什麼？

2. Who is your favorite soccer player?　你最喜歡的足球選手是誰？

3. Why do you watch soccer games?　為什麼要看足球比賽呢？

4. When did you last watch a soccer game?　上一次看足球比賽是何時？

✪ 不用六何法疑問詞來提問

5. Do you like soccer?　喜歡足球嗎？

6. Can you play soccer?　你會踢足球嗎？

STEP 2 反向利用提問來回答

14-2.mp3

如果以前只能簡短回答問題的話，現在試著說出完整的句子吧。將疑問句變成陳述句，就能簡單變成一個句子了。開始練習用句子回答吧！

1. What is your favorite soccer team?　你最喜歡的足球隊是什麼？

   My favorite soccer team is _____.

   我最喜歡的足球隊是 _____ 。

   Real Madrid 皇家馬德里足球俱樂部 ┃ Manchester United FC 曼徹斯特聯足球俱樂部 ┃
   Liverpool FC 利物浦足球俱樂部 ┃ Suwon Samsung Bluewings 水原三星藍翼足球俱樂部

2. Who is your favorite soccer player?　你最喜歡的足球選手是誰？

   My favorite soccer player is _____.

   我最喜歡的足球選手是 _____ 。

   Lionel Messi 梅西 ┃ Cristiano Ronaldo 羅納度 ┃ Didier Drogba 德羅巴

3. Why do you watch soccer games?　為什麼要看足球比賽呢？

I watch soccer games because _____.

我看足球比賽是因為 _____。

❶ I like to share the victory with my team.　我喜歡和支持的隊伍分享勝利的喜悅。

❷ cheering helps me to feel better.　加油打氣能讓我的心情變好。

4. When did you last watch a soccer game?　上一次看足球比賽是何時？

The last time I watched a soccer game was _____.　上一次看足

球比賽是 _____。

in 2008 在 2008 年 ｜ a month ago 一個月前 ｜ last Friday 上週五

5. Do you like soccer?　喜歡足球嗎？

→ Yes, I like soccer. Because _____.

是，我喜歡足球，因為 _____。

❶ it's an exciting game.　是很令人興奮的比賽。

❷ it's a complex game that requires physical strength and good strategies.　是需要體力和

正確戰略的複雜比賽。

→ No, I don't like soccer. Because _____.

不，我不喜歡足球，因為 _____。

❶ I don't like ball games.　我不喜歡球類運動。

❷ I am not athletic and I'm not into sports.　我不擅長運動，所以不喜歡體育競賽。

6. Can you play soccer?　你會踢足球嗎？

→ Yes, I can play soccer. Because _____.

會，我會踢足球，因為 _____。

❶ my brother taught me when I was young.　小時候哥哥有教過我。

❷ I was a member of my high school soccer team.　高中時曾是足球隊成員。

→ No, I can't play soccer. Because _____.

不，我不會踢足球，因為 _____。

❶ I have never tried it.　我沒有踢過。

❷ I am really bad at running.　我跑不快。

確認前面練習的提問如何活用在和母語人士的對話中，請不要忘記一邊聽一邊跟著說。

James　Did you watch the soccer game last night?

Min　Nope, I didn't. Which teams were playing?

James　It was Korea versus Greece. You didn't watch the game?

Min　Nope, I'm **not that into**[①] soccer.

James　So **when did you last watch a soccer game**?

Min　It's embarrassing but the 2002 World Cup was the last time. **Do you like soccer?**

James　Are you kidding me? I'm crazy about soccer.

Min　Really? **What is your favorite soccer team?**

James　In the Korean league, I like Suwon Samsung Bluewings the best.

Min　That's good. Do you watch their games often?

James　Of course I do. I watch most of their games.

Min　If you don't mind me asking, **why do you watch soccer games?**

James　It's exciting to watch games and I get to share the victory, with my team.

Min　Well, I can't **relate to**[②] you completely, but it's nice to see that you have a passionate hobby.

James　Thanks. I am a big fan of soccer. I know most of the players' names, too.

Min　That is impressive. **Who is your favorite soccer player?**

James　My favorite player is Chong Te-se. Do you know him?

Min　Oh, yeh. I **have heard of**[③] him. So **can you play soccer?**

James　I was a member of my high school soccer team. I was a mid-fielder. But I don't think I can play well now.

▶ ▶ ▶ ▶ 解說請見 P282

用 6 句英文，和外國人輕鬆話家常！

① not that into

有部電影叫做 *He's Just Not That Into You*，臺灣譯成《他其實沒那麼喜歡妳》。be into something 有「對～很關心、喜歡」的意思，因此，加入 not，就成了「對～不關心、不喜歡」的意思。

➲ I'm **not that into** cooking.　我不太喜歡料理。

➲ Interestingly, my sister is **not that into** shopping.　很有趣地，我姊姊不太喜歡逛街。

② relate to

大家都知道這是「與～有關聯」的說法，不過在這個對話中，則是用來表示「對～同感、能理解」，類似 sympathize with 的說法。

➲ I can't **relate to** you since I have never experienced it.　由於不曾有過那樣的經驗，我無法體會你的感受。

➲ I like to talk with people who I can **relate to**.　我想和有同感的人說話。

③ hear of

意思是「聽過關於～」，當你想表示「雖然不太理解，但大略聽過內容」時可以使用。

➲ I have heard of the new restaurant downtown.　我聽過那家市區新開的餐廳。

➲ I have never heard of that name.　我沒有聽過那個名字。

Do you watch TV to kill time?

→→→ 你用看電視來殺時間嗎？

　　許多人空閒時會看電視來打發時間，電視看太多的人叫做 **couch potato**，是結合 couch（沙發）與 potato（馬鈴薯）而成的詞彙，如果是每到週末就宅在家裡看電視的人，就可以這樣說：I'm a couch potato on weekends.（我到了週末就會癱在家裡看電視。）

　　最近全世界似乎都很流行真人實境節目，從美國的《美國偶像》（American Idol）到韓國的「Superstar K」，這類可以讓一般人出演、比賽才藝的節目稱作 **reality show**、**survival show** 或是 **talent show**。

　　還有一種無論在哪裡都很受歡迎的節目——喜劇（comedy），這裡要介紹的是 **standup comedy**，這種體裁是主持人站在觀眾面前，用口頭演說的方式來引人發笑。幾年前一位叫做羅素‧彼得斯（Russell Peters）的印度裔加拿大人，在這個領域斬獲了高人氣，他擅長用搞笑的方式呈現各國語言的特徵以及語言相關文化，並以此而聞名。韓國也有類似的節目，不妨找來看看。

STEP 1　我先提出問題

🎧 15-1.mp3

試著用「誰、何時、在哪裡、做什麼、如何做、為什麼」的六何法疑問詞來問問題。直到沒有可以再進一步詢問的疑問詞時，就能更自然地引導對話。

✪ 用六何法疑問詞來提問

1. Where do you watch TV?　你在哪裡看電視？

2. Who decides what to watch in your family?　在家裡要看什麼是由誰來決定？

3. When do you normally watch TV?　通常何時會看電視？

4. What is your favorite TV program?　最喜歡的電視節目是什麼？

✪ 不用六何法疑問詞來提問

5. Do you like to watch TV?　你喜歡看電視嗎？

6. Do you think TV is educational?　你覺得電視有教育性嗎？

STEP 2　反向利用提問來回答

🎧 15-2.mp3

如果以前只能簡短回答問題的話，現在試著說出完整的句子吧。將疑問句變成陳述句，就能簡單變成一個句子了。開始練習用句子回答吧！

1. Where do you watch TV?　你在哪裡看電視？

   I watch TV _____.　我 _____ 看電視。

   at home 在家 ┃ in the living room 在客廳 ┃ in my room 在我房間

2. Who decides what to watch in your family?　在家裡要看什麼是由誰來決定？

   _____ decides what to watch in my family.　我家的遙控器掌控權在 _____ 手上。

   My father 爸爸 ┃ My grandmother 奶奶 ┃ The youngest 最小的人（老么）

3. When do you normally watch TV?　通常何時會看電視？

I normally watch TV _____.　通常 _____ 會看電視。

in the morning 早上 ｜ on weekends 週末 ｜ after work 下班後 ｜ when I'm free 有時間時

4. What is your favorite TV program?　最喜歡的電視節目是什麼？

My favorite TV program is _____.

最喜歡的電視節目是 _____。

a survival program called Superstar K 真人實境節目「Superstar K」 ｜ a drama called
Happy Days 電視劇《幸福的日子》 ｜ a talk show called Radio Star 脫口秀「Radio Star」

5. Do you like to watch TV? 你喜歡看電視嗎？

→ Yes, I like to watch TV. Because _____.

是，我喜歡，因為_____。

❶ I can relieve my stress.　能減輕壓力。

❷ I can get useful information.　能獲得有用的資訊。

→ No, I don't like to watch TV. Because _____.

不，我不喜歡，因為_____。

❶ it is a waste of time.　浪費時間。

❷ TV gives us too much useless information.　有太多不必要的資訊。

6. Do you think TV is educational?　你覺得電視有教育性嗎？

→ Yes, I think TV is educational. Because _____.

是，我覺得電視有教育性，因為 _____。

❶ I can learn about current issues.　可以瞭解時事。

❷ there are many educational documentaries.　有許多具教育意義的紀錄片。

→ No, I don't think TV is educational. Because _____.

不，我不覺得電視有教育性，因為 _____。

❶ most TV programs are fun-oriented.　大部分的電視節目都是以娛樂為主。

❷ all TV programs are used for commercial purposes.　所有電視節目都有商業目的。

確認前面練習的提問如何活用在和母語人士的對話中，請不要忘記一邊聽一邊跟著說。

Min You look tired. What were you up to last night?

James I **stayed up all night**[1] watching the Olympics.

Min Did you? I just went to bed. **Do you like to watch TV?**

James Yes, I do. I think I am addicted to TV.

Min Are you? How often do you watch TV?

James I watch it almost every day. Don't you?

Min Nope. I watch TV once or twice a week. **Where do you watch TV?**

James There are two TVs in my house. One in the living room and the other in my bedroom. So I watch TV in the living room and in my room.

Min You really love TV, don't you? So **what is your favorite TV program?**

James I especially like talk shows. I like listening to celebrities' personal stories.

Min I'm just curious, **who decides what to watch in your family?**

James Well, in the living room, my father decides what to watch, but as I told you, I have a TV in my room too, so I **am free to watch whatever I want**[2].

Min That is convenient. **When do you normally watch TV?** Aren't you busy with work?

James I am busy so I watch TV before I go to sleep.

Min Since you watch TV so much, **do you think it is educational?**

James **To some extent**[3] yes. I can learn about current issues and international affairs. And documentaries are very educational.

解說請見 P283

① stay up all night ···

意思為「熬夜」，表示「為了唸書、看電視或講電話而熬夜」時可以使用。

➲ I'm tired because I had to **stay up all night** and study.　我因為熬夜唸書而非常累。

➲ I have to **stay up all night** to finish my project.　我得熬夜來完成專案了。

② be free to do whatever I/you want ···························

「能自由地做想做的事」，也就是「能隨心所欲去做」的意思。如果改用 as I/you wish，會有更高級的感覺。

➲ My parents are away on a vacation so I **am free to do whatever I want**.　父母去旅行了，所以我可以隨心所欲做我想做的事。

➲ I'll give you a day off. You **are free to do whatever you want**.　我讓你休息一天，你可以自由地去做想做的事。

③ to some extent ··

extent 是「程度」的意思，to some extent 則是「某些程度」，很適合用來表達儘管不是百分之百但仍有某些程度同意。完全同意時，可以說 I absolutely agree.

➲ I think Korean politics is corrupted **to some extent**.　我覺得韓國的政治某些程度是腐敗的。

➲ **To some extent**, I understand why she is upset.　我大概知道她為什麼會生氣了。

Do you want to watch a movie?

→ → → 你要看電影嗎？

　　直至二〇一五年四月之前，全世界觀影次數最多的電影是《阿凡達》（*Avatar*）、《鐵達尼號》（*Titanic*）、《復仇者聯盟》（*Marvel's The Avengers*）、《哈利波特》系列（*the Harry Potter Series*）和《冰雪奇緣》（*Frozen*）。美國的第一名則是《亂世佳人》（*Gone with the Wind*），接著第二名是《星際大戰四部曲：曙光乍現》（*Star Wars: Episode IV - A New Hope*）。

　　許多電影台詞（lines）時常會被自然地運用在日常對話中，最常見的台詞像是 **Houston, we have a problem.**（休士頓，我們有麻煩了），出自電影《阿波羅 13 號》（*Apollo 13*），凡是日常生活出現狀況時都可以使用這句話。

　　《綠野仙蹤》（*The Wizard of Oz*）的 **There is no place like home.**（世界上沒有比家更好的地方），就是經過長途旅行回家後，感受到家和家人的溫暖時所說的話，這句台詞也很知名。

　　在《魔鬼終結者》（*The Terminator*）中，警察告訴魔鬼終結者現在見不到他要找的人，並問他要不要等待時，他說了句 **I'll be back.**（我會再回來），之後便往外走，開著警車往警察局爆衝，以後若想表示「會再回來」的意思就可以使用這句話。

STEP 1　我先提出問題　

16-1.mp3

試著用「誰、何時、在哪裡、做什麼、如何做、為什麼」的六何法疑問詞來問問題。直到沒有可以再進一步詢問的疑問詞時，就能更自然地引導對話。

✪ 用六何法疑問詞來提問

1. When do you normally watch a movie?　通常會在何時看電影？

2. Who do you like to watch a movie with?　喜歡跟誰一起看電影？

3. What is the most recent movie you have watched?　最近你看了什麼電影？

4. Who is the most popular movie star in Korea?　韓國最有名的電影演員是誰？

✪ 不用六何法疑問詞來提問

5. Do you like to watch movies?　喜歡看電影嗎？

6. Would you watch the same movie more than once?　同一部電影會看一次以上嗎？

STEP 2　反向利用提問來回答

16-2.mp3

如果以前只能簡短回答問題的話，現在試著說出完整的句子吧。將疑問句變成陳述句，就能簡單變成一個句子了。開始練習用句子回答吧！

1. When do you normally watch a movie?　通常會在何時看電影？

I normally watch a movie _____.　通常 _____ 會看電影。

on Fridays after work 在週五下班後 ┃ on weekends 在週末 ┃ on my day off 在休假時

2. Who do you like to watch a movie with?　喜歡跟誰一起看電影？

I like to watch a movie with _____.　我喜歡跟 _____ 一起看電影。

my best friend 最好的朋友 ┃ my colleague 同事 ┃ my family 家人

用 6 句英文，和外國人輕鬆話家常！

3. What is the most recent movie you have watched? 最近你看了什麼
電影？

The most recent movie I have watched is _____. 最近看的電影
是_____。

Iron Man 《鋼鐵人》 | Titanic 《鐵達尼號》 | Gone Girl 《控制》

4. Who is the most popular movie star in Korea? 韓國最有名的電影演員
是誰？

The most popular movie star in Korea is _____. 韓國最有名的電
影演員是_____。

Min-sik Choi 崔岷植 | Yeong-ae Lee 李英愛 | Rain 鄭智薰

5. Do you like to watch movies? 喜歡看電影嗎？

→ Yes, I like to watch movies. Because _____. 是，我喜歡看電影，
因為_____。

❶ I can learn about many different things. 能夠學到很多不同的東西。

❷ it is entertaining and stress-relieving. 有趣又能紓解壓力。

→ No, I don't like to watch movies. Because _____. 不，我不喜歡
看電影，因為_____。

❶ I prefer to read books than watch movies. 比起看電影我更喜歡看書。

❷ they are unrealistic and boring. 不是現實的而且無聊。

6. Would you watch the same movie more than once? 同一部電影會看
一次以上嗎？

→ Yes, I would watch the same movie more than once. Because
_____. 是，同一部電影我會看一次以上，因為 _____。

❶ I can understand the movie better. 可以更理解那部電影。

❷ I think a good movie is worth watching several times. 我覺得好電影值得多看幾次。

→ No, I wouldn't watch the same movie more than once. Because
_____. 不，同一部電影我不會看一次以上，因為 _____。

① it is not interesting if I know the ending. 知道結局就沒意思了。

② I think it is a waste of time and money. 感覺是浪費時間和金錢。

STEP 3 和母語人士對話

🎧 16-3.mp3

確認前面練習的提問如何活用在和母語人士的對話中，請不要忘記一邊聽一邊跟著說。

James Hey, have you watched *Lucy*?

Min Not yet. Why do you ask?

James I wanted to ask if you liked it or not. **What is the most recent movie you have watched?**

Min Well, I haven't watched a movie for a while now. **Do you like to watch movies?**

James Yes. I watch a movie once a month.

Min That's quite often. **When do you normally watch a movie?**

James I go to the movies on weekends. I don't get time on weekdays.

Min Yep, **I hear you.**① Our work is a bit demanding. **Who do you like to watch a movie with?**

James I normally go with my wife. We **are** both movie **lovers**②.

Min That's good. Can you recommend a good American movie?

James Sure, what genre do you like?

Min I don't care about the genre, but I would like to watch one with a famous American actor. **Who is the most popular movie star in America these days?**

James Well, I don't know who the most popular star is, but I like Adam Sandler the best.

Min What is your favorite movie? I'll watch that first.

James My favorite Hollywood movie is *Blended*. I have watched it several times.

Min **For real?**[3] Several times?

James Yep. **Wouldn't you watch the same movie more than once?**

Min Never! I guess I don't like movies that much.

 解說請見 P283

① I hear you.

一種表達同意時可以使用的有趣說法，也有「我知道你在說什麼，我聽到你說的了」的意思，簡單地想成「理解」即可。

⊃ A：Do you get what I'm saying? He is totally being biased. 你懂我說的嗎？他太過偏心了。

⊃ B：**I hear you**. What's up with him? 我懂，那個人究竟怎麼了？

② be ~ a lover

非常喜歡某件事物時可以這麼說，就是「愛好者」的意思。例如 I am an ice cream lover.（我很喜歡冰淇淋），在空格中加入喜歡的事物即可。

⊃ **I am a coffee lover.** I drink coffee every day. 我喜歡咖啡，每天都會喝咖啡。

⊃ They **are music lovers** so they enjoy music festivals. 他們喜愛音樂，因此很享受音樂祭。

③ For real?

「當真？真的嗎？」的意思，適合在聽到難以置信的話時使用，類似的說法還有 Seriously?

⊃ A：I'm going to the States this month for good. 我這個月要去美國了。

⊃ B：**For real?** Why didn't you tell me before? 真的嗎？為什麼之前都沒有跟我說？

Music heals pain

➔➔➔ **音樂能治療傷痛**

　　唱歌或是演奏樂器（instrument）時，應該要看得懂樂譜吧？看樂譜的英語是 **read music**，也可以說 **read music notes**。樂團披頭四（Beatles）演奏、演唱的歌曲都是自己創作的，但竟然所有成員都不會看樂譜（None of the Beatles could **read music**.），看起來，會讀樂譜似乎不是當音樂家（musician）的必要條件。

　　看得懂樂譜也不代表歌就唱得好，嚴重的音痴叫做 **tone-deaf**，deaf 為「聽覺障礙」，tone 則是「音調、音色」的意思。如果是音痴的話，可以說 I'm tone-deaf.，更簡單的說法是 I'm a bad singer.；相反地，如果歌唱得好的話，說 I'm a good singer. 就可以囉。

　　那麼，擁有絕對音感的人怎麼說呢？就是 **have a sense of perfect pitch**，pitch 的意思是「音高」，因此高音是 high pitch，低音是 low pitch。

STEP 1 我先提出問題

🎧 17-1.mp3

試著用「誰、何時、在哪裡、做什麼、如何做、為什麼」的六何法疑問詞來問問題。直到沒有可以再進一步詢問的疑問詞時，就能更自然地引導對話。

✪ 用六何法疑問詞來提問

1. When do you listen to music?　何時會聽音樂呢？

2. Who is your favorite musician?　最喜歡的音樂家是誰？

3. What is your least favorite music genre?　最討厭什麼類型的音樂？

4. Which device do you use to listen to music?　用什麼設備來聽音樂呢？

✪ 不用六何法疑問詞來提問

5. Do you like to listen to music?　喜歡聽音樂嗎？

6. Can you recommend good K-pop singers?　可以推薦不錯的韓國歌手給我嗎？

STEP 2 反向利用提問來回答

🎧 17-2.mp3

如果以前只能簡短回答問題的話，現在試著説出完整的句子吧。將疑問句變成陳述句，就能簡單變成一個句子了，開始練習用句子回答吧！

1. When do you listen to music? 何時會聽音樂呢？

   I listen to music _____.　我 _____會聽音樂。

   before going to sleep 睡前 ┃ when I commute 通勤時 ┃ when I'm doing household chores 做家事時

2. Who is your favorite musician? 最喜歡的音樂家是誰？

   My favorite musician is _____.

   我最喜歡的音樂家是_____。

   Madonna 瑪丹娜 ┃ G-Dragon 權志龍 ┃ Bach 巴哈

3. What is your least favorite music genre?　最討厭什麼類型的音樂？

My least favorite music genre is _____.　最討厭的音樂類型
是 _____ 。

rap 饒舌 ｜ heavy metal 重金屬 ｜ classical 古典 ｜ blues 藍調

4. Which device do you use to listen to music?　用什麼設備來聽音樂呢？

I listen to music on my _____.　我用 _____ 聽音樂。

CD player CD 播放器 ｜ MP3 player MP3 播放器 ｜ smartphone 智慧型手機 ｜ car radio 汽
車收音機

5. Do you like to listen to music?　喜歡聽音樂嗎？

→ Yes, I like to listen to music. Because _____.　是，我喜歡聽音樂，

因為 _____ 。

❶ music comforts me when I'm sad.　難過時音樂能安慰我。

❷ I feel better when I listen to good music.　聽好聽的音樂時，心情會變好。

→ No, I don't like to listen to music. Because _____.　不，我不喜歡

聽音樂，因為 _____ 。

❶ music distracts me from concentrating.　會妨礙我無法專心。

❷ I prefer to be quiet when I'm thinking.　我思考時喜歡安靜。

6. Can you recommend good K-pop singers?　可以推薦不錯的韓國歌手
給我嗎？

→ Sure, I would like to recommend _____.

當然，我推薦 _____ 。

Girls Generation 少女時代 ｜ Busker Busker ｜ 2PM

→ Sorry, I don't know any K-pop singers. Because _____.

很抱歉，我不認識韓國歌手，因為 _____ 。

❶ I am not interested in K-pop.　我對韓國流行樂不感興趣。

❷ I just came to Korea last week so I don't know much about the Korean music scene.
我上星期才來韓國，對於韓國的音樂圈不太瞭解。

確認前面練習的提問如何活用在和母語人士的對話中，請不要忘記一邊聽一邊跟著說。

Min   Hey James, what are you listening to?

James   Good morning. I'm listening to some of the latest K-pop songs.

Min   Do you like K-pop?

James   Yes, I do. I don't understand the lyrics, but I think the singers are very talented.

Min   **Who is your favorite musician?**

James   I like CL the most. Do you like to listen to K-pop?

Min   Sure. I like American pop music too. **What is your least favorite music genre?**

James   I guess it's rap because I can't **keep up with**[①] the fast rapping. And sometimes I can't understand what they are saying.

Min   Exactly! So James, **when do you listen to music?**

James   I like to listen to music when I'm in the subway. I think it's the best way to **kill time**[②] in the subway.

Min   **I can't agree more!**[③] So, **which device do you use to listen to music?**

James   I carry a CD player because it has better sound quality than a smartphone.

Min   I didn't know that. Thanks for the information.

James   Min, **can you recommend good K-pop singers?**

Min   Well, I'd like to recommend Akdong Musician. They are two young siblings who won a television audition program a few years ago.

James   They sound interesting. I sure will. Thank you, Min.

 解說請見 P284

① keep up with

keep 是「維持」，up 是「往上」，然後 with 有「和～」的意思，因此把 keep up with 想成「（落後～時）追上」的意思即可。用來表示跟上時間或是跟上事物，例如「知道最新的新聞」、「定期地做～」、「和～保持聯絡」等情況。

⊃ I read the newspaper to **keep up with** the current issues.　我看報紙是為了知道（跟上）時事。

⊃ My mother tries her best to **keep up with** the trends.　我媽媽盡全力地跟上流行。

② kill time

直譯為「殺時間」，揣摩一下意思的話，就是「無所事事地度過時間」。沒有一定要做的事，要打發時間就可以這麼說。

⊃ What do you do to **kill time** in the subway?　在地鐵裡要殺時間會做什麼？

⊃ I watched a movie last night to **kill time**.　昨天晚上看了電影來打發時間。

③ I can't agree more!

「不能再更同意了」，其實就是完全同意的意思。適合用來表達強烈的同意。

⊃ A：Professor Johnson is too strict!　強森教授太嚴格了！

⊃ B：**I can't agree more!**　我完全同意！

I'll take this

→→→ 我要這個

　　來認識一下英語系國家的購物節（shopping day）吧，美國的感恩節隔天 **Black Friday**，和聖誕節的前一個星期六 **Super Saturday** 是最適合購物的時機。由於 Black Friday 有整年最大幅度的折扣（sales），有不少韓國人都會從海外直接購買。因為人們在這一天大量消費，讓這一天成為一年中首次出赤字（red ink）轉為黑字（black ink）的日子，便以 Black Friday 來命名。赤字用紅色來標示，而黑字則用黑色來標示。

　　加拿大和英國的購物節則是聖誕節隔天的 **Boxing Day**，由於這天也有許多折扣，幾乎可以視為固定的購物日了。這天的購物中心（shopping mall）或百貨公司（department store）都會聚集大量人潮，和美國的 Super Saturday 為類似的日子。

　　和購物相關的説法中，eye shopping 並不是正確的英語，**window shopping** 才是正確的説法。如果問對方想不想 eye shopping，就説 Do you want to go **window shopping**?。退款最常用的單字是 **refund**，想要退款時，説 Can I get a refund? 或是 I want to return this. 即可。

試著用「誰、何時、在哪裡、做什麼、如何做、為什麼」的六何法疑問詞來問問題。直到沒有可以再進一步詢問的疑問詞時，就能更自然地引導對話。

✪ 用六何法疑問詞來提問

1. Who do you like to go shopping with?　你最喜歡跟誰一起逛街？

2. When do you normally go shopping?　通常何時會去逛街？

3. Where do you usually go to shop?　主要會去哪裡逛街？

4. What do you shop for most often?　最常購買的是什麼？

✪ 不用六何法疑問詞來提問

5. Do you like shopping?　喜歡購物嗎？

6. Do you prefer online shopping or offline shopping?　你比較偏好網路購物還是實體購物？

STEP 2　反向利用提問來回答

如果以前只能簡短回答問題的話，現在試著說出完整的句子吧。將疑問句變成陳述句，就能簡單變成一個句子了。開始練習用句子回答吧！

1. Who do you like to go shopping with?　你最喜歡跟誰一起逛街？

   I like to go shopping with _____.　我最喜歡跟 _____ 一起去逛街。

   my mother 媽媽 ┃ my boyfriend 男朋友 ┃ my best friend 最好的朋友

   * I like to go shopping alone.　我喜歡一個人逛街。

2. When do you normally go shopping?　通常何時會去逛街？

   I normally go shopping _____.　通常 _____ 會去逛街。

   on weekends 週末 ┃ on my day off 休息的日子 ┃ early in the morning 一大早

3. Where do you usually go to shop?　主要會去哪裡逛街？

I usually go to _____ to shop.　主要會去_____逛街。

an outlet store called 2001 一家叫做 2001 的暢貨中心 ｜ Lotte Department Store 樂天百貨
公司 ｜ the underground shopping complex near my house 我家附近的地下街

4. What do you shop for most often?　最常購買的是什麼？

I shop for _____ most often.　我最常買_____。

clothes 衣服 ｜ cosmetics 化妝品 ｜ groceries 食品 ｜ shoes 鞋子 ｜ stationery 文具

5. Do you like shopping?　喜歡購物嗎？

→ Yes, I like shopping. Because _____.

是，我喜歡購物，因為_____。

❶ it relieves my stress.　能紓解壓力。

❷ I can buy new items. A well chosen new item can make me happy.　可以買新的東西，
仔細挑選的新商品能讓我開心。

→ No, I don't like shopping. Because _____.

个，我不喜歡購物，因為_____。

❶ it is difficult to choose one among many items I want.　很難在那麼多想要的商品中挑選
出一個。

❷ I tend to buy things I don't need.　我很容易買了不需要的東西。

6. Do you prefer online shopping or offline shopping?　你比較偏好網路購
物還是實體購物？

→ I prefer online shopping. Because _____.

我比較偏好網路購物，因為 _____。

❶ I can save time and the product is delivered to my house.　可以節省時間，物品還能配
送到家。

❷ I can read the comments of other consumers and make the best choice.　可以參考其
他顧客的評價選出最好的商品。

→ I prefer offline shopping. Because _____.

我比較偏好實體購物，因為 _____。

❶ I can check the quality of the product and try on clothes.　可以確認物品的品質，衣服
還能試穿。

❷ I can bargain for the price and compare different brands. 可以殺價還能比較不同的牌子。

確認前面練習的提問如何活用在和母語人士的對話中，請不要忘記一邊聽一邊跟著說。

Min Nice shirt! Is it new?

James Thank you. I just bought it last weekend.

Min **Where do you usually go shopping?**

James I like to go to ABC Department Store. I bought this there.

Min **Do you like shopping?** You seem to have many nice clothes.

James Yep. I love shopping especially for clothes.

Min **Who do you like to go shopping with?**

James Well, it depends on what I need to buy. For clothes, I like to go with my best friend. He **has good taste in**[1] clothes.

Min That's good for you. **What do you shop for most often?**

James To be frank, I buy shirts most often. I feel a little embarrassed as I **spend a fortune**[2] on my clothes.

Min **When do you normally go shopping?**

James I like to shop on Fridays because that's when special discounts start.

Min I didn't know that. Have you tried online shopping?

James Yep. I have tried it several times.

Min **Do you prefer online shopping or offline shopping?**

James I definitely prefer offline shopping.

Min Why would you say that?

James I like to try on clothes before I buy them. They might not fit me right **and stuff**[3].

 解說請見 P284

用 **6** 句英文，和外國人輕鬆話家常！

① have good taste in

稱讚對方的感覺或喜好時，可以說 good taste，把欲稱讚的事物接在 in 的後面即可，類似的說法有 have a good sense in。

- ➲ I think she **has good taste in** fashion.　我覺得她很有時尚感。
- ➲ Do you think I **have good taste in** music?　你覺得我的音樂品味好嗎？

② spend a fortune

fortune 除了有「運」的意思，還有「全部財產」的意思，spend a fortune 直譯是「花了全部的財產」，不過實際上有「花了很多錢」之意。

- ➲ **I spent a fortune** on this new bag.　我花了很多錢買這個新包包。
- ➲ I think it is unnecessary to **spend a fortune** on a new car.　我覺得沒有必要花很多錢來買新車。

③ and stuff

「等等，諸如此類」的意思，知道 etc. 吧？原文為 et cetera，但由於不好發音，很多人都不太用，或說 and so on 也可以。

- ➲ I want to celebrate by baking you a cake, giving you a gift **and stuff**.　我想要烤蛋糕還有送你禮物等等，來幫你慶祝。
- ➲ Please bring all the things you need for hiking. Things like hiking shoes, snacks **and stuff**.　請把你需要的登山物品都帶來，像是登山鞋、點心等等。

I'm on a shopping spree

→→→ 購物失心瘋

　　網路購物在不知不覺中成為生活的一部分了，網路購物雖然方便（convenient），但也有風險（risky），以下就來看看有哪些風險吧。

　　因為太便利了，有時會毫無計畫地衝動購物，這樣的情形叫做 **impulse purchase**，impulse 是「衝動」，purchase 就是「購買」。Online shopping encourages **impulse purchases**.（網路購物會使人衝動購物），還有類似的情況，例如年輕人購物時亂買一通，韓國有句話叫做「知凜神[2]降臨」，英語的說法是 **be on a shopping spree**。

　　至於販賣仿冒品的問題，仿冒品的英語怎麼說呢？常用的是 **fake**，或是 **imitation**。It's a fake bag.（這是假的包包），I bought a Fendi bag online and it turned out to be an imitation.（我在網路上買了芬迪的包包，後來才知道是假的），像這樣使用即可。

　　因網購而產生的個資外洩問題也很嚴重，使用網路購物時，請記得這句話：Your personal information can be **leaked** on online shopping websites.（你的個人資料可能會透過購物網站外流），leak 是「洩露、露出」的意思。

2　原文為지름신，會唆使人衝動購物的假想神。

我先提出問題

試著用「誰、何時、在哪裡、做什麼、如何做、為什麼」的六何法疑問詞來問問題。直到沒有可以再進一步詢問的疑問詞時，就能更自然地引導對話。

✪ 用六何法疑問詞來提問

1. When do you shop online?　何時會網路購物？

2. How often do you shop online?　有多常網路購物？

3. Which online shopping mall do you like the most?　你最喜歡哪一個購物網站？

4. What is the biggest advantage of online shopping?　網路購物最大的優點是什麼？

✪ 不用六何法疑問詞來提問

5. Do you think online shopping is safe?　你覺得網路購物安全嗎？

6. Is online shopping better than offline shopping?　網路購物比實體購物好嗎？

 STEP 2

反向利用提問來回答

如果以前只能簡短回答問題的話，現在試著說出完整的句子吧。將疑問句變成陳述句，就能簡單變成一個句子了。開始練習用句子回答吧！

1. When do you shop online?　何時會網路購物？

   I shop online _____.　我 _____ 會網路購物。

   during my lunch break 中午休息時間 ┃ before going to bed 睡前 ┃ on weekends 在週末

2. How often do you shop online?　有多常網路購物？

   I shop online _____.　我 _____ 會網路購物。

   about three times a month 一個月三次左右 ┃ almost every day 幾乎每天 ┃ whenever I need to 每次有需要時

3. Which online shopping mall do you like the most? 你最喜歡哪一個購物網站？

I like _____ the most. 我最喜歡 _____。

Auction | Halfclub | G-market

4. What is the biggest advantage of online shopping? 網路購物最大的優點是什麼？

The biggest advantage of online shopping is _____. 網路購物最大的優點是 _____。

the cheap price 價格便宜 | other consumers' comments 其他消費者的評價 | the delivery service 配送服務

5. Do you think online shopping is safe? 你覺得網路購物安全嗎？

→ Yes, I think it is safe. Because _____.

是，我覺得安全，因為 _____。

❶ I have made several purchases online and I haven't had any problems. 我好幾次都是透過網路購買，而且沒有任何問題。

❷ some online shopping websites are used worldwide and have a long history. 有些購物網站全球都能使用，並且有一定的歷史。

→ No, I don't think it is safe. Because _____.

不，我覺得不安全，因為_____。

❶ I can't see the product and I can't trust the seller. 看不到物品，而且我不相信賣家。

❷ some online shopping websites disappear from time to time. 有些購物網站時不時會消失。

6. Is online shopping better than offline shopping? 網路購物比實體購物好嗎？

→ Yes, online shopping is better than offline shopping. Because _____. 是，網路購物比實體購物好，因為 _____。

❶ I can buy things even late at night. 即使到深夜我也可以買東西。

❷ I can compare different designs and prices easily. 可以輕鬆地比較各種設計和價格。

→ No, offline shopping is better than online shopping.

Because _____.

不，實體購物比網路購物好，因為 _____。

❶ I can get products as soon as I pay for them.　付了錢之後馬上就能擁有商品。

❷ I can check the quality of the product before buying it.　在購買前可以確認物品的品質。

和母語人士對話 19-3.mp3

確認前面練習的提問如何活用在和母語人士的對話中，請不要忘記一邊聽一邊跟著説。

Min Nice hat James. That color **suits you**①.

James Thanks. I bought it online last Saturday. I finally got it yesterday.

Min Do you like online shopping?

James Yes. I love online shopping as I can get special offers.

Min **Is online shopping better than offline shopping?**

James I guess so. They sell the same things, but it's way cheaper. And the delivery is free.

Min It sounds like **a great deal**②. **When do you shop online?**

James After work. And just before going to bed, I check my favorite online shopping websites.

Min **How often do you shop online?**

James I access the websites every day, but I actually make a purchase once or twice a week.

Min That doesn't sound like too often. **Which online shopping mall do you like the most?**

James My favorite one is Halfclub. They have good quality things with special discounts.

Min It sounds like you really like online shopping. So tell me James, **what is the biggest advantage of online shopping?**

James I must say, the price is the biggest advantage. You can usually get a minimum 10% discount.

Min Some people think online shopping is a bit risky. **Do you think online shopping is safe?**

James Sure! I've been doing it for years and I have never had any problems. **As long as**[3] you use big online shopping websites, you are fine.

 解說請見 P285

① suit me / you

suit 有「適合」的意思，也有「西裝」的意思。穿戴上衣服、飾品或鞋子之後，可以用這個片語來表達適不適合。

➲ That blue dress really **suits her**. She looks stunning. 那件藍色的洋裝很適合她，看起來很有魅力。

➲ I don't think these jeans **suit me**. 我不覺得這些牛仔褲適合我。

② a great deal

指「好的交易」，也可以用在購物外的情況，適合用來表示不吃虧的交易。

➲ A 50% discount? What **a great deal**! 五折？真棒的折扣。

➲ I got **a great deal** on this house. 我用不錯的價格買了這個房子。

③ as long as

「只要～的話」的說法，以前有個叫 Backstreet Boys 的團體，他們有首歌 *As Long As You Love Me* 非常有名，裡頭有句歌詞是「只要你愛我的話，我便不在乎你的過去」。

➲ **As long as** you do your household chores, you can get your allowance. 只要你做家事，就能得到零用錢。

➲ We'll go out on a picnic **as long as** the weather is good. 只要天氣好的話就去野餐吧。

I enjoy playing computer games

→→→ 我喜歡玩電腦遊戲

　　每次玩電腦遊戲或電玩遊戲（video game）就會忘了時間，這樣的情況用英語該怎麼表達呢？最常用的説法是 **time flies**，表現出歲月或時間的快速流逝，可以説 When I play computer games, time flies.（玩電腦遊戲時，時間過得飛快。）

　　電腦遊戲大略可以分為 **action games**（動作遊戲）、**simulation games**（模擬遊戲）、**racing games**（競速遊戲）、**adventure games**（冒險遊戲）、**role playing games**（角色扮演遊戲）等。

　　action games 是讓 **player** 成為主角，和敵人對戰、利用武器來打仗的類型。simulation games 是「假裝成～」（pretending）的遊戲，像是建造城市、美少女養成等等，都是有名的模擬遊戲。sports games 是控制（control）籃球、足球等等運動選手的遊戲。racing games 可以想成是汽車遊戲，adventure games 是主角展開探險的遊戲。role playing games 則是擔任某種角色，和多人一起冒險的線上（online）遊戲。

STEP 1 我先提出問題

🎧 20-1.mp3

試著用「誰、何時、在哪裡、做什麼、如何做、為什麼」的六何法疑問詞來問問題。直到沒有可以再進一步詢問的疑問詞時，就能更自然地引導對話。

✪ 用六何法疑問詞來提問

1. How many hours a week do you play computer games? 每週會玩幾小時電腦遊戲呢？

2. Where do you play computer games? 你會在哪裡玩電腦遊戲？

3. What is your favorite computer game? 最喜歡的電腦遊戲是什麼？

4. When do you usually play computer games? 通常何時會玩電腦遊戲？

✪ 不用六何法疑問詞來提問

5. Do you play computer games? 你玩電腦遊戲嗎？

6. Are you good at playing computer games? 你擅長玩電腦遊戲嗎？

STEP 2 反向利用提問來回答

🎧 20-2.mp3

如果以前只能簡短回答問題的話，現在試著說出完整的句子吧。將疑問句變成陳述句，就能簡單變成一個句子了。開始練習用句子回答吧！

1. How many hours a week do you play computer games? 每週會玩幾小時電腦遊戲呢？

I play computer games _____ a week.

我每週會玩 _____ 電腦遊戲。

two to three hours 兩三個小時 ∣ around 10 hours 大約十小時 ∣ more than 25 hours 二十五小時以上

2. Where do you play computer games? 你會在哪裡玩電腦遊戲？

I usually play computer games _____. 通常 _____ 玩電腦遊戲。

at an Internet café near my house 我家附近的網咖 ∣ at my friend's house 在朋友家

用 6 句英文，和外國人輕鬆話家常！

110

3. What is your favorite computer game? 最喜歡的電腦遊戲是什麼？

My favorite computer game is _____.

最喜歡的電腦遊戲是_____。

Star Craft 星海爭霸 ┃ Diablo 暗黑破壞神 ┃ Final Fantasy 最終幻想 ┃ Tetris 俄羅斯方塊 ┃
Minesweeper 踩地雷

4. When do you usually play computer games?　通常何時會玩電腦遊戲？

I usually play computer games _____.　我通常 _____ 會玩

電腦遊戲。

on weekends 週末 ┃ when I meet my friends 和朋友見面時 ┃ when I'm bored 當我無聊時

5. Do you play computer games?　你玩電腦遊戲嗎？

→ Yes, I play computer games. Because _____.　是，我玩電腦遊

戲，因為 _____。

❶ it is fun and I can play with my friends.　很有趣而且可以跟朋友一起玩。

❷ I can kill time and I can relieve stress.　可以打發時間，還能紓解壓力。

→ No, I don't play computer games. Because _____.　不，我不玩電

腦遊戲，因為 _____。

❶ I think it is a waste of time.　感覺很浪費時間。

❷ I am really bad at it so I actually get stressed out.　我真的不太會玩，反而會有壓力。

6. Are you good at playing computer games?　你擅長玩電腦遊戲嗎？

→ Yes, I am good at playing computer games. Because _____.

是，我擅長玩電腦遊戲，因為 _____。

❶ I have been playing ever since I was in middle school.　從中學開始就一直在玩了。

❷ I am good at predicting the other players moves.　我很會預測其他玩家的行動。

→ No, I am bad at playing computer games. Because _____.

不，我不擅長玩電腦遊戲，因為 _____。

❶ I don't play often enough to get better.　不太常玩，所以實力也沒有增加。

❷ there are too many things happening at the same time so I can't concentrate.　同一時
間有太多事情發生，我沒辦法專心。

確認前面練習的提問如何活用在和母語人士的對話中，請不要忘記一邊聽一邊跟著說。

Min What were you up to last night? Your eyes are red.

James I went to bed late last night because I played computer games with my cousins.

Min You need to get some eye drops. They are too red. Do you like computer games?

James Yes, I do. What about you? **Do you play computer games?**

Min Not really. I don't **see the point**[1] of it. Tell me, why do you play computer games?

James It is fun. You should give it a try. It helps you to relieve stress for sure.

Min Seriously? I have never really tried it. **Are you good at playing computer games?**

James I am quite good. If you want, I could **give you some pointers**[2].

Min That is nice of you. **What is your favorite computer game?**

James I **can't deny**[3] that my favorite computer game is Star Craft.

Min I've heard of that game. Is it still popular now?

James It's a classic so it's popularity will never fade.

Min Okay, I get the picture. **When do you usually play computer games?**

James As you know, I only get free time on weekends.

Min **Where do you play computer games?** Do you go to Internet cafés?

James Nope, I usually play at home. I don't like going to Internet cafés.

▶▶▶▶ 解說請見 P285

① see the point

point 除了「點」之外，還有「意見、要點」的意思，see the point 可以用來表示「知道要點，理解原因」之意，因此無法理解要點時，説 I don't see the point. 即可。

⊃ I'm going to give up as I don't **see the point** any more.　感覺沒有什麼意義了，所以我要放棄。

⊃ Why are you reading that? I don't **see the point**.　你為什麼要讀那個？感覺沒什麼重點。

② give ~ some pointers

「給～建議」的意思，pointer 有「忠告、信號、指針」之意。

⊃ Could you **give me some pointers** on improving my math score?　你可以給我一些建議來提高數學成績嗎？

⊃ My friend **gave me some pointers** on being healthy.　我朋友給我一些保持健康的建議。

③ can't deny

deny 的意思是「否認」，反之，在表達意見的時候説 I can't deny ～的話，則有「無法否認～事實」之意。

⊃ **I can't deny** that Yuna Kim is diligent.　我無法否認金妍兒很認真。

⊃ You **can't deny** the fact that English is a basic skill one needs in this globalized world.　你無法否認在這個全球化的時代，英語是必備的基本技能。

Part 3

讓生活更豐富的
休閒活動

隨著平均壽命百歲時代的來臨，健康嗜好的必要性
與閒暇活動的重要性，都變得越來越高了，生活
能否變得豐富多彩，端看如何度過休閒時間了。接下來
試著用六何法疑問詞，來聊聊能提高生活品質的休閒活
動吧？

請掃描 QRCode，
收聽例句的 mp3 音檔吧！
聆聽後跟著複誦一次，
能讓學習效果加倍！

Leisure activities spice up
your life

Relieve stress the right way

➔ ➔ ➔ 好好地消除壓力

　　新聞報導指出韓國人最常使用的外來語是壓力（stress），那麼就來整理一下我們平常會掛在嘴邊，與壓力有關的説法吧。**I'm stressed out.**（感受到壓力）是很基本的表達方式，在某些情況下感到無可奈何，這種感覺（feelings）就是所謂的壓力，因此會説 I'm overwhelmed.（被壓倒，不知該如何是好），或是 I've had it.（忍無可忍），I can't take it anymore. 也是相同的意思，在這種情況下也可以使用。

　　工作太多，感到疲倦時，也會產生壓力，「疲倦」的簡單説法是 **I'm tired.**，高級一點的話也可以用 I'm exhausted.（精疲力盡了）。日常對話中常會用 I'm burned out.，有精力全都用盡、身體癱軟的意思，也會説 I'm beat. 或 I'm worn out.。

　　「消除壓力」多用 **relieve stress**，relieve 也可以換成 release 或 get rid of。詢問別人如何消除壓力，則可以説 **How do you relieve/release/get rid of stress?**。

STEP 1　我先提出問題

🎧 21-1.mp3

試著用「誰、何時、在哪裡、做什麼、如何做、為什麼」的六何法疑問詞來問問題。直到沒有可以再進一步詢問的疑問詞時，就能更自然地引導對話。

✪ 用六何法疑問詞來提問

1. What stresses you out?　什麼讓你感到壓力？

2. How do you relieve stress?　如何消除壓力？

3. Where do you go when you are stressed?　覺得有壓力時會去哪裡？

4. When was the most stressful time of your life?　人生中何時壓力最大？

✪ 不用六何法疑問詞來提問

5. Can you relax at home?　在家裡能放鬆休息嗎？

6. Do you get stressed out easily?　很容易感到壓力嗎？

STEP 2　反向利用提問來回答

🎧 21-2.mp3

如果以前只能簡短回答問題的話，現在試著說出完整的句了吧。將疑問句變成陳述句，就能簡單變成一個句子了。開始練習用句子問答吧！

1. What stresses you out?　什麼讓你感到壓力？

_____ stress(es) me out.　_____ 讓我有壓力。

Examinations 考試 ｜ English 英語 ｜ My supervisor 職場上司 ｜ A traffic jam 交通堵塞

2. How do you relieve stress?　如何消除壓力？

I relieve stress by _____.　我靠 _____ 來消除壓力。

sleeping in 睡懶覺 ｜ going to a good restaurant 去一間好餐廳吃飯 ｜ watching a good movie 看一部好電影 ｜ talking to my friends 和朋友聊天

3. Where do you go when you are stressed?　覺得有壓力時會去哪裡？

I go to _____ when I am stressed.　有壓力時我會去 _____。

a department store 百貨公司 ｜ the park 公園 ｜ the gym 健身中心 ｜ a hair salon 美髮店

4. When was the most stressful time of your life? 人生中何時壓力最大？

_____ was the most stressful time of my life.

_____ 是我人生中壓力最大的時候。

Studying for the national college entrance exam 準備大學入學考試 | Applying for a job 應徵工作 | Preparing for my wedding 準備婚禮

5. Can you relax at home? 在家裡能放鬆休息嗎？

→ Yes, I can relax at home. Because _____. 是，我在家可以放鬆，因為 _____ 。

❶ I have my own space to get total privacy. 有個人的空間可以享有隱私。

❷ my family is always there to support me. 我的家人總是會支持我。

→ No, I cannot relax at home. Because _____. 不，我在家無法放鬆，因為_____ 。

❶ I have work to do around the house. 家裡面到處都有家事要做。

❷ my house is always noisy. 我家總是很吵。

6. Do you get stressed easily? 很容易感到壓力嗎？

→ Yes, I get stressed easily. Because _____. 是，我很容易感到壓力，因為_____ 。

❶ I constantly worry about things. 我老是會擔心。

❷ I have a very sensitive personality. 我的個性很敏感。

→ No, I don't get stressed easily. Because _____. 不，我不容易感到壓力，因為_____ 。

❶ I have a positive personality. 我的個性很樂觀。

❷ I don't worry about things. 我不會擔心事情。

確認前面練習的提問如何活用在和母語人士的對話中，請不要忘記一邊聽一邊跟著說。

Min Are you alright? You **look beat**①.

James I am stressed out a bit. Thanks for asking.

Min Why are you stressed out?

James I have a project due next Monday and I can't **get started**②.

Min You should take a rest for a bit. **Can you relax at home?**

James No, I can't. I live with my parents so my house is always noisy with guests.

Min So **where do you go when you are stressed?**

James I go to the park to take a walk and to think quietly.

Min That sounds like a great way to relieve stress.

James **How do you relieve stress?**

Min I do fun things like shopping, watching a movie and reading a good book.

James Yep, I do those things too. **What stresses you out?**

Min I get stressed by work, mostly. I don't get stressed out easily though. Do you?

James Yes, I do. I'm very sensitive and a bit negative.

Min You should try to **take things easy**③. **When was the most stressful time of your life?**

James I guess it was just before graduating from high school. The national college entrance exam was very stressful.

Min I totally get you.

▶ ▶ ▶ 解說請見 P286

① look beat

很奇妙地，這個説法有「看起來疲倦」的意思，beat 主要的意思是「拍子」或「戰勝」，但 look beat 則和 look tired 的意思相近，常用來形容過了漫長的一天後的疲倦感。

➲ Are you okay? You **look beat.** 還好嗎？你看起來很疲倦。

➲ Didn't you get any sleep last night? You **look beat.** 昨天沒睡嗎？你看起來很疲倦。

② get started

和 start 一樣有「開始」的意思，比起 start，母語人士多使用 get started，説「我們開始吧」時，也比較常用 Let's get started. 的説法。start 之後需要加受詞，但 get started 可以不加受詞，或是用「get started on ＋受詞」。

➲ I was confused about the instructions so I couldn't **get started.** 我對指令感到困惑，因此還沒開始。

➲ Did you **get started** on the assignment? 開始做功課了嗎？

③ take it/things easy

在對話中常會用到的説法，可以解釋成「想得簡單一點、想得輕鬆一點、不要著急」。當對方覺得不安或有壓力時，很適合向對方這麼説。

➲ A：I am behind schedule. I'm so stressed. 我趕不上進度，覺得好有壓力。

➲ B：You should **take it easy**. It's better to make sure you are doing everything right. 不要著急，確定事情都有做好比較重要。

Don't let the bed bugs bite

➜ ➜ ➜ **睡覺時小心不要被蟲咬了**

不少人會因為壓力或是錯誤的睡眠習慣而無法睡得安穩，但為了提升生活品質和創意，最好有充分的睡眠，因此，有句話説「have a good night」。以下就要告訴你可以用來取代 **good night** 的説法。

首先有 **Sleep tight.**，這句話出自從前會用繩子來支撐床墊（mattress），現在則有「睡個好覺」的意思。

還有 **Don't let the bed bugs bite.**，由於英國的濕度高且常下雨，用久的床墊就會出現蟲子（bed bugs），一被咬到就會痛到醒過來，自然無法睡得安穩，便出現了這樣的説法。

此外，**Have a good night's sleep.** 也是常見的説法。現在開始不要總是説 Good night.，試著使用不同的説法來道晚安吧。

STEP 1　我先提出問題

試著用「誰、何時、在哪裡、做什麼、如何做、為什麼」的六何法疑問詞來問問題。直到沒有可以再進一步詢問的疑問詞時，就能更自然地引導對話。

✪ 用六何法疑問詞來提問

1. When do you normally go to sleep?　通常何時上床睡覺？

2. How many hours do you sleep every day?　每天會睡幾小時？

3. What is the most interesting dream you have ever had?　目前為止做過最有趣的夢是什麼？

4. Which bad sleeping habit do you have?　有什麼不好的睡眠習慣嗎？

✪ 不用六何法疑問詞來提問

5. Do you prefer sleeping on the floor or on a bed?　你喜歡睡在地板上還是床上？

6. Have you ever suffered from insomnia?　曾經受失眠所苦嗎？

STEP 2　反向利用提問來回答

如果以前只能簡短回答問題的話，現在試著說出完整的句子吧。將疑問句變成陳述句，就能簡單變成一個句子了。開始練習用句子回答吧！

1. When do you normally go to sleep?　通常何時上床睡覺？

   I normally go to sleep at _____.　我通常 _____ 會上床睡覺。

   midnight 午夜十二點 ┃ 11 pm 晚上十一點 ┃ 2 am 凌晨二點

2. How many hours do you sleep every day?　每天會睡幾小時？

   I sleep _____ every day.　我每天睡 _____。

   6 hours 六小時 ┃ less than 8 hours 不到八小時 ┃ more than 9 hours 超過九小時

3. What is the most interesting dream you have ever had?　目前為止做過最有趣的夢是什麼？

The most interesting dream I have ever had was about _____.

我做過最有趣的是關於 _____ 的夢。

flying monkeys 會飛的猴子 | talking flowers 會說話的花 | a war between humans and apes 人類和人猿的戰爭

4. Which bad sleeping habit do you have?　有什麼不好的睡眠習慣嗎?

My bad sleeping habit is _____.　我的睡眠壞習慣是 _____。

snoring 打鼾 | sleep talking 說夢話 | grinding my teeth 磨牙

5. Do you prefer sleeping on the floor or on a bed?　你喜歡睡在地板上還是床上?

→ I prefer sleeping on the floor. Because _____.　我喜歡睡在地板上,因為 _____。

① the floor in a Korean house heats up so it's warmer than sleeping on a bed.　韓國房子的地板會加熱,比睡在床上更溫暖。

② I have a back problem and the doctor advised me to sleep on the floor.　我有背痛的問題,醫生建議我睡在地板上。

→ I prefer sleeping on a bed. Because _____.　我喜歡睡在床上,因為 _____。

① I like the soft mattress of a bed.　我喜歡床上柔軟的床墊。

② I have always slept on a bed so I'm used to it.　我總睡在床上,已經習慣了。

6. Have you ever suffered from insomnia?　曾經受失眠所苦嗎?

→ Yes, I have. Because _____.　是,我有,因為 _____。

① I was extremely stressed about the national college entrance exam when I was in high school.　高中時因為大學入學考試感到很大的壓力。

② I had a horrible nightmare last year and I couldnt sleep well for several months.　去年做過可怕的噩夢後,好幾個月都沒睡好。

→ No, I haven't. Because _____.　不,我沒有,因為 _____。

① I'm always exhausted at the end of the day.　到了一天要結束時,我總是累癱了。

② I can fall asleep easily.　我很容易入睡。

確認前面練習的提問如何活用在和母語人士的對話中，請不要忘記一邊聽一邊跟著說。

James How are you? You look tired.

Min Thanks for asking. I can't sleep these days.

James **Poor you**[①]. Have you tried warm milk, a hot shower or another solution?

Min Yes, I have. I think I'm just stressed out. **Have you ever suffered from**[②] **insomnia?**

James Nope, I can sleep wherever I am.

Min That is good. Sometimes, I have weird dreams that distract me from getting enough sleep.

James You do? **What is the most interesting dream you have ever had?**

Min Oh, once, I had to go to the army in my dream because somehow the law in Korea changed so everyone had to serve in the army.

James Wow! That sounds exciting and chaotic **at the same time**[③].

Min It was. Do you have any bad sleeping habit?

James Apparently, I do. I didn't know this until recently.

Min **Which bad sleeping habit do you have?**

James It seems I sleep talk from time to time. My friend thought I was awake and talking so he replied.

Min That is hilarious!

James By the way, you always look tired. **How many hours do you sleep every day?**

Min I don't get enough sleep. I sleep for about 5 hours every day.

James That is too little. **When do you normally go to sleep?**

Min After midnight. When I get home from work, I have to do the household chores and then I watch some TV to relax.

用 6 句英文，和外國人輕鬆話家常！

James	Do you prefer sleeping on the floor or on a bed?
Min	I prefer sleeping on a bed. It's cozier and softer.

解說請見 P286

① poor you

用於替對方感到難過時，有「哎喲，好可憐啊」的感覺，最好不要對初次見面的人，或是年紀較大的人說。

- ⊃ A：My boss always blames me for the bad results.　老闆總是將不好的結果怪罪在我身上。
- ⊃ B：**Poor you.** What a bad boss!　真可憐，真是個壞老闆！

② suffer from

「因～遭受痛苦」的說法，from 之後可加上 cancer（癌症）、severe cold（重感冒）、upset stomach（肚子痛）等病名，除了疾病，也可以加上 homework（功課）、endless work（做不完的工作）等困難的事。

- ⊃ I'm **suffering from** my boss' never-ending yelling.　上司永無止境的咆哮讓我覺得很痛苦。
- ⊃ My friend's mother is **suffering from** lung cancer.　朋友的母親受肺癌所苦。

③ at the same time

有「同時」的意思，與 simultaneously 的說法類似，對話中會使用 at the same time。

- ⊃ James and Lisa entered the room **at the same time.**　詹姆士和麗莎同時進入了房間。
- ⊃ Many students answered **at the same time.**　許多學生同時作答。

Do you like to read?

→ → → 喜歡看書嗎？

　　紙本書大致上可以分成精裝（hardcover）和平裝（paperback）兩種形式，平裝書通常以文字為主，而且輕又便宜。以二〇一五年的《哈利波特》系列（*Harry Potter*）為例，精裝本是 15.99 美元（約台幣 485 元），平裝本是 7.48 美元（約台幣 226 元），價格相差兩倍左右，因此，精裝本多為收藏用，相反地，平裝本可以劃線或是折頁角，能夠更隨性地閱讀。

　　先在這邊暫停一下！像這樣書讀到一半，將頁角稍微折起來，英語要怎麼說呢？就是 **dog-ear**，想想小狗耳朵折起來的樣子，真的和折頁角一模一樣吧？不過，對珍貴的書或是尊敬的作者的書，最好還是不要 dog-ear 比較好。

　　再來告訴你，適合送什麼禮物給喜歡書的外國人，就是找到那個人喜愛作家的作品首刷本，當成禮物送他。光從二〇一一年《蜘蛛人》首刷本競價到 110 美元（約台幣 3330 元），《超人》首刷本競價到 150 美元（約台幣 4540 元）來看，就可以知道美國人對於收藏首刷本的狂熱了吧？

🎧 23-1.mp3

試著用「誰、何時、在哪裡、做什麼、如何做、為什麼」的六何法疑問詞來問問題。直到沒有可以再進一步詢問的疑問詞時，就能更自然地引導對話。

✪ 用六何法疑問詞來提問

1. What is your favorite book genre?　最喜歡什麼類型的書？

2. Which author do you like the most?　最喜歡哪位作家？

3. How many books do you read a year?　一年會讀幾本書？

4. Where do you like to read?　喜歡在哪裡看書？

✪ 不用六何法疑問詞來提問

5. Do you like to read?　喜歡看書嗎？

6. Can you recommend a good book to read?　可以推薦一本好書嗎？

🎧 23-2.mp3

如果以前只能簡短回答問題的話，現在試著說出完整的句子吧。將疑問句變成陳述句，就能簡單變成一個句子了。開始練習用句子回答吧！

1. What is your favorite book genre?　最喜歡什麼類型的書？

My favorite book genre is _____.　最喜歡的類型是 _____。

romance novels 羅曼史小說 ┃ adventure novels 冒險小說 ┃ detective novels 推理小說 ┃ self-help books 自我開發書籍

2. Which author do you like the most?　最喜歡哪位作家？

The author I like the most is _____.

最喜歡的作家是 _____。

Stephen King 史蒂芬‧金 ┃ James Patterson 詹姆斯‧派特森 ┃ John Grisham 約翰‧葛里遜

3. How many books do you read a year?　一年會讀幾本書？

I read _____ a year.　一年會讀 _____ 。

about 12 books 大約十二本書 ｜ around twenty books 大約二十本書 ｜ from 10 to 20books 十本至二十本書

4. Where do you like to read?　喜歡在哪裡看書？

I like to read _____.　我喜歡 _____ 看書。

in my room, on my bed 在我房間的床上 ｜ in a coffee shop 在咖啡館裡 ｜ in the subway 在地鐵上

5. Do you like to read?　喜歡看書嗎？

→ Yes, I like to read. Because _____.

是，我喜歡看書，因為 _____ 。

❶ I can gain second-hand experience and expand my perspective.　可以獲得間接經驗並開拓視野。

❷ I can improve my language skills and learn useful facts.　可以提升語言能力並學到有用的知識。

→ No, I don't like to read. Because _____.

不，我不喜歡看書，因為 _____ 。

❶ it takes a lot of time to finish one book.　看完一本書要花太多時間了。

❷ some books are difficult to understand.　有些書很難理解。

6. Can you recommend a good book to read?　可以推薦一本好書嗎？

→ Sure. I strongly recommend you read _____.　當然，我強烈推薦你去看 _____ 。

Dear John by Nicholas Sparks 尼可拉斯・史派克的《分手信》 ｜ *Twilight* by Stephenie Meyer 史蒂芬妮・梅爾的《暮光之城》

→ No, I'm sorry. I can't recommend any. Because _____.　不，很抱歉無法幫你推薦，因為 _____ 。

❶ I don't read much. I don't know any good books.　我不太看書的，不知道有什麼好書。

❷ I can't recall any good book titles right now.　現在想不起來任何書名。

確認前面練習的提問如何活用在和母語人士的對話中，請不要忘記一邊聽一邊跟著說。

Min What are you reading?

James I'm reading *The Da Vinci Code* by Dan Brown.

Min I always see you reading on your lunch break. **Do you like to read?**

James Yes, I love reading. I can experience a whole new world just by **flipping the pages**①.

Min Oh, you really enjoy reading. **What is your favorite book genre?**

James I especially like adventure books.

Min **Which author do you like the most?**

James My favorite author **of all time**② is Dan Brown.

Min Why do you like him?

James I like his story telling techniques and his writing style.

Min I should read one of his books. Besides your lunch breaks, when do you normally read?

James I normally read in the subway, before going to sleep and whenever I'm bored.

Min It sounds like you are reading **the whole day**③. **Where do you like to read?**

James I like reading at a café.

Min **Can you recommend a good book to read?**

James Sure. I recommend the book I'm reading now. I think it's the best book I've read this year.

Min Okay. So tell me, **how many books do you read a year?**

James Not that many. I think I read about 12 books a year, that's one book every month.

 解說請見 P287

① flip the pages

flip 有「翻動、投擲」的意思，有 flip a coin 這樣的說法，意思是把錢幣丟出去，再根據出現哪一面來做決定。上述對話中出現的 flip the pages 則是翻書頁的意思。

- I like the sound when I **flip the pages** of a book.　我喜歡翻書的聲音。
- Don't **flip the page** now. You have to wait for the explanation.　現在還不要翻頁，要等待說明。

② of all time

意指「一直以來、歷史上」，很適合用來表示「到目前為止，在既有的事物中最好的」。

- I think Michael Jackson is the best singer **of all time**.　我覺得麥可‧傑克森是歷史上最棒的歌手。
- What is your favorite movie **of all time**?　你目前為止看過的電影中最喜歡的是哪一部？

③ the whole day

「一整天」的意思，想表示「二十四小時、從早到晚一直～」時，可以使用這個說法。

- I studied for today's test **the whole day** yesterday.　我昨天一整天都在準備今天的考試。
- She waited for you **the whole day**.　她等了你一整天。

用 **6** 句英文，和外國人輕鬆話家常！

130

It's a perfect day to ride a bike!

➔ ➔ ➔ 適合騎自行車的日子！

　　騎自行車叫做 **ride a bicycle**，也可以改變順序寫成 bicycle riding，或是將 bicycle 當成動詞，寫成 Let's go bicycling.，試著用英語説説看：「要不要去騎自行車？」就是 Do you want to **ride a bicycle**? / Do you want to **go bicycle riding**? / Do you want to **go bicycling**?。

　　自行車道的英語是 **bike lane**，加以應用，公車專用道就是 bus lane。停自行車的地方稱作 **bicycle racks**，在美國也有收費的 bicycle racks，公車上或地鐵上都有便利的停車處。雖然騎自行車時戴上安全帽（helmet）比較安全，但法律並沒有嚴格規定。高速公路（freeway）當然是禁止自行車通行。

　　來討論一下自行車的用途吧，若是為了通勤的話，可以説 **I ride a bicycle to commute.**，commute 就是上下班；為了運動而騎，則是 **to exercise**，為了樂趣是 **for fun**；當成交通工具的話，也可以説 **to get to places**。如果有人問你 Why do you ride a bicycle?，挑選上面其中一個説法，再用 I ride a bicycle _____. 來回答即可。

STEP 1 我先提出問題

🎧 24-1.mp3

試著用「誰、何時、在哪裡、做什麼、如何做、為什麼」的六何法疑問詞來問問題。直到沒有可以再進一步詢問的疑問詞時，就能更自然地引導對話。

✪ 用六何法疑問詞來提問

1. How often do you ride a bicycle?　有多常騎自行車呢？

2. Where do you usually ride a bicycle?　主要會在哪裡騎自行車？

3. When did you learn how to ride a bicycle?　何時學會騎自行車呢？

4. Who taught you how to ride a bicycle?　誰教你騎自行車的呢？

✪ 不用六何法疑問詞來提問

5. Can you ride a bicycle?　你會騎自行車嗎？

6. Do you like to ride a bicycle?　喜歡騎自行車嗎？

STEP 2 反向利用提問來回答

🎧 24-2.mp3

如果以前只能簡短回答問題的話，現在試著說出完整的句子吧。將疑問句變成陳述句，就能簡單變成一個句子了。開始練習用句子回答吧！

1. How often do you ride a bicycle?　有多常騎自行車呢？

   I ride a bicycle _____.　我 _____ 會騎自行車。

   every day to commute 每天通勤 ｜ on Saturdays 每星期六 ｜ once or twice a month 一個月一兩次

2. Where do you usually ride a bicycle?　主要會在哪裡騎自行車？

   I usually ride a bicycle _____.　我主要會 _____ 騎自行車。

   at a park 在公園 ｜ in my neighborhood 在我家附近 ｜ along the Han River 沿著漢江

3. When did you learn how to ride a bicycle?　何時學會騎自行車呢？

   I learned how to ride a bicycle _____.　我在 _____ 學會騎自行車。

   last month 上個月 ｜ a decade ago 十年前 ｜ when I was in elementary school 小學時

4. Who taught you how to ride a bicycle? 誰教你騎自行車的呢？

_____ taught me how to ride a bicycle. _____ 教我騎自行車。

My father 我爸爸 ┃ My older brother 我哥哥 ┃ My uncle 我叔叔

5. Can you ride a bicycle? 你會騎自行車嗎？

→ Yes, I can. _____ 是，我會，_____。

① I'm quite good at riding a bicycle. 我自行車騎得還挺好的。

② I recently learned how to ride a bicycle. 最近學會如何騎自行車了。

→ No, I can't. _____ 不，我不會，_____。

① And I don't really want to learn how to ride a bicycle. 而且我真的不想學怎麼騎自行車。

② I'm scared I might fall and get hurt. 我害怕會摔下來受傷。

6. Do you like to ride a bicycle? 喜歡騎自行車嗎？

→ Yes, I like to ride a bicycle. Because _____.

是，我喜歡，因為 _____。

① it is great exercise. 是很棒的運動。

② it feels good when I have a cool breeze on my face. 涼風吹在臉上的感覺很好。

→ No, I don't like to ride a bicycle. Because _____.

不，我不喜歡，因為 _____。

① the air pollution is severe in Seoul. 首爾的空氣污染很嚴重。

② it is very tiring and difficult. 很累人又很困難。

STEP 3 和母語人士對話

🎧 24-3.mp3

確認前面練習的提問如何活用在和母語人士的對話中，請不要忘記一邊聽一邊跟著說。

James Good morning. Isn't that a bicycle helmet?

Min Yes, it is. **Can you ride a bicycle**, James?

James Yep. But I don't ride one often. **Do you like to ride a bicycle?**

Min I do. But I'm not that good at it so I'm practicing.

James Good for you! **How often do you ride a bicycle?**

Min About once or twice a month. I don't get much time to. What about you?

James Same here. There are many other things to do, right?

Min **That's exactly what I mean.**[1] **Where do you usually ride a bicycle?**

James There is a beautiful park near my house so I go there.

Min It must be so nice to have a park nearby. How far have you gone on a bicycle?

James Actually last month, I went to Gilbut Park from Han River on a bicycle. It took me about 4 hours.

Min Wow, that must have been **a bit of a challenge**[2]. Did you get sore muscles?

James Yes, I did. My thighs were burning like crazy so I had to take a rest the next day.

Min But it must have been fun.

James Yes, it was amazing. Min, **when did you learn how to ride a bicycle?**

Min It was ages ago. I can barely remember. James, I'm just curious, **who taught you how to ride a bicycle?**

James My older brother taught me, but I think I got it **just like that**[3].

Min Yep. I remember it not being that difficult.

James Min, shall we go bicycle riding this weekend? What do you say?

Min That's a great idea. I would love to.

解說請見 P287

用 **6** 句英文，和外國人輕鬆話家常！

① That's exactly what I mean.

「我說的就是這個」的意思，適合在完全同意對方說的話時使用。

- ⊃ A：I don't think the government should raise taxes.　我覺得政府不應提高稅金。
- ⊃ B：**That's exactly what I mean**.　我就是這個意思。

② a bit of a challenge

challenge 是「挑戰」，a bit of 是「一點、少量的」之意，母語人士習慣連在一起使用，a bit of a challenge 可以解釋成「頗困難的事」。This task is a challenge.（這個任務很困難）可以改為 This task is a bit of a challenge.。

- ⊃ Hiking is **a bit of a challenge** for me since I'm so unfit.　登山對體力不好的我來說很困難。
- ⊃ **A bit of a challenge** is what I need right now to motivate myself.　為了讓自己有動力，我現在需要某些程度的挑戰。

③ just like that

「就那樣、突然」的意思，沒什麼特別的原因或預期，適合在突然做了什麼或突然發生事情時使用。

- ⊃ My mother-in-law came to my house **just like that.**　我婆婆突然就跑來我家。
- ⊃ She threw away my bag **just like that.**　她沒有任何原因就把我的包包丟了。

Climbing a mountain is fun

➜ ➜ ➜ 登山很有趣

登山或是旅行時，輕便打包行李叫做 **pack light**，When I go hiking, I like to pack light.（去登山時，我喜歡將行李輕便打包。）

登山時要準備什麼呢？當然一定要帶水囉，最好也帶上急救藥品（first-aid medicine），急救箱就叫做 **first-aid kit**，然後最重要的是爬山時帶來能量的零食，像是水果（fruit）、牛肉乾（beef jerky）、穀麥棒（a granola bar）之類的，You need to bring a water bottle, a first-aid kit and snacks.（需要帶水壺、急救箱和零食。）

不只韓國，許多國家的人都很喜歡登山，若要細數幾個登山的優點的話，有 improve muscular fitness（增加體力）、lower the risk of high cholesterol（降低得到高膽固醇的風險）以及 increase bone density（增加骨骼密度）等。Hiking is fun and healthy so you should try it too.（登山既有趣又有益健康，請一定要試試。）

試著用「誰、何時、在哪裡、做什麼、如何做、為什麼」的六何法疑問詞來問問題。直到沒有可以再進一步詢問的疑問詞時，就能更自然地引導對話。

✪ 用六何法疑問詞來提問

1. Why do you like hiking?　為何喜歡登山呢？

2. When do you normally go hiking?　通常何時會去登山？

3. Who do you usually go hiking with?　主要和誰一起去登山？

4. Which mountains have you been to?　爬過哪些山？

✪ 不用六何法疑問詞來提問

5. Do you like hiking?　喜歡登山嗎？

6. Have you ever been to the peak of a mountain?　曾登到山頂過嗎？

STEP 2 反向利用提問來回答

🎧 25-2.mp3

如果以前只能簡短回答問題的話，現在試著說出完整的句子吧。將疑問句變成陳述句，就能簡單變成一個句子了。開始練習用句子回答吧！

1. Why do you like hiking?　為何喜歡登山呢？

I like hiking because _____.　我喜歡登山，因為 _____。

❶ it's great exercise　是很好的運動。

❷ I can enjoy nature　能享受大自然。

2. When do you normally go hiking?　通常何時會去登山？

I normally go hiking _____.　通常 _____ 會去登山。

on weekends 週末 ┃ on my day off 休息的日子 ┃ in spring 春天 ┃ in fall 秋天

3. Who do you usually go hiking with?　主要和誰一起去登山？

I usually go hiking with _____.　主要和 _____ 一起去登山。

my father 我爸爸 ┃ my colleague 同事 ┃ my best friend 最好的朋友

4. Which mountains have you been to?　爬過哪些山？

I have been to _____ and _____.

爬過 _____ 和 _____ 。

Mount Everest 聖母峰、Seorak Mountain 雪嶽山 | Halla Mountain 漢拏山、Mount Fuji 富士山

5. Do you like hiking?　喜歡登山嗎？

→ Yes, I like hiking. Because _____.

是，我喜歡登山，因為 _____ 。

❶ it's a great way to lose weight.　是很好的減肥方式。

❷ I can breathe in fresh air so I feel refreshed.　呼吸新鮮空氣令人覺得舒暢。

→ No, I don't like hiking. Because _____.

不，我不喜歡登山，因為 _____ 。

❶ I don't like outdoor activities.　我不喜歡戶外活動。

❷ I'm afraid of insects in the woods.　我害怕樹林裡的昆蟲。

6. Have you ever been to the peak of a mountain?　曾登到山頂過嗎？

→ Yes, I have been to the peak of a mountain. Because _____.

是，我曾登到山頂過，因為 _____ 。

❶ I think hiking is completed only when you reach the peak.　我覺得到了山頂，登山才算完成。

❷ I get a sense of achievement when I reach the peak of a mountain.　我登到山頂才會有成就感。

→ No, I have never been to the peak of a mountain. Because _____.

不，我不曾登到山頂過，因為 _____ 。

❶ I always run out of energy just before reaching the peak.　我總是在抵達山頂之前就精疲力盡了。

❷ I don't think reaching the peak is that important. I just enjoy nature.　我不覺得到達山頂有那麼重要，只要享受大自然就好。

STEP 3 和母語人士對話

🎧 25-3.mp3

確認前面練習的提問如何活用在和母語人士的對話中，請不要忘記一邊聽一邊跟著說。

James Yeh! Tomorrow is a holiday! I'm so excited!

Min Do you have any special plans?

James I'm going hiking with my friends. **Do you like hiking?**

Min Yes, I do. Can I join you tomorrow?

James Sure, be my guest.

Min Thank you for letting me join you. Just asking, **why do you like hiking?**

James I love nature. And I can **breathe in**[①] fresh air and clear my mind.

Min I totally agree. **When do you normally go hiking?**

James I usually go in spring and fall. Summer is too hot and winter is too dangerous.

Min Yep, **same here**[②]. **Which mountains have you been to in Korea?**

James I have been to Seorak Mountain and Dobong Mountain. I loved them.

Min I've been to those mountains too! Have you ever been to the peaks of those mountains?

James Of course I have. When I go hiking, I always go to the peak. It gives me **a great sense of achievement**[③].

解說請見 P288

讓生活更豐富的休閒活動

① breathe in

「吸氣」的意思，breath 為「呼吸」之意，類似的意思可以用 inhale（吸氣），相反的意思則是 breathe out 或 exhale（吐氣）。

- I like the countryside as I can **breathe in** fresh air.　我喜歡鄉下，因為可以呼吸新鮮空氣。
- When people smoke on the street, I try to hold my breath. I don't like to **breathe in** the smoke.　如果有人在路上抽菸的話，我會試著憋氣，我不想吸到菸。

② same here

意思是「我也是一樣」，用來表達和對方有相同的想法、感情或希望。

- A：I hate listening to noisy rock music.　我討厭聽吵鬧的搖滾樂。
- B：**Same here.** I don't understand why my son likes it.　我也是，我無法理解我兒子為何會喜歡。

③ a sense of achievement

「成就感」的意思，a sense of 後面也可以加其他單字，例如 a sense of identity 是「認同感」，a sense of unity 則有「一致性」的意思。

- Finishing a book gives me **a sense of achievement.**　讀完一本書之後，會很有成就感。
- You will get **a sense of achievement** when you reach the peak of the mountain.　登上山頂的話，會很有成就感。

Exercise is refreshing!

→ → → **運動過後很舒暢！**

「運動」是 exercise 或是 work out。

運動是為了鍛鍊身體（to keep fit）、維持苗條的身材（to keep slim）、保持健康（to keep healthy）等等，有各式各樣的原因。

要形容身材和身體素質好時，可以説 **be in good shape**，變胖且身材走樣是 **be out of shape**。I exercise to **be in good shape**. 則是「我運動是為了讓身材好看和鍛鍊體力」的意思。

接著來看看運動時所需的能力吧，有句英語在韓國不太常用，就是 **hand-eye coordination**，意指反射性地使用手和眼的能力，也可以簡單解釋成「運動神經」。那麼，I have good hand-eye coordination. 是什麼意思呢？就是「擅長球類項目」的意思，因為要手眼並用的運動幾乎都是球類項目。一般説運動神經好的話，用 **I am athletic.** 即可，體力的英語是 **physical strength**，柔軟度則是 **flexibility**，要説「我柔軟度好」的話，用 I am flexible. 即可。

試著用「誰、何時、在哪裡、做什麼、如何做、為什麼」的六何法疑問詞來問問題。直到沒有可以再進一步詢問的疑問詞時,就能更自然地引導對話。

✪ 用六何法疑問詞來提問

1. Why do you exercise?　為何運動呢?

2. When do you work out?　何時會做運動?

3. Where do you go to get some exercise?　會去哪裡做運動?

4. What is your favorite exercise?　最喜歡的運動是什麼?

✪ 不用六何法疑問詞來提問

5. Are you athletic?　運動神經好嗎?

6. Do you exercise regularly?　會規律運動嗎?

STEP **2** 反向利用提問來回答

🎧 26-2.mp3

如果以前只能簡短回答問題的話,現在試著説出完整的句子吧。將疑問句變成陳述句,就能簡單變成一個句子了。開始練習用句子回答吧!

1. **Why** do you exercise?　為何運動呢?

I exercise **because it is** _____.　我運動因為_____。

healthy 健康 ｜ refreshing 能消除疲勞 ｜ relaxing 能放鬆心情 ｜ stress relieving 能消除壓力

2. **When** do you work out?　何時會做運動?

I usually work out _____.　我通常 _____ 會做運動。

in the morning 在早上 ｜ in the evening 在傍晚 ｜ at night 在夜晚 ｜ on weekends 在週末

3. **Where** do you go to get some exercise?　會去哪裡做運動?

I go to _____ to get some exercise.　我會去 _____ 做運動。

the gym 健身中心 ｜ the school playground 學校運動場 ｜ a park near my house 我家附近的公園

用 **6** 句英文,和外國人輕鬆話家常!

4. What is your favorite exercise?　最喜歡的運動是什麼？

My favorite exercise is ＿＿＿＿＿.　最喜歡的運動是 ＿＿＿＿＿。

Pilates 彼拉提斯 ｜ running 跑步 ｜ swimming 游泳 ｜ working out at a gym 健身房運動

5. Are you athletic?　運動神經好嗎？

→ Yes, I am athletic. Because ＿＿＿＿＿.

是，很好，因為 ＿＿＿＿＿。

① I have exercised on a regular basis since I was young.　我從小就開始規律做運動。

② I am a member of a local gym and I work out often.　我是附近健身中心的會員，而且很常運動。

→ No, I am not athletic. Because ＿＿＿＿＿.

不，不好，因為 ＿＿＿＿＿。

① I rarely exercise and I don't like sports.　我幾乎不做運動，也不喜歡運動。

② I don't work out much. My body is not in good shape.　我不常運動，我的身體／身材不太好。

6. Do you exercise regularly?　會規律運動嗎？

→ Yes, I exercise regularly. Because ＿＿＿＿＿.

是，我會規律運動，因為 ＿＿＿＿＿。

① I think it's important for my health. I go to the gym almost every day.　我覺得這對健康很重要，幾乎每天都會去健身房。

② exercise keeps me slim. I take a yoga class twice a week.　運動讓我保持苗窕，我一週會去上兩次瑜伽課。

→ No, I don't exercise regularly. Because ＿＿＿＿＿.

不，我沒有規律運動，因為 ＿＿＿＿＿。

① I don't have the time or energy to work out.　我沒有時間和精力做運動。

② I don't like exercising and I am not athletic.　我討厭做運動，而且運動神經不好。

確認前面練習的提問如何活用在和母語人士的對話中,請不要忘記一邊聽一邊跟著說。

Min Your hair is wet. Did you just have a shower?

James Actually, I went swimming. I didn't have time to dry my hair after my shower.

Min You go swimming? I didn't know that. **Do you swim regularly?**

James I try to. There is an indoor swimming pool near my apartment. I got a membership there recently. Do you exercise often?

Min Yep, I do. I just go to the local gym. Swimming sounds fun. I should try it.

James You should. **When and where do you work out?**

Min I work out in the evening at the gym **after work**[1].

James Aren't you tired after work? I go swimming before work.

Min That sounds more tiring for me.

James Does it? I guess it depends on the person. How often do you exercise?

Min I try to **hit the gym**[2] at least twice a week.

James **What is your favorite exercise?** Do you like working out at the gym?

Min Nope. Actually I really like yoga. Unfortunately there is no decent yoga studio in my neighborhood.

James **That's a shame.**[3] **Are you athletic?**

Min I wouldn't say I am, but I'm quite flexible. Have you tried yoga?

James I don't think it's for guys. It looks and sounds like a girls' exercise.

Min That's absurd. I have seen many guys taking yoga class.

解說請見 P288

① after work

直接看字面意思的話，就是「工作（結束）後」，也可以當成「下班後」的意思。下班後約見面，可以說 Let's meet after work.。

- ➲ I go running every day **after work**.　每天下班後都會跑步。
- ➲ I'm exhausted when I get home **after work**.　下班後回到家都累癱了。

② hit the gym

大家都知道 hit 是「打」的意思吧？不曉得是否聽過 *Hit The Road Jack* 這首歌呢？ hit the road 不是「敲打道路」而是「離開道路、開始旅行」之意。同樣地，hit the gym 就是「去健身中心」的意思，也可以說 Go to the gym and work out.。

- ➲ I am going to **hit the gym** tonight.　我今天晚上要去健身房。
- ➲ You are out of shape. You need to **hit the gym.**　你身材走樣了，你得去健身房了。

③ That's a shame.

shame 有「丟臉、遺憾」之意，That's a shame. 則是「真可惜」的意思。

- ➲ **That's a shame** you can't come to the party tonight.　真可惜你不能來今晚的派對。
- ➲ **That's a shame** you didn't finish your work on time.　真可惜你無法準時完成工作。

Are you good at driving?

→ → → 擅長開車嗎?

　　這一章節來熟悉一下開車的相關用語,首先 **pull over** 是「靠邊停車」,電影中警察要請駕駛停車時,會說 Sir, please pull over your car.(先生,請靠邊停車);若是被人攔下來的情況,變成被動語態 get pulled over 就可以了,如果要說「昨天警察要我靠邊停車」,就是 Yesterday, I got pulled over by the police.。

　　另外,還有兩個常用的詞是 **speed up** 和 **slow down**,是什麼意思應該馬上就能猜出來吧? speed up 是「加快速度」,slow down 是「減慢速度」。想要再多加快一點速度時,是 **step on it**,這裡的 it 是加速器(accelerator),超速罰單則是 speeding ticket。

　　很驚險地避開了交通事故是 **have a near miss**,說 I had a near miss.,就是「我差點要出車禍了」的意思。

我先提出問題

🎧 27-1.mp3

試著用「誰、何時、在哪裡、做什麼、如何做、為什麼」的六何法疑問詞來問問題。直到沒有可以再進一步詢問的疑問詞時，就能更自然地引導對話。

✪ 用六何法疑問詞來提問

1. What was your first car?　你的第一臺車是什麼？

2. Where is a nice place to go for a drive?　哪裡是適合兜風的地方？

3. When did you get your driver's license?　何時考到駕照呢？

✪ 不用六何法疑問詞來提問

4. Are you a good driver?　你是好駕駛嗎？

5. Do you like driving?　喜歡開車嗎？

6. Have you ever had a car accident?　曾經出過車禍嗎？

反向利用提問來回答

🎧 27-2.mp3

如果以前只能簡短回答問題的話，現在試著説出完整的句子吧。將疑問句變成陳述句，就能簡單變成一個句子了。開始練習用句子回答吧！

1. What was your first car?　你的第一臺車是什麼？

My first car was _____.　我的第一臺車是 _____。

a second-hand truck 中古貨車 ｜ a Hyundai Accent 現代的 Accent ｜ a Ford Focus 福特的 Focus

2. Where is a nice place to go for a drive?　哪裡是適合兜風的地方？

_____ is a nice place to go for a drive.　_____ 是適合兜風的地方。

The east coast 東海岸 ｜ The cherry blossom road 櫻花路 ｜ The road along the river 江邊沿岸

3. When did you get your driver's license?　何時考到駕照呢？

I got my driver's license _____.　我在 _____ 考到駕照。

after graduating from university 大學畢業後 | about 5 years ago 大概五年前 | when I was 21 years old 二十一歲時

4. Are you a good driver? 你是好駕駛嗎？

→ Yes, I am a good driver. Because _____. 是，我是個好駕駛，因為 _____。

❶ I abide by all the traffic rules. 我遵守所有的交通規則。

❷ I yield to the other drivers on the road. 我會禮讓其他駕駛。

→ No, I am not a good driver. Because _____. 不，我不是個好駕駛，因為 _____。

❶ I became impatient when I drive. 開車時我沒有耐心。

❷ I drive fast and sometimes I even use foul language. 我開車很快，而且偶爾會罵髒話。

5. Do you like driving? 喜歡開車嗎？

→ Yes, I like driving. Because _____.
是，我喜歡，因為 _____。

❶ I like to be in control of such a powerful machine. 我喜歡駕馭馬力強大的汽車。

❷ I enjoy speed as I can get rid of stress. 我享受速度感，能消除壓力。

→ No, I don't like driving. Because _____.
不，我不喜歡，因為 _____。

❶ the traffic jams in Seoul are too severe. 首爾的交通堵塞太嚴重了。

❷ I'm not very good at driving. 我不太會開車。

6. Have you ever had a car accident? 曾經出過車禍嗎？

→ Yes, I have had a car accident. _____
是，我曾出過車禍，_____。

❶ I was hit by a bus. 我被公車撞到。

❷ I scratched a parked car by accident. 意外刮到停好的車子。

→ No, I have never had a car accident. _____
不，我不曾出過車禍，_____。

❶ I'm very careful when I drive. 我開車時非常小心。

❷ I'm very good at driving. 我開車技術很好。

STEP 3 和母語人士對話

🎧 27-3.mp3

確認前面練習的提問如何活用在和母語人士的對話中，請不要忘記一邊聽一邊跟著說。

Min Hey, is that your driver's license?

James Yes. The picture is from way back. I **look dorky**①.

Min No, I think you look cute in that picture. **When did you get your driver's license?**

James Let me think... I guess it was about 15 years ago.

Min Wow, that's a long time ago. **What was your first car?**

James My first car was actually a truck. My father got it for me on my 16th birthday.

Min So you've been driving for a long time. **Are you a good driver?**

James I must be. I have never had a car accident. **Have you ever had a car accident?**

Min Well, yes. It was a month ago. I scratched a parked car by accident.

James That's okay. You just started driving last year, right? You will **get used to**② it soon.

Min I hope so. I'm still scared of driving. **Do you like driving?**

James I love driving. I like going around Korea to see the hidden beauties.

Min That sounds fun. **Where is a nice place to go for a drive?** Can you recommend a good place?

James You should try driving along the east coast of Korea. It's beautiful.

Min Thank you for the recommendation.

James Sure. I'm going for a drive along the east coast this weekend.

Min Really? If you don't mind, can I tag along?

James Sure, please **be my guest**③.

▶ ▶ ▶ 解說請見 P289

① look dorky

dorky 是會話中使用的俚語，意為「白癡一樣、笨蛋一樣」，因此 look dorky 就成了「看起來像笨蛋一樣」的意思，dork 是「白癡」的名詞。

⊃ With my new haircut, I **look dorky.**　因為新髮型的緣故，我看起來呆呆的。

⊃ I used to **look dorky** in high school.　我上高中時看起來傻傻的。

② get used to

「對於（做）～變熟悉」的意思，to 後面可加名詞或動名詞，可以再變化成 be used to 來使用，就是「對於～熟悉」的意思。

⊃ You will **get used to** cooking.　你對做料理會變得熟練。

⊃ I **am used to** getting lots of attention.　我已經習慣受人矚目了。

③ be my guest

直譯的話是「請成為我的客人」，當對方想做某些行動時，說這句話表示允許對方那麼做。有「請隨心所欲去做吧」的意思，適合在欣然接受對方的要求時使用。

⊃ A：Can I stay in your room for a while?　我可以在你的房間裡待一會兒嗎？

⊃ B：Sure, **be my guest.**　當然，請便。

用 **6** 句英文，和外國人輕鬆話家常！

I like to pat my pet

→ → → 我喜歡摸寵物

喜歡寵物的人一般來說可以分成貓派（a cat person）和狗派（a dog person），下次遇到外國朋友時，不妨問問看對方：**Are you a cat person or a dog person?**

我們通常會繫上牽繩再帶寵物去散步，牽繩的英語是什麼呢？是 **(dog) leash**，和狗狗散步後可以這麼說，I walked my dog on a leash.（我繫牽繩去遛狗了）。

接著來看看有哪些用動物來比喻人或事的說法，最簡單的就是 **copy cat**，一模一樣地模仿別人行為的人就是 copy cat，對那樣的人可以說 You are such a copy cat.（你真是個學人精）。

chicken 有「膽小鬼」的意思，可以說 You are a chicken.，不過這個說法可能會讓對方不開心，請謹慎使用。再加以應用，chicken out 則有「臨陣退縮」的意思。

fishy 又是什麼意思呢？ fish 是魚，fishy 則有「散發出魚腥味」的意思，散發出腥味常用來表示「可疑的」，覺得人事物有可疑之處時，便說 I smell something **fishy**.（好像很可疑的樣子）即可。

我先提出問題

🎧 28-1.mp3

試著用「誰、何時、在哪裡、做什麼、如何做、為什麼」的六何法疑問詞來問問題。直到沒有可以再進一步詢問的疑問詞時，就能更自然地引導對話。

✪ 用六何法疑問詞來提問

1. Who lakes care of your pet? 誰在照顧你的寵物？

2. What can children learn by having a pet? 孩子們透過養寵物能學習到什麼？

3. Which animals do you think are cute? 你覺得什麼動物可愛？

4. When was the last time you went to the zoo? 你上次去動物園是什麼時候？

✪ 不用六何法疑問詞來提問

5. Do you have a pet? 你有養寵物嗎？

6. Are you interested in animal rights? 你關心動物的權益嗎？

反向利用提問來回答

🎧 28-2.mp3

如果以前只能簡短回答問題的話，現在試著說出完整的句子吧。將疑問句變成陳述句，就能簡單變成一個句子了。開始練習用句子回答吧！

1. Who takes care of your pet? 誰在照顧你的寵物？

_____ take(s) care of my pet. _____ 照顧我的寵物。

I 我自己 ┃ My mother 我媽媽 ┃ My younger brother 我弟弟

2. What can children learn by having a pet? 孩子們透過養寵物能學習到什麼？

Children can learn _____ by having a pet. 孩子們透過養寵物能學習到 _____。

responsibility 責任感 ┃ love 愛 ┃ obedience 順從 ┃ loyalty 忠心

3. Which animals do you think are cute? 你覺得什麼動物可愛？

I think _____ , _____ and _____ are cute.

我覺得 _____ 、 _____ 還有_____ 很可愛。

squirrels 松鼠、guinea pigs 天竺鼠、goldfish 金魚 │ pigeons 鴿子、hamsters 倉鼠、
Iguanas 鬣蜥

4. When was the last time you went to the zoo? 你上次去動物園是什麼時候？

The last time I went to the zoo was _____. 我上次去動物園是_____。

last year 去年 │ several years ago 幾年前 │ when I was in elementary school 當我還在念小學時

5. Do you have a pet? 你有養寵物嗎？

→ Yes, I have a pet. Because _____.

是的，我有，因為 _____。

❶ I like animals. They keep me company 我喜歡動物，他們和我作伴。

❷ I've had a pet ever since I was very young. 我從很小開始就有養寵物了。

→ No, I don't have a pet. Because _____.

不，我沒有，因為_____。

❶ I don't like animals. They are messy and noisy. 我不喜歡動物，他們又髒又吵。

❷ I don't have time to take care of a pet. 我沒有時間照顧寵物。

6. Are you interested in animal rights? 你關心動物的權益嗎？

→ Yes, I am interested in animal rights. Because _____.

是，我關心動物權益，因為 _____。

❶ I think it's cruel to use animals for scientific experiments. 我覺得將動物用在科學實驗非常殘忍。

❷ I believe that animals also have souls. 我相信動物也有靈魂

→ No, I am not interested in animal rights. Because _____.

不，我不關心動物權益，因為 _____。

❶ I think it's more important to take care of starving children first.　我覺得幫助飢餓的孩童更重要。

❷ I don't believe that animals have souls.　我覺得動物沒有靈魂。

STEP 3 和母語人士對話

確認前面練習的提問如何活用在和母語人士的對話中，請不要忘記一邊聽一邊跟著說。

Min James, **do you have a pet?**

James Yep. I have a cat. Her name is Sally and she is shy.

Min **Who takes care of your pet?** Aren't you out working most of the time?

James Cats are very independent. They can spend time by themselves.

Min That is nice. My nephew takes care of my puppy when I'm out.

James Your nephew? He lives with you?

Min Nope, but he **lives next door**① to me. I give him some pocket money for taking care of my puppy.

James **What can children learn by having a pet?**

Min I think they can learn responsibility and love by having a pet.

James I agree. They can also learn to appreciate and understand animals.

Min **Which animals do you think are cute?**

James I think squirrels are cute. I want to have one as a pet.

Min It's a silly question, but if you could be any animal, what animal would you choose to be?

James Oh, it is an interesting question. Well, I would like to be a bird and **fly away**②. What about you?

Min I would like to be a dolphin and swim away.

James **That reminds me,**③ do you want to go to the zoo? **When was the last time you went to the zoo?**

用 6 句英文，和外國人輕鬆話家常！

Min	I think it's been 5 years. Let's go to the zoo!
James	By the way, some people say that zoos are cruel places for animals. What do you think?
Min	I never thought about it in that way. **Are you interested in animal rights?**
James	In fact, I am. I am a member of an animal rights group.

 解說請見 P289

① live next door

「住在隔壁」的意思，也可以說 live in the next house。

⊃ My sister **lives next door** so we meet often.　我妹妹住在隔壁，所以我們很常見面。

⊃ I **live next door.** I brought some cookies for you.　我就住在隔壁，帶了一點餅乾過來給你。

② fly away

「飛得遠遠的」之意，away 有「往另一個方向」的意思，和動詞一起使用，加強了「變得遠遠的」的意思，就像 run way 是「逃跑」，walk away 是「離開」一樣。

⊃ I wish I could **fly away** like a bird.　要是能像鳥一樣飛得遠遠的就好了。

⊃ My pet bird **flew away** so I'm really sad.　我養的鳥飛走了，讓我很難過。

③ that reminds me

remind 有「喚起」的意思，因此 that reminds me 就是前面提及或看到的事物，喚起了某些回憶，理解成「這麼一來讓我想到」即可。

⊃ A：Have you seen my history notebook?　你有看到我的歷史筆記嗎？

⊃ B：**That reminds me,** didn't you borrow my mathematics textbook?　這麼一說讓我想到，你不是借走了我的數學課本嗎？

Do you want to be famous?

→ → → **想要出名嗎？**

　　來學學和名聲有關的英語說法吧，首先名聲是 **fame**，有名的人叫做 someone famous，運動選手或藝人等等名人則稱作 **celebrity**。

　　近年有句為人所知的話是 15 minutes of fame（十五分鐘的名氣），出自普普藝術家（pop artist）安迪・沃荷（Andy Warhol）之口，他曾說：In the future, everybody will be world-famous for 15 minutes.（在未來，人人都能成名十五分鐘）。在這個透過 Youtube 就能讓一般人暫時成名的時代來看，這句話似乎所言不假。15 minutes of fame 的意思並不是真的十五分鐘的名氣，而是意指「短暫的名氣」。

　　fame 的延伸說法有 **hall of fame**，意思是「名譽的殿堂」，這個詞最初是從德國的名人堂（Ruhmeshalle）而來，該處是為了紀念光耀德國歷史的人物所設立。後來變成英語，出現了「美國偉人紀念堂」（Hall of Fame for Great Americans），宗旨為紀念在體育、藝術等特定領域中，留下偉大成績並受到尊崇的人士。之前美國設立了不少偉人紀念堂，最近日本、韓國等國家也開始風行。

STEP 1 我先提出問題

🎧 29-1.mp3

試著用「誰、何時、在哪裡、做什麼、如何做、為什麼」的六何法疑問詞來問問題。直到沒有可以再進一步詢問的疑問詞時，就能更自然地引導對話。

✪ 用六何法疑問詞來提問

1. Where can one see celebrities in person?　哪裡可以親眼見到藝人？

2. Which celebrity would you like to meet in person?　你想親眼見到哪位藝人？

3. Why do you think teenagers like celebrities so much?　你覺得為何青少年會喜歡藝人呢？

✪ 不用六何法疑問詞來提問

4. Would you like to be famous?　你想要變有名嗎？

5. Do you know someone famous?　你認識名人嗎？

6. Have you ever seen a celebrity in person?　曾經親眼見過藝人嗎？

STEP 2 反向利用提問來回答

🎧 29-2.mp3

如果以前只能簡短回答問題的話，現在試著說出完整的句子吧。將疑問句變成陳述句，就能簡單變成一個句子了。開始練習用句子回答吧！

1. Where can one see celebrities in person?　哪裡可以親眼見到藝人？

   One can see celebrities in person _____.　可以在 _____ 親自見到藝人。

   at trendy restaurants 引領流行的餐廳 ┃ at broadcasting stations 電視臺 ┃ at famous hair salons 知名的美髮沙龍

2. Which celebrity would you like to meet?　你想親眼見到哪位藝人？

   I would like to meet _____.　我想見到 _____。

   Taylor Swift 泰勒絲（美國歌手）┃ Angelina Jolie 安潔莉娜·裘莉（美國演員）┃ Yoo Jae-suk 劉在錫（韓國諧星）

3. Why do you think teenagers like celebrities so much? 你覺得為何青少年會喜歡藝人呢？

I think teenagers like celebrities so much because _____.

我認為青少年喜歡藝人是因為 _____。

❶ they look glamorous and fashionable on TV　藝人在電視上看起來迷人又有型。

❷ they make a lot of money and many people love them　藝人賺很多錢且備受喜愛。

4. Would you like to be famous? 你想要變有名嗎？

→ Yes, I would like to be famous. Because _____. 是，我想變有名，因為_____。

❶ I could make a lot of money if I became famous.　變有名的話就能賺很多錢。

❷ I could become an influential person.　我想成為有影響力的人

→ No, I would not like to be famous. Because _____. 不，我不想變有名，因為_____。

❶ my privacy would be revealed to the public.　私生活會暴露在大眾面前。

❷ I couldnt behave or speak freely.　無法自由行動或說話。

5. Do you know someone famous? 你認識名人嗎？

→ Yes, I know someone famous. He/She is _____. 是的，我認識，他／她是_____。

a well-known actor/actress 知名的演員 ┃ a famous singer 有名的歌手 ┃ a renowned doctor 著名的醫生

→ No, I don't know anyone famous. 不，我不認識任何名人。

6. Have you ever seen a celebrity in person? 曾經親眼見過藝人嗎？

→ Yes, I have seen a celebrity in person. I saw __（人）__ at __（地點）__. 是，我曾親眼見過藝人，在 _____ 遇見 _____ 了。

❶ Kim Yuna　金妍兒、a Japanese restaurant　日式餐廳

❷ PSY、 a broadcasting station　電視臺

→ No, I have never seen a celebrity in person. Because _____. 不，我不曾親眼見過藝人，因為 _____。

❶ I don't go to crowded or fashionable places much. 我不太去人多或是上流人士聚集的地方。

❷ I don't know many celebrities. 我認識的藝人不多。

STEP 3 和母語人士對話 🎧 29-3.mp3

確認前面練習的提問如何活用在和母語人士的對話中，請不要忘記一邊聽一邊跟著說。

James What's all the fuss about?

Min Oh, a famous Korean actor is here. And his fans are gathered downstairs.

James Sometimes I don't get these teenage fans.

Min I know. They **are** so **crazy about**① celebrities.

James **Why do you think teenagers like celebrities so much?**

Min Well, they want to be like them. They want a high income and a glamorous lifestyle.

James I guess we have also had times when we were big fans of famous singers.

Min We sure have. **Have you ever seen a celebrity in person?**

James Yep, several times. If you live in Seoul, it's not hard to see one.

Min Seriously? How come I have never seen one? **Where can one see celebrities in person?**

James You can see celebrities at trendy restaurants, famous hair salons and obviously at broadcasting stations.

Min I should try going to famous restaurants more often.

James **Which celebrity would you like to meet?**

Min I would really like to meet Yoo Jae-suk. You know, the Korean comedian?

James Yep, I like him too. **Do you know someone famous?**

Min **Let me think.**② Oh, my uncle went to the same school as Park Geun-hye.

James That is cool! **Would you like to be famous?**

Min Not really. I don't want my private life to **be exposed to**[3] the public. What about you?

James I wouldn't mind making a lot of money by being a celebrity.

解說請見 P290

① be crazy about ···

這是很常聽到的說法吧？當你很喜歡某個事物時，就可以這麼說。about 後面可以加上人、行為（動名詞）、物品或場所等等。

⊃ I **am crazy about** ice cream. I can't pass a day without eating it.　我非常喜歡冰淇淋，每天都要吃。

⊃ My brother **is crazy about** Girls Generation. If I make any bad comments about them, he gets upset.　我弟弟非常喜歡少女時代，如果我說了她們的壞話，他會生氣的。

② Let me think. ···

「要稍微想一下」的意思，用法和 Give me a second.（請稍等我一下）相似。還沒想出要怎麼回答，想再借用一點時間，就可以說這句話。

⊃ A：Have you ever been robbed?　你有被搶過嗎？

⊃ B：**Let me think.** Nope, I can't remember being robbed.　讓我想一想，沒有，我不記得有被搶過。

③ be exposed to ···

expose 是「露出」的意思，所以「be exposed」就是「被露出」，be exposed 後面加上 to，可用來表示「暴露在～」。

⊃ Children these days **are exposed to** a lot of violent TV content.　最近孩子們都暴露在暴力的電視節目之下。

⊃ Celebrities' personal lives **are exposed to** the public.　藝人的私生活暴露在大眾面前。

用

6

句英文，和外國人輕鬆話家常！

Let's go to an art exhibition!
→ → → 我們去看展覽吧！

　　旅行時，常常會有參觀博物館（museum）或美術館（art gallery）的行程，每個國家都有知名的博物館，例如美國有大都會藝術博物館（The Metropolitan Museum of Art），法國有羅浮宮（Louvre Museum），英國則有大英博物館（British Museum）。現在就來告訴各位，造訪這些知名的博物館或美術館時，必須掌握哪些祕訣吧。

　　首先，如果是學生的話，出發前請先申請好國際學生證（International Student ID），因為買票時可以享有優惠折扣，只要問售票處 I am a student. Can I get a discount?（我是學生，可以有優惠嗎？）就可以了，出示學生證後，就能購買優惠票券了；年長者（senior）也可享優惠，一定要記得攜帶護照喔。

　　請多利用知名博物館或美術館的 **audio guide**，大部分皆有提供中文的導覽，先詢問服務處 Could I get an audio guide in Chinese?（我可以租借中文的語音導覽嗎？），再抵押證件並支付費用即可。

　　有些地方偶爾能免費看展，以羅浮宮為例，淡季月份的第一個週一為免費參觀，請先至博物館網站仔細查看 **Hours and Admission**。

試著用「誰、何時、在哪裡、做什麼、如何做、為什麼」的六何法疑問詞來問問題。直到沒有可以再進一步詢問的疑問詞時，就能更自然地引導對話。

✪ 用六何法疑問詞來提問

1. Why do you enjoy art? 為何喜歡藝術呢？

2. Who is your favorite painter? 最喜歡的畫家是誰？

3. What style of painting do you like the most? 最喜歡什麼風格的畫作？

4. When was the last time you went to an art exhibition? 上次去看藝術展是什麼時候？

✪ 不用六何法疑問詞來提問

5. Have you ever been to an art gallery? 曾去過美術館嗎？

6. Are you good at drawing? 擅長畫畫嗎？

如果以前只能簡短回答問題的話，現在試著說出完整的句子吧。將疑問句變成陳述句，就能簡單變成一個句子了。開始練習用句子回答吧！

1. Why do you enjoy art? 為何喜歡藝術呢？

   I enjoy art because _____. 我喜歡藝術，因為 _____。

   ❶ I can learn about history by looking at old paintings 可以透過欣賞老畫作來學習歷史。

   ❷ I can calm myself down when I look at beautiful pictures 看著優美的畫作時，能讓我的內心平靜。

2. Who is your favorite painter? 最喜歡的畫家是誰？

   My favorite painter is _____. 我最喜歡的畫家是 _____。

   Picasso 畢卡索 | Cezanne 塞尚 | Van Gogh 梵谷

3. What style of painting do you like the most? 最喜歡什麼風格的畫作？

   I like _____ the most. 我最喜歡 _____。

用 **6** 句英文，和外國人輕鬆話家常！

oil paintings 油畫 | water colors 水彩畫 | still life paintings 靜物畫 | Cubism 立體主義

4. When was the last time you went to an art exhibition? 上次去看藝術展是什麼時候？

The last time I went to an art exhibition was _____. 上次去看展是 _____。

last week 上星期 | several months ago 幾個月前 | ages ago 很久以前

5. Have you ever been to an art gallery? 曾去過美術館嗎？

→ Yes, I have been to an art gallery. Because _____. 是，我去過美術館，因為 _____。

❶ my mother likes art so she has taken me to art galleries many times. 我母親喜愛藝術，因此帶我去過美術館很多次。

❷ it was a high school art class assignment. 是高中美術課的作業。

→ No, I haven't been to an art gallery. Because _____. 不，我不曾去過美術館，因為 _____。

❶ I am not interested in art. 我對藝術沒興趣。

❷ I find art to be boring and dull. 我覺得藝術無聊又沒意思。

6. Are you good at drawing? 擅長畫畫嗎？

→ Yes, I am good at drawing. Because _____. 是，我擅長畫畫，因為 _____。

❶ I went to an art academy in high school. 我高中時有去美術補習班上課。

❷ my mother is a famous artist and I take after her. 我母親是知名藝術家，而我遺傳到她。

→ No, I am not good at drawing. Because _____. 不，我不擅長畫畫，因為 _____。

❶ I have never learned how to draw. 我沒有學過畫畫。

❷ I just don't have any artistic talent. 就是沒有藝術天份。

確認前面練習的提問如何活用在和母語人士的對話中，請不要忘記一邊聽一邊跟著說。

James	Hey, what is that? Did you draw this?
Min	Oh, it's just silly doodling I did.
James	It looks good. **Are you good at drawing?**
Min	I don't think I am good at drawing. But I like art.
James	You do? **Why do you enjoy art?**
Min	Well, there are many reasons but **in a nutshell**①, art makes me happy.
James	So **have you ever been to an art gallery?**
Min	Of course. I go to an art gallery **on a regular basis**②. In fact, I'm going to an art exhibition this Saturday too.
James	Whose exhibition is it?
Min	It's an Andy Warhol exhibition.
James	You like modern art too? I never get modern art.
Min	Yep, many people say that.
James	**What style of painting do you like the most?**
Min	I like oil paintings. I especially like Impressionism.
James	Oh, I know what that is. It is an art movement which was led by painters like Van Gogh and Cezanne, right?
Min	Good for you. I **am impressed**③. Do you enjoy art?
James	Not really. **Who is your favorite painter?**
Min	I have liked Picasso ever since I was little. I think he is a genius.
James	I can't disagree with that. I also learned about Picasso in school.
Min	**When was the last time you went to an art exhibition?**
James	It's been too long to remember.

Min Would you like to join me this Saturday?

James Why not? I'll come along.

► ► ► 解說請見 P291

① in a nutshell

「簡單地」的意思，用來說明將長篇大論整理得簡單明瞭，一種比較高級的說法。put something in a nutshell 表示「簡而言之」的意思。

⊃ It's a long story but to put it **in a nutshell**, I passed the test. 說來話長，簡而言之就是我通過考試了。

⊃ To put it **in a nutshell**, it is a happy ending. 簡而言之，是幸福的結局。

② on a regular basis

「規律地」的意思，和 regularly 同義。適合用於表示反覆、規律地進行某個行為。

⊃ I study English **on a regular basis.** 我定期學習英語。

⊃ My father exercises **on a regular basis.** 爸爸規律地做運動。

③ be impressed

意思為「感到佩服」，覺得感動時也可以使用，如果要說深深地感動，前面加上 deeply 即可。

⊃ I **was impressed** by your performance. 你的表演讓我很感動。

⊃ My brother said that he **was** deeply **impressed** by this book. 我弟弟說他被這本書深深地感動。

Part 4

現實生活及網路世界

現代人過著兩種生活，也就是與人面對面互動的離線（offline）生活，以及透過網路互動的線上（online）生活！在這個沒有網路就幾乎無法生活的時代，online/offline 生活成了最常見的對話素材。那麼，現在就用六何法疑問詞來聊聊現實生活及網路世界吧！

The real and virtual worlds

I reminisce about my college days

→ → → 回憶大學時期

　　來比較一下韓國的大學和美國的大學吧，首先，美國的大學生常在上課時間發表想法，就算教授正在上課，學生也會舉手發問（ask questions）和討論（discuss），比起被動地（passive）聽課，更積極地（active）參與（participate）。

　　韓國的考試分為期中考（mid-term exam）與期末考（final exam），美國則是常有 assignments（作業）、presentation（發表）與 test（考試），因此根本沒辦法 cramming（臨時抱佛腳）。

　　至於和學生主修科系較無關聯的通識課程（general education），韓國的通識課內容多是以理論為主，美國則較多以活動為主，如學習樂器、歌唱、演戲等等。

　　在韓國的學生餐廳用餐，每次都要付錢，美國的學生則是在學期初就加入所謂的 meal-plan，先計算好一學期（semester）會用餐幾次，並預先支付在學生餐廳用餐的費用。

STEP 1 我先提出問題

🎧 31-1.mp3

試著用「誰、何時、在哪裡、做什麼、如何做、為什麼」的六何法疑問詞來問問題。直到沒有可以再進一步詢問的疑問詞時，就能更自然地引導對話。

✪ 用六何法疑問詞來提問

1. What was your major?　你大學主修什麼？

2. When did you graduate from college?　大學何時畢業的呢？

3. Where did you get your college degree?　你在哪裡取得學位？

4. How did you pay for college?　你如何支付大學學費呢？

✪ 不用六何法疑問詞來提問

5. Did you have a girlfriend/boyfriend in college?　大學時有女朋友／男朋友嗎？

6. Were you a member of a club?　你是社團成員嗎？

STEP 2 反向利用提問來回答

🎧 31-2.mp3

如果以前只能簡短回答問題的話，現在試著說出完整的句子吧。將疑問句變成陳述句，就能簡單變成一個句子了。開始練習用句子回答吧！

1. What was your major?　你大學主修什麼？

My major was _____.　我大學主修 _____。

economics 經濟學 ｜ physics 物理 ｜ fine art 純藝術

2. When did you graduate from college?　大學何時畢業的呢？

I graduated from college _____.　我 _____ 大學畢業。

10 years ago 十年前 ｜ in 2001 在 2001 年 ｜ several months ago 幾個月前

3. Where did you get your college degree?　你在哪裡取得學位？

I got my college degree from _____.　我在 _____ 取得學位。

Seoul National University 首爾大學 ｜ the University of Oxford 牛津大學 ｜ Harvard University 哈佛大學

4. How did you pay for college? 你如何支付大學學費呢？

I paid for college _____. 我靠 _____ 來支付大學學費。

by working part time 打工 ┃ by getting a student loan 申請就學貸款 ┃ by borrowing money from my parents 和父母借錢

5. Did you have a girlfriend/boyfriend in college? 大學時有女朋友／男朋友嗎？

→ Yes, I had a girlfriend/boyfriend. We met _____. 是，我有女朋友／男朋友，我們是在 _____ 認識的。

in a club activity 社團活動中 ┃ during the college festival 大學校慶期間 ┃ in French class 法語課上

→ No, I didn't have a girlfriend/boyfriend. Because _____. 不，我沒有女朋友／男朋友，因為 _____。

❶ I had to concentrate on my studies. 我得專注在課業上。

❷ I didn't have any time as I also had a part time job. 我還要打工，沒有時間。

6. Were you a member of a club? 你是社團成員嗎？

→ Yes, I was a member of the _____ club. 是，我是 _____ 社的成員。

debating 辯論 ┃ horse riding 馬術 ┃ sign language 手語

→ No, I wasn't a member of a club. Because _____. 不，我不是社團成員，因為 _____。

❶ I was too busy with my classes. 課業非常繁忙。

❷ I was a TA(teaching assistant) so I didn't have any additional time. 我是助教，完全沒有多餘的時間。

STEP 3 和母語人士對話

31-3.mp3

確認前面練習的提問如何活用在和母語人士的對話中，請不要忘記一邊聽一邊跟著說。

James Good morning. How was your weekend?

Min I had a lot of fun. I went to my college reunion.

James It sounds like you had a blast. **Where did you get your college degree?**

Min I graduated from Gilbut University.

James Wow, you went to a prestigious university. **When did you graduate from college?**

Min I graduated 6 years ago. It was in 2009.

James By the way, I don't even know your major. **What was your major?**

Min I majored in economics. What about you?

James I studied mathematics in college. It was really difficult for me. I don't know how I graduated.

Min Tell me about it. I don't know how I completed economics either.

James **How did you pay for college?** I got student loans. I'm still paying for them.

Min I had to borrow money from my parents. I **paid** it all **back**① just last month.

James Congratulations! You must be so relieved.

Min It is **a weight off my shoulders**②. By the way, **did you have a girlfriend in college?**

James Of course I did. Why, didn't you date?

Min No, I didn't. I was too shy **back then**③. Also, I was a member of many clubs. So I didn't have any extra time.

James It sounds like you had a busy university life.

Min I did. **Were you a member of a club?**

James In fact, I was a member of the magic society. I was interested in magic.

解說請見 P292

① pay back

pay back 有正面和負面兩種用法，負面有「報仇」之意，而正面則有「還款」之意。

⟳ Can you give me a week to **pay** the money **back**?　可以給我一個星期的還款時間嗎？

⟳ I will **pay** you **back** for making me wait so long.　你讓我等了這麼久，我會報仇的。

② a weight off one's shoulders

weight 為「重量」的意思，這裡用來表示「負擔」，意思為「卸下肩膀上的重擔、減少負擔」。要表示相反的意思時，說 a weight on my shoulders 即可。

⟳ Paying off the debt is **a weight off my shoulders.**　還了債務讓我的負擔減少了。

⟳ This project is **a** huge **weight on my shoulders.**　這個專案對我來說是個沉重的負擔。

③ back then

「以前」的意思，回想起過去的時候可以這麼說，即「以前是那樣的」。

⟳ I used to be very flexible **back then**.　我以前柔軟度很好。

⟳ Korea was not divided **back then**.　以前韓國不是分裂的。

用 **6** 句英文，和外國人輕鬆話家常！

Wanna go out on a date?

→ → → 要去約會嗎？

在美國如果要約會（date），男生會將女生當成公主般對待，像是有到家門口接送（pick up）這樣的文化，這個部分就和韓國略有不同了。另外，男女通常不會各付各的（go Dutch），較多是男生請女生的情況。接著來看看在美國約會時，有哪些必須知道的用語吧。

首先，交往叫做 **go out with someone**，go out 原本是「出去外面」的意思，把約會聯想成和某人一起出去就可以了。

求婚時會問對方 Will you marry me?，而「求婚」的英語是 **pop the question**，男友求婚的話，女生可以對親友說 He finally popped the question!（他終於求婚了！）。

關於「另一半」，有個浪漫一點的說法是 **my better half**，意思為「更好的另一半」，這樣的說法很溫暖吧？「完美的一對」的英語為 **a match made in heaven**，中文意思就是「上天撮合的一對」。

試著用「誰、何時、在哪裡、做什麼、如何做、為什麼」的六何法疑問詞來問問題。直到沒有可以再進一步詢問的疑問詞時，就能更自然地引導對話。

✪ 用六何法疑問詞來提問

1. What is your ideal date?　什麼是你理想中的約會？

2. When did you go on your first date?　第一次約會是在何時？

3. Where is your favorite place to go on a date?　你最喜歡的約會地點是哪裡？

4. Why did you break up with your ex-girlfriend/ex-boyfriend?　為何跟前女友／前男友分手？

✪ 不用六何法疑問詞來提問

5. Do you have a girlfriend/boyfriend?　你有女友／男友嗎？

6. Have you ever fallen in love at first sight?　你曾經一見鍾情嗎？

STEP
2 反向利用提問來回答
32-2.mp3

如果以前只能簡短回答問題的話，現在試著說出完整的句子吧。將疑問句變成陳述句，就能簡單變成一個句子了。開始練習用句子回答吧！

1. What is your ideal date?　什麼是你理想中的約會？

   My ideal date is _____.　我理想中的約會是 _____。

   going to a fancy restaurant 去高級餐廳 ｜ watching a good movie 看一部好電影 ｜ visiting a beautiful park 去美麗的公園 ｜ doing something exciting 做些開心的事

2. When did you go on your first date?　第一次約會是在何時？

   I went on my first date _____.　我第一次約會是在 _____。

   8 years ago 八年前 ｜ when I was 我十五歲時 ｜ when I was in high school 高中的時候

3. Where is your favorite place to go on a date?　你最喜歡的約會地點是哪裡？

My favorite place to go on a date is _____.　我最喜歡的約會地點

是 _____ 。

a movie theater 電影院　│　shopping mall 購物中心　│　an exotic restaurant 異國餐廳

4. **Why** did you break up with your ex-girlfriend/ex-boyfriend?　為何跟前女

友／前男友分手？

I broke up with my ex-girlfriend/ex-boyfriend **because** _____.

我和前女友／前男友分手是因為 _____ 。

❶ I moved to a new town.　我搬家了。

❷ we fought frequently.　我們很常吵架。

❸ my girlfriend/boyfriend cheated on me.　女友／男友劈腿。

5. Do you have a girlfriend/boyfriend?　你有女友／男友嗎？

→ Yes, I have a girlfriend/boyfriend. _____.

是的，我有女友／男友，_____ 。

❶ I had a blind date a few months ago and we have been dating ever since.　幾個月前參
加了相親，我們從那時就開始約會了。

❷ Last year my classmate asked me out and I said yes.　去年同班同學問我要不要約會，
然後我就答應了。

→ No, I don't have a girlfriend/boyfriend. **Because** _____.

不，我沒有女友／男友，因為 _____ 。

❶ I recently broke up.　最近分手了。

❷ I am too busy with work to date.　工作太忙了，沒辦法約會。

6. **Have** you ever fallen in love at first sight?　你曾經一見鍾情嗎？

→ Yes, I have fallen in love at first sight. _____.

是，我曾一見鍾情，_____ 。

❶ Last year, I met my ideal girl and I fell in love instantly.　去年我遇見理想的對象，馬上
就陷入愛河了。

❷ When I saw my wife for the first time, I instantly knew I had to marry her.　第一次見到
我太太時，馬上就知道我要和這個女人結婚。

→ No, I have never fallen in love at first sight. Because _____.

不，我不曾一見鍾情，因為 _____。

❶ I don't consider looks to be important.　我不認為外表很重要。

❷ I don't believe in love at first sight.　我不相信一見鍾情。

確認前面練習的提問如何活用在和母語人士的對話中，請不要忘記一邊聽一邊跟著說。

Min   Hey, do you believe in love at first sight?

James   Yes, I do. What about you? **Have you ever fallen in love at first sight?**

Min   Yes, I have. In fact, I **fell in love with**[①] my boyfriend the moment I saw him.

James   That is romantic.

Min   Thank you. **Do you have a girlfriend?**

James   Yes, I do. We've been dating for a few months now.

Min   **Where is your favorite place to go on a date?**

James   I like going to the movie theater. Watching a good movie with a box of popcorn is my ideal date. **What is your ideal date?**

Min   My ideal date is going to an exotic restaurant and going for a walk after a nice dinner.

James   That sounds fun. I should give it a try. Do you remember your very first date?

Min   Of course I do. It was when I was in high school. **When did you go on your first date?**

James   My first date was when I was a freshman in university. We went to watch a play and **things went well**[②]. We went out for 5 years.

Min   That's a long time. **Why did you break up with her?**

James She had to move to another country. We decided it was best to break up.

Min **I'm sorry to hear that.**[3] It must have been hard for both of you.

James Yes, it was. But now we've moved on and we both have new relationships.

解說請見 P292

Part 4

現實生活及網路世界

① fall in love with

「和～陷入愛情」的意思，fall 原本有「摔倒、掉進洞裡」之意。

● When I met Lisa, I **fell in love with** her instantly.　當我遇見莉莎時，馬上就和她陷入了愛河。

● Have you ever **fallen in love with** somebody?　你曾經和誰陷入愛情中嗎？

② things go well

情況進行順利時，會使用 go well；相反地，進行得不太順利時，會用 go wrong 或 go badly。

● **Things went well** so I got a promotion.　因為事情進行得很順利，所以我升職了。

● Did **things go well** for you? You seemed worried.　事情還順利嗎？你看起來很擔心的樣子。

③ I'm sorry to hear that.

「對於～感到遺憾」之意，I'm sorry 有多種意思，做錯事情時用來表示道歉，或是對於他人的無奈情況，表達同理的悲傷、遺憾之意。因此，面對喪家時會說 I'm sorry。

● **I'm sorry to hear that** you failed the test.　很遺憾得知你沒有通過考試。

● **I'm sorry to hear that** your father has passed away.　很難過得知您父親過世的消息。

Holidays are for family

→ → → 假日和家人一起度過

　　每年十一月的第四個週四為美國的重要節日 —— 感恩節，英語為 **Thanksgiving Day**，起源於清教徒一開始移民到美國，為了感謝第一次豐收而舉行的慶典，雖然是宗教性的節日，但現在卻更具有文化上的意義。

　　在感恩節這天，整個家族會聚在一起享用豐盛的晚餐，最具代表性的料理就是烤火雞（turkey），再搭配肉汁（gravy）與馬鈴薯泥、蔓越莓醬（cranberry sauce）、玉米、南瓜派（pumpkin pie）等等。在美國有這樣的迷信（superstition）：火雞的骨頭中有 **wishbone**（幸運骨，即脖子和胸前的 V 字形骨頭），兩個人抓著骨頭的兩側，往自己的方向用力拉扯折斷，折到較長那一邊的人，許下的願望就會實現。

　　每到了感恩節，紐約就會舉行有名的 **Macy's Thanksgiving Day Parade**（梅西感恩節大遊行），據說這是 Macy 百貨公司的員工為了慶祝節日，而開始舉辦的活動。

我先提出問題

🎧 33-1.mp3

試著用「誰、何時、在哪裡、做什麼、如何做、為什麼」的六何法疑問詞來問問題。直到沒有可以再進一步詢問的疑問詞時，就能更自然地引導對話。

✪ 用六何法疑問詞來提問

1. Who do you meet on your holidays?　節日時會和誰見面？

2. Which holiday is your favorite?　你最喜歡那個節日？

3. What are the big holidays in your country?　你的國家有什麼大節日？

4. How did you spend your last holiday?　上一次的節日怎麼度過？

✪ 不用六何法疑問詞來提問

5. Do you like holidays?　你喜歡節日嗎？

6. Are there special foods for each holiday?　每個節日有特別的料理嗎？

反向利用提問來回答

🎧 33-2.mp3

如果以前只能簡短回答問題的話，現在試著說出完整的句子吧。將疑問句變成陳述句，就能簡單變成一個句子了。開始練習用句子回答吧！

1. Who do you meet on your holidays?　節日時會和誰見面？

I meet _____ on my holidays.　節日時我會和 _____ 見面。

my distant relatives 遠房親戚 ▎ my family 家人 ▎ my childhood friends 兒時玩伴

2. Which holiday is your favorite?　你最喜歡那個節日？

My favorite holiday is _____.　我最喜歡 _____。

New Year's Day 元旦 ▎ Thanksgiving Day 感恩節 ▎ Christmas 聖誕節 ▎ Easter 復活節

3. What are the big holidays in your country?　你的國家有什麼大節日？

The big holidays in my country are _____ and _____.

我們國家的大節日有 _____ 和 _____。

(Korean) New Year's Day 韓國春節、Chuseok 韓國中秋節 ▎ Thanksgiving Day 感恩節、
Christmas 聖誕節

4. How did you spend your last holiday? 上一次的節日怎麼度過？

I spent my last holiday _____. 我 _____ 來度過上一次節日。

visiting my grandparents 拜訪祖父母 ┃ resting at home 在家休息 ┃ traveling overseas 去海外旅行

5. Do you like holidays? 你喜歡節日嗎？

→ Yes, I like holidays. Because _____.

是，我喜歡，因為 _____。

❶ I can have delicious traditional foods and meet my relatives. 可以吃到好吃的傳統料理，還能與親戚見面。

❷ I can rest a few days from work and have fun with my family. 可以休息幾天不用工作，並且和家人開心度過。

→ No, I don't like holidays. Because _____.

不，我不喜歡，因為 _____。

❶ the traffic jams are too severe so I don't go anywhere. 塞車太嚴重了，哪裡都不能去。

❷ my aunts and uncles nag me and it is stressful. 叔伯姑嬸的嘮叨讓我有壓力。

6. Are there special foods for each holiday? 每個節日有特別的料理嗎？

→ Yes, we have __（料理）__ on __（節日）__.

是的，我們在 _____ 有 _____。

turkey and mashed potatoes 火雞和薯泥，Thanksgiving Day 感恩節 ┃ rice cakes 年糕，Korean New Year's Day 韓國春節 ┃ chocolate Easter eggs 巧克力蛋，Easter 復活節

STEP 3 和母語人士對話

🎧 33-3.mp3

確認前面練習的提問如何活用在和母語人士的對話中，請不要忘記一邊聽一邊跟著說。

James	Merry Christmas Min!
Min	Merry Christmas James! Happy holidays!
James	Min, it doesn't really feel much like Christmas here.
Min	I know what you mean. Christmas is not really **a big deal**[①] in Korea.

James I kind of got it. So, **what are the big holidays in your country?**

Min The biggest is Korean New Year's Day. And Chuseok, the Korean Thanksgiving Day is also huge.

James **Are you serious?**② Do you only have 2 big holidays?

Min No, we do have other holidays too.

James **Which holiday is your favorite?**

Min I definitely like Chuseok the most.

James Why do you like it the most?

Min It is just when fall starts so the weather is amazing, and you get to have great food with your relatives.

James That sounds like an ideal holiday.

Min **Do you like holidays?**

James Of course I do. I adore Thanksgiving. We celebrate it by having a delicious family dinner, the famous Macy's parade is held in New York and we also watch an American football game.

Min What an exciting day! **Are there special foods for this holiday?**

James Sure there are. We have roasted turkey and pumpkin pie on Thanksgiving Day.

Min I think I saw it on an American drama. **Who do you meet on your holidays?**

James We meet our family, friends and relatives **just like you do**③.

Min Since you are away from your family, **how did you spend your last holiday?**

James I met my friends and we held a party of our own.

 解說請見 P293

① a big deal

deal 當成動詞為「做生意」，名詞為「交易」，a big deal 則是「重要的事、厲害的東西」，也有「大筆交易」的意思。

- ⊃ Halloween is not **a big deal** in Korea.　萬聖節在韓國不是那麼重要的日子。
- ⊃ This contract is **a big deal** for our company.　這筆交易對我們公司來說非常重要。

② Are you serious?

用於難以相信對方的話時，「真的嗎？這是事實嗎？」的意思，和 Are you for real? 同義。

- ⊃ A：I met President Obama at a café last night.　我昨天晚上在咖啡館遇見歐巴馬總統。
- ⊃ B：**Are you serious?** Did you take a picture?　真的嗎？有拍照嗎？

③ just like you (do)

意思為「像你做的一樣」，「just like you」為「像你一樣」，這邊的 like 不是「喜歡」，而是「像～、如同～」的意思。

- ⊃ I get coffee every morning **just like you do.**　像你一樣，我每天也都要來杯咖啡。
- ⊃ I want to be **just like you.**　我想要像你一樣。

I'm happy to have a job

→ → → **有工作很幸福**

　　來認識一些工作場合（at work）會用到的英語說法吧。上班族最喜歡的當然非休假（holiday）莫屬，和休假相關的必學說法是 **take a day off**，休一天是 take a day off，休一個星期則是 take a week off，如果說 I'm taking this Friday off.，意思就是「我這個週五休假」。若有人問 Where is John?（約翰在哪裡？），回答 He is **taking a day off**.（他正在休假）即可。

　　工作中暫時休息一下，可以說 **take a break**，類似的說法有 **unwind**、**take time out**，Let's get coffee and unwind. 就是「我們去喝咖啡休息一下」的意思。

　　美國的聚餐文化和韓國略為不同，在美國如果不是正式的活動，便不會強迫參加，並且會簡單地結束。但如果是正式的聚餐（company dinner）、公司野餐（company picnic）、送別會（farewell party）、生日派對（birthday party），最好還是參加。

我先提出問題

試著用「誰、何時、在哪裡、做什麼、如何做、為什麼」的六何法疑問詞來問問題。直到沒有可以再進一步詢問的疑問詞時，就能更自然地引導對話。

✪ 用六何法疑問詞來提問

1. When did you start working?　何時開始工作的？

2. Which job would you never want to have?　你絕對不想從事哪種職業？

3. How often do you work overtime?　你有多常加班？

4. What do you like the most about your job?　關於你的工作你最喜歡什麼部分？

✪ 不用六何法疑問詞來提問

5. Do you like your boss?　你喜歡你的主管嗎？

6. Is it easy to find a job in your country?　在你的國家找工作簡單嗎？

反向利用提問來回答

STEP 2

如果以前只能簡短回答問題的話，現在試著說出完整的句子吧。將疑問句變成陳述句，就能簡單變成一個句子了。開始練習用句子回答吧！

1. When did you start working?　何時開始工作的？

   I started working _____.　我從 _____ 開始工作。

   in high school 高中時 ┃ after graduating from university 大學畢業後 ┃ when I was 21 years old 二十一歲時

2. Which job would you never want to have?　你絕對不想從事哪種職業？

   I would never want to be a _____.　我絕對不想當 _____。

   farmer 農夫 ┃ fisherman 漁夫 ┃ doctor 醫生 ┃ teacher 老師

3. How often do you work overtime?　你有多常加班？

   I work overtime _____.　我 _____ 會加班。

once in a while 偶爾一次 | almost every day 幾乎每天 | only during the busy season 只有忙季時

4. What do you like the most about your job? 關於你的工作你最喜歡什麼部分？

I like _____ the most. 我最喜歡 _____。

my colleagues 同事們 | the working conditions 工作環境 | the generous salary 優渥的薪水 | the benefits 福利

5. Do you like your boss? 你喜歡你的主管嗎？

→ Yes, I like my boss. Because _____. 是的，我喜歡我的主管，因為 _____。

❶ he is very understanding. 他非常善解人意。

❷ she is very professional. 她非常專業。

→ No, I don't like my boss. Because _____. 不，我不喜歡我的主管，因為 _____。

❶ he is very emotional. 他太過情緒化了。

❷ she makes us work overtime every day 她每天都要我們加班。

6. Is it easy to find a job in your country? 在你的國家找工作簡單嗎？

→ Yes, it is easy to find a job. Because _____. 是，找工作很簡單，因為 _____。

❶ the economy is doing well now. 現在的經濟景氣不錯。

❷ many companies are expanding right now. 很多公司現在正在擴展事業。

→ No, it is not easy to find a job. Because _____. 不，找工作不簡單，因為 _____。

❶ the unemployment rate is high. 失業率高。

❷ the competition among applicants is fierce. 求職者之間的競爭激烈。

確認前面練習的提問如何活用在和母語人士的對話中，請不要忘記一邊聽一邊跟著說。

Min Hey, you seem busy. What are you up to these days?

James I'm trying to get a new job.

Min Why are you trying to get a new job?

James My current job is good, but the pay is horrible. I want to get a better salary.

Min Yep, the salary is important. It keeps the workers motivated.

James That's exactly what I mean. **When did you start working?**

Min I started working right after university.

James If you don't mind me asking, **do you like your boss?**

Min Well, I don't really like him but I can put up with him.

James That's good. **What do you like the most about your job?**

Min I love the working hours. They are flexible and I rarely **work overtime**[1].

How often do you work overtime?

James At my present job, I'm always working overtime. Is your company hiring?

Min Let me ask. By the way, **which job would you never want to have?**

James I would never want to be a gardener. I'm terrible at taking care of plants.

What about you?

Min Well, I puke whenever I see blood so being a doctor is **out of the question**[2] for me.

James I understand. **Is it easy to find a job in your country?**

Min Not really. The unemployment rate in my country is very high right now.

James Same in my country. I guess the global **economy is down**[3].

▶ ▶ ▶ 解說請見 P293

用 **6** 句英文，和外國人輕鬆話家常！

① work overtime

「加時工作」就是 work overtime。韓國的夜景之所以美麗，是因為公司都在加班的緣故，英文翻譯為 Korea's night view is beautiful because of all the people working overtime in their offices.，不曉得你是否看過這樣的照片呢？

➲ I'm tired because I **worked overtime** last night.　我很疲憊，因為昨晚加班。

➲ I rarely **work overtime** so I can go to yoga class in the evenings.　我幾乎不加班，因此晚上能去上瑜伽課。

② out of the question

意思為「不可能的」，無論再怎麼討論或煩惱都沒有解答，適合用來表達強烈認為不可能的事。刪掉 the 的話，out of question 是「必定、當然」，意思完全不同，請特別注意。

➲ Skipping class is **out of the question.**　我絕對不可能缺課。

➲ Due to the latest problem, plan A is **out of the question.**　由於最近出現的問題，計畫 A 是不可能達成了。

③ economy is down

「經濟不好、經濟停滯」之意，也可以使用 bad，如 bad economy、the economy is bad、the economy is doing badly，有很多種說法。

➲ The **economy is down** so the unemployment rate is high.　由於經濟不景氣，失業率很高。

➲ Do you remember a few years ago when the **economy was down**?　你還記得幾年前經濟不景氣的時候嗎？

It's payday!

➔➔➔ 發薪日！

　　很多人都知道 salaryman 是上班族，不過這是日語的說法，雖然英語系國家的人現在也都聽得懂，但不是正確的說法，上班族是 employees 或 workers。上班族可以分成領時薪（hourly pay）的人和領月薪（salary）的人，月薪制度的上班族稱作 salaried workers。

　　所有上班族都期待的日子── payday！就是領工資的日子，工資稱作 paycheck，月薪雖然叫做 salary，但 paycheck 和 salary 的意義不太相同，月薪是事先在契約書上制定好，金額和工作量及業績無關，但是工資的金額則是做多少拿多少。

　　再告訴大家一個與月薪相關的有趣說法，少得像老鼠尾巴一樣的月薪，用英語怎麼說呢？你一定很好奇有沒有這樣的說法吧？很少的錢叫做 chicken feed，因此當月薪真的很少的時候，說 My salary is chicken feed. 就可以了。

STEP 1 我先提出問題

🎧 35-1.mp3

試著用「誰、何時、在哪裡、做什麼、如何做、為什麼」的六何法疑問詞來問問題。直到沒有可以再進一步詢問的疑問詞時，就能更自然地引導對話。

✪ 用六何法疑問詞來提問

1. Who manages your money? 誰來管理你的錢？

2. When did you get your first salary? 何時領到第一筆月薪？

3. How much do you save every month? 每個月存多少錢？

4. What did you buy with your first salary? 用第一筆薪水買了什麼？

5. Why are you saving money? 為什麼存錢呢？

✪ 不用六何法疑問詞來提問

6. Are you happy with your salary? 對於現在的薪水滿意嗎？

STEP 2 反向利用提問來回答

🎧 35-2.mp3

如果以前只能簡短回答問題的話，現在試著說出完整的句子吧。將疑問句變成陳述句，就能簡單變成一個句子了。開始練習用句子回答吧！

1. Who manages your money? 誰來管理你的錢？

_____ manage(s) my money. _____ 管理我的錢。

I 我 ┃ My mother 媽媽 ┃ A fund manager 基金經理人

2. When did you get your first salary? 何時領到第一筆月薪？

I got my first salary _____. _____ 我領到第一筆月薪。

9 years ago 九年前 ┃ in 2005 在 2005 年 ┃ when I was 27 years old 二十七歲時

3. How much do you save every month? 每個月存多少錢？

I save _____ every month. 我每個月存_____。

one quarter of my salary 月薪的四分之一 ┃ one third of my pay 月薪的三分之一 ┃ half of my income 收入的一半

4. What did you buy with your first salary? 用第一筆薪水買了什麼？

I bought _____ with my first salary.

我用第一筆薪水買了 _____。

my parents gifts 父母的禮物 ┃ a luxury bag 名牌包 ┃ an expensive watch 昂貴的手錶

5. Why are you saving money? 為什麼存錢呢？

I am saving money for _____. 我存錢是為了 _____。

my wedding 我的婚禮 ┃ my retirement 退休 ┃ a beautiful house for my future family 給未來的家人住好房子

6. Are you happy with your salary? 對於現在的薪水滿意嗎？

→ Yes, I am happy with my salary. Because _____. 是，我滿意我的薪水，因為 _____。

❶ I think I get paid well for my working hours. 我覺得和工作時間相比，我的收入算是不錯的。

❷ I also get sufficient bonuses. 我還有收到足夠的獎金。

→ No, I am not happy with my salary. Because _____. 不，我不滿意我的薪水，因為 _____。

❶ I always work overtime and don't get any extra pay. 我一直在加班，卻沒有領到額外的津貼。

❷ I think I work way more than I should. 我覺得我做得比分內的事要來得多。

STEP 3 和母語人士對話

🎧 35-3.mp3

確認前面練習的提問如何活用在和母語人士的對話中，請不要忘記一邊聽一邊跟著說。

Min Tomorrow is payday! Yeh~

James I know! I am always broke just before payday.

Min Are you? **Who manages your money?**

James I do. I manage my money. Do you?

Min	I guess I do. But I get counseling from my mother and I normally follow her suggestions.
James	If you don't mind, **how much do you save every month?**
Min	Let me see... I think I save one third of my salary. Do you think that's a lot or a little?
James	I think that's reasonable. **Why are you saving money?**
Min	Well, I need to save up for my wedding, a house, a car and so on.
James	Wow, you **have a lot on your mind**[①].
Min	**Come to think of it,**[②] I do have a lot on my mind.
James	Hey, **when did you get your first salary?** Do you remember?
Min	Of course I do. It was 7 years ago. I bought a designer handbag with it. **What did you buy with your first salary?**
James	I bought gifts for my parents.
Min	Aww, **that is so sweet of you!**[③] Just asking, **are you happy with your salary?**
James	More or less, yes. I can't complain since the unemployment rate is so high these days.
Min	You are an optimist!

▶ ▶ ▶  解說請見 P294

① have a lot on one's mind

mind 可以解釋成「頭腦」，on one's mind 則可以理解成「腦海中的」，或是「費心」。因此這個片語就是「費心的事很多」，心裡有掛念的事情時，可以用這個說法。

➲ I have a presentation coming up and my son is sick. I **have a lot on my mind.**
發表會就近在眼前，但我兒子卻生病了，煩心的事好多。

➲ My team leader is in charge of so many things. I'm sure he **has a lot on his mind.** 我們這組的組長負責的事情真的很多，我想他一定很費心。

② come to think of it

「這麼看來」的意思，適合在突然想起什麼的時候使用。

➲ **Come to think of it,** James said he is going out of town today. 這麼一說，詹姆士說他今天要出城。

➲ **Come to think of it,** I have a meeting today. 這麼看來，我今天有個會議。

③ That is so sweet of you!

sweet 不只有「甜蜜」的意思，也能表示親切，因此這句話的意思就是「你真的好親切！」

➲ A：I helped an old lady cross the street. 我幫忙一位老奶奶過馬路。

➲ B：**That is so sweet of you!** 你好親切啊！

A meeting can be productive!
➜ ➜ ➜ 開會可以更有效率！

　　各位對於開會有什麼看法呢？由於每家公司、各個組織或部門，都有不同的會議文化，因此很難概括而論，但有不少人覺得美國公司的會議文化要比韓國公司來得發達。

　　因此，最近有不少韓國公司引進美國知名企業的會議文化並加以應用，其中最有名的 **stand-up meeting**，就是所有人都站著進行會議，據說能防止會議變得無謂、冗長，由跨國企業佳能公司最先開始採用並廣為流傳。

　　在美國的會議中，大家最重視的便是 **be on time**（遵守時間），也就是要在預計的時間開始並結束會議。有許多公司不會根據職等（status）來分配發言權，而是不拘泥於職等，積極地討論。此外，討論時也偏好明確地以 Yes 或 No 來回答，對於提問也會給予肯定的態度，而且不能打斷別人的發言。稱呼上司或會長時，要說 second name，也就是對方的姓氏，Mr. So-and-so（某某先生）、Ms. So-and-so（某某女士）這麼說就可以了。

STEP **1** 我先提出問題

試著用「誰、何時、在哪裡、做什麼、如何做、為什麼」的六何法疑問詞來問問題。直到沒有可以再進一步詢問的疑問詞時,就能更自然地引導對話。

✪ 用六何法疑問詞來提問

1. Why do you have meetings?　為什麼開會呢?

2. How often do you have a meeting?　有多常開會?

3. Where do you have meetings?　在哪裡開會?

4. When do you think it's a good time to have meetings?　你覺得何時適合開會?

✪ 不用六何法疑問詞來提問

5. Do you think it's good to have many meetings?　你覺得常開會好嗎?

6. Are you a talker or a listener in meetings?　開會時,你是勇於發言或是聆聽的人呢?

STEP **2** 反向利用提問來回答

如果以前只能簡短回答問題的話,現在試著說出完整的句子吧。將疑問句變成陳述句,就能簡單變成一個句子了。開始練習用句子回答吧!

1. Why do you have meetings?　為什麼開會呢?

   We have meetings because _____.　我們為了 _____ 開會。

   ❶ we need to come up with new ideas　要激發出新的點子

   ❷ we need to check the work procedure　要確認工作流程

2. How often do you have a meeting?　有多常開會?

   We have a meeting _____.　我們 _____ 開會。

   almost every day 幾乎每天 ┃ once a week 一週一次 ┃ biweekly 隔週

3. Where do you have meetings?　在哪裡開會?

   We have meetings _____.　我們在 _____ 開會。

in the meeting room 會議室裡 ┃ in the conference room 會議廳裡 ┃ at a café 咖啡館

4. When do you think it's a good time to have meetings? 你覺得何時適合開會？

I think it's a good time to have meetings __（時間）__ ,

because __ ____.

我覺得 _ ____適合開會，因為 _____ 。

❶ in the morning 早上，we can plan the day's work accordingly 可以根據開會內容來規劃當天的工作。

❷ after lunch 午餐時間後，we get sleepy after lunch so a discussion can keep us awake 午餐後總是昏昏欲睡，討論可以讓我們保持清醒。

5. Do you think it's good to have many meetings? 你覺得常開會好嗎？

→ Yes, I think it's good to have many meetings. Because _____.

是，我覺得常開會很好，因為 _____ 。

❶ we can prevent making mistakes. 可以預防出錯。

❷ members can check each others work. 成員可以確認彼此的工作。

→ No, I don't think it's good to have many meetings. Because _____.

不，我不覺得常開會很好，因為 _____ 。

❶ it can be a waste of time. 可能會浪費時間。

❷ too many meetings can distract people from working. 太多會議可能會妨礙人們工作。

6. Are you a talker or a listener in meetings? 開會時，你是勇於發言或是聆聽的人呢？

→ I am a talker in meetings. Because _____. 我是勇於發言的人，因為_____ 。

❶ I like to express my opinion. 我喜歡表達意見。

❷ I think a meeting can be productive if we talk a lot. 我覺得要多說話，會議才有效益。

→ I am a listener in meetings. Because _____. 我是聆聽的人，因為 _____ 。

❶ I don't have many ideas. 我的想法不多。

❷ I don't like to be seen as a talkative person. 我不想被看成多話的人。

確認前面練習的提問如何活用在和母語人士的對話中，請不要忘記一邊聽一邊跟著說。

| James | Why didn't you pick up the phone yesterday? |

Min Oops, sorry. I was in a meeting and I **meant to**[①] call back but I forgot.

James That's okay. You seem to have many meetings.

Min We do. Don't you? **How often do you have a meeting?**

James We only have a meeting once a week.

Min Seriously? We have meetings every day.

James Every day seems a bit too much. **Where do you have meetings?**

Min Conveniently, we have a meeting room on our floor.

James When do you normally have meetings?

Min We have meetings in the morning **at** 9 am **sharp**[②]. We can't come late because of the meeting.

James That must be stressful. **Why do you have so many meetings?**

Min We have to present our work process every day. I don't like having so many meetings. What about you? **Do you think it's good to have many meetings?**

James Nope. I think it is a waste of time if you are not prepared for the meeting.

Min Exactly. It's like you are reading my mind.

James **Are you a talker or a listener in meetings?**

Min Definitely a listener. In Korea, it's better to be quiet and listen if you want to have a good reputation.

James That is sad.

Min In your opinion, **when is a good time to have a meeting?**

196

James Well, I like morning meetings. I can plan my day's work according to the meeting we had.

Min Yep, you **make a** valid **point**[3].

 解說請見 P294

① meant to (*do*)

「原本打算要做〜」的意思，meant 為 mean 的過去式，I meant to call you 就是「我原本打算要打電話給你」。

⊃ I **meant to** study after taking a nap.　我原本打算小睡一會後要唸書。

⊃ I **meant to** apologize to you, but I didn't get the chance.　我原本打算要道歉的，但是沒有機會。

② at 時間 sharp

用來表示準確的時間，有「準時」的意思，沒有晚一分一秒，正好那個時間。

⊃ Please come to the office **at 8 am sharp**.　請早上八點準時來辦公室。

⊃ Our first lecture starts **at 9 am sharp**.　第一堂課在早上九點準時開始。

③ make a point

「主張，強調某事」的意思，適合在說服對方接受意見時使用。

⊃ Can I **make a point** before we continue with this meeting?　在會議繼續進行之前，我可以提出一個意見嗎？

⊃ She tried to **make a point**, but nobody understood it.　她試著讓大家接受她的意見，但沒有人能理解。

A little bird told me

→ → → **我聽到傳聞了**

　　由於 *Gossip Girls* 這齣非常知名的美劇，讓 **gossip** 成為廣為人知的單字，gossip 意思為稍微誇大且可能有誤的傳聞，可以當成名詞和動詞使用，進一步解釋的話，就是 **talk behind one's back**，意即在某人的背後說話。

　　散播傳聞（rumor、gossip）時，可以說 **A little bird told me.**，很可愛的說法吧？舉例來說，**A little bird told me** that Jack and Lisa broke up.（我聽到八卦說傑克和麗莎分手了）。

　　有趣的八卦是 **juicy gossip**，juicy 原本是「多汁」的意思，可以說 I have some **juicy gossip** for you.（我有個有趣的消息要告訴你）。想聽別人的祕密（secret）時，只要說 **kiss and tell** 即可，意思就是「跟我說就好～」。

　　有趣的八卦雖然好玩，但是 Please remember, what goes around comes around.，也就是「種瓜得瓜，種豆得豆」，對於別人的八卦議論紛紛的話，總有一天自己也可能成為八卦的主角。

STEP 1 我先提出問題

 🎧 37-1.mp3

試著用「誰、何時、在哪裡、做什麼、如何做、為什麼」的六何法疑問詞來問問題。直到沒有可以再進一步詢問的疑問詞時，就能更自然地引導對話。

✪ 用六何法疑問詞來提問

1. Who gossips more: men or women?　男生和女生誰比較愛講八卦？

2. What are the most common themes for gossip?　最常見的八卦話題是什麼？

3. Where are some places people like to gossip?　人們喜歡在哪些地方講八卦？

4. Why do you think people like to listen to gossip?　人們為什麼會喜歡聽八卦？

✪ 不用六何法疑問詞來提問

5. Do you like to gossip?　你喜歡講八卦嗎？

6. Has someone ever spread a rumor about you? If Yes, how did you react?　曾有人散佈關於你的謠言嗎？有的話，你怎麼應對？

STEP 2 反向利用提問來回答

🎧 37-2.mp3

如果以前只能簡短回答問題的話，現在試著說出完整的句子吧。將疑問句變成陳述句，就能簡單變成一個句子了。開始練習用句子回答吧！

1. Who gossips more: men or women?　男生和女生誰比較愛講八卦？

I think ＿＿（性別）＿＿ gossip more because ＿＿＿＿＿.

我覺得 ＿＿＿＿＿ 比較八卦，因為 ＿＿＿＿＿。

❶ men, I heard that boys share all their secrets with each other.　男生，我聽說男生會跟彼此分享所有的祕密。

❷ men, I know a group of boys who spend hours and hours talking.　男生，我認識一群男生會花好幾個小時聊天。

③ women, girls spend a lot of time on their phones talking to their friends.　女生，女生會和朋友花很長的時間講電話。

④ women, if I tell a secret to my girlfriend, all her friends are aware of it in a week.　女生，如果我跟女友講了一個祕密，一星期之內女友的朋友全都知道了。

2. What are the most common themes for gossip?　最常見的八卦話題是什麼？

I think the most common themes for gossip are _____.　最常見的八卦話題是 _____。

love and relationships 戀愛和人際關係 | money and the economy 金錢和經濟 | celebrities and their personal lives 名人及他們的私生活

3. Where are some places people like to gossip?　人們喜歡在哪些地方講八卦？

The place where people like to gossip is _____.

人們喜歡在 _____ 講八掛。

a café 咖啡館 | the staff room 茶水間 | the office building staircase 辦公大樓的樓梯間

4. Why do you think people like to listen to gossip?　人們為什麼會喜歡聽八卦？

I think people like to listen to gossip because _____.　我覺得人們喜歡聽八卦是因為 _____。

❶ people are curious about others lives.　好奇別人的生活。

❷ some want to feel good about themselves by bringing others down.　有人想要靠貶低他人來提升自己的優越感。

5. Do you like to gossip?　你喜歡講八卦嗎？

→ Yes, I like to gossip. Because _____.　是，我喜歡講八卦，因為 _____。

❶ I like being aware of other peoples lives.　我喜歡知道別人的生活。

❷ it is interesting and also it is stress relieving.　很有趣又能紓解壓力。

→ No, I don't like to gossip. Because _____.　不，我不喜歡講八卦，因為 _____ 。

　① I don't like talking about others.　我不喜歡談論別人。

　② I think that it is useless and rude.　我覺得毫無意義而且沒有教養。

6. Has someone ever spread a rumor about you?　If Yes, how did you react?　曾有人散佈關於你的謠言嗎？有的話，你怎麼應對？

→ Yes, someone has spread a rumor about me. I reacted by _____.　是，有人曾散佈關於我的謠言，我的應對方式是 _____ 。

ignoring it completely 完全無視 ┃ confronting the person who started the rumor 直接去見那個開始散佈謠言的人

→ No, no one has ever spread a rumor about me.　不，不曾有人散佈關於我的謠言。

STEP 3 和母語人士對話

 37-3.mp3

確認前面練習的提問如何活用在和母語人士的對話中，請不要忘記一邊聽一邊跟著說。

Min　Did you hear the latest office gossip?

James　Yes. It's a shame that Mr. Thompson had to be fired.

Min　Do you think it's all true? Stories about Mr. Thompson?

James　I wouldn't know. But I feel bad that people are talking about him.

Min　**What do you think are the most common themes for gossip?**

James　I think people mostly talk about others' reputations. What do you think?

Min　I agree. People also love to talk about celebrities. **Where are some places people like to gossip?**

James　Well, a coffee shop is the main place and the staff room is also a good place to talk.

Min	Yes. Tell me James, **who gossips more: men or women?**
James	I think it's definitely women. They are so talkative.
Min	I have to disagree. My male friends are just as talkative as I am.
James	Are they? Well, **don't take it personally**[①]. I didn't mean to offend you.
Min	I know. Anyway, **why do you think people like to listen to gossip?**
James	Gossip is interesting. And some people are just nosy.
Min	**Do you like to gossip?**
James	**I wouldn't say**[②] I like to, but it's like a natural habit for me now. Everybody gossips and I just listen.
Min	**Has someone ever spread a rumor about you?**
James	Yes. When I was in high school, a girl started a rumor telling others that I was dating two girls at once.
Min	How did you react?
James	I confronted her. I asked her where she got that idea from and she apologized for **making things up**[③].

解說請見 P295

① don't take it personally

說的話可能引起對方誤會時，若想表示自己沒有那樣的意圖，只是實話實說時可以使用這個說法，可以解釋成「說這些話不是為了要傷害你，聽的時候不要覺得受傷」。

⊃ **Don't take it personally,** but I disagree with your opinion.　希望你聽了不要誤會，但我不認同你的意見。

⊃ **Don't take it personally,** but boys smell bad especially in summer.　聽了請不要往心裡去，但到了夏天，男生的味道更是難聞。

② I wouldn't say

「不會説～」的意思，若要婉轉敘述對方聽了可能會不舒服的話時，可以使用這個説法。

◐ **I wouldn't say** you're completely wrong.　我不會說你完全都錯了。

◐ **I wouldn't say** no to your request.　我不會說要拒絕你的請求。

③ make things up

「編造」的意思，編造傳聞時常用的片語，雖然也有「～製作、構成」之意，但在前述對話所使用的 make things up，則是「編造傳聞」的意思。

◐ The story about Jake is not true. It seems that Lisa **made things up.**　關於傑克的傳聞不是事實，看起來是麗莎編造出來的。

◐ I don't like people who **make things up.** I just can't trust them.　我討厭會編造故事的人，就是沒辦法信任他們。

Are you computer-literate?

➜ ➜ ➜ 你會用電腦嗎？

　　識字且會寫字的人叫做 literate，相反地，不識字也不會寫字的則是 illiterate。那麼試著延伸到電腦吧，很會用電腦的人就是 computer-literate，反過來說不會用電腦的人則是 computer-illiterate，因此，假使有人問你 Are you computer-literate?（你會用電腦嗎？），如果擅長使用電腦，可以說 I am computer-literate.，不會的話則說 I am computer-illiterate.。

　　接著來說明桌上型電腦（desktop）和筆記型電腦（laptop）的差異，桌機是放在 desk（書桌）上來作業，筆電則是放在 lap（大腿）上來使用，由此衍生出它們的名字。laptop 的另一個名稱則是 notebook，由於 notebook 也常用來表示筆記本，因此用 laptop 會比較好，不然的話，乾脆稱作 notebook computer，在後面加上 computer 較適當。

　　電腦的作業系統叫做 O.S.（Operating System），通常會使用 Microsoft 或 Mac 兩者之一。雖然 Mac 在韓國還不算普遍，但在美國非常普及，因此，如果能熟悉這兩種作業系統的話，在美國唸書或工作會相當有幫助。

STEP 1 我先提出問題

 38-1.mp3

試著用「誰、何時、在哪裡、做什麼、如何做、為什麼」的六何法疑問詞來問問題。直到沒有可以再進一步詢問的疑問詞時，就能更自然地引導對話。

✪ 用六何法疑問詞來提問

1. Which do you like better: desktops or laptops?　你比較喜歡哪一個：桌上型電腦或筆記型電腦？

2. Who taught you to use a computer?　誰教你使用電腦的方法？

3. What software program do you use most often?　你最常使用的軟體程式是什麼？

4. When did you first start using a computer?　第一次開始使用電腦是在什麼時候？

✪ 不用六何法疑問詞來提問

5. Do you remember your first computer? Did you like it?　還記得你的第一臺電腦嗎？你喜歡嗎？

6. Have you ever studied English using your computer?　你曾利用電腦來學習英語嗎？

STEP 2 反向利用提問來回答

 38-2.mp3

如果以前只能簡短回答問題的話，現在試著說出完整的句子吧。將疑問句變成陳述句，就能簡單變成一個句子了。開始練習用句子回答吧！

1. Which do you like better: desktops or laptops?　你比較喜歡哪一個：桌上型電腦或筆記型電腦？

I like ＿＿（電腦）＿＿ better because ＿＿＿＿＿＿.

我比較喜歡＿＿＿＿＿＿，因為 ＿＿＿＿＿＿。

① desktops, they have better functions and bigger storage　桌上型電腦，功能比較好而且儲存容量比較大。

② laptops, they are small and portable　筆記型電腦，體積小且容易攜帶。

2. Who taught you to use a computer? 誰教你使用電腦的方法？

_____ taught me to use a computer. 是 _____ 教我使用電腦的方法。

My older brother 我哥哥 | My school teacher 學校老師 | My friend 朋友

3. What software program do you use most often? 你最常使用的軟體程式是什麼？

I use _____ most often. 我最常使用 _____ 。

Microsoft Office 微軟辦公軟體 | Internet Explorer 網頁瀏覽器

4. When did you first start using a computer? 第一次開始使用電腦是在什麼時候？

I first started using a computer _____. 我第一次開始使用電腦是在 _____ 。

about 10 years ago 大約十年前 | when I was in middle school 中學時期

5. Do you remember your first computer? Did you like it? 還記得你的第一臺電腦嗎？你喜歡嗎？

→ Yes, I do. It was __（電腦品牌）__ and I liked it because _____.
是的，我記得是 _____ ，而且我很喜歡它，因為 _____ 。

❶ a Samsung laptop, it had many useful functions 三星的筆記型電腦，有許多實用的功能。

❷ an Apple computer, it was fast and I could run many programs at once 蘋果電腦，速度快而且能一次執行很多程式。

→ No, I don't remember. Because _____.
不，我不記得了，因為 _____ 。

❶ it was too long ago. 是很久以前的事了。

❷ I have had so many computers that I can't remember what the first one was. 我有過很多臺電腦，所以不記得哪一個是第一臺。

6. Have you ever studied English using your computer? 你曾利用電腦來學習英語嗎？

→ Yes, I have. Because _____. 是，我有，因為 _____。

  ❶ I like watching online lectures to study English.　我喜歡收看網路課程來學習英語。

  ❷ it is cheaper than attending offline classes.　線上授課比實際授課要來得便宜。

→ No, I haven't. Because _____. 不，我沒有，因為 _____。

  ❶ to be honest, I am computer-illiterate.　事實上我不太會用電腦。

  ❷ I don't think it's as effective as offline classes.　我不覺得和實際授課會有同樣的效果。

STEP 3 和母語人士對話

 38-3.mp3

確認前面練習的提問如何活用在和母語人士的對話中，請不要忘記一邊聽一邊跟著說。

Min What's wrong? Your eyes are red.

James I know. I've been staring at the computer screen for too long.

Min How often do you use a computer?

James Every day. I feel like I'm getting addicted to the computer.

Min **Join the club.**[①] It is bad to use a computer all the time but we **can't help it**[②].

James **Which do you like better: desktops or laptops?**

Min I definitely prefer laptops as I can carry them around. **When did you first start using a computer?**

James I first started using a computer when I was 10 or 11.

Min **Do you remember your first computer? Did you like it?**

James Of course I remember my first computer. It was a huge desktop that **took up** a lot of **space**[③] in my room. I liked it since it was my first time to have a computer.

Min Did you play games with it?

James I did play games. I was quite good at playing them.

Min I can't picture you playing computer games. **Who taught you to use a computer?**

James I attended a computer class in school.

Min That must have been helpful. **What software program do you use most often?**

James Microsoft Office, for sure. Isn't it the same for you?

Min Yep, but I also have a blog. So I use Internet Explorer as often as I use Microsoft Office.

James I didn't know you have a blog. Min, **have you ever studied English using your computer?**

Min In fact, yes I have. I used to watch lectures online.

▶ ▶ ▶ 解說請見 P296

① Join the club.

這句話不能直譯成「參加俱樂部」,而是在自己和對方經歷了相同的情況時, 用來表示「我也是相同的遭遇」。

➲ A：I have so much to do. I don't think I can sleep tonight.　要做的事太多了, 感覺今天不能睡了。

➲ B：**Join the club.** Let's get some coffee.　我也是,我們去喝咖啡吧。

② can't help it

這個說法有「沒辦法」的意思,it 也可以用詳細的物品或情況來代替,舉例來 說,可以說 I can't help the ice melting.(我沒有辦法阻止冰塊融化)。

➲ A：Stop eating those chocolate cookies.　不要再吃那些巧克力餅乾了。

➲ B：They are so delicious. I **can't help it.**　太好吃了,我沒辦法啊。

③ take up space ·······························

「占據位置」之意，當傢俱或物品占據位置時，可以說 take up space，占了很多空間時，就像對話中一樣說 take up a lot of space 即可。

○ My piano doesn't **take up** a lot of **space** in the living room. 鋼琴沒有占掉客廳太大空間。

○ I don't like buying things that **take up** a lot of **space**. 我不喜歡買占很多空間的物品

I can't live without the Internet!

➔ ➔ ➔ 沒有網路活不下去！

你知道 **Google** 可以當作動詞使用嗎？如果説 Google it. 的話，就是「用 Google 來搜尋看看」的意思，這也代表「Google」的 **search engine**（搜尋引擎）真的很有名。如果有要搜尋的東西，美國人會馬上用 Google 來尋找。

提供免費郵件信箱、個人網頁服務、新聞、留言板等等功能的網站，叫做 **portal site**（入口網站），韓國以「NAVER」和「Daum」較受歡迎，而美國最受歡迎的入口網站則是 Google 和 **Yahoo**，Yahoo 最常被使用的功能是電子郵件（email），Yahoo Korea[3] 雖然沒什麼人氣，但在美國或其他國家卻是很熱門的入口網站。

另外還有人氣網站 **Wikipedia**，這個名字是由 wiki（網路使用者能修訂、編輯內容的網站）與 encyclopedia（百科全書）組成的複合詞，即網路世界的百科全書，任何人都能連上網站親自上傳知識與資訊，也能要求修改內容。要用英語搜尋資訊時，不妨利用 Wikipedia，也可以翻譯成其他語言。

■ 3　Yahoo Korea 已於 2012 年底終止服務。

我先提出問題

 39-1.mp3

試著用「誰、何時、在哪裡、做什麼、如何做、為什麼」的六何法疑問詞來問問題。直到沒有可以再進一步詢問的疑問詞時，就能更自然地引導對話。

✪ 用六何法疑問詞來提問

1. How often do you use the Internet?　有多常使用網路呢？

2. When did you first use the Internet?　第一次使用網路是在什麼時候？

3. Who uses the Internet the most in your family?　家人之中誰最常使用網路？

4. What problems does the Internet create?　網路會造成什麼問題？

✪ 不用六何法疑問詞來提問

5. Do you access the Internet with your smartphone?　你會使用手機上網嗎？

6. Is it dangerous to meet people on the Internet?　網路交友危險嗎？

STEP
2
反向利用提問來回答

 39-2.mp3

如果以前只能簡短回答問題的話，現在試著說出完整的句子吧。將疑問句變成陳述句，就能簡單變成一個句子了。開始練習用句子回答吧！

1. How often do you use the Internet?　有多常使用網路呢？

   I use the Internet _____.　我 _____ 會使用網路。

   all the time 總是 ┃ almost every day 幾乎每天 ┃ once or twice a week 一週一兩次

2. When did you first use the Internet?　第一次使用網路是在什麼時候？

   I first used the Internet _____.

   我第一次使用網路是在 _____。

   in the late 1990s 1990 年代後期 ┃ when I was a middle school student 中學時期 ┃ when I was 20 二十歲時

3. Who uses the Internet the most in your family?　家人之中誰最常使用網路？

_____ uses the Internet the most in my family.

家人之中 _____ 最常使用網路。

My younger brother 我弟弟 | My husband 我丈夫 | My daughter 我女兒

4. What problems does the Internet create?　網路會造成什麼問題？

I think the Internet _____.　我覺得網路 _____。

makes people waste their time 使人們浪費時間 | gives too much unnecessary information 提供太多不必要的資訊 | makes children get addicted to online games 讓孩子對網路遊戲成癮 | exposes children to r-rated videos 讓孩子暴露在限制級影片的威脅中

5. Do you access the Internet with your smartphone?　你會使用手機上網嗎？

→ Yes, I access the Internet with my smartphone. Because _____.

是，我用手機上網，因為 _____。

❶ I can make a better use of my commuting time.　能更靈活運用通勤時間。

❷ it is convenient and saves a lot of time.　很方便而且能節省時間。

→ No, I don't access the Internet with my smart-phone.

Because _____.　不，我不用手機上網，因為 _____。

❶ I don't like reading on a small screen.　我不喜歡用小螢幕閱讀東西。

❷ I get a headache if I look at my smartphone for too long　手機看太久的話我會頭痛。

6. Is it dangerous to meet people on the Internet?　網路交友危險嗎？

→ Yes, I think it is dangerous to meet people on the Internet.

Because _____.　是，我覺得網路交友危險，因為 _____。

❶ people can easily fake their true identity and then commit crimes.　人們很容易捏造身分和犯罪。

❷ you can't be sure of the other persons background.　無法確認他人的背景。

→ No, I don't think it is dangerous to meet people on the Internet.

Because _____.　不，我不覺得網路交友危險，因為 _____。

❶ I know a few couples who got married after meeting on the Internet.　我認識幾對夫妻是在網路上認識後結婚的。

❷ these days, some sites carefully check that posts are true.　最近有些網站會詳加確認貼文的真實性。

STEP 3 和母語人士對話

確認前面練習的提問如何活用在和母語人士的對話中，請不要忘記一邊聽一邊跟著說。

Min You look tired today. What's wrong?

James I was up late last night.

Min **What were you up to?**[①]

James I was reading articles online and I lost track of time.

Min It seems like you use the Internet a lot. **How often do you use the Internet?**

James Every day. At least three hours per day.

Min What do you do on the Internet?

James I read articles, watch interesting video clips, and so on.

Min **Do you access the Internet**[②] **with your smartphone?**

James Yes I do. I access the Internet on my smartphone when I commute.

Min **When did you first use the Internet?** I think for me, it was in the late 1990s.

James Same here. I first used the Internet when I was in middle school.

Min **Who uses the Internet the most in your family?**

James I use the Internet the most in my family.

Min Don't you think the Internet also causes problems?

James Of course I do. I think the Internet does have some **negative effects**[③] on society.

Min **What problems does the Internet create?**

James Well, many kids are becoming addicted to online games and they are also exposed to r-rated videos.

Min I agree. What about online dating? Have you tried that?

James Nope, not yet. What do you think, **is it dangerous to meet people on the**

Internet?

Min I definitely think that it is dangerous. People can easily fake their identity on the Internet. I don't think it's safe.

解說請見 P296

① What are you up to?

和 What are you doing right now? 的意思相同，可理解成「在做什麼呢？」，是能和關係親近的對象使用的日常說法。

⊃ A：John, **what are you up to?**　約翰，你在做什麼？

⊃ B：I'm just getting ready for my meeting in 20 minutes.　我正在準備 20 分鐘後的會議。

② access the Internet

意思為「連接網路」，如果要說「使用網路」時，則是 use the Internet，使用 access 的話則有「連接」上網路之意。

⊃ Can you **access the Internet** from your house?　家裡可以上網嗎？

⊃ Korea is a country where you can **access the Internet** from anywhere.　韓國是個到處都能連上網路的國家。

③ negative effect

effect 為「影響」之意，因此 negative effect 的意思就是「負面的影響」，請注意，不會說成 bad effect，至於正面的影響則是 positive effect。

⊃ I think online games can have a **negative effect** on children.　我覺得網路遊戲會給孩子負面的影響。

⊃ What are the **negative effects** of watching porn?　看色情片會有什麼不好的影響？

Do you use SNS?

→ → → 有用社群網站嗎？

　　在韓國也很知名的 **Social Networking Services**（**SNS**），有利用「按讚」來對貼文表示同感的 **Facebook**、可以分享照片的 **Instagram**，還有將特定的貼文「Retweet」以分享意見的 **Twitter**。年輕的社群網站使用者會利用社群網站來規劃活動（event planning）、邀請（invitation）還有回應（RSVP），可以累積人脈（make personal connections），還能交換資訊（exchange information）。不過，隨著利用社群網站上的個人資訊犯罪的情況越來越多，謹慎使用的文化也正在形成中。美國人認為洩漏個人資訊（personal information）並用來犯罪是很嚴重的問題，因此，相較於韓國人來說，美國人就比較不會在社群網站上暴露自己的位置和休假計畫等等。像是 Facebook 的創始人馬克‧祖克柏，就買下了他和家人住家附近的 4 間房子，用來保護私生活（privacy protection）。

　　根據統計，美國的網路使用者（online user）使用電子郵件（email）和網路購物（online shopping）的次數比社群網站要來得多，社群網站並不會影響和家人共處的時間，看起來似乎已逐漸形成健康的文化了。

STEP **1** 我先提出問題

🎧 40-1.mp3

試著用「誰、何時、在哪裡、做什麼、如何做、為什麼」的六何法疑問詞來問問題。直到沒有可以再進一步詢問的疑問詞時，就能更自然地引導對話。

✪ 用六何法疑問詞來提問

1. Why do you use SNS?　為什麼用社群網站呢？

2. How do you access your social network account?　你如何登入你的社群網站帳號？

3. Which SNS do you use?　你使用哪個社群網站？

4. What type of information do you put on SNS?　你會上傳什麼種類的資訊到社群網站？

✪ 不用六何法疑問詞來提問

5. Are you addicted to SNS?　你對社群網站成癮嗎？

6. Do you have a blog?　你有部落格嗎？

STEP **2** 反向利用提問來回答

🎧 40-2.mp3

如果以前只能簡短回答問題的話，現在試著說出完整的句子吧。將疑問句變成陳述句，就能簡單變成一個句子了。開始練習用句子回答吧！

1. Why do you use SNS?　為什麼用社群網站呢？

   I use SNS ＿＿＿＿＿＿.　我用社群網站來 ＿＿＿＿＿＿ 。

   to keep in touch with my friends 和朋友保持聯絡 ┃ to get useful information 獲得實用資訊 ┃ to post my opinions 發表我的意見

2. How do you access your social network account?　你如何登入你的社群網站帳號？

   I access my social network account by using ＿＿＿＿＿＿.

   我用 ＿＿＿＿＿＿ 登入我的社群網站帳號。

   my smartphone 智慧型手機 ┃ my computer 電腦 ┃ my tablet computer 平板電腦

3. Which SNS do you use?　你使用哪個社群網站？

I use _____ and _____.　我用 _____ 和 _____。

Pinterest 繽趣、Facebook 臉書 ┃ Twitter 推特、Naver blog Naver 部落格 ┃ Kakao Talk、
Instagram

4. What type of information do you put on SNS?　你會上傳什麼種類的資
訊到社群網站？

I put _____ on SNS.　我會上傳 _____ 到社群網站。

my daily life 日常生活 ┃ funny pictures 好笑的照片 ┃ interesting videos 有趣的影片 ┃
international news 國際新聞

5. Are you addicted to SNS?　你對社群網站成癮嗎？

→ Yes, I am addicted to SNS. Because _____.　是，我對社群網站
成癮，因為 _____。

❶ I constantly check Facebook posts.　我會不斷地查看臉書貼文。

❷ I get nervous if I can't check my blog every hour or so.　如果無法每小時查看部落格的
話，就會感到不安。

→ No, I am not addicted to SNS. Because _____.　不，我沒有對社
群網站成癮，因為 _____。

❶ I rarely check my Facebook.　我很少查看臉書。

❷ I'm not interested in SNS.　我對社群網站不感興趣。

6. Do you have a blog?　你有部落格嗎？

→ Yes, I have a blog. Because _____.

是的，我有部落格，因為 _____。

❶ I like to post and share my opinions and ideas.　我喜歡上傳並分享自己的意見和想法。

❷ it is my hobby and I can make many friends.　這是我的興趣，而且可以交到很多朋友。

→ No, I don't have a blog. Because _____.

不，我沒有部落格，因為 _____。

❶ I think it is a waste of time.　感覺很浪費時間。

❷ I don't know what to write about.　不曉得該寫些什麼。

確認前面練習的提問如何活用在和母語人士的對話中，請不要忘記一邊聽一邊跟著説。

Min Good morning, James.

James Good morning. You seem like you **are in a good mood**①. What's up?

Min Oh, I **got in touch**② with a high school friend through Facebook.

James It must have been nice to talk to your friend after so long.

Min It was good. Do you use Facebook?

James Oops, sorry. I don't use Facebook.

Min You don't? **Which SNS do you use?**

James I use Instagram.

Min I have that too. **Do you have a blog?**

James Nope, I don't have a blog. Do you?

Min Yes, I do. I post information about restaurants in Seoul. **What type of information do you put on SNS?**

James I like posting beautiful pictures of my neighborhood.

Min Please tell me the address. I shall **check** it **out**③.

James Sure. I'll write it down for you. Min, you seem to be into SNS. **Why do you use SNS?**

Min I use SNS to keep in touch with my friends. Some of them are abroad so I can't see them often.

James **How do you access your social network account?**

Min I use my smartphone as it is convenient. Don't you?

James Nope. I use my computer because a smartphone screen hurts my eyes.

Min **Do you think you are addicted to SNS?**

James Nope. I'm not that into SNS. I use it only when I need to.

用 **6** 句英文，和外國人輕鬆話家常！

▶ ▶ ▶ 解說請見 P297

① be in a good mood

mood 有「心情、氣氛」的意思，be in a good mood 則是「心情好」，將 good 改成 bad 的話，be in a bad mood 就是「心情差」。

⊃ When I woke up this morning, I **was in a good mood**. 我今天早上起床時心情很好。

⊃ My daughter's smile always makes me **be in a good mood**. 女兒的笑容總是能讓我的心情很好。

② get in touch

「取得聯繫」的意思，將 get 改成 stay 或是 keep 的話，就有「保持聯絡」的意思。

⊃ You need to **get in touch** with your classmates. 你需要和班上同學聯繫。

⊃ Tom sent an email to **get in touch** with me. 湯姆寄了電子郵件和我聯繫。

③ check out

意思為「確認」，直接用眼睛查看，來確認事物。很常聽到 Check it out! 吧？就是「確認某事」的意思。

⊃ You should **check out** the new restaurant. 你應該要看看那間新餐廳。

⊃ I want to **check out** your blog. 我想查看你的部落格。

Part 5

人生的重要瞬間與日常

什麼是人生？不就是由那些早已習慣的微小日常所匯集而成的嗎？每一天雖然很相似，卻都是不同的日子。稍微瞭解一下別人怎麼生活的也無妨，那麼，就用六何法疑問詞來聊聊那些看起來微不足道，卻又珍貴的日常吧？

請掃描 QRCode，
收聽例句的 mp3 音檔吧！
聆聽後跟著複誦一次，
能讓學習效果加倍！

Precious moments in life

I learn current issues in the news

→ → → 從新聞瞭解時事

Do you read or watch a lot of news?（你會讀或看很多新聞嗎？）美國知名的新聞頻道有 CNN、ABC、FOX、NBC，在韓國也很知名的 CNN 常會報導國際新聞（international news），ABC、FOX、NBC 則較多報導美國國內新聞（domestic news）。CNN 在美國被評為最具客觀性的新聞頻道，美國民眾覺得新聞頻道大部分都是 **liberal**（開放自由的），但有不少人覺得 FOX 比較 **conservative**（保守的）。至於美國最知名的報紙則有 *The Wall Street Journal*、*The New York Times* 和 *USA Today*。

接著來認識一下新聞的種類吧，除了國際、國內新聞，還有地方新聞（local news）、政治（politics、government）、經濟（business、finance、economy）、社會（society、people）、健康（health、medicine）、娛樂或影視相關（entertainment）、體育（sports）、氣象（weather）等等，而報紙上除了新聞以外，還有學生族群最常閱讀的社論（opinion、editorial）。

STEP 1　我先提出問題

🎧 41-1.mp3

試著用「誰、何時、在哪裡、做什麼、如何做、為什麼」的六何法疑問詞來問問題。直到沒有可以再進一步詢問的疑問詞時，就能更自然地引導對話。

✪ 用六何法疑問詞來提問

1. Where do you get most of your news?　最常從哪裡獲取新聞？

2. How often do you watch or read the news?　有多常看電視新聞或閱讀報紙？

3. When do you normally read the news?　通常何時會讀新聞？

4. What section of the newspaper do you like to read?　你喜歡看報紙的什麼版？

✪ 不用六何法疑問詞來提問

5. Do you keep up with current issues?　你關注時事嗎？

6. Is watching the news a good way to improve your English?　看新聞是提升英語能力的好方法嗎？

STEP 2　反向利用提問來回答

🎧 41-2.mp3

如果以前只能簡短回答問題的話，現在試著說出完整的句子吧。將疑問句變成陳述句，就能簡單變成一個句子了。開始練習用句子回答吧！

1. **Where** do you get most of your news?　最常從哪裡獲取新聞？

   I get most of my news from _____.　我最常從 _____ 來獲取新聞。

   TV 電視 ┃ smartphone news apps 智慧型手機的新聞 APP ┃ the Internet 網路 ┃ the newspaper 報紙

2. **How often** do you watch or read the news?　有多常看電視新聞或閱讀報紙？

   I watch the news on TV _____ and I read the news _____.

我 ＿＿＿＿＿ 會看電視新聞，然後 ＿＿＿＿＿ 會閱讀報紙。

on weekends 週末，almost every day 幾乎每天 | once or twice a day 一天一兩次，about three times a week 一週三次左右

3. When do you normally read the news? 通常何時會看新聞？

I normally read the news ＿＿＿＿＿. 我通常 ＿＿＿＿＿ 會看新聞。

while having breakfast 吃早餐時 | when I'm commuting 通勤時 | before going to bed 在睡覺前

4. What section of the newspaper do you like to read? 你喜歡看報紙的什麼版？

I like to read ＿＿＿＿＿ section of the newspaper.

我喜歡看報紙的 ＿＿＿＿＿ 版。

the international news 國際新聞 | the national news 國內新聞 | the economy 經濟

5. Do you keep up with current issues? 你關注時事嗎？

→ Yes, I keep up with current issues. Because ＿＿＿＿＿.

是，我關注時事，因為 ＿＿＿＿＿。

❶ I need it for my job. 工作需要。

❷ I am interested in current issues. 我對時事感興趣。

→ No, I don't keep up with current issues. Because ＿＿＿＿＿.

不，我不關注時事，因為 ＿＿＿＿＿。

❶ the news makes me depressed. 新聞讓我感到沮喪。

❷ I'm not concerned about social problems. 我不關注社會問題。

6. Is watching the news a good way to improve your English? 看新聞是提升英語能力的好方法嗎？

→ Yes, it is a good way to improve your English. Because ＿＿＿＿＿.

對，是提升英語能力的好方法，因為 ＿＿＿＿＿。

❶ the anchors pronunciation is good and clear. 主播的發音正確且清楚。

❷ the grammar is perfect and the content is educational. 文法完美而且內容有教育性。

→ No, it isn't a good way to improve your English. Because ＿＿＿＿＿.

不，不是提升英語能力的好方法，因為 ＿＿＿＿＿。

❶ the content is too difficult to understand. 內容難以理解。

❷ the anchor speaks too fast and the words are too difficult. 主播說話速度太快，而且用字太艱澀。

STEP 3 和母語人士對話

🎧 41-3.mp3

確認前面練習的提問如何活用在和母語人士的對話中，請不要忘記一邊聽一邊跟著說。

James **Do you keep up with the current issues?**

Min Yes, I do. In fact, this morning I read a newspaper story about the earthquake in Japan yesterday.

James I saw that on the TV news last night. I'm a bit worried. **Where do you get most of your news?**

Min I don't like watching TV news programs. I read the newspaper in the subway on my way to work.

James That's a bit **old-fashioned**①. I didn't think you were a newspaper person.

Min **Why would you say that?**②

James I thought you would just use a news app on your smartphone or something like that.

Min That is prejudice. Anyway, **how often do you watch the news or read the news?**

James Almost every day. **What section of the newspaper do you like to read?**

Min I love the international news section. I'm very interested in different things happening around the world.

James Wow, that is impressive. **Is reading the newspaper a good way to improve your English?**

Min I definitely think so. The grammar is perfect and the content is very educational.

James You have a very **positive attitude**③ towards the news, don't you?

Min Yes, I do. I have benefited a lot by reading the news.

▶ ▶ ▶ 解說請見 P298

用 **6** 句英文，和外國人輕鬆話家常！

① old-fashioned

意思為「以前的、舊式的」，這裡的 fashion 包含了所有流行，因此 old fashion 也可以用來形容衣服以外的事物。

⊃ I don't want people to think that I am **old-fashioned**.　我不想讓別人覺得我很老派。

⊃ My father gave me a 9 pm curfew. He is such an **old-fashioned** man.　我爸爸定了晚上九點的門禁時間，他好老派。

② Why would you say that?

意思是「為何說這樣的話」，適合在無法明確理解對方的話，或是想要確認話語中真正的意思時使用。

⊃ A：I don't think you are fit for that position.　我不覺得你適合那個位置。

⊃ B：I disagree. **Why would you say that?**　我不同意，為何會這麼說呢？

③ positive attitude

「積極的態度」之意，前面可接動詞 have 或 keep。

⊃ I believe that a **positive attitude** is the key to success.　我相信正面的態度是成功的鑰匙。

⊃ How do you keep a **positive attitude** when you are sad?　當你難過時要如何保持正面的態度？

What a beautiful day!

→ → → 天氣真好！

　　美國本來就是個幅員遼闊的國家，因此不同地區的氣候也極為不同，南部地區（the South）炎熱，因此人們有著慵懶的個性；中西部地區（the Midwest）寒冷且常下雪；西部（West）由於面臨太平洋（the Pacific）的緣故，以溫和的（temperate）氣候而聞名；有許多韓國人居住的 L.A. 就位在西部，至於紐約所在的東部則是四季分明。

　　用英語談論氣溫（temperature）時，有特別需要注意的地方，我們使用的是 **Celsius**（攝氏），但英語系國家較常使用 **Fahrenheit**（華氏），提到氣溫時一定要表明是攝氏或是華氏。舉例來說，假設今天的氣溫是 20 度的話，應該要說 It's 20 degrees Celsius today.，一定要加上 degrees Celsius，攝氏 20 度為華氏 68 度，說 It's 68 degrees Fahrenheit. 即可。

　　和外國人初次見面時，天氣是最常見的 small talk 主題，天氣好時可以說 **Beautiful day, isn't it?**，好像會下雨時則說 **It looks like it's going to rain.**。如果能先這樣熟悉天氣的英語說法，就能輕鬆化解尷尬的初次見面了。

STEP 1 我先提出問題

試著用「誰、何時、在哪裡、做什麼、如何做、為什麼」的六何法疑問詞來問問題。直到沒有可以再進一步詢問的疑問詞時,就能更自然地引導對話。

✪ 用六何法疑問詞來提問

1. How is the weather today?　今天的天氣如何?

2. What is your favorite season?　你最喜歡什麼季節?

3. When is the best season to visit Korea?　什麼時候是最適合造訪韓國的季節?

4. Which do you like better: hot weather or cold weather?　你比較喜歡哪一個:天氣熱或天氣冷?

✪ 不用六何法疑問詞來提問

5. Do you watch the weather forecast?　你看天氣預報嗎?

6. Has the weather ever affected your plan?　天氣曾經對你的計畫造成影響嗎?

STEP 2 反向利用提問來回答

42-2.mp3

如果以前只能簡短回答問題的話,現在試著說出完整的句子吧。將疑問句變成陳述句,就能簡單變成一個句子了。開始練習用句子回答吧!

1. How is the weather today?　今天的天氣如何?

It is _____ today.　今天是 _____ 天。

rainy 下雨 ┃ sunny 晴 ┃ cloudy 陰 ┃ chilly 涼涼的 ┃ pleasant 天氣好的

2. When is the best season to visit Korea?　什麼時候是最適合造訪韓國的季節?

__(季節)__ is the best season to visit Korea. Because _____.

在 _____ 最適合造訪韓國,因為 _____。

用 **6** 句英文,和外國人輕鬆話家常!

❶ Spring, we have famous cherry blossom festivals.　春天，我們有知名的櫻花季。

❷ Summer, you can enjoy water sports.　夏天，可以享受水上活動。

❸ Fall, the tree leaves turn colorful and the weather is perfect for outdoor activities.　秋天，樹葉變得五彩繽紛，天氣非常適合進行戶外活動。

❹ Winter, you can enjoy winter sports such as skiing and snowboarding.　冬天，可以享受滑雪和單板滑雪等冬季運動。

3. Which do you like better: hot weather or cold weather?　你比較喜歡哪一個：天氣熱或天氣冷？

I like ＿＿（天氣）＿＿ weather better. Because ＿＿＿＿＿＿.

我比較喜歡天氣 ＿＿＿＿＿＿ ，因為 ＿＿＿＿＿＿ 。

❶ hot, I like water sports. I can't enjoy water sports when it is cold.　熱，我喜歡水上運動，天氣冷的話就無法享受水上活動了。

❷ hot, I was born in summer and I can't handle the cold well.　熱，因為我是夏天出生的，受不了冷天氣。

❸ cold, I like winter sports such as skiing and snowboarding.　冷，我喜歡滑雪或是單板滑雪之類的冬季運動。

❹ cold, I love snow.　冷，我喜歡雪。

4. Do you watch the weather forecast?　你看天氣預報嗎？

→ Yes, I watch the weather forecast. Because ＿＿＿＿＿＿.

是，我看天氣預報，因為 ＿＿＿＿＿＿ 。

❶ I want to dress according to the weather.　我想配合天氣來穿衣服。

❷ I can check if I need to take an umbrella.　可以確認要不要帶雨傘。

→ No, I don't watch the weather forecast. Because ＿＿＿＿＿＿.

不，我不看天氣預報，因為 ＿＿＿＿＿＿ 。

❶ I don't trust the weather forecast.　我不相信天氣預報。

❷ I don't have time to.　我沒有時間。

5. Has the weather ever affected your plan?　天氣曾經對你的計畫造成影響嗎？

→ Yes, the weather has affected my plan. Because ＿＿＿＿＿＿.

有，天氣曾影響我的計畫，因為 ＿＿＿＿＿＿ 。

❶ it rained when I wanted to go on a picnic.　我想去野餐時卻下雨了。

❷ it snowed when I wanted to go hiking.　我想去登山時卻下雪了。

→ No, the weather has never affected my plan. Because _____.

沒有，天氣不曾影響我的計畫，因為 _____。

❶ whatever the weather is, I don't mind doing outdoor activities.　不管天氣如何，我都願意從事戶外活動。

❷ I always check the weather forecast before I make a plan.　在擬定計畫之前，我總是會確認天氣預報。

STEP 3 和母語人士對話

 42-3.mp3

確認前面練習的提問如何活用在和母語人士的對話中，請不要忘記一邊聽一邊跟著說。

Min　James, you are all wet. Didn't you bring an umbrella?

James　Nope, I didn't know it would rain today.

Min　They said it would rain today. **Don't you watch the weather forecast?**

James　I don't have time to. And I don't trust the weather forecast.

Min　You are so cynical. They are incorrect at times, but I think it's better to be prepared.

James　So Min, do you know what the weather will be tomorrow?

Min　It **is supposed to be**① sunny tomorrow.

James　That is a relief. I don't like the rain or the cold winter.

Min　**What is your favorite season then?**

James　I like summer as I love water sports. The Korean winter is too cold. What about you? **Which do you like better: hot weather or cold weather?**

Min　I also prefer the hot weather. I love to go swimming.

James　We should go swimming together next summer.

Min I would love to. James, **when do you think is the best season to visit Korea?**

James Even though I like summer the most, I think spring is the best season to visit Korea. I think the beautiful cherry blossoms are **worth**[2] seeing.

Min I also agree with you. And I'm proud of Korea's four distinct seasons.

James **You should be.**[3] Hey, **has the weather ever affected your plan?**

Min Yes, several times. Last Saturday, I wanted to go on a picnic, but it rained so I just stayed home.

James That is a shame. We should always check the weather forecast before making any plans.

 解說請見 P298

① be suppose to (*do*) ·····················

「決定要做～」或是「應該要～」的意思，如果原本的計畫沒有按照預定進行時，常會這麼使用。

⊃ My brother is **supposed to** come home by 5 pm.　我弟弟應該要在五點回家。

⊃ Lisa is **supposed to** be the main speaker at the seminar.　麗莎應該是研討會的主講。

② worth ··························

worth 當作名詞為「價值」，當作動詞則是「有～價值」的意思，對話中的 worth seeing 就是「有值得看的價值」之意。

⊃ The Bible is **worth** reading.　《聖經》值得閱讀。

⊃ This hotel is **worth** visiting.　這家飯店值得造訪。

③ You should be.

本來使用 should 時有「應該要～」的意思，用法類似 must 和 have to，在這個對話中，you should be 則是「你必須要這麼做」的意思。

⊃ A：I am so embarrassed that I am the only one who didn't finish the homework. 只有我沒有完成作業，真的太丟臉了。

⊃ B：**You should be.** I am quite disappointed in you.　你的確要感到丟臉，我真的對你很失望。

Public transportation is efficient

→ → → 大眾交通工具很有效率

　　世界各國的主要大眾交通工具為巴士和地下鐵，巴士大致上分成三種，舉例來説，連接京畿道與首爾的長途客運，英語叫做 **express bus** 或 **inter-clty bus**；市內公車是 **bus** 或 **intra-city bus**；接駁車則是 **village bus** 或 **shuttle bus**。

　　地下鐵則是隨著各國地下鐵系統而有不同的稱呼，美國的城市地下鐵系統是 **subway**，英國是 **underground**，法國是 **metro**，因此説英式英語的人也會稱美國地鐵為 subway，稱巴黎等歐洲地鐵為 metro。

　　以美國為例，不同地區的車資與支付方式略有不同，不過大部分都要先購買交通票卡（transit pass），才能使用地鐵和巴士，票卡分成一個月（monthly pass）、一週（weekly pass）、一天（day pass）的期間。

　　美國在大眾交通方面特別體貼殘疾人士，這部分值得我們學習，像是他們的公車幾乎為低底盤公車，殘疾人士可享車資優惠，路人也不會特別盯著身體不便的人看。

試著用「誰、何時、在哪裡、做什麼、如何做、為什麼」的六何法疑問詞來問問題。直到沒有可以再進一步詢問的疑問詞時,就能更自然地引導對話。

✪ 用六何法疑問詞來提問

1. How do you get to work/school? 你如何去上班／學校?

2. When do you dislike using public transportation? 什麼時候會不想搭大眾交通工具?

3. Which do you prefer: taking a bus or the subway? 你比較喜歡哪一個:巴士或是地下鐵?

4. What do you usually do when taking public transportation? 搭大眾交通工具時通常會做什麼?

✪ 不用六何法疑問詞來提問

5. Do you use public transportation? 你搭大眾交通工具嗎?

6. Is parking a problem in your country? 在你的國家有停車問題嗎?

如果以前只能簡短回答問題的話,現在試著說出完整的句子吧。將疑問句變成陳述句,就能簡單變成一個句子了。開始練習用句子回答吧!

1. How do you get to work/school? 你如何去上班／學校?

I go to work/school ＿＿＿＿＿. 我 ＿＿＿＿＿ 去上班／學校。

on foot 走路 ┃ by taking the bus 搭公車 ┃ by riding my bike 騎自行車

2. When do you dislike using public transportation? 什麼時候會不想搭大眾交通工具?

I dislike using public transportation ＿＿＿＿＿. 我 ＿＿＿＿＿ 會不想搭大眾交通工具。

用 **6** 句英文,和外國人輕鬆話家常!

late at night 深夜 | when it rains or snows 下雨或下雪時 | when it is too crowded 太過擁擠時

3. Which do you prefer: taking a bus or the subway?　你比較喜歡哪一個：巴士或是地下鐵？

I prefer taking ＿＿＿（交通工具）＿＿ because ＿＿＿＿＿.

我比較喜歡搭 ＿＿＿＿＿，因為 ＿＿＿＿＿。

❶ a bus, I can enjoy the view through the window.　巴士，可以透過車窗欣賞風景。

❷ a bus, I don't like walking down the stairs into the subway station.　巴士，我不喜歡去地鐵站還要下樓梯。

❸ the subway, it is faster than taking a bus. The subway is always on time.　地下鐵，比巴士要快，而且地鐵一般來說都會準時抵達。

❹ the subway, the subway stations are warm in winter and cool in summer.　地下鐵，地鐵站冬暖夏涼。

4. What do you usually do when taking public transportation?　搭大眾交通工具時通常會做什麼？

I usually ＿＿＿＿＿ when taking public transportation.　搭大眾交通工具時，我通常會 ＿＿＿＿＿。

read a book 看書 | listen to music 聽音樂 | sleep 睡覺 | use my smartphone 滑手機

5. Do you use public transportation?　你搭大眾交通工具嗎？

→ Yes, I use public transportation. Because ＿＿＿＿＿.　是的，我搭大眾交通工具，因為 ＿＿＿＿＿。

❶ it's cheaper than driving.　比開車要來得便宜。

❷ it's faster than driving.　比開車快。

→ No, I don't use public transportation. Because ＿＿＿＿＿.　不，我不搭大眾交通工具，因為 ＿＿＿＿＿。

❶ I don't like waiting for a bus or the subway.　我不喜歡等公車或地鐵。

❷ I like to drive.　我喜歡開車。

6. Is parking a problem in your country? 在你的國家有停車問題嗎？

→ Yes, parking is a problem in my country. Because _____.

有，我的國家有停車問題，因為 _____。

❶ we don't have enough parking spaces. 沒有足夠的停車位。

❷ there are too many cars. 車子太多了。

→ No, parking is not a problem in my country. Because _____.

沒有，我的國家沒有停車問題，因為 _____。

❶ we have enough parking spaces. 有足夠的停車位。

❷ there arent many cars. 車子不多。

STEP 3 和母語人士對話

 43-3.mp3

確認前面練習的提問如何活用在和母語人士的對話中，請不要忘記一邊聽一邊跟著說。

James I'm sorry I'm late.

Min It's okay. You are only 5 minutes late.

James There was a severe traffic jam. After parking, I ran through the corridor.

Min Sit down and **catch your breath**①. You look tired.

James Thanks. I normally take the bus, but today I felt like driving.

Min Yeh, that happens at times.

James **How do you get to work?**

Min I always take public transportation to get to places, including my work.

James **Why do you use public transportation?**

Min To be honest, I'm a horrible driver. I don't know how I even got my driver's license.

James I'm sure you are not that bad. **How often do you use public transportation?**

Min Almost every day. I drive only when I'm going **out of town**②. But sometimes, I dislike using public transportation.

James   When do you dislike using public transportation?

Min   When it rains, there are too many people in the subway and it's even more crowded with all the wet umbrellas.

James   I imagine the floor is wet and slippery.

Min   Yep, that's exactly what I dislike.

James   Which do you prefer: taking a bus or the subway?

Min   I guess I prefer the subway as it is faster. The subway **is always on time**③ whereas buses can be late when there is a traffic jam.

James   That's true. I like driving but in Korea, parking takes such a long time.

Min   I know. **Is parking a problem in your country, too?**

James   Nope. In my country, we have plenty of parking spaces.

 解說請見 P299

① catch one's breath

運動過後氣喘吁吁時,用來表示「喘口氣」的説法。

⮊ I ran for half an hour. Let me sit down and **catch my breath.**   我跑了半小時,讓我坐下來喘口氣吧。

⮊ You are panting. Take a seat and **catch your breath.**   你氣喘吁吁的,坐下來喘口氣吧。

② out of town

town 原本是小鎮的意思,而慣用語 out of town 則是「離開(現在住的)城市」之意,到其他城市出差或是旅行時,也可以説 go out of town。

⮊ Mr. James is **out of town** on a business trip right now.   詹姆士現在出差(到外縣市)去了。

⮊ How often do you **go out of town**?   你有多常到外縣市去?

③ be on time

意思為「遵守時間」，和 punctual 的意思相同。

- I like taking the subway because it **is** always **on time**. 我喜歡搭地鐵因為總是會準時抵達。

- So many people are waiting for you so you have to **be on time**. 有很多人在等你，所以你一定要準時。

Healthy habits keep you healthy

→ → → 健康的習慣讓你身體健康

　　人們為了保持健康（health）付出很多努力，在提及健康重要性的俗諺中，有句話是 **Good health is above wealth.**，意思為「健康比財富更重要」，還有一句是 **You are what you eat.**，意思就是「人如其食」，告誡我們選擇吃什麼的重要性。

　　由此看來，英語系國家進行的 **"5 a day"** 健康運動（health campaign），鼓勵「一天吃五份水果或蔬菜」，可以說是非常適切。

　　還有一些和健康飲食相關的知名俗諺，例如 **An apple a day keeps the doctor away.**，「一天一蘋果，醫生遠離我」，也就是「不用去醫院（hospital）」的意思，就像韓國也有「早上吃的蘋果是金蘋果」的說法。另外有句俗語是 **Sound body sound mind.**，這裡的 sound 意指「健康的」，意思就是「身體健康，心裡也會健康」。

試著用「誰、何時、在哪裡、做什麼、如何做、為什麼」的六何法疑問詞來問問題。直到沒有可以再進一步詢問的疑問詞時，就能更自然地引導對話。

✪ 用六何法疑問詞來提問

1. What do you do to stay healthy?　你做什麼來保持健康？

2. When was the last time you were sick?　上次生病是什麼時候？

3. How often do you get a medical examination?　有多常接受健康檢查？

4. Where do you get information about health?　從哪裡獲得健康資訊？

✪ 不用六何法疑問詞來提問

5. Are you a health-conscious person?　你是有健康意識的人嗎？

6. Do you take medicine on a regular basis?　你有定期服藥嗎？

STEP 2 反向利用提問來回答

🎧 44-2.mp3

如果以前只能簡短回答問題的話，現在試著說出完整的句子吧。將疑問句變成陳述句，就能簡單變成一個句子了。開始練習用句子回答吧！

1. What do you do to stay healthy?　你做什麼來保持健康？

   I _____ to stay healthy.　我靠 _____ 來保持健康。

   exercise regularly 規律運動 ｜ have balanced meals 均衡飲食 ｜ drink plenty of water 喝足夠的水

2. When was the last time you were sick?　上次生病是什麼時候？

   The last time I was sick was _____.　上次生病是在 _____。

   last weekend 上週末 ｜ a few months ago 幾個月前 ｜ a couple of years ago 幾年前

3. How often do you get a medical examination?　有多常接受健康檢查？

   I get a medical examination _____.　我 _____ 接受一次健康檢查。

   once a year 一年一次 ｜ every two years 每兩年 ｜ once in a while 偶爾一次

4. Where do you get information about health? 從哪裡獲得健康資訊？

I get information about health from _____. 我從 _____ 獲得健康資訊。

TV health programs 電視健康節目 ┃ various websites 各種網站 ┃ the people around me 身邊的人

5. Are you a health-conscious person? 你是有健康意識的人嗎？

→ Yes, I think I am health-conscious. Because _____.

是，我覺得我有健康意識，因為 _____。

❶ I exercise on a regular basis. 我會規律地運動。

❷ I don't drink or smoke. 我不抽菸也不喝酒。

→ No, I don't think I am health-conscious. Because _____.

不，我不覺得我有健康意識，因為 _____。

❶ I drink and smoke a lot. 我大量地抽菸喝酒。

❷ I eat a lot of fast food. 我常吃速食。

6. Do you take medicine on a regular basis? 你有定期服藥嗎？

→ Yes, I take medicine on a regular basis. Because _____.

是，我會定期服藥，因為 _____。

❶ I have low blood pressure. 我有低血壓。

❷ I have some chronic health problems. 我有慢性健康問題。

→ No, I don't take medicine on a regular basis. Because _____.

不，我沒有定期服藥，因為 _____。

❶ I don't believe in medicine. 我不相信藥物。

❷ I am healthy so I don't need to take any medicine. 我很健康，不用服藥。

確認前面練習的提問如何活用在和母語人士的對話中，請不要忘記一邊聽一邊跟著說。

James Hey Min, would you like some vitamins?

Min Thanks. **Do you take medicine on a regular basis?**

James Yes. I have high blood pressure so I take my medicine every day.

Min It sounds like you take good care of yourself. **Do you think you are a health-conscious person?**

James Sure, I think I'm very conscious about my health.

Min What makes you say that?

James I exercise every day, **stay away from**[①] fast food and I don't smoke.

Min Wow, you do have a healthy lifestyle. **Where do you get information about health?**

James I read many books on health, exercise and food. Do you want me to recommend some books for you?

Min I would love that. Thank you.

James **No problem.**[②] **Min, what do you do to stay healthy?**

Min Well, I do small things like drinking plenty of water and staying away from soft drinks.

James That's good enough. Do you get sick often? **When was the last time you were sick?**

Min I guess it was last winter. I had a severe stomachache so I went to the hospital.

James You should go to the hospital regularly. **How often do you get a medical examination?**

Min Once a year? You know, the one our company pays for.

James Oh, yep. Have you ever had a health problem show up in examination result?

Min Not yet. But I do get scared every time I take a health examination.

James Same here. Who is the healthiest person in your family?

Min I guess it's my father. He **is** always **conscious about**[3] his health.

解說請見 P299

Part 5

人生的重要瞬間與日常

① stay away from

away 有「離開」之意，而 stay 則有「維持」的意思，stay away from 就是「保持離開～」，也就是「遠離～」的意思。

⊃ I try to **stay away from** alcohol. 我試著努力戒酒。

⊃ My father **stays away from** oily food. 爸爸對油膩的食物忌口。

② No problem.

可代替 You're welcome. 的說法，可以解釋成「完全不成問題、沒關係」。當你接受別人的請求後，對方表示謝意時，你可以這麼回答。

⊃ A：Thank you for doing me a favor. I owe you big. 謝謝你答應幫我，我欠你一份人情。

⊃ B：**No problem**. 別客氣。

③ be conscious about

conscious 意思為「意識」，前面加上 be 的話，be conscious about 就是「意識到～」，看旁人臉色、不太自在時可以說 be self-conscious。

⊃ Jane **is** very **conscious about** her weight. She is always on a diet. 珍很在意自己的體重，她總是在節食。

⊃ My boss **is** very **conscious about** his health. 我的主管很有健康意識。

Let's get educated!

→ → → 一起去上學吧!

　　美國的學校系統使用的是 **K-12** 體制,K 是 kindergarten,為幼稚園的意思,12 為十二年級,代表高三的意思,K-12 就是從幼稚園到高三。小學是 **elementary school**、中學為 **junior high school**、高中則是 **high school**,美國的五十州都有其各自獨立的教育系統。

　　美國學校也有課後活動,通常叫做 **after school activities**,或是 **extracurricular-activities**。由於雙薪家庭多,學校正規的課程結束後,就會開設課外活動課程給學生參加,年紀小的學生則會送到托兒所(daycare center)。除此之外,美國也有私立學校(private education)。

　　美國的大學入學能力考試叫做 **SAT**,推理測驗(Reasoning Test)會考數學、英語(critical reading, writing),各大題計分為 200 ～ 800 分。其他科目則是依照自己的志願,再各自加考特定的科目,像是物理、化學、歷史等等。美國的高中學歷證明檢定 GED(General Educational Development),則是考英語(閱讀及寫作)、社會、科學、數學。

我先提出問題

 45-1.mp3

試著用「誰、何時、在哪裡、做什麼、如何做、為什麼」的六何法疑問詞來問問題。直到沒有可以再進一步詢問的疑問詞時，就能更自然地引導對話。

✪ 用六何法疑問詞來提問

1. Who was your favorite teacher?　你最喜歡的老師是誰？

2. What subject were you good at?　你擅長什麼科目？

3. Which school is the best school you have attended?　在你讀過的學校中，你最喜歡哪一所？

4. How many students were in your class in high school?　高中時班上有幾個學生？

✪ 不用六何法疑問詞來提問

5. Do you still keep in touch with your high school friends?　和高中朋友還保持聯絡嗎？

6. Would you go back to school if you had a chance?　如果有機會的話，會想重返校園嗎？

STEP
2
反向利用提問來回答

 45-2.mp3

如果以前只能簡短回答問題的話，現在試著說出完整的句子吧。將疑問句變成陳述句，就能簡單變成一個句子了。開始練習用句子回答吧！

1. Who was your favorite teacher?　你最喜歡的老師是誰？

My favorite teacher was _____.　我最喜歡的老師是 _____。

Miss. Smith who taught science 教科學的史密斯老師 ┃ Mr. Longfield who taught math 教數學的朗菲爾德老師

2. What subject were you good at?　你擅長什麼科目？

I was good at _____.　我擅長 _____。

Korean 韓語 ┃ English literature 英語文學 ┃ world history 世界史

3. Which school is the best school you have attended?　在你讀過的學校中，你最喜歡哪一所？

The best school I have attended is ＿＿（學校）＿＿, because ＿＿＿＿＿.

我最喜歡 ＿＿＿＿＿，因為 ＿＿＿＿＿。

❶ my elementary school, I made many good friends　我的小學，交到很多好朋友。

❷ my high school, I met an amazing teacher who helped me to decide my career　我的高中，我遇到很棒的老師幫助我決定職業。

4. How many students were in your class in high school?　高中時班上有幾個學生？

There were ＿＿＿＿＿ in my class in high school.

高中時班上有 ＿＿＿＿＿。

around 20 people 大約二十人 | about 55 students 大約五十五人 | less than 40 pupils 少於四十位學生

5. Do you still keep in touch with your high school friends?　和高中朋友還保持聯絡嗎？

→ Yes, I keep in touch with my high school friends. ＿＿＿＿＿

是，我和高中朋友還保持聯絡，＿＿＿＿＿。

❶ We have regular meetings.　我們會定期聚會。

❷ We still live near each other so it's easy to meet up.　我們仍住得很近，很容易見面。

→ No, I don't keep in touch with my high school friends. ＿＿＿＿＿

不，我和高中朋友沒有聯絡了，＿＿＿＿＿。

❶ We all live in different cities so it is hard to meet up.　因為住在不同城市，不容易碰面。

❷ There was a serious disagreement a few years ago so we don't see each other anymore.　由於幾年前發生了嚴重的意見不合，現在都不見面了。

6. Would you go back to school if you had a chance?　如果有機會的話，會想重返校園嗎？

→ Yes, I would go back to school if I had a chance. Because ＿＿＿＿＿.

是，有機會的話，我會想重返校園，因為 ＿＿＿＿＿。

① I want to study more about my field.　我想針對自己專攻的領域再進修。

② I would like to try a different major.　我想挑戰其他主修科目。

→ No, I wouldn't go back to school even if I had a chance.

Because _____.

不，有機會的話，我不會想重返校園，因為 _____ 。

① I don't want to take tests anymore.　我再也不想考試了。

② I prefer working to studying.　我喜歡工作更甚於唸書。

STEP 3 和母語人士對話

🎧 45-3.mp3

確認前面練習的提問如何活用在和母語人士的對話中，請不要忘記一邊聽一邊跟著說。

James This is my high school yearbook. You want to see?

Min Sure. I see you had a different hairstyle back then.

James I did. **Do you still keep in touch with your high school friends?**

Min Yes I do. In fact, one of them is my best friend now.

James That's great. Since graduation, **it has been hard for me to**① keep in touch with my high school friends.

Min I know it isn't easy, but you should try. When you were in high school, **what subject were you good at?**

James Hmm. I was kind of good at English, math and science.

Min Wow, those are all my **least favorite**② subjects. **Who was your favorite teacher?**

James I used to like my math teacher. She was really good at explaining difficult concepts.

Min Do you keep in touch with her?

James Yes I do. I keep in touch with her through Facebook.

Min Good. **How many students were in your class in high school?**

James	In my high school, there were about 20 students in one class.
Min	That's not fair. We had 40 students in one class.
James	That must have been one crowded classroom.
Min	**You can't imagine.**③ **Which school is the best school you have attended?**
James	I really liked my university. I made good friends there and we still meet regularly.
Min	That is nice. **Would you go back to school if you had a chance?**
James	Nope. Studying is too stressful.

▶ ▶ ▶ 解說請見 P300

① it's hard for *one* to (*do*)

「對（某人）來說做～很困難」的意思，在 to 之後加上動詞即可，也可以把 hard 換成 difficult。

- ➲ **It's hard for me to** talk to strangers.　對我來說，要和初次見面的人說話很困難。
- ➲ **It's hard for her to** be a working mom.　對她來說，當一個職業婦女很難。

② least favorite

「最不喜歡」也就是「最討厭」的意思，「討厭、不喜歡」有許多種說法，動詞的話有 dislike，強烈一點則是 hate，假設要用形容詞的話，可以說 least favorite。

- ➲ Math was my **least favorite** subject in high school.　高中時我最討厭的科目是數學。
- ➲ What is your **least favorite** way of staying healthy?　你最討厭什麼維持健康的方法？

③ You can't imagine. ∙∙

「無法想像」的意思，由於彼此的經驗不同或是背景不同，適合在感覺對方完全無法理解自己的話時使用。

⊃ **You can't imagine** how difficult it was for mc to study English.　你無法想像對我來說學英語有多困難。

⊃ **You can't imagine** how hot it is in India in summer. You have to go there to experience it.　你無法想像印度的夏天有多熱，你應該過去體驗看看。

Would you marry me?

→ → → 要跟我結婚嗎？

　　接下來要介紹的是英語系國家非常知名的一種婚禮（wedding）文化，就是 Something old, Something new, Something borrowed, Something blue，新娘（bride）結婚時要帶這四樣物品：一個繼承來的舊物品、一個新買的物品、一個借來的物品、一個藍色的物品，這項傳統的英語是 four **"somethings"**，也叫做 **bridal rhyme**。

　　那麼就一個一個來看這四樣物品的意義吧，Something old means continuity.（舊的物品代表持續性），Something new means optimism for the future.（新的東西代表積極迎向未來），Something borrowed means borrowed happiness.（借來的物品表示借來幸福），Something blue means purity, love and fidelity.（藍色的物品意指純真、愛情以及對伴侶的忠貞）。

　　由於這四樣物品並沒有固定要是什麼，所以每個新娘都不會一樣，舉例來說，新娘穿著新買的禮服，將奶奶傳承下來的緞帶繫在腰上，穿上向朋友借來的鞋子，再戴上藍色的耳環。每個新娘根據自己的情況，將四種意義賦予在四種物品上。

我先提出問題

46-1.mp3

試著用「誰、何時、在哪裡、做什麼、如何做、為什麼」的六何法疑問詞來問問題。直到沒有可以再進一步詢問的疑問詞時，就能更自然地引導對話。

✪ 用六何法疑問詞來提問

1. When do you want to get married? 你想在何時結婚？

2. What kind of man/woman do you want as a husband/wife? 你想要什麼樣的男人／女人當丈夫／太太？

3. What are some important qualities for a spouse? 什麼是伴侶需要具備的重要素質？

4. How long should a couple date before getting married? 結婚前應該要交往多久？

✪ 不用六何法疑問詞來提問

5. Do you want to have children? 你想要孩子嗎？

6. Would you marry someone from another country? 你願意和不同國家的人結婚嗎？

反向利用提問來回答

46-2.mp3

如果以前只能簡短回答問題的話，現在試著說出完整的句子吧。將疑問句變成陳述句，就能簡單變成一個句子了。開始練習用句子回答吧！

1. When do you want to get married? 你想在何時結婚？

   I want to get married _____. 我想 _____ 結婚。

   in 5 years 五年後 │ when I'm 30 到了三十歲時 │ when I get a decent job 當我找到體面的工作時

2. What kind of man/woman do you want as a husband/wife? 你想要什麼樣的男人／女人當丈夫／太太？

   I want a _____ man/woman as a husband/wife.

Part 5

人生的重要瞬間與日常

我想要 _____ 男人／女人當丈夫／太太。

kind 親切的 ┃ loving 可愛的 ┃ diligent 勤奮的 ┃ competent 有能力的

3. What are some important qualities for a spouse?　什麼是伴侶需要具備的重要素質？

I think an important quality for a spouse is _____.

我覺得 _____ 是伴侶需要具備的重要素質。

honesty 誠實 ┃ humbleness 謙虛 ┃ thriftiness 樸實 ┃ generosity 大方

4. How long should a couple date before getting married?　結婚前應該要交往多久？

I think a couple should date for _____ before getting married.

我覺得婚前應該要交往 _____。

6 months 六個月 ┃ at least a year 至少一年 ┃ about 2 years 大約兩年

5 Do you want to have children?　你想要孩子嗎？

→ Yes, I want to have children. Because _____.

是，我想要孩子，因為 _____。

❶ I like children and I have always wanted to have kids.　我喜歡小孩，而且一直都想要有小孩。

❷ I want my children looking just like my husband and me.　我想要我的孩子長得像丈夫和我一樣。

→ No, I don't want to have children. Because _____.

不，我不想要孩子，因為 _____。

❶ my career is more important than having children.　工作比生小孩更重要。

❷ I don't like children and I just want to enjoy life with my spouse.　我不喜歡小孩，而且只想和伴侶一起享受生活。

6. Would you marry someone from another country?　你願意和不同國家的人結婚嗎？

→ Yes, I would marry someone from another country.

Because _____.

可以，我願意和不同國家的人結婚，因為 _____ 。

❶ I get along well with people from different countries.　我和不同國家的人相處得很好。

❷ I would like to raise my children in a multi-cultural environment.　我想讓孩子在多元文化的環境中成長。

→ No, I wouldn't marry someone from another country.

Because _____.

不，我不想和不同國家的人結婚，因為 _____ 。

❶ my parents wouldnt allow an international marriage.　我的父母不會允許跨國婚姻。

❷ I would like to provide a typical Korean home for my children.　我想給孩子一個典型的韓國家庭。

STEP 3　和母語人士對話

 46-3.mp3

確認前面練習的提問如何活用在和母語人士的對話中，請不要忘記一邊聽一邊跟著說。

James	Hey, what are you doing this weekend?
Min	I have to go to my friend's wedding on Saturday and I'm going to rest on Sunday.
James	It is a wedding season, huh?
Min	It definitely is. **When do you want to get married?**
James	When I meet the perfect woman. **I'm just kidding.**[①] When I'm ready.
Min	**What kind of woman do you want as a wife?**
James	I want a sweet and kind lady. It will be even better if she can cook well.
Min	I know a girl who can cook really well. She is Korean. **Would you marry someone from another country?**

James　Sure, I don't mind marrying someone from another country.

Min　**In your opinion**[2]**, how long should a couple date before getting married?**

James　I don't think the length of the dating period matters much. Do you?

Min　Well, I think you should date for at least a year to really get to know the other person.

James　That sounds reasonable. **Now you tell me.**[3] **What are some important qualities for a spouse?**

Min　For me, I would say responsibility. He should be a responsible breadwinner.

James　**Do you want to have children?**

Min　Of course I do. I want to have at least 3 children. What about you?

James　I also want many children. I want to have a big family.

解說請見 P300

① I'm just kidding.

「只是開玩笑」的意思，類似的說法有 I'm just messing with you.，「只是逗你玩的」，I'm just pulling your leg. 則是「只是跟你鬧著玩的」。

⊃　A：Do you like this dress?　你喜歡這件洋裝嗎？

⊃　B：I think it looks horrible. **I'm just kidding.** It looks good.　我覺得看起來很怪。開玩笑的，很漂亮。

② in your opinion

「就你的意見」的意思，適合在好奇對方的意見時使用，如果是 in one's opinion，改變所有格的話，就成了「以～的意見」的意思。

- **In your opinion,** will this project take off?　在你看來，這個專案會成功嗎？
- **In my opinion,** this TV show is lame.　在我看來，這個電視節目不怎麼樣。

③ Now you tell me. ····················

在持續陳述自己想法的情境中，如果中途好奇對方的意見時，可以使用這個說法，意思是「那麼換你告訴我」。

- **Now you tell me.** What do you think about this picture?　換你告訴我，你覺得這幅畫怎麼樣？
- **Now you tell me.** How would you solve this problem?　換你告訴我，如果是你的話會怎麼解決這個問題？

Are you feeling alright?

→ → → 身體沒事吧？

　　在美國旅行或是留學的時候，假設要到醫院看病，一定很不便吧？來學學在醫院裡會用到的句子和單字吧。首先要預約醫院，用電話掛號時，説 **I'd like to make an appointment.** 即可，接下來要説身體哪邊不舒服，先説身體部位之後再加上 **ache** 就可以了，舉例來説，像 I have a headache.，在 head 後面加上 **ache** 即可。如果是背痛的話，在 back 後面加上 ache，説 I have a backache. 即可。假使發生意外事故，則是用 I had an accident. 來開頭。

　　在美國如果沒有保險（insurance），醫藥費會非常可觀，因此若不是很嚴重的情況，建議先到藥局買藥服用。若是在美國長途旅行，或是要住在那裡，就一定要加入保險，才能避免醫藥費暴增。

　　打電話預約後，去醫院時一定要帶好護照（passport）和保險卡（insurance card），事後醫院會郵寄醫藥費的帳單（medical bill），來請你支付費用。如果預約了卻不去的話，可能要繳交罰金（fine），請一定要去電取消（cancellation call）。

試著用「誰、何時、在哪裡、做什麼、如何做、為什麼」的六何法疑問詞來問問題。直到沒有可以再進一步詢問的疑問詞時,就能更自然地引導對話。

✪ 用六何法疑問詞來提問

1. How often do you go to the hospital?　你有多常去醫院?

2. When was the last time you saw the doctor?　上次去醫院是什麼時候?

3. What do you think is a serious health problem in Korea?　你覺得什麼是韓國嚴重的健康問題?

4. What kind of doctor do you see most often?　你最常看什麼科的醫生?

✪ 不用六何法疑問詞來提問

5. Do you like to go to the hospital?　你喜歡去醫院嗎?

6. Have you ever been hospitalized?　你曾經住院嗎?

Part 5

人生的重要瞬間與日常

如果以前只能簡短回答問題的話,現在試著說出完整的句子吧。將疑問句變成陳述句,就能簡單變成一個句子了。開始練習用句子回答吧!

1. How often do you go to the hospital?　你有多常去醫院?

I go to the hospital _____.　我 _____ 會去醫院。

once a month 一個月一次 ┃ once or twice a year 一年一兩次 ┃ about four times a year 一年四次左右

2. When was the last time you saw the doctor?　上次去醫院是什麼時候?

The last time I saw the doctor was _____.

上次去醫院是 _____。

last Friday 上週五 ┃ several weeks ago 幾個星期前 ┃ last year 去年

3. What do you think is a serious health problem in Korea? 你覺得什麼是韓國嚴重的健康問題？

I think a serious health problem in Korea is _____. 我覺得韓國嚴重的健康問題是 _____。

air pollution 空氣污染 ┃ the smoking and drinking culture in companies 公司裡的抽菸喝酒文化

4. What kind of doctor do you see most often? 你最常看什麼科的醫生？

I see _____ most often. 我最常看 _____。

a dermatologist 皮膚科醫生 ┃ a dentist 牙醫師 ┃ a plastic surgeon 整型外科醫生

5 Do you like to go to the hospital? 你喜歡去醫院嗎？

→ Yes, I like to go to the hospital. Because _____.

是，我喜歡去醫院，因為 _____。

❶ I know Ill get better after getting some advice or medicine. 我知道聽了建議或拿了藥之後就會好一點。

❷ I can know what my problem is. 我可以知道問題是什麼。

→ No, I don't like to go to the hospital. Because _____.

不，我不喜歡去醫院，因為_____。

❶ I don't like the smell of hospitals. 我討厭醫院的味道。

❷ I feel that I could get infected by being around sick patients. 感覺和病人待在一起會被傳染。

6. Have you ever been hospitalized? 你曾經住院嗎？

→ Yes, I have been hospitalized. Because _____.

是，我曾住院，因為 _____。

❶ I had a severe fever when I was 10. 我十歲時曾發過嚴重的高燒。

❷ I got injured in a car accident 5 years ago. 我五年前發生交通事故受傷。

→ No, I have never been hospitalized. Because _____.

不，我不曾住院，因為 _____。

❶ I have never been seriously ill.　我不曾生過重病。

❷ I never had an accident.　我沒有發生過意外。

STEP 3 和母語人士對話
🎧 47-3.mp3

確認前面練習的提問如何活用在和母語人士的對話中，請不要忘記一邊聽一邊跟著說。

James　Hey, do you want to have dinner tonight?

Min　Sorry, I'm visiting my grandmother at the hospital.

James　Is she okay? I hope it's nothing serious.

Min　She had a small accident so she's been hospitalized for a week.

James　I hope she feels better soon.

Min　Thank you. **Have you ever been hospitalized?**

James　Nope, I'm very healthy and I have never had an accident yet. **Knock on wood.**① **When was the last time you saw the doctor?**

Min　A month ago? I had my annual checkup.

James　**How often do you go to the hospital?**

Min　I think I go to the hospital fewer than 5 times a year. What about you?

James　I go to hospitals quite often.

Min　**What kind of doctor do you see most often?**

James　I recently got my braces removed so I would say the dentist.

Min　**Do you like to go to the hospital?**

James　Yes, why not? I know I will get better when I visit the doctor.

Min　**That's the spirit!**② Do you think Koreans are healthier than Americans?

James　Nope, I think on average, Americans are healthier.

Min　Seriously? I thought the other way around. Americans on TV are so fat. No offense.

259

James	Well, we are bigger, but I think Americans are more health-conscious.
Min	**What do you think is a serious health problem in Korea?**
James	I think people drink too much. I don't like the drinking culture at work.
Min	**I understand where you are coming from.**③

解說請見 P301

① knock on wood

這是英語系國家的一種迷信，為了不讓壞事發生而唸的咒語，一邊說著 knock on wood，一邊用手輕敲附近的木頭，相信這樣不幸就不會降臨，並且會維持好運。

- ⊃ A：What if there is an accident?　發生意外的話該怎麼辦？
- ⊃ B：Don't say that. We will be fine, **knock on wood.**　不要說這種話，會沒事的，上帝保佑。

② That's the spirit!

可以解釋成「就是這個！這想法很好！」，加油打氣時常會使用的說法，適合在對方表現出積極正面的態度時，用來表示聲援的說法。

- ⊃ A：I will try my best to win this competition.　我會盡全力贏得這次比賽。
- ⊃ B：You go girl! **That's the spirit!**　加油！就是這樣！（這麼想就對了！）

③ I understand where you are coming from.

表示理解對方的意見，「我理解你為何會這麼想」的意思。

- ⊃ A：That's why I disagree with Tom. Do you get me?　這就是我反對湯姆的原因，你能理解嗎？
- ⊃ B：**I understand where you are coming from.**　我理解你為何會這麼想。

Religions influenced our cultures

→ → → 宗教會影響文化

英語（English）為英國（Great Britain）的語言，基督教（Christianity）文化也影響著英語，因此要理解西方文化時，先認識基督教就會容易許多。接下來就看看以基督教為基礎，過去、現在都很常用的英語說法。

首先，有句話說 **be poor as a church mouse**，意思就是「像教會的老鼠一樣貧窮」，由於十七世紀的教會過於窮困，沒有廚房也沒有倉庫，老鼠就算進入教會裡，也沒有東西可吃，因此有了 be poor as a church mouse 這樣的說法。

不曉得你是否聽過 **cross one's fingers** 這個片語呢？這是「祈求好運」的意思，要一邊說這句話，一邊將食指和中指 cross，交叉成十字架的模樣。

另外還有 **doubting Thomas**，意思為「多疑的多馬」，多馬是《聖經》（Bible）中不相信耶穌復活（Jesus' resurrection）的門徒 Thomas，doubt 則是「懷疑」之意，因此 doubting 就是「懷疑的」，現在形容多疑的人就會說 doubting Thomas。

我先提出問題

 48-1.mp3

試著用「誰、何時、在哪裡、做什麼、如何做、為什麼」的六何法疑問詞來問問題。直到沒有可以再進一步詢問的疑問詞時，就能更自然地引導對話。

✪ 用六何法疑問詞來提問

1. How do you practice your religion?　你如何實踐自己的信仰？

2. Who influenced you about your religious beliefs?　誰影響了你的信仰？

3. Why do you think people have a religion?　你覺得人為何要有信仰？

4. What is the main religion in your country?　你的國家主要宗教是什麼？

✪ 不用六何法疑問詞來提問

5. Do you have a religion?　你相信宗教嗎？

6. Is religion important to you?　宗教對你來說重要嗎？

反向利用提問來回答

48-2.mp3

如果以前只能簡短回答問題的話，現在試著說出完整的句子吧。將疑問句變成陳述句，就能簡單變成一個句子了。開始練習用句子回答吧！

1. **How** do you practice your religion?　你如何實踐自己的信仰？

   I practice my religion by _____.　我靠 _____ 來實踐自己的信仰。

   going to church 上教會 | doing volunteer work 從事公益活動 | doing good deeds 做善事

2. **Who** influenced you about your religious beliefs?　誰影響了你的信仰？

   _____ influenced me about my religious beliefs.

   _____ 影響了我的信仰。

   My spouse 我的伴侶 | My parents 父母 | My teacher 我的老師

3. **Why** do you think people have a religion?　你覺得人為何要有信仰？

I think people have a religion because _____.　我覺得人有信仰是

因為 _____。

❶ they want miracles to happen　他們希望發生奇蹟。

❷ it soothes them when they are in trouble　遇到困難時能安撫心靈。

4. What is the main religion in your country?　你的國家主要宗教是什麼？

The main religion in my country is _____.　我的國家主要宗教

是 _____。

Christianity 基督教 | Buddhism 佛教 | Confucianism 儒教

5 Do you have a religion?　你相信宗教嗎？

→ Yes, I have a religion. I am ＿（宗教）＿. Because _____.

是，我相信宗教，我是 _____，因為 _____。

❶ a Christian, I was raised as a Christian.　基督徒，我從小就被培養成基督徒。

❷ a Buddhist, my family members are all Buddhists.　佛教徒，我所有家人都是佛教徒。

→ No, I don't have a religion. Because _____.

不，我不相信宗教，因為 _____。

❶ I am an atheist. I don't believe in God.　我是無神論者，我不相信神。

❷ I never thought about having a religion.　我不曾想過要有信仰。

6. Is religion important to you?　宗教對你來說重要嗎？

→ Yes, it is important to me. Because _____.

是，對我來說很重要，因為 _____。

❶ it's a big part of my life.　是我人生中很重要的部分。

❷ I have experienced a miracle of God.　我曾經歷過神蹟。

→ No, it is not important to me. Because _____.

不，對我來說不重要，因為 _____。

❶ I don't think religion affects my life.　我不覺得宗教會影響我的人生。

❷ I think religion is just a superstition.　我覺得宗教只是迷信而已。

確認前面練習的提問如何活用在和母語人士的對話中，請不要忘記一邊聽一邊跟著說。

James	Hey Min. Is that your bible?
Min	This book? Yes, I am a Christian.
James	**How do you practice your religion?**
Min	I go to church, read the bible and pray.
James	I see. **Is religion important to you?**
Min	Yes. My whole life is affected by my religion. The way I think, speak and make decisions.
James	So you are a devout Christian. **Who influenced you about your religious beliefs?**
Min	I **was born into**① a Christian family. So my parents influenced me a lot.
James	Didn't you have questions about religion when you were growing up?
Min	I did but Christianity **made sense**② to me. **Do you have a religion?**
James	Nope. I used to be a Buddhist, but now I'm an atheist.
Min	Interesting! How did you get interested in Buddhism **in the first place**③?
James	Oh, I read a book about Buddhism when I was young.
Min	As far as I know, Buddhism is not common in your country, right?
James	You are right. I was the only Buddhist in my family.
Min	**What is the main religion in your country?**
James	Definitely Christianity. Most Americans are either Christians or atheists.
Min	**Why do you think people have a religion?**
James	I think people have a religion because they want some supernatural power to help them.
Min	I can't disagree with that. I also pray for miracles to happen.

▶ ▶ ▶　解說請見 P302

① be born into

意思為「從～出生」，常用的說法有 be born into a Christian family，就是「出生在基督教的家庭」，be born into wealth 是「出生在有錢人家」。

⊃ I **was born into** a family of 10 children.　我出生在一個有十個孩子的家庭。

⊃ Jane **was born into** a Buddhist family.　珍出生在佛教家庭。

② make sense

「意思相通、能理解」的意思，話說得通時就是 make sense，話說不通時則是 don't/doesn't make sense。

⊃ This sentence doesn't **make sense.**　這句子前後說不通。

⊃ When my boss is drunk, his words don't **make sense.**　當主管喝醉時，他說的話很難理解。

③ in the first place

「首先、一開始、最先」的意思，想要強調「最一開始」時使用，聽起來會感覺很厲害。

⊃ You should have apologized **in the first place.**　你一開始就應該要道歉了。

⊃ What made you upset **in the first place**?　你一開始為什麼生氣呢？

You can overcome your addictions

➔➔➔ 戒除上癮症

　　現代人的生活多多少少都會對某種東西上癮，就我身邊的例子來說，很多人對智慧型手機上癮，對電視、酒、菸或咖啡上癮的人也不少。上癮是 **addiction**，對什麼成癮則是 **be addicted to**。

　　最近網路成癮的情況更是嚴重，上網可以留言（posting comment）、寫部落格（blogging）、確認電子郵件（checking email）、聊天（chatting）、網路購物（doing online shopping）、玩遊戲（playing video games）、賭博（gambling）等等，消磨很多時間。還有一些遊戲、色情網站，青少年若對其上癮將帶來不好的影響，因此，也有人在討論該使這類成癮性活動（addictive activities）非法化。

　　想要戒除上癮的話，該怎麼做才好？在美國找心理醫生（psychiatrist）諮詢是很普遍的現象，最近韓國也漸漸有這樣的趨勢。

　　團體治療（group therapy）也很常見，團體治療是將受成癮而苦的人們聚集起來，藉由分享想法和心情來彼此安慰，並有助於戒除成癮症，又稱作支持團體（support group）。此外，也有結交朋友，分組幫助彼此遠離成癮症的治療方式。

試著用「誰、何時、在哪裡、做什麼、如何做、為什麼」的六何法疑問詞來問問題。直到沒有可以再進一步詢問的疑問詞時,就能更自然地引導對話。

✪ 用六何法疑問詞來提問

1. What are you addicted to?　你對什麼上癮?

2. Why do some people become addicted to alcohol/smoking/computer games?　為何有些人會對酒╱菸╱電腦遊戲成癮?

3. How did you overcome your addiction?　你如何戒除成癮症?

4. When do you know you're addicted to something?　你何時知道自己對某種事物上癮了?

✪ 不用六何法疑問詞來提問

5. Are you addicted to watching TV?　你看電視上癮了嗎?

6. Do you think online addictive activities should be illegal?　你覺得有成癮性的網路活動應該非法化嗎?

STEP 2 反向利用提問來回答

🎧 49-2.mp3

如果以前只能簡短回答問題的話,現在試著說出完整的句子吧。將疑問句變成陳述句,就能簡單變成一個句子了。開始練習用句子回答吧!

1. What are you addicted to?　你對什麼上癮?

I am addicted to _____.　我對 _____ 上癮。

shopping 購物 ｜ watching TV 看電視 ｜ fizzy drinks 碳酸飲料

2. Why do some people become addicted to alcohol?　為何有人會對酒成癮?

I think people become addicted to alcohol because _____.　我覺得人對酒成癮是因為 _____。

❶ it is comforting 給人帶來慰藉。

❷ it is easy to buy 容易購買。

3. How did you overcome your addiction? 你如何戒除成癮症？

I overcame my addiction by _____.

我靠 _____ 來戒除成癮症。

finding a healthier hobby such as jogging 尋找更健康的習慣，像是慢跑 | getting help from a doctor 尋求醫生的幫助

4. When do you know you're addicted to something? 你何時知道自己對某種事物上癮了？

I know I'm addicted to __(事物)__ when _____.

當我 _____，我就知道我對 _____ 上癮了。

❶ my smartphone, I get nervous if I can't find it 智慧型手機，找不到手機便會感到不安。

❷ coffee, my hands shake if I skip my morning coffee 咖啡，早上沒喝咖啡的話手會抖。

5. Are you addicted to watching TV? 你看電視上癮了嗎？

→ Yes, I'm addicted to watching TV. Because _____.

是，我看電視上癮了，因為 _____。

❶ I watch dramas every day. 我每天都要看電視劇。

❷ I get nervous when I don't watch TV. 我不看電視的話會覺得緊張。

→ No, I'm not addicted to watching TV. Because _____.

不，我沒有對電視上癮，因為 _____。

❶ I rarely watch TV. 我幾乎不看電視。

❷ I think that watching TV is a waste of time. 我覺得看電視是浪費時間。

6. Do you think online addictive activities should be illegal? 你覺得有成癮性的網路活動應該非法化嗎？

→ Yes, I think so. Because _____.

是，我這麼覺得，因為 _____。

❶ if online gambling is illegal; there will be less temptation for weak people. 線上賭博非法化的話，就不會有那麼多意志力薄弱的人被誘惑了。

❷ it can protect children from harmful exposure to them. 可以保護孩子避免暴露在有害的活動中。

→ No, I don't think so. Because _____.

不，我不這麼覺得，因為 _____ 。

❶ we should respect peoples rights and choices.　我們應該尊重個人的權利和選擇。

❷ it will only increase offline gambling and other harmful activities.　這樣只會助長線上賭博和其他有害活動。

 STEP 3 和母語人士對話　　🎧 49-3.mp3

確認前面練習的提問如何活用在和母語人士的對話中，請不要忘記一邊聽一邊跟著說。

Min	Hey, James. Do you smoke?
James	Nope, not anymore. Why do you ask?
Min	Yesterday, I read an article about addiction.
James	I was addicted to smoking before, but I overcame my addiction.
Min	**How did you overcome your addiction?**
James	I got professional help. I went to a clinic. **What are you addicted to?**
Min	I think I'm addicted to my smartphone. Do you think you are addicted to your smartphone?
James	Nope, I don't think so. I can go outside without my smartphone.
Min	That's not normal. How can you contact people?
James	I know all my family's and friends' phone numbers.
Min	That is amazing. I don't know any phone numbers **by heart**[①], except mine of course.
James	Do you like to drink alcohol?
Min	Sure. I like to drink **now and then**[②].
James	**Why do you think some people become addicted to drinking?**
Min	Well, many people say that they like to celebrate with friends and bond with them.

James I think when you drink, people become vulnerable and that's when they have a **heart-to-heart**[3] talk and build intimacy.

Min **When do you know that you're addicted to something?**

James I know I am addicted to coffee when my hands shake if I miss my morning coffee.

Min **Do you think online addictive activities should be illegal?**

James Definitely. I don't want children to access any gambling sites by accident. We need to protect them by having firm regulations.

解說請見 P302

① by heart

by heart 用來表示「背下來、默記」的意思，by heart 前面可以加各種動詞，尤其又以 I know by heart、learn by heart 和 memorize by heart 最常使用。

⊃ Do you know your mother's phone number **by heart**?　你記得你媽媽的手機號碼嗎？

⊃ How can we remember all these **by heart**?　我們怎麼能把這些全都記下來？

② now and then

意指「有時、偶爾」，和 sometimes、from time to time 的意思類似。

⊃ My brother and I have arguments **now and then**.　我弟弟和我偶爾會有爭執。

⊃ I go swimming **now and then**.　我偶爾會去游泳。

③ heart-to-heart

意思為「開誠布公、不隱瞞」，適合在彼此要坦誠對話時使用，另外也常被拿來當作電視節目的名稱。

⊃ Can we have a **heart-to-heart** talk?　我們可以開誠布公地說嗎？

⊃ In Korea, people purposely get drunk to have a **heart-to-heart** talk.　在韓國，人們為了要坦誠對話會故意喝醉酒。

Know yourself!

→ → → 認識你自己吧！

一起來學習要形容一個人的個性或特徵時，有哪些有趣的説法吧。

1. 有個説法是 **busy body**，不是忙的意思，而是指「喜歡干預別人事情的人」。She is such a busy body.（她很愛干涉別人的事。）

2. **cheapskate** 的 cheap 意思和「便宜的」相關，意指不管什麼都想要撿便宜的「鐵公雞」。He is a cheapskale. He would never pay.（他是個鐵公雞，絕對不會花錢的。）

3. **goody-goody** 是「善良的人」，指的是行動或説話善良，並且遵守規則的人，常用來指「裝作善良的孩子」，帶有負面的語意。My sister is a **goody-goody**. She will never disobey rules.（我妹妹很乖，絕對不會違反規定。）

4. **know-it-all**，意思是不管什麼都「裝懂的人」，Mr. Johnson is a **know-it-all**. He talks endlessly and tries to teach us all the time.（強森一副萬事通的樣子，老是説個不停，還想要指導我們。）

試著用「誰、何時、在哪裡、做什麼、如何做、為什麼」的六何法疑問詞來問問題。直到沒有可以再進一步詢問的疑問詞時，就能更自然地引導對話。

✪ 用六何法疑問詞來提問

1. When are you happy?　你何時會覺得快樂？

2. How do you make yourself happy?　如何讓自己開心？

3. Where do you go when you are sad?　難過時會去哪裡？

4. What do you think your personality is?　你覺得自己是什麼個性？

✪ 不用六何法疑問詞來提問

5. Is your personality suited to your job?　你的個性適合你的工作嗎？

6. Do you want to change your personality?　你想要改變個性嗎？

STEP 2 反向利用提問來回答

 50-2.mp3

如果以前只能簡短回答問題的話，現在試著説出完整的句子吧。將疑問句變成陳述句，就能簡單變成一個句子了。開始練習用句子回答吧！

1. When are you happy?　你何時會覺得快樂？

I'm happy ＿＿＿＿＿＿.　＿＿＿＿＿＿，我覺得快樂。

① when I'm reading a book quietly by myself 當我一個人安靜地看書時

② when I travel 當我去旅行時

③ when I have fun with my friends 當我和朋友一起玩時

2. How do you make yourself happy?　如何讓自己開心？

I make myself happy ＿＿＿＿＿＿.　我 ＿＿＿＿＿＿ 讓自己開心。

by treating myself to a nice meal 招待自己好好吃一頓 ┃ by allowing myself a break 給自己一段休息的時間 ┃ by listening to good music 聽好聽的音樂

3. Where do you go when you are sad?　難過時會去哪裡？

用 **6** 句英文，和外國人輕鬆話家常！

I go to _____ when I am sad. 難過時我會去 _____。

church 教會 | the shopping center 購物中心 | the park near my house 我家附近的公園

4. What do you think your personality is? 你覺得自己是什麼個性？

I think I am _____. 我覺得我是 _____。

an extrovert 外向的人 | an introvert 內向的人 | outgoing 愛交際的 | shy 害羞的 |
positive 樂觀的 | negative 悲觀的

5. Is your personality suited to your job? 你的個性適合你的工作嗎？

→ Yes, my personality is suited to my job. Because I am __(個性)__ and I work as a __(職業)__ .

是，我的個性適合我的工作，因為我 _____ 而且我的工作是 _____。

kind 很親切，flight attendant 空服員 | cynical 憤世嫉俗，media critic 媒體評論家 |
patient 有耐心，teacher 老師

→ No, my personality is not suited to my job. Because I am __(個性)__ and I work as a __(職業)__ .

不，我的個性不適合我的工作，因為我 _____ 而且我的工作是 _____。

outgoing 愛交際，office worker 上班族 | shy 害羞，sales person 銷售人員 | rude 粗魯，
server 服務生

6. Do you want to change your personality? 你想要改變個性嗎？

→ Yes, I want to change my personality. Because _____.

是，我想改變個性，因為 _____。

❶ I want to be more active and outgoing. 我想要更活潑、更外向一點。

❷ I am unhappy with my personality. 我不滿意自己的個性。

→ No, I don't want to change my personality. Because _____.

不，我不想改變個性，因為 _____。

❶ I am satisfied with my personality. 我很滿意自己的個性。

❷ my friends compliment my personality. 我的朋友都稱讚我的個性。

確認前面練習的提問如何活用在和母語人士的對話中，請不要忘記一邊聽一邊跟著說。

Min Our boss is a **loose cannon**①. He is so moody!

James Mine, too! My boss is also unpredictable.

Min Why can't they be sane like us?

James I know! You have such a wonderful personality!

Min Do I? Thank you. I don't really know my personality.

James Okay, let's **figure it out**②. **When are you happy?**

Min Well, lately, I'm happy when I'm alone in my room. Quiet and just resting.

James That could mean that you are an introvert.

Min Really? What about you? **How do you make yourself happy?**

James I am a typical extrovert. I like to go out and **hang out**③ with my friends. That makes me happy.

Min **Where do you go when you are sad?**

James I go to a café and talk to my friends when I am sad. Talking helps me sort out my problems.

Min That does sound like an extrovert.

James So think about it. **What do you think your personality is?**

Min I think I am a bit reserved, sometimes shy and I like things to be laid out and planned.

James Yep, that does sound like you. **Is your personality suited to your job?**

Min Sure. I am just an office worker so my personality is perfect for my job.

James If you could, **do you want to change your personality?**

Min No way. I am used to who I am. I don't want to change myself now.

▶ ▶ ▶ 解說請見 P303

① loose cannon

指的是「常做突發行為的人、不曉得會跑哪去的人」，loose 是「鬆散的」之意，cannon 則是「大砲」。假設船上的固定裝置鬆脫，大砲從支架上落下來並到處滾動，砲彈便會飛到我軍方向，由此衍生出 loose cannon 的說法。

⊃ John is like a **loose cannon**. We have to watch out for his unpredictable behavior.　強森是個脫韁野馬，我們得要注意他難以捉摸的行為。

⊃ The media calls him a **loose cannon**.　媒體稱他為難以捉摸的人。

② figure out

有「理解、弄清楚」之意，也會用來表示「想出來（come up with an idea）」、「計算（calculate）」的意思。

⊃ I need to **figure out** what I did wrong.　我應該要弄清楚自己做錯了什麼。

⊃ She has to **figure out** the answer in 3 hours.　她要在三個小時內算出答案。

③ hang out

hang out 的意思是「度過時間」，後面接上「with ＋人＋ at ＋場所」的話，就有「和誰在哪裡度過時間」的意思。

⊃ I like **hanging out** with you. You are fun to be with.　我喜歡和你一起玩，和你在一起很開心。

⊃ Would you like to **hang out** at the shopping mall today?　今天你想要在購物中心度過嗎？

PART 1
Eating and drinking well

01 | Let's eat out today!

==== 解 說 ====

小敏	嘿，詹姆士，沒想到這麼巧會碰到你，過得怎麼樣？
詹姆士	早安，小敏！都還不錯，我過得很好，你呢？
小敏	我很好。你看了昨晚的料理節目嗎？
詹姆士	是，我看了，我喜歡看料理節目。
小敏	節目裡最喜歡哪位廚師呢？
詹姆士	嗯，昨晚的節目嗎？這個嘛……我好像最喜歡金夏瑛，總有一天我想要去他的餐廳。
小敏	那一定很不錯，你通常會在什麼時候外食？
詹姆士	通常會在週末，週間則是在家裡吃。
小敏	你喜歡去哪裡外食呢？
詹姆士	我喜歡去知名的餐廳，我會在網路上搜尋再挑選要去的餐廳。
小敏	聽起來很有趣！最喜歡什麼料理呢？
詹姆士	嗯，我喜歡吃日式、韓式、義式料理，又特別喜歡披薩和義大利麵之類的義式料理。
小敏	披薩和義大利麵一定很美味！你會做披薩和義大利麵嗎？你喜歡做菜嗎？
詹姆士	嗯，我不太會做菜，所以做的料理不好吃。
小敏	沒關係，我也不太會，對了，你可以推薦我不錯的餐廳嗎？
詹姆士	那當然，公司前面有家叫「Kiku」的壽司店，這是那家餐廳的名片。
小敏	謝謝，這個星期六我會去試試。

==== 單 字 ====

eating out 外食／ normally 主要、通常／ cuisine 料理、飲食

recommend 推薦／ ingredient 材料／ business card 名片

02 | Delivery food is convenient

==== 解 說 ====

小敏	詹姆士，你喜歡點外送餐點來吃嗎？
詹姆士	那當然囉！其實我理想的週末就是在家看一場好電影，邊吃著外送餐點。
小敏	一定很美味又舒服，有多常叫來吃呢？
詹姆士	雖然有點丟人，但真的幾乎是一個星期一次。
小敏	那又沒什麼，通常什麼時候會叫外送餐點呢？
詹姆士	主要是懶得做菜的週末。
小敏	最喜歡的外送餐點是什麼？
詹姆士	我喜歡叫中華料理還有炸雞，那你呢？
小敏	我也喜歡炸雞，不過我不太喜歡外送餐點。
詹姆士	為什麼呢？你覺得太常吃外送餐點對身體不好嗎？
小敏	對，老實說我的確這麼想，外送餐點通常都會危害健康，讓人發胖又很油膩。
詹姆士	某些程度上的確如此，但真的很好吃啊。
小敏	這我無法否認，話說回來，外送餐點有什麼優點？
詹姆士	嗯，首先不用做菜，之後也不需要收拾，此外還能吃到自己做不出來的異國料理。

==== 單 字 ====

exotic 異國的／ decent （水準、品質）還不錯／ unhygienic 不衛生的／ artificial 人工的

seasoning 調味料／ deep fried 炸得太焦／ I must say （強調意見時）確實、真的

fattening （食物）使人發胖／ greasy 油膩

03 | Coffee wakes me up!

解 說

詹姆士	早安，小敏，要去喝杯咖啡嗎？
小敏	嗨，詹姆士，好啊。
詹姆士	你最喜歡什麼咖啡呢？
小敏	我喜歡喝拿鐵，你呢？
詹姆士	我最喜歡美式咖啡，還挺常喝的。
小敏	你好像真的很喜歡咖啡呢，會在家裡親自煮咖啡嗎？
詹姆士	會，其實我家裡有臺咖啡機，每天早上我會幫我太太煮咖啡。
小敏	你真體貼，何時會喝咖啡呢？
詹姆士	起床後會喝一杯，還有在兩餐之間也會喝，算是喝滿多的。
小敏	感覺是呢，有多常喝呢？
詹姆士	平均來說一天大約四杯左右。
小敏	真的很多耶，這麼說來你覺得自己對咖啡上癮了嗎？
詹姆士	是，的確如此，沒有咖啡我活不下去，無法專注。
小敏	如果你不介意我問的話，為何要喝咖啡呢？
詹姆士	咖啡幫助我集中精神，還有疲倦時也能趕走睡意。
小敏	這樣我就理解了。

單 字

be addicted to　對～上癮／ keep awake　保持清醒／ concentrate　集中、專心

craving (for)　渴望、熱切盼望／ average ~ out　取～平均／ definitely　明確、確實

04 | It is a plate of heaven

解 說

小敏	嘿，詹姆士！過來吃點蛋糕吧。
詹姆士	謝謝。（咬了一口）好吃！這個很好吃耶！這是誰做的呢？
小敏	嗯，雖然不太想炫耀，但這是我親自做的。
詹姆士	好厲害！我不知道你還會烤麵包！
小敏	嗯，是興趣啦，你喜歡甜點嗎？
詹姆士	那當然！大家都喜歡吧？
小敏	好像是呢，有多常吃甜點呢？
詹姆士	一星期一到兩次？
小敏	那還不算太常！我幾乎每天都要吃！
詹姆士	每天？太頻繁了吧！全部都是自己做的嗎？還是用買的？
小敏	有自己烤的也有買的。
詹姆士	你喜歡在哪裡買甜點呢？
小敏	我喜歡市政府前面一家叫做「A to Z」的甜點咖啡館。
詹姆士	我也想去看看，你最喜歡那裡的什麼甜點？
小敏	我很喜歡巧克力舒芙蕾，真的很好吃。
詹姆士	那你可以帶我去不錯的甜點咖啡館嗎？剛剛說的地方怎麼樣？
小敏	好啊，現在就去吧！跟我來！

單 字

plate　料理；盤子／ apartment complex　公寓社區／ have a sweet tooth　喜歡甜食

lose weight　減肥／ stay away from　避開、遠離／ mention　提及

05 | What do I love to eat?

===== 解 說 =====

小敏	吃點年糕吧。
詹姆士	謝謝，好吃！這個好吃耶，這個年糕叫什麼名字？
小敏	我們稱作糯米糕或麻糬。
詹姆士	我沒有吃過這個，這是你最喜歡的年糕嗎？
小敏	是的，沒錯，你最喜歡的韓國食物是什麼？
詹姆士	我最喜歡的韓國食物是泡麵。
小敏	為什麼泡麵是你最喜歡的韓國食物呢？
詹姆士	感覺就是最棒的，麵條和辣湯總是能讓我流口水。
小敏	第一次吃韓國泡麵是在什麼時候呢？
詹姆士	讓我想想，好像是三年前吧。
小敏	第一次吃韓國泡麵是在哪裡呢？
詹姆士	和朋友去露營時，我們吃泡麵當成晚餐，真的非常完美。
小敏	我知道這是個笨問題，但你覺得泡麵健康嗎？
詹姆士	我不這麼覺得，大家都說有害健康，我也知道原因，有太多的味精，對吧？
小敏	對，沒錯，所以不要太常吃。
詹姆士	我會這麼做的，你好像我媽。
小敏	喔喔，抱歉。你會煮泡麵嗎？
詹姆士	那當然了，簡直易如反掌，五分鐘內就能煮好。

===== 單 字 =====

local （當下說的或是自己住的特定）區域的、當地的／ recipe 料理方法、食譜

glutinous 黏的、有韌性的／ contain 有著、包含

06 | A home cooked meal is the best!

===== 解 說 =====

詹姆士	為何這麼匆忙？
小敏	今天要去我媽媽家。
詹姆士	她一定很開心，是什麼日子啊？
小敏	是我弟弟的生日，全家要聚在一起吃晚餐。
詹姆士	好羨慕啊，一定很有趣。
小敏	一定的，我很興奮可以吃到媽媽做的菜，你喜歡家常菜嗎？
詹姆士	當然囉，我覺得家常菜最棒了。
小敏	我完全同意，你為何會喜歡家常菜呢？
詹姆士	最重要的是很健康，媽媽用的是最好的材料，而且家常菜比餐廳的食物更加衛生。
小敏	說得很對，你會做好吃的家常菜嗎？
詹姆士	嗯，雖然比不上媽媽，但我找了一些食譜，能做出幾道還不錯的料理。
小敏	那麼很常做菜囉？有多常吃家常菜呢？
詹姆士	幾乎每天都吃。
小敏	你有時間嗎？主要會在何時吃家常菜啊？
詹姆士	我每天都在家裡做早餐。
小敏	這是很健康的習慣，你覺得家常菜的優點是什麼？
詹姆士	我覺得最大的優點是材料新鮮，外食的話，你無法知道材料放了多久。
小敏	我非常同意。

===== 單 字 =====

home cooked 在家中烹調的／ hygienic 衛生的／ get off work 下班／ gather 聚集／ way 更加

用 6 句英文，和外國人輕鬆話家常！

07 | Fast food is delicious!

=== 解 說 ===

小敏	終於到午餐時間了！感覺早上好像永遠都過不完。
詹姆士	就是說啊，真的好餓。
小敏	午餐想吃什麼呢？
詹姆士	今天想要吃漢堡，你喜歡速食嗎？
小敏	嗯，我喜歡，我們去樓下的速食餐廳吧。
詹姆士	好啊，你最喜歡的速食是什麼？
小敏	最喜歡的是漢堡，你呢？
詹姆士	我也喜歡漢堡，我最愛的是酥脆炸雞堡。
小敏	那個感覺也很美味，你會去哪裡吃速食呢？
詹姆士	我家前面有家還不錯的速食餐廳，每次想吃速食時，我都會去那裡。
小敏	通常什麼時候會吃速食呢？
詹姆士	應該是週末不想做菜時，會比較偏好吃速食。
小敏	我雖然很喜歡速食，但不想讓孩子太常吃，你覺得呢？速食對孩童不好嗎？
詹姆士	我很同意，速食會讓人發胖，營養也不夠充分，我真的覺得對孩子不好。
小敏	是啊，我姪子胖嘟嘟的，感覺就是吃了太多速食，兒童肥胖是很嚴重的問題。
詹姆士	對，但偶爾吃一次速食的話還不錯。

=== 單 字 ===

nutrient　營養素、養分／ obesity　肥胖／ be starving　快餓壞了

crispy　酥脆的／ lack　不足

08 | Cooking can be fun!

=== 解 說 ===

小敏	這是你的便當嗎？你會準備便當？
詹姆士	是的，我會，我很常做菜，所以會從家裡帶食物過來。
小敏	真是不錯，我不曉得你喜歡做料理。
詹姆士	是的，我喜歡做料理，這是我的興趣之一。
小敏	如果你不介意我問的話，你為何要做料理？
詹姆士	嗯，優點有很多，確實比較健康，而且常自己做菜也能省錢。
小敏	原來如此，主要是為了誰做菜呢？和家人一起住嗎？
詹姆士	不，我自己住，所以是做料理給自己吃。
小敏	一邊要上班一邊還要做料理，一定很辛苦，通常何時會做料理呢？
詹姆士	是啊，沒錯，週間比較忙，通常在週末才做料理。
小敏	真是聰明，你最擅長煮什麼呢？
詹姆士	我最擅長做韓式咖哩，簡單、快速又美味，你也該試試看。
小敏	我雖然料理不太行，但會挑戰看看。那麼，你覺得在家做菜比外食來得好，對吧？
詹姆士	那當然囉！自己做菜的話可以減肥，同時還能省錢呢。

=== 單 字 ===

packed lunch　便當／ economical　經濟的／ full-time job　全職工作

09 | Would you like to go out for a drink?

==== 解 說 ====

詹姆士	嘿，小敏，上週末你做了什麼？
小敏	早安，詹姆士！我和丈夫一起愉快地度過了。
詹姆士	做了什麼？再多說一點。
小敏	我們去了我家前面新開的酒吧。
詹姆士	不錯啊，那裡怎麼樣呢？
小敏	我們喝了清酒，真的很好喝，你喝過清酒嗎？
詹姆士	還沒喝過，是日本酒沒錯吧？我之後想喝喝看。
小敏	一定要的。你喜歡喝啤酒嗎？
詹姆士	是的，我很喜歡。
小敏	喜歡跟誰一起喝啤酒呢？
詹姆士	我喜歡和朋友、同事、家人之類的一起喝，應該只是喜歡喝酒吧。
小敏	我懂，最喜歡什麼酒呢？
詹姆士	嗯，我覺得是葡萄酒，最近喜歡喝白酒。
小敏	我也喜歡葡萄酒，通常什麼時候會去酒吧呢？
詹姆士	通常在生日、紀念日以及有要慶祝的事情時會去。
小敏	原來如此，那麼主要會去哪裡呢？
詹姆士	主要會去公司附近的酒吧喝酒，我不喜歡去太遠的地方。
小敏	下個週末一起喝個酒吧，你覺得呢？
詹姆士	好啊，打電話給我。

==== 單 字 ====

colleague　同事／ spouse　配偶、伴侶／ filling　易填飽肚子的／ recently　最近／ get together　聚集

10 | Let's talk about street food!

==== 解 說 ====

小敏	好漫長的會議，你吃過午餐了嗎？
詹姆士	嗯，我吃過了，但還是有點餓，要吃點心嗎？
小敏	好啊，肚子好餓啊，我想吃路邊小吃，你喜歡路邊小吃嗎？
詹姆士	當然，真是心有靈犀，你最喜歡的路邊小吃是什麼？
小敏	我喜歡辣炒年糕和魚板，是很完美的組合。
詹姆士	感覺很好吃，我們去吃吧。
小敏	你有多常吃路邊小吃呢？
詹姆士	我真的很喜歡辣炒年糕，所以滿常吃路邊小吃的，大概一週一次左右？
小敏	那還不算太常，通常何時會吃路邊小吃呢？
詹姆士	想吃辣的東西時，偶爾會對辣炒年糕嘴饞。
小敏	我不曉得你那麼喜歡辣的食物，你都去哪裡吃路邊小吃呢？
詹姆士	我喜歡去一家叫做「Jaw's」的小吃店，是很有名的地方。
小敏	既然你那麼喜歡路邊小吃，那麼你會在家裡做路邊小吃嗎？
詹姆士	會，我會做辣炒年糕，應該算做得不錯吧。
小敏	我想也是，有機會的話我想嘗嘗看。

==== 單 字 ====

affordable　負擔得起的、便宜的／ proper　正常的、適合的／ grab　抓、理解

PART 2

Hobbies make who you are

11 | Bon voyage!

解 說

詹姆士	小敏，休假過得怎麼樣？做了什麼呢？
小敏	很棒，我和丈夫一起去了泰國，玩得很開心。
詹姆士	哇，聽起來你真的很享受假期。
小敏	是，我們喜歡旅行，你喜歡旅行嗎？
詹姆士	當然，我也喜歡出國旅行。
小敏	喔，真的嗎？有多常出國旅行呢？
詹姆士	嗯，一年至少要出國一次吧。
小敏	真好，你一定去過很多地方，目前為止你最喜歡的旅行是什麼？
詹姆士	目前為止我最喜歡去西班牙的旅行，是幾年前去的。
小敏	我也好想去西班牙，跟誰去的呢？
詹姆士	和最好的朋友一起去的，你喜歡跟誰一起旅行？
小敏	我嗎？嗯，我喜歡跟家人一起旅行。那詹姆士，你下次想去哪裡旅行？
詹姆士	明年夏天計畫要去希臘旅行，我一直很想去。
小敏	真棒，你覺得韓國是旅行的好去處嗎？
詹姆士	嗯，好像是又好像不是。韓國雖然有許多有趣的歷史遺跡可以欣賞，但是有時沒有英語標示，對外國人來說，要找路比較困難。

單 字

numerous 許多／ historical monument 遺跡／ at least 至少

12 | Be smarter with a smartphone

解 說

小敏	昨天晚上為什麼沒有回我訊息？
詹姆士	智慧型手機壞了，得拿去修理了。
小敏	你用智慧型手機嗎？為何使用智慧型手機呢？
詹姆士	因為方便，我想要可以常常確認電子郵件。你有智慧型手機嗎？
小敏	我用一般手機，你第一次買智慧型手機是在什麼時候？
詹姆士	滿久以前了，第一支是在五年前買的，你怎麼不用智慧型手機呢？
小敏	我看到朋友浪費很多時間在玩遊戲之類的。
詹姆士	嗯，沒錯，我用智慧型手機時也是不知不覺就忘記時間了。
小敏	你有多常使用智慧型手機呢？
詹姆士	每個小時都會確認手機。
小敏	不過那是用來工作吧？你最喜歡的 APP 是什麼？
詹姆士	我最常使用我公司的 APP，很輕鬆就能確認電子郵件、訊息以及通知。
小敏	看吧，你是用來工作，那麼下個問題是，你有手機成癮症嗎？
詹姆士	嗯，我想我有，沒有手機的話就無法工作。
小敏	你覺得智慧型手機是必需品還是奢侈品呢？
詹姆士	對我來說是必需品，因為我用來做很多工作，你覺得是奢侈品嗎？
小敏	對，對我來說好像沒有必要，我用一般手機和筆記型電腦就能工作了。

單 字

necessity 必需品／ luxury item 奢侈品／ every single day 每天／ once in a blue moon 非常少見

regular 一般的、平凡的／ notification 通知／ laptop 筆記型電腦

13 | I want to be beautiful

詹姆士	衣服很不賴！今天要去什麼特別的地方嗎？
小敏	謝謝，今天只是想打扮一下，沒有什麼特別的計畫。
詹姆士	我第一次看到你盛裝打扮。
小敏	我偶爾會打扮一下，不過要上班時就不會了。
詹姆士	這樣嗎？有多常打扮呢？
小敏	一個月一兩次，要去參加婚禮或是晚宴時。
詹姆士	原來如此，通常會穿什麼類型的衣服呢？
小敏	只要是看起來端莊的衣服都可以，主要會穿簡單的裙子還有罩衫。
詹姆士	嗯，你真的穿得很端莊，你通常在哪裡買衣服呢？
小敏	我喜歡去我家附近的暢貨中心。
詹姆士	喜歡跟誰一起去買衣服呢？
小敏	主要是跟媽媽一起去，我媽媽很有時尚感。
詹姆士	真不錯，那麼很常去逛街嗎？
小敏	算是吧，一個月至少會去一次。
詹姆士	你覺得自己是購物狂嗎？
小敏	完全不是！我不會買負擔不起的東西。
詹姆士	真是明智！一年會花多少錢買衣服呢？
小敏	這問題有點敏感，讓我想想，一年大概花一百萬韓元（約二萬七千元台幣）來買衣服吧。
詹姆士	還算合理，你會看時尚雜誌嗎？
小敏	會，我喜歡從雜誌中獲得時尚穿搭的祕訣。

afford 負擔／ informative 有情報／ dress up 打扮／ reasonable 適當的、不貴的

14 | Let's cheer for my soccer team!

詹姆士	你看了昨晚的足球比賽嗎？
小敏	不，我沒看，是哪些隊伍的比賽？
詹姆士	韓國對希臘，你沒看嗎？
小敏	沒有，我沒有很喜歡足球。
詹姆士	那麼上一次看足球比賽是何時？
小敏	說來慚愧，不過上一次是二〇〇二年世界盃，你喜歡足球嗎？
詹姆士	你在開玩笑吧？我超熱愛足球。
小敏	真的嗎？你最喜歡哪一隊？
詹姆士	韓國足球聯賽中最喜歡水原三星藍翼足球俱樂部。
小敏	很好啊，經常看那一隊的比賽嗎？
詹姆士	當然囉，幾乎都會看。
小敏	如果你不介意我問的話，你為何看足球比賽呢？
詹姆士	看比賽很刺激，還能分享自己支持的隊伍勝利的喜悅。
小敏	嗯，雖然我無法完全體會，但是很高興看到你有熱愛的嗜好。
詹姆士	謝謝，我是足球的瘋狂粉絲，選手的名字也幾乎都知道。
小敏	真讓人佩服，你最喜歡哪位選手？
詹姆士	我最喜歡鄭大世，你知道他嗎？
小敏	喔，是，我聽過他。那麼你會踢足球嗎？
詹姆士	我高中時曾是足球隊隊員，我是中場球員，但現在應該踢得不好了。

單字

complex　複雜的／ physical strength　體力／ athletic　擅長運動的／ embarrassing　令人尷尬的、羞愧的
passionate　熱情的

15 | Do you watch TV to kill time?

解 說

小敏	你看起來很累，昨天晚上做了什麼？
詹姆士	我為了看奧運熬夜了。
小敏	是喔？我就去睡了，你喜歡看電視嗎？
詹姆士	是，我喜歡，我覺得我應該有電視成癮症。
小敏	是喔？你有多常看電視呢？
詹姆士	幾乎每天都看，你不是嗎？
小敏	不是，我一星期只看一兩次。你都在哪裡看電視？
詹姆士	家裡有兩臺電視機，客廳裡一臺，我房間裡一臺，所以在客廳還有我房間的時候都會看。
小敏	你真的很愛看電視，對吧？那麼你最喜歡什麼節目？
詹姆士	我特別喜歡脫口秀，我喜歡聽名人說自己的故事。
小敏	我只是好奇，你們家裡的遙控器掌控權在誰手裡？
詹姆士	嗯，在客廳是爸爸決定要看什麼，不過像我剛剛說的，我房間裡有電視，所以可以隨心所欲地看。
小敏	很方便，通常何時會看呢？工作不忙嗎？
詹姆士	因為很忙所以都在睡前看。
小敏	既然你這麼常看電視，你覺得電視有教育性嗎？
詹姆士	某些程度上算是，能夠瞭解時事和國際事務，還有紀錄片也很有教育性。

單 字

current issues　時事／ commercial　商業的／ purpose　目的／ international affairs　國際事務

16 | Do you want to watch a movie?

解 說

詹姆士	你看過《露西》這部電影了嗎？
小敏	還沒看，為什麼這麼問呢？
詹姆士	我想問你喜不喜歡，你最近看了什麼電影？
小敏	嗯，我有好一陣子沒看電影了，你喜歡看電影嗎？
詹姆士	是啊，一個月會看一次。
小敏	還挺常的呢，通常何時會看電影呢？
詹姆士	週末會去看電影，週間沒有時間。
小敏	是，我能理解，我們的工作太緊繃了。你喜歡和誰一起去看電影呢？
詹姆士	通常和太太一起去，我們兩個都很愛看電影。
小敏	真好，能推薦我一部好看的美國電影嗎？
詹姆士	當然，你喜歡什麼類型的？
小敏	什麼類型都可以，我想看有知名美國演員出演的電影。最近美國最有名的電影演員是誰呢？
詹姆士	嗯，我不清楚誰是最有人氣的演員，但我最喜歡亞當‧山德勒。
小敏	你最喜歡的電影是什麼？我要先看那部。
詹姆士	最喜歡的好萊塢電影是《當我們混在一起》，我看了好幾次。
小敏	真的嗎？好幾遍？
詹姆士	對，同一部電影你不會看一遍以上嗎？
小敏	絕對不會！我應該沒有這麼喜歡電影吧。

entertaining　娛樂／ stress-relieving　釋放壓力／ demanding　負擔大、要求多

blended (family)　混合式（家庭）

17 | Music heals pain

小敏	嘿，詹姆士，你在聽什麼？
詹姆士	早安，我正在聽一些新的韓國流行歌曲。
小敏	你喜歡韓國流行樂嗎？
詹姆士	是啊，我喜歡，雖然聽不懂歌詞，但歌手們感覺很有才華。
小敏	你最喜歡的歌手是誰？
詹姆士	我最喜歡 CL，你喜歡聽韓國流行樂嗎？
小敏	當然，我也喜歡美國流行樂，你最不喜歡什麼音樂類型？
詹姆士	我應該最不喜歡饒舌吧，因為我跟不上快速的饒舌，偶爾聽不出來在唱什麼。
小敏	沒錯！那麼詹姆士，你都何時聽音樂呢？
詹姆士	我喜歡在搭地鐵時聽音樂，感覺是在地鐵裡殺時間最好的方法。
小敏	我完全同意。那麼，你都用什麼設備來聽音樂呢？
詹姆士	我會攜帶 CD 播放器，因為音質比智慧型手機要來得好。
小敏	這我就不清楚了，謝謝你告訴我。
詹姆士	小敏，你可以推薦我不錯的韓國歌手嗎？
小敏	嗯，我推薦樂童音樂家，是幾年前在電視選秀節目中獲勝的一對年輕兄妹。
詹姆士	聽起來真有意思，我一定會聽的，謝謝你，小敏。

least　至少、最少的／ distract　（精神）無法集中／ talented　有才華的／ sound quality　音質

siblings　兄弟、姐妹、兄妹

18 | I'll take this

小敏	襯衫很好看！是新的嗎？
詹姆士	謝謝，我上週末剛買的。
小敏	你通常會去哪裡購物呢？
詹姆士	我喜歡去 ABC 百貨公司，這個也是在那裡買的。
小敏	你喜歡逛街嗎？你似乎有不少好看的衣服。
詹姆士	是，我特別喜歡買衣服。
小敏	你喜歡跟誰一起逛街呢？
詹姆士	嗯，這要看我需要買什麼而定，買衣服時我喜歡和最好的朋友一起去，他很有時尚感。
小敏	那很不錯啊，你最常買的是什麼？
詹姆士	老實說我最常買襯衫，說來有點不好意思，我花太多錢在衣服上了。
小敏	通常何時會去逛街呢？
詹姆士	我喜歡星期五去，因為會開始有特別的折扣。
小敏	這我不知道呢，你試過網路購物嗎？
詹姆士	是，我買過幾次。
小敏	你比較偏好網路購物還是實體購物？
詹姆士	當然是實體購物囉。
小敏	為什麼？
詹姆士	我喜歡在買之前可以試穿，因為有可能會不合身之類的啊。

consumer　消費者／tend to　有～的傾向／bargain　講價

19 | I'm on a shopping spree

小敏	帽子很好看耶，詹姆士，顏色很適合你。
詹姆士	謝謝，我上個星期六在網路上買的，昨天終於收到了。
小敏	你喜歡網路購物嗎？
詹姆士	是，我喜歡網路購物，因為有特別的折扣。
小敏	網路購物比實體購物好嗎？
詹姆士	好像是呢，同樣的東西卻便宜許多，而且免運費。
小敏	感覺很不錯，你何時會網路購物呢？
詹姆士	下班後還有睡前，我會確認一下我喜歡的購物網站。
小敏	你有多常網路購物呢？
詹姆士	我雖然每天都會瀏覽網站，但一週大約只會購買一兩次。
小敏	那還不算太頻繁，你最喜歡哪一個購物網站？
詹姆士	我最喜歡 Halfclub，東西品質好，還會有特別折扣。
小敏	感覺你真的很喜歡網路購物，那麼詹姆士，你覺得網路購物最大的優點是什麼？
詹姆士	再怎麼說價格都是最大的優點，一般最少都有 10%的優惠。
小敏	有些人覺得網路購物有風險，你覺得網物購物安全嗎？
詹姆士	那當然！我已經買了好幾年了，而且沒有任何問題，只要是利用大型購物網站就不會有問題。

tempt　唆使（去做不好的事）／special offer　特價販售／make a purchase　買東西

tell me　那個、話說（要提問時的發語詞）

20 | I enjoy playing computer games

小敏	昨天晚上做了什麼？你眼睛紅紅的。
詹姆士	我和表弟玩電腦遊戲，以至於太晚睡了。
小敏	你需要點一些眼藥水，眼睛太紅了。你喜歡電腦遊戲嗎？
詹姆士	是啊，你呢？你玩電腦遊戲嗎？
小敏	我還好，我不知道意義在哪裡，對了，你為何要玩電腦遊戲？
詹姆士	很有趣啊，你應該試試看的，確實可以紓解壓力。
小敏	真的嗎？我沒有真正玩過，你很擅長電腦遊戲嗎？
詹姆士	我還算屬害，需要的話我可以給你一些建議。
小敏	你人真好，你最喜歡什麼電腦遊戲？
詹姆士	我最愛的是星海爭霸。
小敏	我有聽過，這遊戲現在還很受歡迎嗎？
詹姆士	因為是經典所以人氣不會消退的。
小敏	是啊，可以理解。通常何時會玩電腦遊戲呢？
詹姆士	如你知道的，我只有週末才有空閒時間。
小敏	都在哪裡玩電腦遊戲呢？會去網咖嗎？
詹姆士	不會，通常都在家玩，我不太喜歡去網咖。

Internet café　網咖／relieve　紓解、使放鬆／predict　預測／eye drop　眼藥水

附錄

解說與單字

PART 3

Leisure activities spice up your life

21 | Relieve stress the right way

——————————— 解 說 ———————————

小敏	還好嗎？你看起來很累的樣子。
詹姆士	我覺得有點壓力，謝謝你的詢問。
小敏	為何會覺得有壓力呢？
詹姆士	下週一之前有個專案要完成，但我還沒動工。
小敏	你應該要休息一下，你在家能放鬆休息嗎？
詹姆士	不行，我無法，我和父母同住，總是有吵鬧的客人。
小敏	那麼有壓力時會去哪裡？
詹姆士	我會去公園走一走，安靜地思考。
小敏	感覺是很不錯的紓壓方法。
詹姆士	你如何消除壓力呢？
小敏	我會做有趣的事，像是逛街、看電影和讀一本好書之類的。
詹姆士	是啊，我也會做這些。什麼會讓你有壓力呢？
小敏	主要是工作，不過我不太容易感到壓力，你呢？
詹姆士	我很容易感到壓力，我的個性很敏感又有點悲觀。
小敏	你應該要試著放輕鬆。人生中何時感到壓力最大呢？
詹姆士	應該是高中畢業之前，大學入學考試給我很大的壓力。
小敏	我完全可以理解。

——————————— 單 字 ———————————

relax　休息／ supervisor　監督者、管理者、上司／ sensitive　敏感／ personality　個性、人格

22 | Don't let the bed bugs bite

——————————— 解 說 ———————————

詹姆士	你好嗎？你看來很累。
小敏	謝謝你這麼問，最近沒睡好。
詹姆士	真可憐，有試過熱牛奶、熱水澡或是其他的方法嗎？
小敏	是啊，有試過，好像是因為壓力的緣故，你曾經受失眠所苦嗎？
詹姆士	沒有，我在哪裡都能睡得很好。
小敏	真好，我有時會做奇怪的夢，以至於睡不飽。
詹姆士	這樣啊？你做過最有趣的夢是什麼？
小敏	喔，有一次我夢到要去當兵，因為韓國修了法律，每個人都要當兵。
詹姆士	哇！一定很興奮又讓人感到混亂。
小敏	是啊，你有什麼不好的睡眠習慣嗎？
詹姆士	好像有，但不知道最近還會不會。
小敏	是怎麼樣的睡眠壞習慣呢？
詹姆士	好像偶爾會說夢話，朋友還以為我醒了並且跟我對話。
小敏	真搞笑！
詹姆士	話說回來，你看起來總是很累，每天睡幾小時呢？
小敏	我都沒睡飽，每天睡五小時左右。
詹姆士	太少了吧，你通常都幾點上床睡覺？
小敏	超過十二點，工作結束回到家還要做家事，然後邊看電視邊休息。
詹姆士	你喜歡睡在地板上還是床上？
小敏	我比較喜歡睡在床上，因為比較柔軟舒服。

insomnia　失眠症／ be used to　對～熟悉／ distract　無法集中、為難／ hilarious　非常好笑（很搞笑）

23 | Do you like to read?

小敏	你在看什麼？
詹姆士	丹・布朗的《達文西密碼》。
小敏	常看到你在午休時間看書，你喜歡看書嗎？
詹姆士	是，我喜歡看書，只要透過翻頁就能體驗全新的世界。
小敏	喔，你真的很愛閱讀呢，你最喜歡什麼類型的書？
詹姆士	我特別喜歡冒險小說。
小敏	最喜歡的作家是誰？
詹姆士	目前為止我最喜歡的作家是丹・布朗。
小敏	為何會喜歡他呢？
詹姆士	我喜歡他說故事的技巧與寫作風格。
小敏	我應該要來看看他的書了。除了午餐時間，你通常會在何時看書呢？
詹姆士	我通常會在地鐵上、睡前還有覺得無聊時看書。
小敏	聽起來像是整天都在看書。你喜歡在哪裡看書呢？
詹姆士	我喜歡在咖啡館裡看書。
小敏	可以推薦值得看的好書給我嗎？
詹姆士	那當然，我推薦我正在看的這本書，應該是今年讀過最好的一本書了。
小敏	好的，那麼你一年會看幾本書呢？
詹姆士	沒有很多，一年差不多看十二本左右吧，一個月一本。

genre　種類／ expand　擴大、增加／ perspective　觀點／ recall　記得、想起

24 | t's a perfect day to ride a bike

詹姆士	早安，那是自行車安全帽嗎？
小敏	對，是的。詹姆士，你會騎自行車嗎？
詹姆士	會，不過不太常騎，你喜歡騎自行車嗎？
小敏	喜歡，不過騎得不太好所以在練習。
詹姆士	一定可以的！你多常騎自行車呢？
小敏	大約一個月一兩次，我不太有時間。那你呢？
詹姆士	我也是啊，有很多其他的事要做，對吧？
小敏	就是說啊，你主要會在哪裡騎自行車呢？
詹姆士	我家附近有個美麗的公園，我會去那裡。
小敏	附近有公園的話，一定很棒吧。曾騎自行車到多遠的地方呢？
詹姆士	其實上個月我騎自行車到了漢江的 Gilbut 公園（譯註：非實際存在的公園，而是原出版社的名稱），大概花了四個小時。
小敏	哇，一定很辛苦吧，會肌肉痠痛嗎？
詹姆士	會啊，一定的，大腿像燒起來一樣非常刺痛，隔天就得休息了。
小敏	但還是很有趣吧。

附錄

解說與單字

詹姆士	是的，非常有趣。小敏，你何時學會騎自行車呢？
小敏	很久以前，記不太清楚了。詹姆士，我只是好奇，是誰教你騎自行車的呢？
詹姆士	我哥教我的，但感覺是自己突然就開竅了。
小敏	對啊，我記得沒有那麼難。
詹姆士	小敏，這個週末要不要去騎自行車？你覺得呢？
小敏	這是個好主意，好啊。

=== **單 字** ===

decade　十年／ severe　極其嚴重／ like crazy　可怕的氣勢、非常

barely　吃力地、好不容易／ curious　好奇

25 ｜ Climbing a mountain is fun

=== **解 說** ===

詹姆士	耶！明天放假！真開心！
小敏	你有什麼特別的計劃嗎？
詹姆士	我要和朋友去登山，你喜歡登山嗎？
小敏	是啊，我喜歡，明天可以一起去嗎？
詹姆士	當然，來吧。
小敏	謝謝你讓我同行。我想問，你為何會喜歡登山呢？
詹姆士	我愛大自然，而登山能呼吸新鮮空氣並調整自己的思緒。
小敏	我完全同意。你通常何時會去登山？
詹姆士	主要是春天和秋天，夏天太熱，冬天又太危險了。
小敏	對，我也覺得。你爬過韓國哪些山？
詹姆士	我去過雪嶽山和道峰山，我真的很喜歡。
小敏	我也爬過那些山！你有登上山頂過嗎？
詹姆士	那當然囉，登山時一定要攻頂，因為會有很大的成就感。

=== **單 字** ===

peak　頂峰、山峰／ complete　完全／ reach　到達／ clear　清理、變清澈

26 ｜ Exercise is refreshing!

=== **解 說** ===

小敏	你的頭髮濕了，剛剛沖過澡嗎？
詹姆士	其實我是去游泳了，沖完澡後沒時間把頭髮吹乾。
小敏	你去游泳嗎？這我還真的不知道呢，你會固定去游泳嗎？
詹姆士	我試著這麼做，我公寓附近有個室內游泳池，最近還加入了那邊的會員。你常運動嗎？
小敏	是，但只是去附近的健身房，游泳感覺很有趣，我應該要試試。
詹姆士	試試看吧，你何時會去哪裡做運動呢？
小敏	我傍晚下班後會去健身房運動。
詹姆士	下班後不會很累嗎？我是上班前去游泳。
小敏	那感覺會更累。
詹姆士	是嗎？每個人的情況應該不太一樣。你有多常運動？
小敏	我試著一個禮拜至少去健身房兩次。
詹姆士	最喜歡什麼運動呢？你喜歡在健身房運動嗎？
小敏	不，其實我最喜歡瑜伽，但運氣不好，附近沒有不錯的瑜伽教室。

詹姆士	真可惜，你的運動神經好嗎？
小敏	雖然稱不上好，但很柔軟，你做過瑜伽嗎？
詹姆士	感覺瑜伽不是男生做的運動，看起來或聽起來都像是女生的運動。
小敏	你這麼說太荒謬了，我就看過很多男生上瑜伽課。

單 字

wórk óut　運動／indoor　室內／unfortunately　不幸地／flexible　柔軟的／absurd　荒謬的、不像話的

27 ｜ Are you good at driving?

解 說

小敏	嘿，你有駕照嗎？
詹姆士	有啊，這是以前的照片，看起來好呆。
小敏	不會啦，我覺得照片中的你看起來很可愛。你何時考到駕照的呢？
詹姆士	讓我想想……好像是十五年前左右。
小敏	哇，很久了呢，你的第一臺車是什麼車？
詹姆士	我的第一臺車其實是貨車，在我十六歲生日時爸爸買給我的。
小敏	那麼你真的開車很長一段時間了，你是個好駕駛嗎？
詹姆士	那還用說，我從來沒有發生過事故，你曾發生過車禍嗎？
小敏	嗯，有的，是一個月前，不知怎麼就刮到停好的車了。
詹姆士	沒關係，你去年才開始開車，對吧？一定很快就能熟悉的。
小敏	我也希望，我還是會怕開車。你喜歡開車嗎？
詹姆士	非常喜歡，我喜歡走遍韓國發現隱藏的美景。
小敏	聽起來真有趣，哪裡適合兜風呢？能推薦我不錯的地方嗎？
詹姆士	你應該試試沿著韓國東海岸兜風，很美麗。
小敏	謝謝你的推薦。
詹姆士	別客氣，這個週末我要去東海岸兜風。
小敏	真的嗎？沒關係的話，我可以跟嗎？
詹姆士	當然，隨時歡迎。

單 字

abide by　根據（法律、協商等）／yield to　（在馬路上對其他車）禮讓／foul language　低俗的話、髒話
scratch　刮、被刮／hidden beauty　隱藏的美景

28 ｜ I like to pat my pet

解 說

小敏	詹姆士，你有寵物嗎？
詹姆士	是的，我有一隻貓，牠叫莎莉，非常害羞。
小敏	誰在照顧你的寵物呢？你為了工作不是幾乎沒有時間了嗎？
詹姆士	貓咪都很獨立，牠們可以自己待著。
小敏	真不錯，我出門時是姪子幫我照顧小狗。
詹姆士	你的姪子？他跟你一起住嗎？
小敏	沒有，他住在隔壁，我給他一些零用錢請他照顧小狗。
詹姆士	孩子們透過養寵物能學習到什麼？
小敏	我覺得能學習到責任感和愛心。
詹姆士	我同意，還能學習珍惜並暸解動物。

小敏	你覺得什麼動物可愛呢？
詹姆士	我覺得松鼠很可愛，我想養一隻當寵物。
小敏	這問題雖然有點蠢，但如果能變成動物的話，你想變成什麼？
詹姆士	喔，這是個有趣的問題，嗯，我想變成鳥翱翔天際，你呢？
小敏	我想變成海豚游得遠遠的。
詹姆士	這讓我想到，你想去動物園嗎？上次去動物園是什麼時候？
小敏	好像已經五年了，我們去動物園吧！
詹姆士	話說回來，有些人覺得動物園是殘忍的地方，你覺得呢？
小敏	這我倒是沒有想過，你關心動物權益嗎？
詹姆士	是，其實我是動物權益團體的成員。

═══════════════ **單 字** ═══════════════

independent　獨立的／ by oneself　自己、獨自／ pocket money　零用錢／ responsibility　責任感

29 ｜ Do you want to be famous?

═══════════════ **解 說** ═══════════════

詹姆士	怎麼這麼吵？
小敏	啊，有位知名的韓國演員來了，所以粉絲們都聚集在樓下。
詹姆士	我有時候不太能理解青少年粉絲。
小敏	沒錯，太過度喜愛藝人了。
詹姆士	青少年為何會那麼喜歡藝人呢？
小敏	嗯，想成為那樣的人啊，想要有高收入和華麗的生活吧。
詹姆士	我們應該也有過那麼瘋狂喜愛知名歌手的時候。
小敏	當然囉，你親眼見過名人嗎？
詹姆士	有啊，好幾次，住在首爾要見到並不困難。
小敏	真的嗎？我怎麼一次都沒見過？要去哪裡才能親眼見到呢？
詹姆士	知名餐廳或是美髮沙龍，還有電視臺當然也可以看到。
小敏	看來我得更常去知名的餐廳了。
詹姆士	你想遇見哪位名人呢？
小敏	我真的很想遇見劉在錫，韓國的諧星你知道嗎？
詹姆士	知道，我也喜歡他，你認識名人嗎？
小敏	讓我想想，啊，我叔叔和朴槿惠（南韓前總統）上同所高中。
詹姆士	真酷！你想變有名嗎？
小敏	不太想，我討厭私生活暴露在大眾面前，你呢？
詹姆士	成為名人賺了很多錢之後，就沒差囉。

═══════════════ **單 字** ═══════════════

glamorous　魅惑的、華麗的／ fashionable　追隨流行的、最新的／ influential　有影響力／ reveal　顯露

renowned　著名的、有名聲的／ fuss　興奮、吵鬧／ private　私人的／ the public　大眾

=== 解 說 ===

詹姆士	嘿，那是什麼？你親手畫的嗎？
小敏	喔，只是隨便的塗鴉而已。
詹姆士	很不錯耶，你擅長畫畫嗎？
小敏	我不覺得我很會畫畫，不過我喜歡藝術。
詹姆士	是嗎？你為何喜歡藝術呢？
小敏	嗯，原因有很多，不過簡單來說，藝術讓我覺得幸福。
詹姆士	那麼你去過美術館嗎？
小敏	當然囉，我會固定去美術館，其實這個星期六我也要去看展。
詹姆士	誰的畫展呢？
小敏	安迪·沃荷的畫展。
詹姆士	你還喜歡現代藝術啊？我看不懂現代藝術。
小敏	是啊，很多人都這麼說。
詹姆士	你最喜歡什麼風格的畫作？
小敏	我喜歡油畫，特別喜歡印象派。
詹姆士	喔，那個我知道，是由梵谷和塞尚等畫家所帶領的藝術運動，對吧？
小敏	沒錯，你很厲害呢，你喜歡藝術嗎？
詹姆士	我還好，你最喜歡哪位畫家？
小敏	我從小就很喜歡畢卡索，我覺得他是天才。
詹姆士	我完全同意，我念書時也有學過畢卡索。
小敏	你上次看展是什麼時候？
詹姆士	太久了，記不太得。
小敏	這個週六要不要一起去？
詹姆士	好啊，我們一起去。

=== 單 字 ===

exhibition　展覽／ dull　無趣的／ Cubism　立體主義

take after　像～／ doodle　塗鴉／ Impressionism　印象派

附錄

解說與單字

PART 4

The real and virtual worlds

31 | I reminisce about my college days

================ 解 說 ================

詹姆士	早安，週末過得怎麼樣？
小敏	非常開心，我去了大學同學會。
詹姆士	感覺你玩得很盡興，你是哪所大學出身的呢？
小敏	我是 Gilbut 大學畢業的。
詹姆士	哇，是名校出身呢，你什麼時候大學畢業的呢？
小敏	六年前畢業，是二〇〇九年。
詹姆士	對了，我還不曉得你的主修科目，你主修什麼？
小敏	我主修經濟學，你呢？
詹姆士	我大學主修數學，真的很難，都不曉得我是怎麼畢業的。
小敏	我懂你的意思，我也不知道我怎麼修完經濟學的。
詹姆士	你怎麼支付大學學費呢？我是申請就學貸款，現在還在還款。
小敏	我是向父母借的，上個月終於還清了。
詹姆士	恭喜你！一定覺得很輕鬆吧？
小敏	負擔終於減輕囉。不過，你大學時有女友嗎？
詹姆士	那當然，怎麼，你沒約會嗎？
小敏	是啊，沒有，我當時太害羞了，然後又加入好幾個社團，所以沒有多餘的時間。
詹姆士	聽起來你大學生活過得很忙碌呢。
小敏	是啊，你有加入社團嗎？
詹姆士	其實我是魔術社的成員，我對魔術很感興趣。

================ 單 字 ================

college degree 學士學位／ student loan 就學貸款／ debate 討論／ TA(teaching assistant) 助教

reunion 同學會／ tell me about it （我也有過同樣的經驗）我懂你的意思／ have a blast 玩得很盡興

32 | Wanna go out on a date?

================ 解 說 ================

小敏	你相信一見鍾情嗎？
詹姆士	是啊，我相信，你呢？曾經一見鍾情過嗎？
小敏	是的，我有過，事實上我一見到我男友就陷入愛河了。
詹姆士	真浪漫。
小敏	謝謝，你有女友嗎？
詹姆士	嗯，我有，我們交往幾個月了。
小敏	你最喜歡的約會地點是哪裡？
詹姆士	我喜歡去電影院，我理想中的約會就是看部好電影，再一邊吃著爆米花。你理想中的約會是什麼呢？
小敏	我理想中的約會是去異國餐廳，吃一頓還不錯的晚餐，然後再去散個步。
詹姆士	聽起來真有趣，我也要試試。還記得你的第一次約會嗎？
小敏	當然囉，那是我高中的時候。你的第一次約會是在什麼時候？
詹姆士	是在我大一的時候，我們會去看舞臺劇，而且交往得很順利，在一起五年。
小敏	很長一段時間呢，為何會分手呢？
詹姆士	她要搬到別的國家，我們決定分手是最好的方式。
小敏	真是遺憾，兩位一定都很難熬。
詹姆士	是啊，沒錯，不過現在我們都有所成長，並且都各自擁有一段新關係了。

用 6 句英文，和外國人輕鬆話家常！

單字

fancy 華麗的、昂貴的／exotic 異國的／cheat on 劈腿
ideal 理想的／move on 成長／relationship （戀人）關係

33 | Holidays are for family

解說

詹姆士	聖誕快樂，小敏！
小敏	聖誕快樂，詹姆士！假期快樂！
詹姆士	小敏，這裡不太有聖誕節的氣氛。
小敏	我懂你的意思，聖誕節在韓國不是重要的節日。
詹姆士	我大概理解，那麼你們國家的重要節日是什麼？
小敏	最大的是春節，然後是中秋節，韓國的感恩節也很重要。
詹姆士	真的嗎？節日只有兩個嗎？
小敏	不是的，也有其他節日。
詹姆士	你最喜歡哪個節日？
小敏	最喜歡的當然是中秋節。
詹姆士	為什麼最喜歡呢？
小敏	由於是初秋，天氣好得沒話說，還可以跟親戚們一起吃很棒的料理。
詹姆士	聽起來是很理想的節日。
小敏	你喜歡節日嗎？
詹姆士	當然囉，我很喜歡感恩節，能和家人一起吃美味的晚餐，知名的梅西大遊行會在紐約舉辦，還有美式足球比賽。
小敏	超有趣的日子啊！感恩節有什麼特殊的料理嗎？
詹姆士	當然有囉，感恩節要吃烤火雞和南瓜派。
小敏	好像曾在美國電視劇中看過，你節日都會和誰見面呢？
詹姆士	跟你一樣，會和家人、朋友、親戚們相聚。
小敏	不過你現在和家人分開了，上一個節日是怎麼度過的呢？
詹姆士	我和朋友見面，然後我們舉辦了自己的派對。

單字

relative 親戚／nag 嘮叨

34 | I'm happy to have a job

解說

小敏	嘿，你似乎很忙，最近在做什麼？
詹姆士	我正在找新工作。
小敏	為什麼要換新工作？
詹姆士	目前的工作是還不錯，但薪水很糟，我想要好一點的薪水。
小敏	是啊，薪水很重要，那可是上班族工作的動力啊。
詹姆士	就是說啊，你何時開始工作的呢？
小敏	大學畢業後馬上就開始了。
詹姆士	如果你不介意我問的話，你喜歡你的主管嗎？
小敏	嗯，雖然不是很喜歡但還可以忍受。
詹姆士	那就好，關於你的工作你最喜歡什麼？

小敏	我喜歡工作的時間，上下班時間很自由，而且幾乎不加班。你有多常加班呢？
詹姆士	現在的工作總是要加班，你的公司有要找人嗎？
小敏	我來問問。不過你絕對不想做什麼工作？
詹姆士	我完全不想要當園丁，我真的很不會照顧植物，你呢？
小敏	嗯，因為我每次看到血都會吐，當醫生是絕對不可能的。
詹姆士	我懂，在你的國家找工作容易嗎？
小敏	不太容易，我們國家目前的失業率很高。
詹姆士	我們國家也是，感覺全球經濟都不景氣。

單 字

horrible　很糟糕／motivated　被激勵／flexible　有流通性／puke　嘔吐

35 │ It's payday!

解 說

小敏	明天是發薪日！耶～
詹姆士	對呀！我老是正好在發薪日之前就把錢用完了。
小敏	是嗎？誰在管理你的錢？
詹姆士	是我，我自己來管理的，你呢？
小敏	我也算是，不過我會和媽媽商量，幾乎都會遵循她的建議。
詹姆士	如果這麼問你不介意的話，你一個月存多少錢呢？
小敏	這個嘛……差不多存月薪的三分之一，你覺得這算多還是少？
詹姆士	我覺得很合理，你為何要存錢呢？
小敏	嗯，存錢是為了結婚、買房子、車子等等。
詹姆士	哇，你真的考慮得很多。
小敏	這麼看來，我真的想得很多。
詹姆士	嘿，你何時收到第一筆月薪？還記得嗎？
小敏	當然囉，是在七年前，我買了名牌手提包。你用第一筆月薪買了什麼呢？
詹姆士	我買了父母的禮物。
小敏	喔，真的好貼心啊。我只是問問，你滿意你的薪水嗎？
詹姆士	馬馬虎虎吧，但最近的失業率太高了，我也沒什麼好抱怨的。
小敏	你真是個樂天派！

單 字

retirement　退休／sufficient　足夠／overtime　加班、夜班／reasonable　適當的
more or less　幾乎／unemployment rate　失業率／optimist　樂天派

36 │ A meeting can be productive!

解 說

詹姆士	你昨天怎麼沒接電話？
小敏	啊，對不起，當時在開會，原本要打給你的但我忘了。
詹姆士	沒關係，你好像很常開會。
小敏	是啊，你不是嗎？有多常開會呢？
詹姆士	我們一星期只開一次。
小敏	真的嗎？我們每天都要開會。
詹姆士	每天感覺有點多，在哪裡開會呢？

用 6 句英文，和外國人輕鬆話家常！

小敏	我們這層樓有會議室，很方便。
詹姆士	通常何時開會呢？
小敏	九點準時開會，因為要開會所以不能遲到。
詹姆士	一定很有壓力，為何要這麼常開會呢？
小敏	每天都要報告工作進度，我不喜歡太常開會，你呢？你覺得常開會好嗎？
詹姆士	不好，如果沒有做好會議準備的話，感覺很浪費時間。
小敏	沒錯，感覺你懂我的想法。
詹姆士	開會時，你是勇於發言的人或是聆聽的人呢？
小敏	當然是聆聽的人，在韓國想要獲得好觀感的話，還是安靜聆聽比較好。
詹姆士	真是難過。
小敏	你覺得何時適合開會？
詹姆士	嗯，早上開會很不錯，可以根據會議來規劃當天的工作啊。
小敏	對，你說得沒錯。

===== 單 字 =====

come up with　拿出、找出／ procedure　過程／ prevent　防止／ productive　有效率的

sharp　準時／ process　過程／ reputation　評判、名聲／ valid　合理的

37 | A little bird told me

===== 解 說 =====

小敏	你聽過最近公司裡的八卦了嗎？
詹姆士	有，很遺憾湯普森先生要被解雇了。
小敏	你覺得都是事實嗎？關於湯普森先生的事？
詹姆士	我不清楚，不過對於別人談論他的事，我覺得很不好。
小敏	你覺得最常見的八卦話題是什麼？
詹姆士	最常說的應該是評論他人吧，你覺得呢？
小敏	我同意，人們也喜歡談論名人的事。什麼地方適合閒聊呢？
詹姆士	嗯，咖啡館是主要的地方，員工休息室也是適合聊天的所在。
小敏	是啊，對了詹姆士，男生和女生誰比較愛講八卦？
詹姆士	當然是女生吧，話很多啊。
小敏	我的想法不一樣，我的男性朋友也跟我差不多長舌。
詹姆士	是嗎？請不要誤會，我不是故意冒犯你的。
小敏	我知道，總之，你覺得人們為何會喜歡聽八卦呢？
詹姆士	很有趣啊，然後有些人就只是愛管閒事。
小敏	你喜歡講八卦嗎？
詹姆士	不能說是喜歡，但現在已經成為很自然的習慣了，因為大家都會說，而我就只好聽了。
小敏	曾經有人散布關於你的傳聞嗎？
詹姆士	有，讀高中時有個女生散布我同時跟兩個女生交往的八卦。
小敏	你怎麼應對？
詹姆士	我直接去找她，問她為什麼會這麼想，她就對編造這件事向我道歉了。

===== 單 字 =====

be aware of　知道關於～／ confront　面對、追究／ talkative　長舌的、話多的／ nosy　愛管閒事

38 | Are you computer-literate?

小敏 怎麼啦？你眼睛紅紅的。

詹姆士 是啊，電腦螢幕看太久了。

小敏 你有多常用電腦呢？

詹姆士 每天啊，差不多是電腦成癮了。

小敏 我也一樣，雖然老是用電腦不好，但也沒辦法，因為太好玩了。

詹姆士 你比較喜歡桌機還是筆電？

小敏 比較喜歡筆電，因為可以隨身攜帶。第一次開始使用電腦是在什麼時候？

詹姆士 我十歲還是十一歲時開始使用電腦。

小敏 還記得你的第一臺電腦嗎？你喜歡嗎？

詹姆士 第一臺電腦我當然記得囉，由於是很大臺的桌上型電腦，在我房間裡占了很大的空間，因為是自己擁有的第一臺電腦，我很喜歡。

小敏 你玩遊戲嗎？

詹姆士 我的確有玩遊戲，還玩得很好。

小敏 實在無法想像你玩電腦遊戲的模樣，是誰教你使用電腦的方法？

詹姆士 我去上學校的電腦課。

小敏 一定很有幫助吧。你最常使用的軟體程式是什麼？

詹姆士 微軟的辦公軟體，你不也一樣嗎？

小敏 是啊，不過我有部落格，所以網頁瀏覽器也和微軟辦公軟體一樣經常使用。

詹姆士 我不知道你還有部落格。小敏，你曾利用電腦來學習英語嗎？

小敏 事實上有的，我常收看網路上的課程。

storage　（資訊的）儲存／ portable　容易攜帶、攜帶用的／ effective　有效果的

stare at　盯著看、凝視／ get addicted　上癮

39 | I can't live without the Internet!

小敏 你今天看起來很累，有什麼事嗎？

詹姆士 我昨晚很晚才睡。

小敏 你在做什麼呢？

詹姆士 在看網路新聞就忘記時間了。

小敏 你似乎很常上網，有多常使用網路呢？

詹姆士 每天都會，一天至少三小時。

小敏 在網路上做什麼呢？

詹姆士 看新聞或是有趣的影片等等。

小敏 你用手機上網嗎？

詹姆士 對，上下班時會用手機上網。

小敏 你第一次使用網路是在什麼時候？我應該是在九〇年代後半。

詹姆士 我也是，中學時第一次使用。

小敏 你們家誰最常使用網路？

詹姆士 我自己最常使用。

小敏 你不覺得網路也會造成問題嗎？

詹姆士 當然會，我認為網路的確給社會帶來一些負面影響。

用 **6** 句英文，和外國人輕鬆話家常！

小敏	網路會造成什麼問題呢？
詹姆士	嗯，會讓孩子對網路遊戲成癮，以及暴露在限制級影片的威脅中。
小敏	我同意，網路約會呢？你有嘗試過嗎？
詹姆士	沒有，還沒試過，你怎麼看呢，網路交友危險嗎？
小敏	當然是危險的，網路上人們很容易捏造身份，感覺並不安全。

━━━━━━━━━ **單 字** ━━━━━━━━━

r-rated （電影）限制級的／ unnecessary 不必要的／ fake 假裝

identity 身份／ commit 肇（事）、犯（罪）／ crime 罪行

40 | Do you use SNS?

━━━━━━━━━ **解 說** ━━━━━━━━━

小敏	早安，詹姆士。
詹姆士	早安，你好像心情很不錯，有什麼事嗎？
小敏	喔，我透過臉書和一個高中朋友連絡上了。
詹姆士	能和那麼久的朋友聊天一定很開心吧。
小敏	開心啊，你用臉書嗎？
詹姆士	喔，很抱歉我不用臉書。
小敏	你不用嗎？那你使用哪個社群網站？
詹姆士	我用 Instagram。
小敏	我也有，你有部落格嗎？
詹姆士	不，我沒有部落格，你有嗎？
小敏	是的，我有，我會上傳首爾的餐廳資訊，你會在社群網站上分享什麼種類的資訊？
詹姆士	我喜歡上傳我家附近漂亮的照片。
小敏	請告訴我網址，我要來看看。
詹姆士	好啊，我寫給你。小敏，你好像很喜歡社群網站，你為什麼用社群網站呢？
小敏	為了和朋友保持聯絡，因為有幾個人住在國外，無法經常見面。
詹姆士	你用什麼登入社群網站呢？
小敏	我用智慧型手機，因為很方便，你不是嗎？
詹姆士	不，我是用電腦，因為智慧型手機會讓我眼睛痛。
小敏	你覺得自己對社群網站成癮嗎？
詹姆士	不會，我沒那麼喜歡社群網站，有需要時才會用。

━━━━━━━━━ **單 字** ━━━━━━━━━

constantly 不斷地／ nervous 不安的／ through 透過

Precious moments in life

41 | I learn current issues in the news

— 解 說 —

詹姆士	你關注時事嗎？
小敏	是的，我有，其實今天早上我才看了昨天日本地震的新聞報導。
詹姆士	我是昨天晚上從電視新聞看到的，有點擔心。你最常從哪裡獲取新聞？
小敏	我不喜歡看電視新聞節目，我會在上班搭地鐵時讀報紙。
詹姆士	有點老派呢，我不覺得你是會讀報紙的人。
小敏	為何這麼說呢？
詹姆士	感覺你會用手機 APP 之類的來看新聞。
小敏	這是你的偏見，總之，你有多常看電視新聞或讀報紙？
詹姆士	幾乎每天，你喜歡看報紙的哪一版？
小敏	我最喜歡國際新聞版，世界各地發生的各式各樣事情非常有趣。
詹姆士	哇，真令人印象深刻。看新聞是提升英語能力的好方法嗎？
小敏	我確實這麼認為，文法完美而且內容有教育性。
詹姆士	你對新聞抱持著相當肯定的態度，對吧？
小敏	是啊，沒錯，讀新聞的好處不少呢。

— 單 字 —

depressed　憂鬱的／ earthquake　地震／ benefit　獲益

42 | What a beautiful day!

— 解 說 —

小敏	詹姆士，你都淋濕了，你沒帶雨傘嗎？
詹姆士	沒有，我不知道今天會下雨。
小敏	有說今天會下雨啊，你沒看天氣預報嗎？
詹姆士	我沒有時間，還有我也不相信天氣預報。
小敏	你真是偏激呢，雖然偶爾會不準，但準備起來還是比較好吧。
詹姆士	那麼小敏，你知道明天天氣怎麼樣嗎？
小敏	明天應該會是晴天。
詹姆士	幸好，我討厭下雨也討厭寒冷的冬天。
小敏	那麼你最喜歡什麼季節？
詹姆士	我喜歡水上運動，所以我喜歡夏天，韓國冬天太冷了，你呢？喜歡天氣熱還是天氣冷？
小敏	我也喜歡熱天，我很愛去游泳。
詹姆士	明年一起去游泳吧。
小敏	我很樂意。詹姆士，你覺得何時是最適合造訪韓國的季節？
詹姆士	雖然我最喜歡夏天，但覺得春天最適合來韓國，我覺得一定要看美麗的櫻花。
小敏	我也同意，而且我很自豪韓國的四季分明。
詹姆士	應該要的。嘿，天氣曾經影響你的計畫嗎？
小敏	是啊，有過幾次，上個星期六原本想去野餐的，結果下雨只能待在家裡。
詹姆士	真是可惜，訂好計畫前應該要確認天氣預報啊。

單字

pleasant　舒適的、心情好的／ cherry blossom　櫻花／ outdoor activity　戶外活動

handle　安排／ cynical　譏諷的／ incorrect　不明確的／ distinct　明顯的、分明的

43 | Public transportation is efficient

解 說

詹姆士	對不起我遲到了。
小敏	沒關係，你只有遲到五分鐘。
詹姆士	塞車塞得很嚴重，我停好車後就穿過走道跑過來了。
小敏	坐下來喘口氣吧，你看起來很累。
詹姆士	謝謝，我通常都會搭公車，但今天突如其來想要開車。
小敏	是啊，偶爾會有這樣的時候。
詹姆士	你如何去上班？
小敏	我總是會搭大眾交通工具去目的地，也包括公司。
詹姆士	為何搭大眾交通工具呢？
小敏	老實說是我開車實力不佳，我也不曉得是怎麼考到駕照的。
詹姆士	應該沒那麼糟糕吧。你有多常使用大眾交通工具？
小敏	幾乎每天，只有到外縣市才會開車，不過偶爾會不想搭大眾交通工具。
詹姆士	什麼時候不想搭大眾交通工具？
小敏	下雨的時候，地鐵裡人太多了，再加上濕雨傘，又更混亂了。
詹姆士	地板濕掉一定很滑吧。
小敏	是啊，我就是討厭那個。
詹姆士	你比較喜歡搭巴士還是地鐵？
小敏	我偏好地鐵，因為比較快，地鐵總是會準時抵達，巴士如果塞車的話就可能會遲到。
詹姆士	的確如此，我雖然喜歡開車，但在韓國停車要花太多時間了。
小敏	沒錯，在你的國家有停車問題嗎？
詹姆士	沒有，我國家的停車位很多。

單 字

corridor　走道／ at times　偶爾／ whereas　相反的／ plenty of　許多

44 | Healthy habits keep you healthy

解 說

詹姆士	嘿，小敏，你要吃點維他命嗎？
小敏	謝謝，你定期服藥嗎？
詹姆士	是，我因為有高血壓每天都要吃。
小敏	感覺你很注意健康，你是有健康意識的人嗎？
詹姆士	當然，我覺得我很有健康意識。
小敏	為什麼這麼說呢？
詹姆士	我每天都會運動，避免吃速食，也不抽菸。
小敏	哇，你的生活習慣真的很健康，你從哪裡獲得健康資訊？
詹姆士	我看很多關於健康、運動及飲食的書籍，要推薦書給你嗎？
小敏	好啊，謝謝你。
詹姆士	不用謝啦，小敏，你做什麼來保持健康？
小敏	嗯，我都是做一些小事，像是喝很多水、避免喝飲料之類的。

詹姆士	這樣已經很足夠了，你常生病嗎？上次生病是什麼時候？
小敏	好像是去年冬天，胃很痛所以就去醫院了。
詹姆士	應該要定期去醫院才行，你有多常接受健康檢查？
小敏	一年一次吧？你知道的，我們公司會安排。
詹姆士	喔，對。檢查結果曾出現健康問題嗎？
小敏	目前沒有，不過每次健康檢查時還是會害怕。
詹姆士	我也是。你的家人中誰最健康？
小敏	應該是我爸爸，他總是很注意健康。

=== 單 字 ===

medical examination　健康檢查／ on a regular basis　規律地／ balanced　均衡的

45 | Let's get educated!

=== 解 說 ===

詹姆士	這是我的高中畢業紀念冊，要看嗎？
小敏	好啊，你當時的髮型和現在不一樣呢。
詹姆士	是啊。你和高中朋友還有保持聯絡嗎？
小敏	是的，我有，事實上其中一位還是我現在最好的朋友。
詹姆士	真好，我畢業後就很難和高中朋友繼續聯絡了。
小敏	我知道不容易，但還是得試試。你高中時最擅長的科目是什麼？
詹姆士	嗯，我比較擅長英語、數學和科學。
小敏	哇，是我最討厭的科目。最喜歡的老師是誰呢？
詹姆士	最喜歡數學老師，她真的很擅長解釋困難的概念。
小敏	和那位老師還保持聯絡嗎？
詹姆士	是的，透過臉書來聯繫。
小敏	真好。你高中時班上有幾個學生？
詹姆士	高中時一班有二十個人左右。
小敏	真不公平，我們班有四十個人。
詹姆士	教室一定很擠吧？
小敏	你無法想像的。在你讀過的學校中，你最喜歡哪一所？
詹姆士	我最喜歡大學，我在那裡交到好朋友，到現在還會固定見面。
小敏	真不錯。如果有機會的話，會想重返校園嗎？
詹姆士	不會，唸書的壓力太大了。

=== 單 字 ===

career　職業／ pupil　學生／ field　領域／ graduation　畢業

46 | Would you marry me?

=== 解 說 ===

詹姆士	嘿，你這個週末要做什麼？
小敏	星期六要去朋友的婚禮，星期天就休息。
詹姆士	結婚季到了，對吧？
小敏	沒錯。你想在何時結婚？
詹姆士	當遇到完美的女人時，開玩笑啦，準備好的時候。
小敏	你想要什麼樣的女人當太太呢？

詹姆士	溫柔、善解人意的淑女，如果擅長料理的話會更好。
小敏	我認識一個女生真的很會做菜，她是韓國人，你願意和不同國家的人結婚嗎？
詹姆士	那當然，我不在意和不同國家的人結婚。
小敏	就你的看法，結婚前應該要交往多久？
詹姆士	我覺得交往的時間並不是那麼重要，你覺得重要嗎？
小敏	這個嘛，我覺得至少要交往一年才能真正理解對方。
詹姆士	還滿合理的，那麼換你告訴我，什麼是伴侶需要具備的重要素質？
小敏	就我而言是責任感，他得是個有責任感的一家之主。
詹姆士	你想要有小孩嗎？
小敏	當然囉，我想生至少三個，你呢？
詹姆士	我也很想要小孩，我想要組一個大家庭。

=== 單 字 ===

competent　有能力的／humbleness　謙虛／thriftiness　節儉／generosity　慷慨、大方

typical　典型的、代表性的／breadwinner　一家之主

47 ｜ Are you feeling alright?

=== 解 說 ===

詹姆士	嘿，晚上要不要一起吃晚餐？
小敏	很抱歉，我要去醫院看奶奶。
詹姆士	沒事吧？希望情況不會太嚴重。
小敏	出了點小意外，要住院一個星期。
詹姆士	希望她能盡快康復。
小敏	謝謝。你住院過嗎？
詹姆士	沒有，我很健康而且不曾發生過意外，上帝保佑。你上次去醫院是什麼時候？
小敏	一個月前嗎？我會接受定期的檢查。
詹姆士	你有多常去醫院？
小敏	一年應該不到五次吧，你呢？
詹姆士	我還滿常去醫院的。
小敏	你最常看什麼科的醫生？
詹姆士	最近因為拿掉矯正器的緣故，應該要屬牙科了。
小敏	你喜歡去醫院嗎？
詹姆士	是啊，為何不呢？我知道去了醫院之後身體就會痊癒。
小敏	這麼想就對了！你覺得韓國人比美國人健康嗎？
詹姆士	不，我覺得平均來說美國人比較健康。
小敏	真的嗎？我倒不這麼想，電視上出現的美國人都胖胖的，我沒有冒犯的意思。
詹姆士	嗯，雖然美國人體型比較大，但感覺比較有健康意識。
小敏	你覺得什麼是韓國嚴重的健康問題？
詹姆士	我覺得是過量飲酒，我不太喜歡職場的飲酒文化。
小敏	我懂你的意思。

=== 單 字 ===

be hospitalized　住院／get infected　被感染／get injured　受傷／annual　年度例行的、每年的

48 | Religions influenced our cultures

=== 解 說 ===

詹姆士 嘿，小敏，那是你的《聖經》嗎？
小敏 這本書嗎？對，我是基督徒。
詹姆士 你如何實踐自己的信仰呢？
小敏 上教會、讀《聖經》還有禱告。
詹姆士 原來如此，宗教對你來說重要嗎？
小敏 是的，我整個人生都受到宗教影響，包括思考模式、說話還有做決定。
詹姆士 所以你是虔誠的基督徒，誰影響了你的信仰？
小敏 我出生在基督教的家庭，所以受到父母很大的影響。
詹姆士 成長過程中沒有對宗教產生疑問嗎？
小敏 有過，但我能理解基督教。你有信仰嗎？
詹姆士 沒有，我曾是佛教徒，但現在是無神論者。
小敏 真有趣！一開始是怎麼對佛教產生興趣的？
詹姆士 喔，我年輕時讀過關於佛教的書。
小敏 就我所知，佛教在你的國家並不常見，對吧？
詹姆士 沒錯，我的家族中只有我是佛教徒。
小敏 你的國家主要宗教是什麼？
詹姆士 當然是基督教啊，美國人大部分都是基督徒，不然就是無神論者。
小敏 你覺得人為何要有信仰？
詹姆士 我覺得人們有信仰是希望能借助某種超自然力量。
小敏 我非常贊同，我也會祈禱奇蹟發生。

=== 單 字 ===

volunteer 義工／ deed 行為／ soothe 安撫內心、鎮定
atheist 無神論者／ affect 造成影響／ supernatural 超自然的

49 | You can overcome your addictions

=== 解 說 ===

小敏 嘿，詹姆士你抽菸嗎？
詹姆士 沒有，不再抽了，為何這麼問？
小敏 昨天我讀到關於成癮的報導。
詹姆士 我以前有菸癮，但現在已經戒掉了。
小敏 你如何戒除的呢？
詹姆士 我尋求專家的幫助，去了專門的診所。你有對什麼上癮嗎？
小敏 我好像對智慧型手機成癮了，你覺得自己對智慧型手機上癮嗎？
詹姆士 沒有，我不這麼覺得，我可以不帶智慧型手機出門。
小敏 很少見呢，你怎麼跟別人聯絡呢？
詹姆士 我記得家人和朋友的電話號碼。
小敏 好驚人，我記不得任何人的電話號碼，當然我自己的除外。
詹姆士 你喜歡喝酒嗎？
小敏 當然囉，我喜歡偶爾小酌一下。
詹姆士 你覺得為何有些人會對酒成癮？
小敏 嗯，很多人說喜歡和朋友一起慶祝，而且能產生歸屬感。
詹姆士 我覺得是喝了酒之後能放下戒心，然後能坦誠地對話、累積親密感。

小敏	你何時知道自己對某種事物上癮了？
詹姆士	當我早上沒喝咖啡的話手會抖，我就知道我對咖啡成癮了。
小敏	你覺得有成癮性的網路活動應該非法化嗎？
詹姆士	那當然啊，我不希望讓孩子不小心接觸到線上賭博，應該以嚴格的法律來保護孩童。

單 字

overcome　克服／ fizzy drinks　有氣泡的（碳酸）飲料／ bond　紐帶、聯繫

vulnerable　脆弱的、軟弱的／ intimacy　親密感

50 | Know yourself!

解 說

小敏	我的主管很難捉摸，情緒起伏太大了！
詹姆士	我的也是！我主管也是難以捉摸。
小敏	為何他們不像我們這麼理智呢？
詹姆士	沒錯！你的個性真的很好！
小敏	我嗎？謝謝，我不是很清楚自己的個性。
詹姆士	那就來弄清楚吧，你何時會覺得快樂？
小敏	嗯，最近是一個人待在房間裡時會覺得快樂，就只是安靜地休息。
詹姆士	那代表你是內向的人。
小敏	真的嗎？那你呢？如何讓自己開心？
詹姆士	我是典型外向的人，我喜歡出去和朋友混在一起，那讓我很開心。
小敏	你難過時會去哪裡？
詹姆士	會去咖啡館和朋友聊聊，聊一聊有助於釐清問題。
小敏	感覺你真的很外向。
詹姆士	那麼來思考一下吧，你覺得自己是什麼個性？
小敏	有點寡言，偶爾會很害羞，喜歡事情井然有序並做好規劃。
詹姆士	對，那聽起來就像你，你的個性適合你的工作嗎？
小敏	當然，我只是一般上班族，我的個性正適合我的工作。
詹姆士	可以的話會想改變自己的個性嗎？
小敏	絕對不要，我很習慣我自己了，現在不會想要改變自己。

單 字

extrovert　外向的（人）／ introvert　內向的（人）／ reserved　拘謹的／ lay out　展開、排列

Easy 輕鬆學　輕鬆學系列 030

用 6 句英文，和外國人輕鬆話家常！
——職場、旅遊、交友都萬用，最快上手的英語會話學習術！
육하원칙 영어회화：6개 의문사로 네이티브와 막힘없이 대화하기

作　　　者	周銀卿
譯　　　者	黃薇之
總 編 輯	何玉美
責 任 編 輯	陳如翎
封 面 設 計	走路花工作室
內 文 排 版	theBAND・變設計— Ada

出 版 發 行	采實文化事業股份有限公司
行 銷 企 劃	陳佩宜・黃于庭・馮羿勳
業 務 發 行	盧金城・張世明・林踏欣・林坤蓉・王貞玉
會 計 行 政	王雅蕙・李韶婉
法 律 顧 問	第一國際法律事務所　余淑杏律師
電 子 信 箱	acme@acmebook.com.tw
采 實 官 網	http://www.acmebook.com.tw
采實粉絲團	https://www.facebook.com/acmebook01/

I S B N	978-957-895-050-4
定　　　價	360 元
初 版 一 刷	2018 年 8 月
劃 撥 帳 號	50148859
劃 撥 戶 名	采實文化事業股份有限公司
	104 台北市中山區建國北路二段 92 號 9 樓
	電話：(02)2518-5198
	傳真：(02)2518-2098

國家圖書館出版品預行編目 (CIP) 資料

用 6 句英文，和外國人輕鬆話家常！：
職場、旅遊、交友都萬用，最快上手的英語會話
學習術！/ 周銀卿作；黃薇之譯 .
-- 初版 . -- 臺北市：采實文化，2018.08
　面；　公分 . -- (輕鬆學系列；30)
ISBN 978-957-8950-50-4(平裝)

1. 英語 2. 會話

805.188　　　　　　　　　　107010636

Original Title: 육하원칙 영어회화
5W1H English by Joo Eun-kyeong
Copyright © 2015 Joo Eun-kyeong
All rights reserved.
Original edition published by Gilbut Eztok, Seoul, Korea
Traditional Chinese Translation Copyright © 2018 by ACME Publishing Co., Ltd.
This Traditional Chinese edition published by arranged with Gilbut Eztok through Eric
Yang Agency

采實出版集團
ACME PUBLISHING GROUP

版權所有，未經同意
不得重製、轉載、翻印